MW01225284

Thanks for
being you.

A Judge,

an Irishman

and a Hot Dog Vendor

go into a Bar

Love,

Rock

A Novel by Roderick Brooks

Copyright © June 2013

Xmas 2013

Author's Note

'*A Judge, an Irishman and a Hot Dog Vendor go into a Bar*' is a work of fiction. It is based on a tragic real life event, the terrorist bombing of Pan Am Flight 103 over Lockerbie, Scotland, on December 21, 1988. The story, dialogue and all characters with the exception of known public figures are products of the author's imagination and are not to be construed as real. Out of respect for the 270 Lockerbie victims and their survivors, great care has been taken to provide an accurate technical and historical context for the flight and its loss. In all other respects, any resemblance to persons living or dead is entirely coincidental.

Rod Brooks
September 2013

For Valerie

Prologue

Monday, March 12, 1990 – 10:13 a.m. EST
26 Federal Plaza, 23rd Floor, New York, NY

IN THE END it's a contest of personal will. When you sit where you're told in an interview room, by default you're a suspect, and Jimmy Kenneally was having no part of that. He rose with his cup of FBI coffee and walked away from the table.

The room was no windowless box like most you will find anywhere in policing. It was a glass-walled corner office and it had a view: a sprawling canvas of lower Manhattan in late winter gray. A commuter plane plied an airway above the East River. An earnest red, white and black tug tried to muscle a barge against current and tide. And below, a stream of cars, mostly yellow, and trucks trailing plumes of exhaust, inched their way along Duane toward the Centre Street loop and destinations uptown.

"Shall I repeat the question?" asked Winters, irritated.

Shall? Isn't this perfect. "You'd get the same answer," Kenneally replied, blowing steam from his cup.

"Okay then, let's try it like this. On the night of the first of September last year, your surveillance at Sullivan's Bar. Luongo arrives at eight-thirty, alone. Waits outside, has a smoke. Moments later a stranger arrives. Luongo greets him, they enter together. And at this point, you haven't a clue who the second man is. Is that fair to say?"

Sanctimonious shit.

The FBI special agent was young. Early thirties. He had those slit-narrow eyes, fixed in an annoyingly permanent squint. White shirt, imported cotton, school tie, business suit off the rack—buttoned up and as crisp as a new dollar bill, sitting perched on the edge of his chair.

Kenneally turned from the window.

"I didn't know the identity of our second subject until I was back in the car with Ahearn," he said, formally. "Otherwise, yes, I might have given more weight to gaining something from their conversation."

Winters brightened.

"Then Ahearn did know this man."

Kenneally groaned. "Fucksakes, he knew of him. Didn't make the connection himself right away."

He chose to return to the table.

"Division of duties," Kenneally explained. "Ahearn had the camera and drove. I caught the legwork and notes. When I returned to the car, I said I couldn't make either one of the others. Couldn't get close. They were in a booth at the back of the bar, a pool table between us. Anyway, Kev gets this look. 'A judge!' he says. The subject he'd seen through the camera lens. He remembered his face from the papers. A federal judge."

It was true. Ahearn had spent years at the Bureau of Alcohol, Tobacco and Firearms on high-profile arms trafficking cases. In and out of the federal courts all the time. City cops like Kenneally, you recognize faces from collars you've made, from the subway, the corner bodega, not from the marble halls down at 500 Pearl or the society page of the Times.

Winters produced one of the photographs Ahearn had taken. "Elliott," he said. "Judge Randolph Owens Elliott. United States District Court for the New York Southern District. Manhattan bench."

"Yeah. We learned that once we were back in the barn."

The other two stirred. The Tall One leaned over and whispered behind his palm to Fat Little Fed Number Three.

Kenneally studied the photograph. A night shot from about fifty yards. Tight depth of field with a Nikkor telephoto stopped wide open. Features illuminated by the bar's entrance lighting just off to the left. A head shot of a white male, maybe sixty, wearing an open-collared checked shirt under his jacket and a worn New York Mets baseball cap. He was gaunt with an angular face and strong jaw, light stubble, close cropped gray hair and wire-framed rimless eyeglasses. An expressionless face. No, there was something in the man's eyes. A sadness that he recognized.

Winters straightened in his chair, a calculated change in posture and body language.

"Didn't it seem curious to you that your surveillance target was meeting a federal judge? A man appointed to the bench by the President of the United States."

"No," said Kenneally. "We had intell that Luongo was making a meet with a Patriarca capo, Gino Testaverde. Even you've heard of him. The East Coast King of stolen plastic explosives? Anyway, he didn't show. So we didn't care. They could've been pals from the Knights of Columbus out for a couple of beer."

The Tall One and Fat Boy perked up.

"Look, Sal Luongo had been a pet project of Kevin's for years. It was an ATF thing. Connections to the Boston and Providence mob, to families from Philly right down to New Orleans. He had him in gun-running files going back to the Sixties."

Winters snorted. "Luongo, the Hot Dog Vendor. What's that? Booze-Smokes-and-Guns humor?"

"Jesus, Winters, you're thick. The man has a Sabrett cart in Foley Square. Centre at Pearl. Right across from the courthouse, and he's only been at it about twenty years. Pull your head from your J. Edgar ass and you'd trip over detail like that."

Winters was unfazed. He read from a stapled three-page typewritten report. Kenneally's report.

"The third man ... " he began.

Kenneally cut him short.

"He was Ulster Irish, that's all I knew."

Jimmy was born in Belfast, Northern Ireland and his family had emigrated when he was eight years of age. They settled in the deeply Irish neighborhood of Windsor Terrace, Brooklyn, and so it was he had grown up immersed in the same Irish lilt he had heard from the cradle. On a coast with six times the population of Irish as the island of Erin itself, their man's heritage would be known for a fact from the moment he opened his mouth.

"Yes," Winters sniffed. "You don't I.D. this one either."

He continued to read. "Caucasian male, mid-thirties, five-ten, dark features, the build of a boxer. Ulster born by his accent, you say. You conclude your report with this subject unknown. And no follow up for the file?"

"What don't you get? No Testaverde, no interest. It was a tip that went bust. As soon as Luongo departed, we folded our tent and went home."

"Right. Pals from the Knights of Columbus."

He pulled another document from the file. Through the back of the single sheet of paper, Kenneally could see a portrait and profile mug shot under what was clearly a British crown imprint.

Winters dished it up like dessert.

"Well, your Irishman was known to someone."

The British Security Service notice was flagged in typical Brit understatement: 'Approach Subject With Caution'.

"Martin Quinn," Winters continued. "Identified last week from this poster by one, Molly Geary, a server that night. Born in Armagh, Northern Ireland, on December 4th, 1954. Became a member of the Provisional IRA in 1974 at the height of the 'Troubles'. A prodigious bomb maker, linked to at least thirty bombings in Ulster and England, including one that killed a British Royal, Lord Louis Mountbatten. Dropped out of sight in the mid-eighties. Thought to have become a private contractor. Sighted variously in Europe and North Africa ... and, barely six months ago, in a Hell's Kitchen bar that was under surveillance by you."

Fucksakes. If these clowns only knew. So, so near, the abyss. Choose to turn over rocks and there is no avoiding the things that crawl out. Jimmy learned that lesson himself on that night in September, unwittingly opening Pandora's Box—and Ahearn, never quick to upbraid, had even got laughing about it as they were driving away.

"Good start to a joke for you, Jimmy," he said with that grin. "A Judge, an Irishman and a Hot Dog Vendor go into a Bar ..."

Chapter 1

CHRISTMAS GARLANDS AND stenciled foam snowflakes decorated the departure lounge at Gate 14, Terminal Three, Heathrow Airport. Every one of its three hundred fiberglass seats appeared to be taken as passengers bound for a snowy New York cluttered the space around them with their winter coats, bags of shopping, or both. Gate agents in Pan Am blue fretted behind the desk, reconciling the checked-in list against reservations, as 'We Wish You a Merry Christmas' rang cheerily through the lounge. It was past sunset, and beyond the halogen glow of Heathrow airport, the low rolling countryside of London's westernmost borough was awash with pinpoints of light—suburban windows warmly ablaze on the first winter night of the year.

At Gate 14, the distinctive white nose of a Boeing 747 filled the windows next to the jetway—*Clipper Maid of The Seas*—Pan Am Flight 103, set to depart for New York.

"Hey!" snapped a young woman in a seat at the crowded end of her row.

"Hey!" she repeated to the man who had sat down beside her. "That's my jacket, and you sat on my chips."

"I *am* sorry," the man said apologetically.

He was British, perhaps fifty, tall and distinguished in a suit and tie and a navy blue Burberry raincoat. He rose and handed the jacket and brightly-bagged snack to the girl.

"Crisps," he said.

"Thank you ... what?" she replied, smiling.

"Your chips."

"Oh, right. Sorry, there aren't a lot of free seats. Everyone's got so much stuff."

"Indeed. Stuff," he agreed, quickly occupying himself with a copy of the Daily Telegraph.

End of conversation.

Fine. Diana Jane Elliott was content to keep to herself, never much one for idle chatter with strangers in transit.

She opened the yellow fifty-pence bag of potato crisps and nibbled. Beef flavored, its packaging claimed. They were, if only vaguely. There had been nothing comfortingly familiar to be found in the vending machines. No barbeque, salt and vinegar, no nacho cheese. A strange taste in snacks have these Brits. She shuddered at the possibility of steak and kidney, tripe or herring and munched on her crushed bits of chip.

AT TWENTY-TWO, Diana Elliott was a seasoned traveler and had been since her middle school years. She was an only child and had been thirteen when her parents went through their first separation, the sad result of which saw her exiled for three years to a boarding school in Switzerland. *Le Sommet* was an exclusive academy founded in 1880 and its select student body had their school year divided between a manorial estate on Lake Geneva and its alpine winter program in the jet set resort of Gstaad. Her summers during this unhappy time had been spent back in Westchester County, New York, where her parents had a Tudor mansion facing Long Island Sound in suburban Port Chester. While the marriage had reconciled during her first term at Le Sommet, her father had remained as unapproachable as ever, and her mother returned to the love that had driven the couple onto the rocks—stiff vodka martinis, light on Vermouth.

Diana's mother, Charlotte Adeline Elliott, nee Burke, had been a belle from Cumberland County, North Carolina. Her family had tobacco money and once had owned slaves.

An aspiring writer, Charlotte Burke had earned a degree in American literature from Duke University in 1957. She returned home that summer and had settled into her writing when she met Randolph Owens Elliott, a Marine Corps lieutenant at nearby Camp Lejeune. Elliott was dashing, gregarious and a catch for any one of the girls on the local society circuit. He was a northerner but as Charlotte would say, a rare breed of Yankee. Charming, well-spoken and damnably handsome.

Charlotte had been handsome herself, polite idiom at the time for attractive women of girth. Any excess weight she did carry barely showed on young Charlotte, but its potential did. In the badinage of southern gentlemen since the Confederacy: "There are, sadly, just two varieties of southern belle. Young or fat."

Still, she'd seemed a wisp of a bride when a year later she joined Lieutenant Elliott at the altar—she a vision in magnolia lace, and he a clear eyed ramrod resplendent in his Marine Corps dress blues—leaving the chapel together through a phalanx of Mameluke swords on the day he returned to civilian life.

Randolph Elliott completed a four-year short service stint in 1958 and entered law school at Yale, his undergrad alma mater. There, he and Charlotte enjoyed three happy years in a small but comfortable apartment in New Haven while he engrossed himself in his studies and she ambitiously returned to her writing. And Charlotte could write.

Short stories had flown from her vintage Remington typewriter, simply plotted morality tales of a genteel South, full of eloquent imagery that conjured gala cotillions, laneway cottonwoods draped in Spanish moss and mint juleps sipped on the porch. Her first recognized effort, 'The Carriage', was the dark account of the rape of a plantation owner's daughter by a malevolent suitor her family had courted, and her heroine's descent into madness when she discovers that she had been sacrificed. It was published in 1960 on first submission to The Antioch Review, a literary journal known for showcasing upcoming new writers. Within months, a collection of eight of Charlotte's short stories—with 'The Carriage' as its cornerstone piece—was in production at a small New York publishing house. It would enjoy modest success in the literary book market the following year.

The critics had been generous and agents had begun to call. When would we see more? Her subsequent efforts, however, were rejected, critiqued as stale, or less flatteringly, an uninspired dredging of earlier themes.

That same year, Harper Lee of Monroeville, Alabama arrived on the national writing scene. Her Pulitzer Prize-winning novel 'To Kill a Mockingbird' became an instant American literary classic, and it gave those who even bothered to look at her work, a new and impossible yardstick for measuring Charlotte.

It was at about this time in her life that cocktail hours for author C. A. Elliott had begun to slip from five o'clock to four, then to three, and occasionally into the mornings on those days that her writer's block would be manifested with actual pain. Creeping alcoholism and creative listlessness seemed to foil any project she started. She would spend weeks tinkering with turns of a phrase, rarely sober enough to perfect them. By the time Charlotte and Randolph Elliott, Esq., attorney at law, settled into a midtown Manhattan brownstone, his star was rising and hers had crashed to the ground.

Randolph Elliott became a respected litigator with the Wall Street firm of Fenn, Wilkeshire and Duke, practicing in the dry but highly visible arena of trade and tariffs law. He had found success in his profession, but his wife's well-known failings became fodder for office gossips and in the social circles of the firm's partners and clients. Looks of commiseration whenever her name was uttered, or when Elliott attended functions and Manhattan galas alone.

Then, in July 1966, Charlotte gave birth to a daughter, Diana Jane. She would be their only child. Complications in childbirth would be her standard lie when asked about it over the years. In truth, after three miscarriages since they had come to New York, she had her tubes tied to avoid the anguish of ever losing a baby again.

DIANA ELLIOTT'S DECISION to fly to England with no destination or actual plan was, while consistent with her capricious nature, less a whim and more a reaction to her last disastrous parental encounter. When it came to discourse with her parents, she had learned early in life to follow the path of least resistance. As a child she would withdraw to her room and her books, pain assuaged by the writings of Andersen, Dickens and Twain. Later in her adolescence, she would seek consolation in booze and promiscuous sex, one routinely compelling the other.

As a girl she had always been pretty and plenty would say that not in spite of her size, Diana had blossomed into an attractive young woman. Taller than most at five-foot-nine, with what the fashion industry unflatteringly termed as a 'brick' body type. But she carried it well. Curves in all the right places, gentle rolls in the rest. *Rubenesque*, the buxom epitome of female perfection for baroque Flemish painters, yet painfully out of place in her Swiss boarding school world of the lithe and lovely.

Her trump was her mother's Liz Taylor looks. An oval face that was symmetric perfection. Complexion of pale porcelain. High, flushed cheeks and an aquiline nose, a wide mouth with full ruby lips that showcased a brilliant smile. She wore her coal black hair the same way since a dorm room makeover when she was sixteen: parted over her left eye, bobbed at the back, and hanging precociously down both sides of her face to her chin. It framed her most compelling feature, her eyes—wide and deep blue, and with the right makeup and lighting, exotic. Her eyes got your attention and she knew it.

She had kept her virginity until she was seventeen and living back home in the States, choosing to lose it on a Christmas Break ski trip with friends to Sugarloaf Mountain in Maine. On a fireside rug in an A-frame chalet after too many glasses of wine. And on a twenty year-old Dartmouth junior and would-be moguls racer named Eddie. His finesse on the slopes hadn't been his only talent, although speed and control didn't translate as well. Even so, from that first encounter she recognized sex as addictive.

Diana would become enigmatic to classmates and casual friends. Weight, like her moods, buoyed and fell, but she remained consistently compelling to potential lovers of either gender. It took self-confidence found rarely in youth to cruise Diana and score. She could be crushingly cold. She set her own agenda and made all the rules, choosing her moments and partners on impulse—like the diner who's dithering over the menu when a server sweeps past with an appealing entrée, and—"Oooh, that looks good!" she might say. "I think I'll have that tonight."

In a rare bonding moment her mother once told her: "My grandmother, Diana, confided to me that she faced her frustrations with gin. Glowing daily from noon until night. My own mother? She laid any man who would look at her twice, from field hands to boys home on furlough from Camp Lejeune. As for myself, I am a modern woman. Free to choose my own vices, to be indiscreet and to bear the consequences."

That had been on Diana's eighteenth birthday and it became for her that seminal moment when the child recognizes the parent is human, mere mortal and flawed. Seriously flawed, Diana had decided, and beyond salvation.

IN THE EARLY morning of November 19, 1988, Diana lay in the emergency room of Bellevue Hospital on the lower east side of midtown Manhattan. Her father had been awakened at home in Port Chester by the ER clerk, with the simple message that his daughter Diana had been mugged.

Judge Elliott hadn't bothered to rouse his wife. She was drunk and snoring on a living room sofa where he had left her hours earlier before turning in. He had dressed quickly and drove for an anxious hour into the city from Westchester County.

When he arrived in the Emergency Room it was as if he had stepped into Saturday night on an alien planet. The ER was a crush of desperate people, all colors, all ages, shapes and sizes, some bleeding, some crying, most angry.

Bewildered, Judge Elliott made his way to a reception desk and asked after his daughter by name. A young woman in blue paisley scrubs simply pointed down the hall toward a congregation of cops.

A paunchy NYPD sergeant was standing by the first of a long row of curtained triage cubicles, an aluminum report case in hand, chatting with two young patrolmen. As Elliott approached him, the cop quickly guessed from his dress and deportment that this was the girl's father, a federal judge, as Diana had obstreperously advised.

"Judge Elliott, is it?" he asked.

"I am. My daughter?"

The sergeant cleared his throat. "She's okay, first of all, sir. Hasn't been hurt. Doc says she's gonna be fine."

"Tell me what happened."

"We, uh, at around one-twenty we received a 9-1-1 call about a woman found in an alley off Jackson Square. A couple came across her and thought she'd been mugged, maybe raped. Officers Chicorelli and Lord, here, were the nearest sector unit and responded in minutes. Didn't know what they had at first." The sergeant glanced uncomfortably at his notes.

"I was told she'd been mugged," pressed the Judge.

"Well, no, that's what was called in. Can I be frank, Judge? The caller thought she was a hooker at first. A trick gone bad or maybe a mugging? She was bleeding from the mouth and, uh, between her legs."

"Bleeding? Has she been assaulted or not?"

"No sir, that's how it looked at the time."

The Judge sighed heavily.

"What do you mean they thought she was a hooker?"

The sergeant wished he could look anywhere else than into the older man's face. But he braced himself. "The thing is, Judge, she was made up and dressed kinda provocatively. You know? Blouse, mini-skirt, boots. No jacket, only her purse. Complainants figured a hooker."

"What did happen, Sergeant?" persisted the Judge.

The officer went on to explain the occurrence as best he could. After initial enquiries at the scene it was quickly established that the young woman had left a bar on the same block. Drunk. Off to hail a cab, a club doorman said. Not a hooker at all, just a college girl on the town.

"And the blood?" the Judge asked.

"Medical issues. Not a criminal matter, at least no assault. I'm sure the doctor can fill you in."

Judge Elliott thanked the sergeant and walked down the hall to engage the doctor. Sikh, he concluded, tall and bearded, in sky blue scrubs and a turban.

The Judge introduced himself and again asked after his daughter. The doctor had a comforting manner and spoke with a cultured English accent.

"I'm afraid your daughter is grossly intoxicated. She had vomited a substantial amount of red blood and, without further tests, I'd suspect an upper G.I. ulcer. Does she ordinarily drink heavily? Binges? That sort of thing?"

The Judge winced and nodded.

"As for the pregnancy," the doctor continued, "I'm afraid she's miscarried. From the fetal mass and the nature of blood loss, I'd estimate two months along."

Randolph Elliott felt as if he had been stabbed in the heart. He thanked the doctor and slipped through the curtain into Diana's cubicle.

His daughter lay under the fluorescent white glare of overhead lights, connected to intravenous plasma and oxygen, on a treatment bed with its head slightly raised and hers pressed into a blood-stained white pillow. An immodest open-backed gown and a hospital blanket were twisted around her. Raven hair disheveled. Mascara blackening her eyes.

Diana lay conscious but groggy, eyes listlessly closed. She stirred, sensing the aroma of his pipe tobacco and feeling his stare. She opened her eyes to see him standing, splendid as always in his cashmere overcoat, stone-faced and studying her with icy detachment.

"They said you'd been assaulted."

"Oh, I'm sorry," she replied scornfully. "And you drove all the way into the city."

The Judge fumed.

"You're an embarrassment, Diana. To me. To yourself. Passed out drunk in an alley, dressed like a common ..."

"Whore, Daddy?" she interjected, slurring her words. "No siree, ask around, anybody'll tell you I never charge for it. Must be genetic, what do you think? And like Momma, too, seems I can shed inconvenient life in the way of a party."

"Goddammit, Diana!" he hissed. "Pregnant? And the father?"

Diana brushed her bangs from her face. At least there was a spark in the old bastard's eyes.

"The father," she began coyly. "Let's see. That doctor, don't you just love his accent? He said I was probably nine weeks along. Middle of September? Hmmm ... Identity's more the issue. Could have been one of five or six boys. But you know? I was drinking a lot. Could've been more. Not such a big deal now, though, is it Daddy?"

Judge Elliott stiffened and buttoned his overcoat. Speechless for an awkward moment. "You've turned into a drunken slut, Diana," he said coldly. "Get a damned grip on your life!"

And with that, he left.

Chapter 2

Wednesday, December 21, 1988 – 12:10 p.m. EST
White Plains Airport, Westchester County, NY

THE GRUMMAN GULFSTREAM III is the best goddamned business jet in the world. Transatlantic range with eight passengers. Cruise at Flight Level 450 at 500 knots, nearly Mach One at that altitude. A flight deck like the space shuttle and Moroccan leather in back, appointed to impress a sultan, corporate hotshot or pimp.

"I *love* this airplane," thought Danny Halliday, running his fingers along the leading edge of the port wing of Grumman Gulfstream NG399X as it sat on the Dixon Flight Services ramp at White Plains airport.

It was a cold afternoon, 39 degrees with a crisp nip in the air that spelled Christmas. He blew on his fingers and ducked under the wing to inspect the port landing gear.

At twenty-nine, Halliday was barely one year out of the Navy, where he'd tallied more than 3,500 flying hours, mostly at the controls of an S3A Viking sub hunter. More than four hundred carrier launches and landings, everywhere from the waters off Norfolk to the eastern Med. Now he had made his way to his goal of piloting corporate jets. First officer, at least. But the Idaho farm boy had patience. As of the previous week, fifty-two hours on type with the Grumman, one of four pilots on staff with Bakker Worldwide Inc., a global high finance firm out of Manhattan with billions, he'd heard, in overseas dealings. Not bad for a shit heel from Coeur d'Alene.

Danny pulled up the fleece collar of his flight jacket to fend off a gusting northerly wind as he crouched to inspect the tire and strut oleo. Something caught his eye as he glanced up into the darkened wheel well.

"Jesus Christ!" he cursed, reaching up into the gear bay and pulling out an oily blue cotton rag. He put it into his jacket pocket, pulled a cigar-thin Maglite from an upper arm sheath and shone its bright beam around, looking for anything else out of place. Nothing. He swore again under his breath and continued his walkaround with eyes like a hawk, but without further dismay.

"Look at this!" he exclaimed as he entered the cabin and stood at the cockpit door.

He waved the oily blue cloth.

Rick "The Stick" Cunningham, the aircraft captain, was sitting in the co-pilot's seat, checking his Jeppesen charts for their flight. He looked back at Danny, surprised.

"I found this in the port gear well," Halliday said angrily. "A grease nipple rag! Goddamn Dixon, they hire the handicapped, Skipper."

Cunningham smiled.

"Find anything else?" he asked calmly.

"No. But it pisses me off."

Danny started to take off his jacket.

"Not so fast," chirped the captain. "If you're in the left seat today, you gotta stand at the stairs and greet the Boss."

The Navy boy grimaced and cinched up his tie.

"I'll tell ya, someday those cheap sons-a-bitches are gonna get somebody killed."

Halliday descended the airstairs as two Mercedes limos cruised onto the ramp and stopped beside the tan Grumman. The first discharged three women and a thin little man who was dressed for success. From the second, two older men scrambled like bull riders shot from the gate. One, pudgy and balding, laughed as he ran twenty yards onto the tarmac, while the other, a rail in a white Stetson, tossed him a football. It was a bobbled but completed pass.

"Touchdown!" cheered the Boss, pumping his fist. "See, you're not so drunk, Bucky! Should a bought a pro ball team when you had the chance!"

Danny greeted the Boss and his entourage before helping the chauffeurs to load up the luggage. Bags stowed, he signaled to the Dixon ramp hand to remove the wheel chocks, and took a last look around as the limousines glided away. As he entered the aircraft, he glanced back into the cabin. The Boss was already holding court, with Penny, his Number One Girl, serving stiff drinks all around.

Texas born millionaire Teddy Bakker was the son of a Midland wildcatter, a Korean War ace and former airline CEO, now investing his time and money in oil, real estate and manufacturing all over the world.

"Get me to London for breakfast, Navy boy!" Bakker called out boisterously, patting the ass of his Number One Girl as she wiggled past to her seat.

AT 12:41 P.M. Eastern time, nearly a quarter to six in London, Gulfstream NG399X lifted off from White Plains and climbed out over Long Island Sound. The jet nosed onto its flight-planned route: a first waypoint east of Cape Cod, then direct to an airway intersection above the Grand Banks, before a transatlantic great circle route to Britain with landfall over the Irish coast.

Teddy Bakker was on his second bourbon when North America slipped away unnoticed under the port wing of his jet. He had gotten right down to business with Buck Peyton, a friend and an old school oilman from Houston, who faced him in a sumptuous leather throne.

"Buck, you're the biggest lease holder in the Gulf from Biloxi to Brownsville. Which is why you're aboard."

"But not on board, son," Peyton replied, waggling one thick finger from a grip on cut crystal. "You've been playing this thing pretty close to your chest."

"Had to play it that way! Had to cut you from your herd of directors before I could open my mouth."

Buck Peyton snickered. That pretty much summed up his board back in Houston. Bunch of pencil-necked bankers and country club cousins his mother had dug in around her when she had the Chair. Never done a lick of real work in their lives, except for counting their money. *His* money.

"Albion Petroleum," Bakker announced.

"I figured it was AP you had on the line."

Teddy Bakker continued, "AP has been a big North Sea player for years. Largest gas station chain across Britain. Now, this won't hit the news until Friday, but they just agreed to acquire all the remaining shares of Standard of Ohio. Gonna be just as big stateside, and that's one helluva chance for us both to get richer!"

Bakker explained. Earlier in the month he had met with the AP chairman in London. Their acquisition of Standard's chain of Gulf Oil service stations had them hungry for an oil resource in the region. In their sights were Amoco and Atlantic Richfield, the two biggest players in the Gulf of Mexico, with both companies planning a heavy investment in offshore exploration. And if the reserves prove out at the estimate levels? Anyone spudding a hole in the Gulf would become the next blue-eyed sheikh.

Teddy Bakker had quickly seen the value in bringing AP and Peyton together. He learned that Buck was about to sell off his Gulf of Mexico oil and gas leases to fund a refinery expansion in Houston. At least that was the intelligence he had received from a source on Buck Peyton's own board.

"Here's what we have in mind. Keep those Gulf leases for another ten years ..." Bakker waved off a sputter of protest. "Hang on, hear me out. I know you're looking to expand your capacity down in Channelview. Another hundred thousand barrels a day? Smart move if the Gulf pans out like they say."

"How in the hell ..."

Bakker smiled and signaled to Penny to refill their glasses.

"C'mon now, Buck. You don't buy jet fuel like I did at Pan Am without making friends. Got plenty of birdies who vie for my ear."

Bakker laid out the plan he had already set with AP. Were Peyton to sell all his leases, he would raise nearly a quarter billion, clear profit, having acquired those rights back in the 1950s, long before seismic barges were plying the Gulf. But an offer of sale would open the floodgates to competitive bidding. And although Amoco and ARCO had aggressive plans for the region, their conservative boards would scuttle themselves with pennywise cherry picking. To be contenders, the two oil companies would need all the rights that Buck Peyton was holding.

An alternative, Bakker suggested, was that he option those rights, and to just those two giants alone. Exclude all of the others completely.

"No way, son!" Peyton shot back. "Options would fetch me two bits on the dollar. Some might go double that, if we're talking ten years. Thing is, I need that whole dollar now."

"Federal tax incentives?"

Peyton's jowls shook as he laughed.

"Goddamn! Well, that's right. And there's an important point here. I gotta break ground on expansion in this fiscal year. Which means funding the damn thing with no borrowed money, it's only the tax break that makes it worthwhile. Hell of a gamble, building for capacity that ain't already proved. The Gulf might look fine on paper, but I'll tell you what, there's a whole ton of people who think it'll fail!"

Peyton paused to wet his whistle.

"I'm not looking for partners on the refining side," he continued. "Never needed one. But going the financing route? With today's interest rates? Blows the balance sheet out of the water. So, there you are. I'm between a rock and a hard place on this thing. If I sell off those leases, I'm set. Amoco and ARCO are gonna go low, still, selling to those two makes sense for my refinery business. But option? That means nowhere near enough money. No expansion. End of story."

Still, Buck Peyton was grinning.

"Unless some smartass has already come up with a plan."

Teddy Bakker glanced at his finance VP, Mark Salzberg, who rose and delivered a thin legal file to the Boss.

"Financing costs on your build. No partners, straight lending. What kind of numbers are we talking about?"

Peyton answered directly.

"Five years fixed interest on a quarter billion, minus the depreciation on capital assets. We did those numbers, and on the short side, ninety-one million."

Bakker set the folder aside and looked Peyton in the eye.

"Call it an even hundred. Ten-year options to Amoco and ARCO could net you fifty. If there was unencumbered new cash to cover the shortfall, leaving you with your leases in hand, offsetting your capital debt? Would that smell more like a winner?"

"I'm listening."

AP would pay Buck Peyton a one time fee of fifty million dollars for the right of first refusal on the eventual sale of his lease holdings, provided all were optioned to Amoco and ARCO exclusively for ten years. During that time, AP would evaluate the region's proved reserves—and if the numbers look good, it would be their intention to acquire both oil companies and become *the* player in the Gulf of Mexico.

"And if the Gulf comes up dry?"

Bakker chuckled. "Then you'll have a nice new refinery gatherin' dust. But we both know that ain't gonna happen."

THEODORE RUMSFELD BAKKER still had the first dollar he ever made, in a frame on the wall of his Manhattan office. He'd been nine, and in dusty Midland, Texas at the height of the Depression, he invested two dollars in the lemonade stand of a schoolmate whose father made ice. His contribution, beyond the core funding for lemons and sugar, had been his intellect. A fine place to offer cold drinks, Teddy ventured, would be the labor dispatch center for roughnecks working the local oilfield. Four shifts a day came and went, dozens of men with parched throats and a nickel or two. Within a week, his cut of the profits had been eight bucks. By the end of the war, his father had earned millions as an oil patch wildcatter. Young Teddy had made thousands from lemonade and he still had that first dollar bill.

Bakker went on to the University of Texas at Austin, earning a degree in business as well as a reputation as a dogged Longhorns cornerback. Graduating in 1948, he disappointed his oilman father by taking a position with an upstart Texas regional airline.

Trans-West Airlines operated a commercial service out of Austin, with six DC-3s on scheduled routes serving Austin, Fort Worth, Houston, Amarillo and Oklahoma City. It quickly grew to a fleet of fifty surplus DC-3s, DC-4s and cargo versions of the Curtiss C-46 Commando. Skilled aircrews were a dime a dozen and under Ted Bakker, Trans-West had extended its daily service as far as Phoenix in the west, Little Rock to the north, and eastward to Atlanta.

In January 1950, at twenty-four years of age, Bakker earned his commercial pilot's license, married his first wife, Eloise, a former Miss Texas, and became the vice-president of Trans-West. Six months later, with war in Korea, he walked into an Air Force recruiting office on a whim and asked if they needed somebody like him. They did. That's when he made the decision to serve his country like his daddy had as a doughboy back in the Great War.

Bakker trained on the F-51D Mustang and F-86 Sabre jet in New Mexico before being deployed overseas at Christmas that year. Flying with the 35th Fighter-Interceptor Wing from Johnson Air Base, Japan, he got his first two kills over Korea on March 11, 1951. His flight had been escorting a wing of B-29s on a high altitude bombing mission, and he had been the first to spot an approaching squadron of North Korean MIG-15s. On his own, low on fuel, he took a dogfight down to treetop level, gunning down the first MIG before pulling up through nine-Gs in a high yo-yo maneuver, putting him on the tail of the wingman. Three seconds. Long enough to empty his .50-cal load until the only sound of his guns was a cycling click. Two kills in one day. Lieutenant Teddy Bakker had six more by the end of his eighteen-month tour. A true jet Ace.

When he returned to the States in early 1953, he left the Air Force to join Pan American World Airways in Los Angeles. He and Eloise had long since divorced; her infidelity, it was claimed, in spite of the fact he had banged everything in a skirt from Albuquerque to Pusan, Korea and back.

In 1956, at thirty-one years of age, he was promoted to Pan Am Vice President, Western North America and the Orient. He made friends easily in the aviation business. His advice to buy McDonnell-Douglas DC-8 jets—the cheaper competitor to the popular Boeing 707—and to concentrate maintenance in the western U.S. had been a business coup worth hundreds of millions of dollars. The charismatic Los Angeles ace was becoming a star at Pan American Airlines. By 1968, with a second ex-wife, Bakker became its Vice President of Business Development, based in New York—and four short years later, its President and CEO.

The Airline Deregulation Act of 1978, and Teddy's ability to lobby sinners on Capitol Hill, helped international carriers like Pan Am get the domestic routes they had wanted for years. His first move was to spend on new aircraft from Airbus in France, to the chagrin of his friends in the domestic aircraft manufacturing sector. Soon after that was his purchase of New York Air's shuttle service linking New York, Boston and Washington. It was the first of several regional airline acquisitions across the States and throughout Europe, under the Pan Am Shuttle banner.

Pan Am entered the 1980s as a global symbol of the United States, which made it a target for terrorists. As CEO, Teddy

Bakker promoted a new security scheme with a subsidiary company, Alert Management Systems, which promised to address two growing international concerns: gate based screening of passengers, and the matching of baggage to persons on board. The promise proved hollow. In May 1986, Bakker issued a confidential directive that security be kept to a minimum. It must not inconvenience passengers. It must not lose business. Nor could it increase the cost of individual flights at departure. No exceptions.

Bakker struggled with the security whiners as profits steadily fell. Soon, enough was enough. In July 1987, he quit Pan Am and left the airline industry to go into business himself—Bakker Worldwide, Inc.—with corporate offices in sight of the Pan Am headquarters building in midtown Manhattan.

And one of the first things he did was to open his checkbook and buy a Grumman Gulfstream III from a bored Saudi prince. Bakker himself took delivery and was at the controls in the right-hand seat all the way from Jeddah to White Plains.

Chapter 3

Wednesday, December 21, 1988 – 5:29 p.m. GMT
Heathrow Airport Terminal Three, London

"LADIES AND GENTLEMEN, we now wish to commence general boarding for Pan Am Flight 103 to New York JFK. Please check your boarding passes for your row and seat assignment, as we will be boarding in sections from the rear of the aircraft forward," announced a confident feminine voice over the public address system at Gate 14.

"Would passengers seated in rows 41 through 57 please come forward at this time. Rows 41 through 57 only. Please form an orderly queue, and thank you for choosing Pan Am."

Diana Elliott breathed a sigh of relief as she moved with her jacket and Harrods shopping bag in hand toward the departure gate. She had been assigned seat 56-J, the same window seat she enjoyed on the flight from New York. Starboard side, second last row from the rear of the plane.

Boarding at Kennedy three weeks earlier had been a nightmare. After First Class and Clipper Class had been called, the remaining Economy rabble in rows 16 through 57 had been called in no particular order at all. A *nightmare.* At least at Heathrow today they were using their heads.

Diana trudged down the jetway and, once welcomed aboard, marched unimpeded all the way down the starboard aisle to the rear of the aircraft and Row 56.

She placed her jacket and bag in the overhead bin, settled into her window seat, and again sighed with relief as it began to look as if the cabin around her would be sparsely settled. There might be a chance, sometime during the night, to claim an unoccupied center row and stretch out to sleep. Hope springs eternal.

As the last of the travelers straggled in and the cabin lights lowered, Diana noticed a latecomer making her way down the aisle. A peculiar tenseness began to grow in her chest as the young woman approached. She was cradling a baby.

On any other day, Diana's eyes would have rolled in dismay. She'd have felt that *Casablanca* sense of passenger angst—in all of the aircraft cabins in all of the world, a baby is waltzed into mine. Yet, what unsettled Diana wasn't the prospect of a seven-hour flight with a newborn wailing nearby; as the young mother drew closer she could see she was smiling, as blissfully content as the cooing baby she had snuggled against her breast. Rather, it was an acutely painful sense of remorse over her own circumstances and what might have been.

IT WAS HER head, not her heart, that had compelled Diana nearly five years earlier to leave her parents and all things Westchester behind. At eighteen she had needed control—of her life, of herself, of her very existence. It became singularly important to her as she moved on to college. It began with a place of her own, a cramped third floor walk-up on the *upper* Upper East Side—East 117th Street between Park Avenue and Lexington—so far up Lex, as some New Yorkers would say, that on a clear day you can see Puerto Rico.

A crumbling apartment block in Spanish Harlem would hardly have been the Elliott's choice for their daughter. But Diana had truly been emancipated, coming into an inheritance from the estate of her maternal grandmother—a southern society matron who had sworn that the daughter of her only daughter would be free to pursue any dream she chose. It was a trust fund of one million dollars, established to pay for her education, with the remainder invested and inaccessible until she turned twenty-five. Its annual interest was paid to her as a monthly living allowance. So it was thanks to a benefactor who had died before Diana was three, that she was financially independent, never needing a cent from her parents.

She came alive as a student.

In June, Diana had received her undergrad Arts degree magna cum laude with a major in history from Barnard College, Columbia University, Manhattan, earning a 4.7 GPA average. Her thematic concentration in history had been Empires and Colonialism—from merchants, pirates, slaves and the making of Atlantic capitalism from the 1600s to globalized business as a modern proxy for both. The irony of her choice of studies had not escaped her, barely four generations removed from the slave-owning tobacco rich; her education bought by blood and sweat in the mud of the plantation Carolinas.

For four years she had thrown herself into academics and thrived. She had an incisive mind, rare even at exclusive Barnard, where the majority of undergrads remained vacuous sponges, regurgitators of fact, content to cruise through the history of civilization as an easy ride to straight C scholastic mediocrity.

Once in her junior year, a bright bulb in her study group had quipped, "They want us to embrace a contentious issue. Every damn topic's been studied to death. All we need to do this term is buy into a half decent, dusty perspective and just milk it. Are we agreed?"

"Fuck off," she had said. Hardly a debate counterpoint that would have earned her team kudos at Le Sommet.

"History is a living thing!" she continued, to the guffaws of her classmates. "A continuum. Like Professor Gaudreau said about Gorbachev de-Stalinizing the Soviet Union. Did you read Thatcher's quote in the Times? 'I like Mr. Gorbachev. We can do business together.' *That's* history. Russia could be the next great capitalist empire. Who knows, in five or ten years? Maybe the Chinese."

"Fuck off, yourself, Diana," Josh Eisner had groaned, the study group's leader and big man on campus whom she'd bedded once, surprisingly completely sober. "We all think it's time you were leaving the group. Start one of your own. Maybe with Jose Cuervo, Jack Daniels and the rest of your friends."

She had gotten up from her chair in the seminar room where they had been meeting all year, in Fayerweather Hall, just off Morningside Park on the Columbia campus.

"It's Jack *Daniel*, moron," she said as she'd collected her books. "You'd drop the apostrophe 'S'." Then she quietly left.

ON MONDAY, NOVEMBER 28th, barely a week out of hospital, Diana had risen at noon, packed one bag, hailed a cab and simply said to the driver, "JFK, please."

Even as she entered the overseas departure concourse at Kennedy Terminal One, she had no idea where she might end up. She looked right: Air India, Singapore Airlines, further along, Turkish Airways. Looking left: Lufthansa, Air France and a couple of others. Pan Am was closest. It had the shortest ticket lines, and so she marched directly over and joined one at random.

Electronic boards had listed impending departures, a dozen choices from London to Capetown to Delhi. London was leaving in less than an hour. Museums and pubs and pasty-faced men with bucked teeth. Timing in the end was the deciding factor and when she took her turn before a smiling Pan Am agent, she said: "London, return. Economy please, and back to New York before Christmas."

Eight hours later, just after six a.m. local time, Diana arrived at Heathrow Airport just west of London. She breezed through customs and, after studying tourist information and the commuter train route map for the city, selected Kensington in London's west end as her next destination. It had Hyde Park, which she'd always wanted to see. Museums, hotels and a nightlife. Walking distance of the city center and sights. Where better to start?

It was 8:30 when Diana ascended the stairs from the Gloucester Road Underground station into bright sunlight and, strangely, onto a traffic island in the intersection of Gloucester and Cromwell Roads.

Both streets were lined with four-story Georgian townhouses in a whitewashed eclectic mix of private homes, shops, cafés, and bed and breakfast hotels. Diana walked north on Gloucester Road for a block when she noticed the flickering neon 'Vacancy' sign in the lead-paned front window of a B&B called The Harrington. It had a pillared entrance with marble steps up from the sidewalk to double oak doors. Its frontage was lined by a low wrought iron fence, glistening with layers of black enamel paint which might first have been daubed in Queen Victoria's time. Diana excused herself to the river of pedestrians parting around her and went in.

That first morning, Diana stowed her luggage away and set out to explore Hyde Park, four blocks to the north. She enjoyed it immensely. Kensington Gardens, strolling the Serpentine, Speakers Corner—where she stood for a while in a small crowd of locals, listening to some loudmouth spout off about the Red Menace and *perestroika*. By noon, jet lag had set in, and after a coffee at a sidewalk café near the park, she returned to her hotel and slept for the rest of the day.

She woke at just past dinnertime and wandered three blocks down Cromwell Road, ending up in a pub called 'The Parchment and Quill'. There she stood at the bar, as one does in an English pub, and ordered a pint of draught apple cider. The choice intrigued a middle-aged man who was standing beside her, sipping a pint of brown ale. They talked and in time were exchanging life stories. His name was McColl—*just McColl*—a tour bus driver from Manchester whose group was bedded down for the night at a B&B a few blocks away.

McColl had a daughter, fifteen, named Amber, who lived with her mother in Chester, three hours north of London. His ex-wife was a bitch. She'd left him when he was a soldier, a corporal in the Green Howards, an infantry regiment, while he'd been serving his second tour in Northern Ireland. He liked American jazz and dreamed of owning a bar in Ibiza— it's a Spanish island in the Mediterranean, but Diana knew that. Good sense of humor. An engaging smile. As last orders were called at eleven p.m., Diana gave McColl a kiss on the cheek, which he accepted with grace, and then she left alone, feeling more content and clear headed than she had for ages.

Over the three weeks that followed, Diana spent most of her days touring museums—of civilization, science and art. And every night she found a new pub within walking distance of her hotel and almost always found someone like McColl. Men of various ages, looks and intentions, whom she would enjoy through hours of casual conversation, and leave at the post at the end of the night, unhappily marking their cards 'Did Not Finish'.

Chapter 4

Wednesday, December 21, 1988 – 6:04 p.m. GMT
Heathrow Airport Terminal Three, London

"CLIPPER 103, HEATHROW Ground, cleared to push back at Kilo fourteen. Standby for airways." The Heathrow air traffic controller responsible for ground movement on the airport was busy. She had eighteen aircraft maneuvering on the thirty-five miles of tarmac and taxiways at Britain's busiest airport. Pan Am Flight 103 was just one that she had to work into her mix.

"Clipper 103, roger," the co-pilot replied.

With 'push back' cleared, the crew of the Boeing 747 was authorized to back away from the terminal jetway, to hold on the ramp and await further instructions. 'Airways' is ATC jargon for a flight's clearance to travel through controlled airspace from its point of departure to their destination. It is based on a flight plan filed in advance by the crew.

Pan Am Flight 103 was planned on a scheduled route that would take it outbound from Heathrow on what was locally known as a 'Daventry Departure'—climbing northward to its flight altitude over Scotland, then west along a pre-determined oceanic track across the Atlantic to the North American coast south of Boston, and finally south to New York JFK. With its four turbofan engines generating power, the jumbo jet inched away from its parking spot as its flight crew watched the conical orange flashlights of the marshaller signaling all clear and waving them back.

"Clipper 103, Heathrow, airways."

"Clipper 103, go ahead."

There was a pause as the Heathrow ground controller collected her thoughts.

"ATC clears Clipper 103 to the New York Kennedy airport via Heathrow, a Daventry departure, flight level three-one-zero, your flight planned route. Depart runway two-seven right, turn right direct the Burnham VOR, climb to six thousand and turn right to a heading of three-five-zero direct Bovingdon, to cross Bovingdon at six thousand or below and standby for further."

The co-pilot read back the ATC clearance correctly.

"Clipper 103, Heathrow Ground, cleared to taxi to runway two-seven right via the inner Whiskey taxiway. Hold short of two-seven right for take-off. Be advised, there is construction activity on the outer taxiway."

"Ground, Clipper 103, roger. Taxi to two-seven right via the inner and we acknowledge the work on the outer."

The Boeing 747-120, registered as N739PA, had begun its travels that morning nearly eight thousand miles away in San Francisco, California. It had been flown by two different crews of sixteen, each comprised of three cockpit crew and thirteen flight attendants. The aircraft itself was eighteen years old, having been built in Everett, Washington in 1970. On this day it had 72,464 flying hours on its airframe, having completed a total of 16,497 take-offs and landings—average usage for a working wide-bodied jet of its age.

As it taxied away from parking spot K-14 at Heathrow, Pan Am Flight 103, Clipper Maid of the Seas, weighed in at just over 713,000 pounds. It carried nearly a quarter million pounds of fuel and it prepared to leave Heathrow with, as they say in the industry, 259 souls on board.

Wednesday, December 21, 1988 – 6:25 p.m. GMT

DIANA FELT THE huge aircraft gently heave and shudder as it accelerated down the runway. Its engines roared as she watched white runway lights quickly speed past her window. The shuddering grew stronger and climactically stopped as the ribbon of lights fell away, the view swiftly replaced by a twinkling patchwork of neighborhoods and motorways spreading off to the horizon. She relaxed and settled into her seat as the 747 climbed silkily into the night sky, the roar of its engines throttling back to a low comforting rumble.

The cabin of the Boeing had been darkened for its takeoff climb, but the scattered soft cones of light from overhead reading lamps and the banter and laughter she heard gave it a warm Christmas feel. Outside, the brilliant spread of London's suburbs began disappearing behind dark, scudding cloud—then, in an instant, they vanished completely as the aircraft climbed into a thick fog-like layer of low stratus.

Diana looked up the aisle as the cabin lights raised and saw flight attendants busying themselves in the timeless routine of bringing the first drinks around. She decided she would drink tonight. They wouldn't have tequila, would they? What the hell, they'd have bourbon. She'd order a double.

Within days of arriving in London, Diana had called home to Westchester and spoke with her mother. It had been just after breakfast New York time and Mommy Dearest had been sober and lucid. She had nearly expressed her surprise at that before she stopped herself. If she was going to make an attempt to change, to really work on their relationship, heartlessly dismissing her mother as she so often had would be the first impulse she'd need to control.

"London? England?" her mother exclaimed. "Jesus, Diana, you might have said you were going abroad. And just out of the hospital? Was that really wise?"

Neither the recovery from her miscarriage, nor the purpose, quality and length of her stay had been details that came up in their conversation. Diana had cut to the chase, explaining simply that she had needed to spend some time away—from New York, from her life—just to get some perspective, some time on her own just to think. It was a motivation that Charlotte Elliott well understood. Nothing more needed to be said. The brief call had concluded when

Diana said she would return before Christmas. She promised that she would phone again with her plans. Both women came away from the call with a simmering feeling of warmth. For once they had managed to be genuinely civil to one another.

Diana had kept her promise, calling home before leaving her hotel for the airport. This time, however, her heart sank when it was quickly apparent her mother was drinking. Not quite noon in New York. Still, Diana had passed on the details of her flight and had asked about the possibility of a family Christmas at home in Port Chester. It was a legitimate question, as her family, such as it was, had taken to observing the holiday with a restaurant brunch in Manhattan.

A long pause had followed and Diana thought she heard her mother utter a sob. "Darling," her mother had said, "that would be the best gift I could ever imagine. You know I've really missed you, sweet girl."

"And Daddy?"

"More than you could know."

"Okay, Momma. I'll be home tomorrow," Diana had replied brightly, instantly needing to finish the call. "See you then."

Wednesday, December 21, 1988 – 6:56 p.m. GMT

PAN AM FLIGHT 103 leveled off at its cruising altitude of Flight Level 310—thirty-one thousand feet above the lowland moors of northwest England, forty miles to the east of the coastal resort city of Blackpool on the Irish Sea. It was nearing the end of the first leg of its journey, having just passed overhead the Pole Hill VOR, an omni-directional radio beacon transmitting near the town of Burnley, County Lancashire. The black dome of the night sky overhead was ablaze with stars and a nearly full moon shone down, illuminating the countryside and the tops of lower cloud layers with an ethereal silvery glow.

Diana lowered her chair back table and smiled at the prim middle-aged stewardess who set down two short glasses, one filled with ice, a small bottle of spring water, and two miniatures of Jim Beam bourbon. It was intuitive service in response to Diana's cryptic two-finger signal as she had mouthed the word 'bourbon'. Sad to see a seasoned boozer in someone so young, the airline hostess had thought.

The smoky wet newspaper taste of bourbon sipped neat had Diana wrinkling her nose. It had been weeks since she had allowed herself to indulge in her preferred evil spirit. Glass in hand, she settled back in her seat and her thoughts shifted from Christmas and the prospect of an Elliott reunion to the dilemma that had dogged her since graduating from Barnard in June—choosing a university where she would continue her scholarly studies.

"You have the finest mind I've encountered in years, dear Diana," Professor Philippe Gaudreau had said, kissing her cheek on the morning of her degree convocation.

Her professor of modern history had enjoyed that brief moment of intimate contact, having dutifully resisted a romantic fixation with Diana since becoming her academic advisor in her junior year. Gaudreau had encouraged her to pursue the lofty goal of national policymaking, to further her education to the master's and doctoral level in the analysis, management and leadership of public policy.

The Kennedy School at Harvard would be an excellent choice, and with his recommendation and contacts her acceptance was more than assured. Consider the London School of Economics, he had added. The Department of International Studies at the LSE is a recognized world leader and its alumni include ministers of government, diplomats and senior decision makers from London to Tokyo. Or perhaps his own first field of study and alma mater: political science at the University of Paris-Sorbonne. Her linguistic abilities would serve her well there. As would, he had joked, her talent in drinking lesser mortals under the table.

"Follow the important road, Diana," Gaudreau had urged. "Become what I am certain you were born to be: the conceiver, the creator of the policy of nations, and not simply as I am, regrettably, its impotent student."

"Cher professeur," she had teased in reply. *"Je doute que l'impuissance est un mot qui pourrait décrire vous."* No. Impotent wasn't a word that would have come to mind in describing Gaudreau, she'd always imagined him as anything but.

Diana did consider the LSE and had visited it briefly during her stay in London. She had strolled around its compact campus, smack dab in the center of the city, collecting some student information, taking nothing much more than a cursory look. Soon after arriving and even before touring the school, she had mentally struck LSE off the list. London, like New York, was too vibrant and interesting a city for someone like her. Too many distractions. The Sorbonne wasn't off the list yet and she was considering a trip to Paris, possibly early in the New Year. Still, it would present the same impediments if not more. If she were to settle down and dedicate herself to scholarly pursuits, her best bet, she had already guessed, would likely be Harvard.

"Well," Diana thought as she sipped her bourbon once more. "Gaudreau would be impressed with my logic."

It was 6:58 p.m. GMT and in the cockpit of Pan Am 103 the first officer selected the ATC frequency for the Shanwick Oceanic Control Area—a broad section of airspace over the North Atlantic to the west of Ireland and the British Isles—controlled jointly by an ATC center in Shannon, Ireland and another in Prestwick, Scotland. He pressed the transmit button on his controls and made the required initial contact, identifying his flight and reporting its altitude.

"Good evening Scottish, Clipper 103, we are level at three-one-zero," he said brightly.

Six miles below and more than one hundred ahead, a controller in the Prestwick area control center near Ayrshire, Scotland, had been following the computer generated icon representing Flight 103 at the bottom of his radar display. He tapped a forefinger on the tiny square on the screen with its trailing data flag—the plane's callsign, assigned and actual altitude, returned electronically from the aircraft by radio transponder.

He moved a tan plastic sleeve—containing a paper flight data strip with computer generated information about Pan Am 103, its flight plan and clearance—from a stack representing high level flights coming into his area, and set it into the tray of those he was actively controlling.

"One-oh-three, you are identified," he replied. He now had control of the flight through his airspace.

Wednesday, December 21, 1988 – 7:01 p.m. GMT

DIANA GLIMPSED THE young mother and her baby seated in 56G, just slightly ahead in the right-hand seat in the center block of her row. She had heard that young babies can only focus their vision to a maximum of eighteen inches, which must be why, she supposed, that adults for millennia have gotten right into their faces with their bloody goo-goos and gaa-gaas, as the young woman did. Repeatedly brushing her child's nose with her own, side to side, drawing back and alternating between cutesy fart-like raspberries and soft puffs of air. Always with a renewed wide-eyed look of wonder. And each time, the baby would smile. It would actually smile.

Diana bit her lip at having just thought of the baby as *it*. She didn't know whether the child was a girl or a boy, swaddled in a gender neutral yellow cotton blanket in the woman's arms. And it wasn't as if those cherubic features— bright blue eyes, button nose and sparse dark curls of impossibly fine hair—gave a clue as to whether it was little Johnny or Janie. *Simply it.*

It, she thought darkly, is an object, not a person. An animal or thing previously mentioned or under discussion. A neuter personal pronoun in the third person singular. Not a live, growing being, a human entity with a developing mind and a soul or the prospect of either.

Tears welled in her eyes and she wiped them away.

She took a large mouthful of whiskey and swallowed it hard. *It* was a thing she had lost when she had miscarried. Not a person, not yet. Never meant to exist. Never …

Diana didn't get the chance to complete that thought.

At seconds short of 7:03 p.m. GMT, preceded by a loud muffled bang, the Boeing 747 lurched violently to the left. Diana's head slammed against the cabin window and she was knocked unconscious.

Screams filled the cabin of Pan Am Flight 103.

Those in the rear of the aircraft around Diana Elliott watched in horror as the cabin ahead bucked and twisted, shuddering first to the left, then hard to the right. And then, suddenly, to the shriek of rending metal, it opened to the night sky as a fireball exploded toward them.

Chapter 5

Wednesday, December 21, 1988 – 7:03 p.m. GMT
Lockerbie, Scotland

"HOLD YOUR HORSES, Dearie," Keith Brunskill cooed as he opened the door to the mud room. It was a porch at the rear of his brick townhouse home on Victoria Road in Lockerbie, Scotland—a sleepy rural town of four thousand in the district of Dumfries and Galloway, just twenty miles north of the border with England.

"Don't piss on mummy's clean floor," he said, completing his admonishment to the skittish female Border Collie that he and his wife Maggie had had since she'd been a pup. Now fourteen, grey and old, Dearie scratched anxiously at the door as her master attached a leash to her collar.

"It's a blustery night out there, old girl, and I need to put on a cap," he said, rummaging through a shelf of ball caps over the mud room door. The fifty-two year old long-haul lorry driver selected his most recent favorite: a black New York Yankees cap that his nephew had given him on his birthday that year after a honeymoon trip to the States.

"We're set now, let's go," he said, pausing for a moment to shout over his shoulder: "Maggie, sweetheart, we're out for our walk. Back soon, love ye later."

Brunskill's wife of thirty-three years was in their parlor, sitting wrapped in the blanket he'd just put around her, in front of their telly with a cup of tea. She was dying from fiber-induced interstitial fibrosis, a lung disease she had contracted as a girl working in the fabric mill sweatshops of Glasgow. Maggie had been diagnosed as terminal that summer, with a year to live, maybe more. Once a bright eyed and vibrant woman who had raised their two children, she had been reduced to a skeleton shrouded in grey leathery skin. She had wasted to eighty-five pounds, with hardly the strength to shift from that chair to the bed that Keith had set up for her in their parlor. Lately, more often than not, she was the one and not Dearie who pissed on the floor.

Brunskill stepped out into the dark windy night and tugged Dearie along as he headed out onto Victoria Road, overlooking the town center of Lockerbie, lying in a broad valley in the Scottish lowlands.

Dearie stopped as they turned in the middle of the broad suburban street and looked to the south. She whined and wouldn't move, sitting strangely alert on her haunches.

"Come now, little lass," Keith said, trying to tug her along. "This is no place to do your business."

Something made him look up into the sky.

He heard a low rumbling sound. It couldn't be thunder, not this time of the year, and there wasn't much cloud on the bright starry night. He turned up the collar of his jacket against the stiff gusty wind and cocked an ear, hearing a distant roar. He looked ahead over the town and saw what looked like dark snow falling onto the rooftops just south of Victoria road.

"What the hell?" he wondered aloud.

Then he heard what sounded like dustbin lids clattering on pavement. Dearie continued to whine and refused to move.

"What the hell!" he repeated, as dark objects fell from the sky and bounced off the roadway, maybe fifty yards ahead. That was when his attention was suddenly drawn to a bright light in the sky. A comet streaking toward the earth, toward the town, with a long line of boiling orange white flame and a roar that grew louder and louder.

Keith watched in awe as the comet came screaming down and hit just south of town center. By the A74 motorway, Sherwood Crescent, he reckoned. The impact came with a brilliant explosion, like holiday fireworks, sending dozens of bright spikes of flame hundreds of feet into the sky. It was followed by the thundering boom of its impact and a shock wave he felt over the gusting wind. And now in the distance, a surreal mushroom cloud of rolling flame.

Keith dropped Dearie's leash and started to jog down Victoria Road. At 245 pounds, with a beer belly that sagged over his forty-two inch waist, the former British Army medic hadn't run for years. But now he was breaking a sweat. A meteorite, he thought. Or perhaps a satellite, one of those bloody Russian or American satellites that keep thundering down onto innocent people. Good Lord! An explosion like that in the center of town, the toll must be horrific. He could help and was determined he would.

He ran south onto tree lined Saint Bryde's Terrace which would cross Dumfries Road in about three hundred yards. As Brunskill ran, gasping for breath, the fireball ahead had begun to subside. Still, a raging inferno brightened the night sky like a monumental bonfire.

Another five minutes along, as he neared Sherwood Crescent, he stopped, out of breath. It was the first time he had noticed the debris that littered the asphalt at his feet. He gasped, took a moment with his head dipped to his knees and slowed his heart rate. In seconds he stood erect. This wasn't a dream. The raging flames from Sherwood Crescent were real. He could feel, smell and taste them.

A piece of paper blew in the gusting wind past him and he instinctively stamped his foot down and trapped it. Exhaling loudly, he bent over and retrieved it. He didn't know what to make of it at first. A scorched piece of paper. What was this? Some kind of ticket? He adjusted his sweat-steamed eyeglasses and peered down at the paper he held. It was a Pan Am airlines boarding pass. It bore someone's name. Today's date. A flight from LHR—he knew that was London Heathrow—to JFK, which he knew from Robbie and Cilla's honeymoon trip was New York Kennedy airport. In an instant it all came together.

"Jesus!" Brunskill exclaimed. "It's a crash."

Wednesday, December 21, 1988 – 8:35 p.m. GMT

GULFSTREAM NG399X WAS cruising as smoothly as oil on glass, three hundred miles southeast of Nova Scotia at Flight Level 390. It was three hours out from White Plains, New York, and local time for those on board was only 3:35 p.m. Eastern Standard Time—yet it was dark and well after cocktail hour for Teddy Bakker and guests.

Bakker sat smugly assured that his plan for Buck Peyton and Albion Petroleum was well in hand. Chitchat after their important business had been reduced to speculation on the Longhorns winning their conference this season, the relative merits of his G3 business jet versus Peyton's Lear 35, and the odds that Bakker's Number One Girl—Miss February 1980— would flash her tits at Peyton if Teddy just asked.

"You know, Buck," Bakker said, sucking down the vestiges of Old Fitzgerald bourbon in his crystal glass. "I think you're gonna like these Brits. Buy into this deal, I'll do my thing on Wall Street, and in ten years we'll be billionaires."

"Don't count your money yet," Peyton replied. Bakker had tossed around numbers that seemed too good to be true. He wished he could put them to Jeffrey Lowe, the bean counter who'd hovered over his shoulder for years.

"I'd be a lot happier," Peyton said, "if I could run your numbers past my top kick in Houston."

Bakker belched and politely excused himself. His eyes lit up like a kid's at Christmas. "I'd be happy to connect you, old buddy," he said, opening a door in the bulkhead next to his seat and extracting a telephone handset.

"Satellite telephone service!" Bakker announced. "Just like your car radio phone in the back forty, but this one connects you worldwide. And it's portable too. The size of a briefcase and plugs in like Lego. I first had this one installed in my turboprop Cessna. Wanna give it a try?"

Peyton threw him a dismissive wave. "Naw, gimme another drink. I'll call him from London."

Penny appeared out of nowhere with another glass of Bakker's best bourbon. A moment later, a red light flashed on the bulkhead next to Bakker's left hand.

"Now, look at that! Middle of the Atlantic and I'm getting a call. You will excuse me, Buck, if I answer this thing?"

With ceremony he put the handset to his ear and answered, "This is Bakker."

William Thurston, his vice-president of operations, was calling from Bakker's Manhattan office.

"It's Bill. About ninety minutes ago, a Clipper 747 went down in southern Scotland ... It was out of Heathrow for Kennedy. It's all over the news. They're showing footage on CNN right now. Christ, Ted, it crashed into a village. This does not look good."

"I see," Bakker replied soberly.

He lowered his voice to a whisper. "Keep me updated tonight. We'll be arriving in London in about four hours. You have the itinerary. Now listen carefully, Bill. Call Gerry Weinstein at home. I want him to dump all my Class-A Pan Am. First thing in the morning."

"Pan Am shares. Dump all your Pan Am?"

"That's right. At the opening bell."

Wednesday, December 21, 1988 — 5:48 p.m. EST
21 Rye Road, Port Chester, New York

JUDGE RANDOLPH OWENS Elliott was smiling as he entered the study of his Port Chester home. He set his briefcase down on an oxblood leather chair, one of two facing his massive mahogany desk—once the prized possession of his father, Lieutenant General William Randolph Elliott, deputy commandant of the Marine Corps when Hoover was commander-in-chief.

Earlier that afternoon, Charlotte had contacted him in his chambers and she'd sounded so girlishly giddy that he assumed she was drunk. Soon, though, it became clear that Diana had called. She was hoping to spend Christmas at home and Charlotte sounded more excited than she had in years. He was even more surprised when she greeted him at the door with a kiss on the cheek, martini in hand but a welcome reception nonetheless. Elliott returned the surprise with a hug, watching as she returned to the living room, knelt next to their Christmas tree, and attended to wrapping a mountain of gifts. She had even shooed him away to his study, to his routine of working over a drink before dinner, when there was dinner to be had. More often than not his evening meals were a sandwich alone with Charlotte passed out on the sofa. But tonight he could smell a pot roast.

His court had recessed for the holiday season earlier in the week, but Judge Elliott had spent the day in his chambers, drafting his charge to the jury in the civil case presently before him. For three weeks he had been hearing the convoluted case of Gursky v. The Sorsheim Gallery, Janus Sorsheim, et al.

In her claim, Julia Gursky, of Brooklyn, New York, plaintiff, alleged that the Sorsheim Gallery of Manhattan and its principal owner, Janus Sorsheim, had presented a painting for sale—'A Girl with Apples', by the late Polish artist Jerzy Wisniewski—with the full knowledge that it had been stolen during the Nazi occupation of Poland in 1941. A theft perpetrated by persons unknown from the estate of Solomon Gursky, a Jew and resident of Warsaw, deceased.

The claim maintained that its rightful owner, the estate of Solomon Gursky and its sole legal heir, Julia Gursky, should redeem the work with the full color of original title.

A goddamned painting stolen by Nazis.

He had seen it, and in his estimation the bloody thing wasn't even that good. Not the work of what he would consider a master, and valued at thirteen million dollars? Its value wasn't material here. The federal court had jurisdiction over the matter as it was alleged the artwork was brought into the country as wartime loot.

The case itself was annoying.

Attorneys for the plaintiff had ridden in on the high horse of Nazi war crimes—the looting of the intimate and valued possessions of the tragically doomed, wrapped in the barbed wire embrace of the Holocaust. One press wag had quipped: "A court case like this one in New York, New York? If you can't make it there, you can't make it anywhere. "

But, and there's always a but, the plaintiff had the onus of proving the artwork had been stolen in the first place and that Sorsheim had knowledge of its original title, of its subsequent theft and of claims to its ownership since.

Her legal argument was thin, but if the jury believed it, Julia Gursky—a woman whom Judge Elliott had found to be detestable—would get the windfall of a multimillion dollar work of art once owned by an uncle she'd never known. Or, if the jury chose to accept the evidence of the defendant's experts, a slimy art dealer from Soho with a comb over as bad as his affected English accent would reap spoils on the ashes of a Holocaust victim. Either way, his charge to the jury would be judicially sage, and as to the outcome of Gursky v. Sorsheim, Judge Randolph Elliott was more than completely impartial—he could not have cared less who prevailed.

Judge Elliott stood at the credenza behind his desk and poured himself two fingers of good single malt scotch and laid the case file on his desk.

Sitting in his chair as he usually did this time of the day, he picked up the remote control to the television fitted into a bookcase on the opposite wall, clicked on the power and turned down the volume. The New York PBS station was showing a nature documentary and in moments it would air its national news program, *The MacNeil/Lerher News Hour*. He thumbed through the file on his desk and picked up the mike to his Dictaphone.

"Andy, this continues the first draft of my charge to the jury on Sorsheim," he began, clearing his throat and taking a sip of scotch.

"Paragraph six. In citing Lussier, add the reference here, the defendant argues that the failure of the United States to criminally indict under the National Stolen Properties Act is, on the face of it, evidence that the painting was not stolen but, rather, subject to a genuine ownership dispute. He further contends that Polish law is unclear as to the painting's provenance. These arguments are even less persuasive now than they were in the motion to dismiss stage. Full stop. Excerpt the motion ruling here. I continue: This court has already found that the documentary evidence of severalty, at plaintiff's Exhibit 17, provides ..."

His attention was distracted by a television image of flaming disaster and he paused from dictating to turn up the sound.

"... clearly as devastating as it has been tonight," the male announcer said gravely, shuffling papers before him.

"To recap this story, a Pan American Airways Boeing 747, believed to have departed this evening from London for New York's John F. Kennedy airport, has crashed in southern Scotland with as many as three hundred on board. We're not sure at this point just how many American passengers may have been on the flight. We're showing scenes here live from the village of Lockerbie, Scotland. Total devastation, as you can see. We're told that the prospect for survivors is not looking good. In a moment, we'll go to BBC correspondent Roger Goodale at Heathrow Airport in London."

Judge Elliott dropped the microphone to his recorder and gaped at the television. An icy ball of alarm began to form in his chest and at the same moment he heard Charlotte's anguished cry from the living room.

"Oh, no, no!" he stammered aloud, rising to his feet as Charlotte appeared in the doorway, trembling and white as a sheet. He could hear the newscaster's voice echoing eerily from down the hall.

"Pan American, Char?" he gasped. "Did you say Pan Am? Tonight home from London? There must have been plenty of flights. Not just this one, surely!"

Elliott put his arm around his wife's shoulders as they stood numbly staring at the images on the television.

Flames rose against a night sky. Rows of quaint stone and brick cottages, narrow cobblestone streets littered with smoking debris. Men in wool coats and stocking caps looking on somberly. Plainly dressed women wearing kerchiefs, sobbing and wringing their hands. It was a surreal scene, almost as if it were newsreel footage of the wartime blitz.

And they cried.

THAT EVENING, RANDOLPH and Charlotte Elliott came to experience the uniquely disconsolate hell of parents with unconfirmed news of the loss of a child. They sat in their living room, with the irony of its holiday splendor mercifully going unnoticed, transfixed by continuous television coverage of the crash aftermath on CNN cable news. The Judge paced. Charlotte's sobs ebbed to mournful irregular sighs and then to silence as the disaster images began to repeat at the top and bottom of each passing hour.

The telephone calls began just after eight.

First was Judge Elliott's sister, Dr. Annabel Freeman, a gerontologist who lived with her husband and family in their nearby birthplace of East Fishkill. Charlotte had called her that morning with the news of Diana's homecoming, and an invitation to the Christmas Day dinner she had excitedly begun to plan. Belle had always been a level headed woman, thrifty with words and emotions, but tonight her voice trembled. Were they certain that this had been Diana's flight? The Judge replied with fact: they didn't know, but it seemed likely. CNN had reported that it was the only Pan Am flight out of Heathrow for Kennedy that dinnertime. Belle offered hope and promised to call again.

The second came soon afterward from Andrew Connachie, Judge Elliott's doting clerk, who had spent the day working with him on Gursky v. Sorsheim. At twenty-eight, the young lawyer, who was also a Yalie, was as devoted a law clerk as any in the Southern District. More so, having a personal affinity for Judge Elliott, a surrogate father figure in his eyes.

"Sir, I have taken the liberty of contacting the airline on your behalf," Connachie began. "I know that your daughter had been … independent, and that your information as next of kin might not have been, well, readily available. They have it now and will call you at home as details become clearer."

"Thank you, Andy," Judge Elliott replied sincerely. It hadn't occurred to him that the airline would have no immediate way of connecting Diana to her parents. "As usual, you are one step ahead. I don't know what I … what we would do without your presence of mind."

"If there is anything else I can do?" Connachie asked, rhetorical assurance that he too would be fretting through the night. "Susan and I are thinking of you both."

Judge Elliott's heart leapt at just after nine when the third call of the evening came. Now he was expecting Pan Am, expecting the worst, but it was the warm feminine voice of his boss, Livna Geller, Chief Judge for the Southern District.

"Liv?" he inquired with surprise.

"Andy Connachie called," she began. Mystery solved.

"I am so, so hopeful that this is all …" she continued, her voice breaking, and uncharacteristically at a loss for just the right words.

"I'm doubtful, frankly," Judge Elliott said, lowering his voice as he noticed tears welling again in Charlotte's eyes. He walked out of earshot with the portable phone.

"She didn't give Charlotte the flight number. Just that it was Pan Am out of Heathrow tonight," he continued. "The news suggests it was their only ... well, the facts seem to be clearly indicating the worst."

"How is Charlotte bearing up?" she asked, more genuinely than he expected. In the five years that they had worked with each other, Liv Geller's world-class charm had never extended to much more than tight lipped acceptance that poor Randy's alcoholic shrew of a wife was his cross to bear.

"I don't know. I can't tell. But today, I'd never seen her so buoyant. She'll fall even harder."

"Just hold her, Randy," was her parting advice.

He did. It wasn't enough.

At around ten o'clock, Charlotte wobbled to her feet after barely saying a word the whole evening. She knocked over an untouched drink and—as was her way—smiled weakly with unfocused eyes, and trotted off straight up to bed.

It was nearly midnight when the phone rang again. It was an operations manager from Pan American asking for Mr. Randolph Elliott. He had the sad duty to inform him that his daughter, Diana Jane Elliott had been confirmed as a passenger on its Flight 103 out of Heathrow, which had been accidentally lost this evening with little hope of survivors. He expressed the sincerest sympathies of the Pan Am family and provided a toll free number which Mr. Elliott could call in the morning for updated information. The Judge thanked him and said goodnight.

Judge Elliott switched off the Christmas tree lights and the television before darkening the living room and trudging through their cavernous kitchen. It was all secure with the pot roast where they'd left it on the counter.

He continued into his study.

The PBS channel he'd last been watching had gone off the air. He meant to switch off the television but hit the wrong buttons on that damned remote and a local news station appeared with the same images of burning wreckage in Lockerbie. The glass of scotch he'd been drinking was just where he left it. He gulped it back as he watched the news for a moment before switching it off.

He changed into pajamas, washed his face and brushed his teeth in the master bedroom ensuite bath, nightly ablutions that were automatic, and slipped into bed beside Charlotte, who was asleep and still fully dressed. She sensed him beside her and rolled against him, swung her arm over and snuggled her face into his chest.

"She's gone isn't she, Randy," she murmured sleepily, without opening her eyes.

"Yes," was all he could muster, clearing tears from his throat and holding her tighter.

"My sweet baby girl," Charlotte mewed, and in seconds she was softly snoring.

Randolph Elliott lay awake for an eternity, comforted by Charlotte's embrace but unable to rid his mind of the last spiteful words he had said to his daughter.

It was absolute anguish no parent should feel.

Chapter 6

Thursday, December 22, 1988 – 6:06 a.m. EST
21 Rye Road, Port Chester, New York

JUDGE ELLIOTT WOKE with a start at six minutes past six, having slept fitfully for just under four hours. His pillow was soaked with cold sweat, and inhaling with a loud gasp was his first conscious act of the day. His next was to stifle a sob, with the events of the previous night all too clear in his mind. Charlotte was already up. He heard the sound of her running a shower behind the closed door of their master bathroom.

On any other weekday morning, Randolph Elliott would have donned his running gear and set off from their Port Chester waterfront home to run precisely a mile and a half. His circuit for years had been exactly the same—west from their gated drive at the end of Rye Road, up to connect with Grace Church Street, winding south past Kirby Pond and around on the north circuit of Manursing Island before retracing his route back home. One and a half miles. Not a jog but a run; a morning routine he'd begun in Marine Corps officers basic and one that had stuck with him since. A mile and a half in under the Corps standard of thirteen minutes, and even at age fifty-eight, one he could still meet without breaking that much of a sweat.

But today Elliott skipped his run. Instead he slipped on a clean, plain gray USMC tracksuit and socks and quietly made his way to the kitchen. He put on a pot of coffee, leaving it percolating over a low gas flame as he moved on to his study and, hesitating a moment, turned on the television.

CNN cable news continued its coverage of the Pan Am crash. Grim crash footage from Lockerbie—smoldering wreckage, devastated homes, lines of policemen in checkerboard caps traversing the low rolling countryside, examining and tagging pieces of wreckage, flagging what likely had to be bodies or body parts. Judge Elliott muted the sound. He couldn't bear to hear the newscaster's account, which only rehashed what they had heard the previous night.

At just short of six-thirty, he returned to the kitchen to get a cup of coffee. Charlotte should be down by now, he thought, sadly wondering how she'd be coping this morning and how he would need to react. He fixed two coffees, his black, hers with cream and two sugar, before heading back upstairs to their bedroom.

Just as when he had risen, he could hear the shower still running in the ensuite bathroom.

"Charlotte?" he called out, knocking lightly on the oak paneled door. There was no reply.

A feeling of dread elevated his heart rate as he set down the coffees and tried the knob. It wasn't locked. He called out again as he turned it and started to open the door. It opened a few inches before meeting resistance.

Dread quickly turned to alarm.

"Charlotte!" he shouted anxiously, firmly shoving the door with his shoulder and catching sight of her in the mirror, lying naked on the bathroom floor. He pushed harder, the door sweeping open to clear her obstructing legs.

"Oh goddamn you, Char ..." he cried as he entered, his hands starting to tremble and knees going weak.

Charlotte was lying peacefully supine on the cold tile floor, her left arm across her chest, head tilted to the right side and her eyes not quite open or closed.

It was her unfocused stare that startled him most. He knelt unsteadily over his wife and checked her right wrist for a pulse. Finding none, he fought to control a sudden onrush of panic, held his breath, and laid his head on her chest. It was impossible to discern a heartbeat or breathing, but she seemed to exhale as he pressed his ear down. An involuntary spasm? He rose and pressed his thumb firmly into the nerve plexus behind her left ear. There was no reaction at all.

Randolph Elliott collapsed and sat for what seemed an eternity with his back to the marble wall, Charlotte's body pulled to him as he cradled her head. Tears ran down his cheeks as he absently stroked her hair. Suicide, Charlotte? Damn you, he thought in anguish, you're made of much sterner stuff! All these years? All the pain we've endured from each other. Losing Diana ... Now, both of you gone.

Twenty minutes passed by the time he collected himself and got up from the floor. Elliott covered his wife from her breasts to her knees with a thick white bath towel before lightly drawing her eyelids closed with trembling fingertips.

He stood and exhaled deeply, regaining his composure, and spotted two orange pill bottles lying uncapped in her sink in the marble vanity top. He examined them both. They were empty. Elavil: amitriptyline, 100 milligrams. Seconal: secobarbital, 100 milligram capsules, quantity 30. One as required for insomnia; no more than one capsule daily. This one dated 12/17/1988—five days since it was filled and there were none left. These alone, Elliott knew, would have been fatal. Reds, he had heard them called, the barbiturate overdose choice of rock stars and society sophisticates.

He stepped over Charlotte and shut off the shower, which had been running cold all along. She'd not used it. He made his way from the bathroom to Charlotte's bedside table, picked up the receiver of her telephone and dialed 9-1-1.

TWO MARKED PATROL units of the Port Chester Police Department arrived at the Elliott home at 7:14 a.m., just over five minutes after the 911 call. The first carried two uniformed patrolmen, day shift partners who ordinarily would have responded alone to the report of an overdose suicide. The second was their Road Sergeant, who had been alerted early on by dispatch in Valhalla that the caller from 21 Rye Road was none other than Judge Randolph Elliott of the federal court in Manhattan. This escalated the first serious call of the day to what cops called a "red ball"—a reference to the single red light atop old-time police cruisers—now slang for any case likely to attract high profile attention. In sleepy Port Chester, with its force of some sixty sworn officers, there were shit storms, the odd cluster fuck, but not many real red balls at all.

Sergeant Ben Hurley arrived with the EMS ambulance hot on his heels, and discovered that the gates at the end of the driveway had stopped his men in their tracks. No one had answered the intercom, prompting a flurry of radio traffic aimed at getting dispatch to reconnect with the caller. Hurley, a thirty-year veteran of policing the wealthy suburb, had already guessed about the gate's emergency override—911 calls from the home would have automatically disengaged its lock. He drew sheepish looks from his stymied patrolmen when he ambled past them, gave the gate a firm shove and pushed it wide open.

"I'll get the doorbell too, boys," he said, chewing on his walrus mustache as he returned to his car and led the small emergency convoy up the drive.

"Judge Elliott?" he asked as the front doors to the sandstone-clad mansion opened and he met Elliott eye to eye. The two men were nearly equal in height, in age, and in their distinguished and sober demeanor.

"Yes, sergeant," Judge Elliott replied.

"My name's Ben Hurley, sir. Port Chester police. I'm sorry we couldn't have gotten here sooner."

Elliott nodded. Behind the sergeant he saw two young policemen standing about ten feet away, each at angles to the doorway keeping him in clear view, and each with their gun hands discreetly close to their holsters. Well back in the drive was an ambulance with its engine running. Procedure, he presumed. Safety first.

"Please come in," he said and ushered the sergeant inside.

Sgt. Hurley motioned with a hand signal for his officers to follow as he joined the Judge in the spacious front foyer. He asked Elliott to remain beside him as the patrolmen entered, and asked whether anyone apart from his wife was in the home. No. Where was she located? The Judge gestured straight up the staircase, indicating which room and the route. The younger officers trundled off up the stairs, eyeing the layout of the home as they disappeared through the open door of the master bedroom.

Hurley stayed with the Judge and gently asked him to recount what he'd told 911. The Judge, he quickly concluded, was distressed but in control of his emotions. He correctly guessed much from the bold U-S-M-C on the man's sweatshirt. Hurley was listening as the Judge replied, not attuned to every word but picking up on the salient points, nodding on cue, or sadly shaking his head. His radio crackled a transmission from his men upstairs. Seconds later, the paramedics came through the front door, left their gurney in the foyer, and headed upstairs with their crash bags in hand.

A moment later, Hurley saw Patrolman Jenner appear on the landing. Hand signals again: Jenner held one finger up, then he turned a thumb down. Hurley nodded and asked aloud: "Is that coffee I smell, your Honor?"

Elliott smiled weakly. "Yes, maybe an hour old."

"Still fresh! Lead the way, sir? I could sure use a cup."

In the kitchen, the two men fixed their coffee and Elliott turned off the pot.

Sgt. Hurley managed a sip of the burnt brew. "I'm afraid the paramedics have confirmed that your wife has passed. I'm sorry for your loss."

"What happens now?" Elliott asked.

"It's an unnatural death," the sergeant began. "We have been on to the medical examiner in Valhalla. They've dispatched a team. Our detective squad will have their boys here too, along with a crime scene unit for photos and all that forensic stuff."

"Crime scene?" Elliott was startled.

Hurley tweaked coffee from his mustache.

"I'm sure you understand, Judge, but we have to treat a suicide like a crime scene until the M.E. and our detectives conclude otherwise."

Elliott nodded, poured the dregs of the coffee into the sink and busied himself fixing another pot. Was it six scoops for twelve cups? One to one? He couldn't remember and split the difference at eight and one-half.

"In your call to 9-1-1," Hurley continued, "you mentioned something about your daughter. Can I ask about that?"

"Our daughter Diana had been in England since the end of November," he replied, putting the pot on a burner and turning up the gas.

"She was on a flight home last night from London," he said, sighing as he looked again at the sergeant. It struck him that this lean, wiry man with compassionate eyes was likely not only a father but a grandfather as well—the sort who bounced cherished tots on his knee, and taught the apples-of-his-eye to catch fastballs and fish. Not the sort of man whose last words to his only child would have been to call her a slut.

Randolph Elliott began to shake. He clung to the granite counter on both sides of the range, head down, shoulders sagging.

"She was aboard that Pan Am flight that crashed in Scotland," he said weakly, but with measured words. "They confirmed it at midnight. And Charlotte drinks, you see. Drunk when she went up to bed around ten. When I joined her, she roused, still half asleep and asked if Diana was gone. I told her she was."

"How did she react?" asked the sergeant.

Elliott cleared his throat.

"Well, ah, she cuddled me closer. We've … we haven't been all that intimate lately, and she sighed 'my sweet baby girl'. That's what she always called her. Charlotte's southern, you see. Then she went straight back to sleep. Quickly snoring, you know? Like she does …"

Hurley saw anguish in Elliott's eyes.

"I am sorry, Judge." he said quietly with a palm on Elliott's shoulder. "I can't begin to imagine ..."

Jenner entered the kitchen and kept a respectful distance as Hurley and the Judge turned their attention his way. In the foyer behind him, the ambulance crew busily packed up their empty gurney and were preparing to leave.

Judge Elliott refocused himself on watching the coffee pot, wishing like hell it would boil, which it didn't.

Sgt. Hurley excused himself to join Jenner and the men spoke discreetly together. Incident checklist complete. Dead maybe two hours the medics had said, nothing could have been done in the way of resuscitation. Empty pill bottles, left in situ for Crime Scene. Likely scene disturbance by the husband. The decedent had been found modestly covered. But no apparent red flags. The ME and the Dicks had been called, ETA ten minutes. The Watch Commander had radioed for a 10-21, a phone call, and Jenner had checked in using the householder's bedroom phone. The Lieutenant had said he would be calling the Chief Judge of the Southern District with a heads up. He had advised the police chief and mayor. All bases covered. Not even a shit show today. At least not yet.

Hurley thanked Jenner and steered him toward the foyer. He told him to set up at the gate with his partner to keep the vultures at bay. Any media enquiries were to be directed to the Watch Commander at the station. No exceptions. And no one was coming onto this man's property without his personal clearance. Not from the Dicks, not the Watch Commander, not God, but from him.

Chapter 7

Thursday, December 22, 1988 – 8:35 a.m. EST
21 Rye Road, Port Chester, New York

LIV GELLER HAD been in her limousine on the Long Island Expressway, westbound through Queens from her home in Sagaponack, when she learned that Charlotte Elliott had committed suicide. The demure fifty-three year old redhead sank back with shock so apparent that her driver thought she was having a stroke. She directed him to divert to Port Chester and they arrived at the Elliott home at just before eight-thirty. Uniformed officers at the gate had radioed for clearance for her to come to the house and waved them on.

By then, the medical examiner had completed his work and had left with the body. The Crime Scene Unit was just wrapping up, and the Marlboro Man with police sergeant's stripes had met her at the door. He escorted her into the living room and explained that his detectives were with Judge Elliott in his study and were nearly done taking his statement. She declined an offer of coffee and he left the room.

Liv sat alone, occupying the farthest of two low-backed chairs which, with the matching leather sectional sofa, formed a conversation space in front of the whitewashed brick fireplace. The room was masterfully decorated, so she thought the first time she'd seen it in this, its latest iteration. That would've been barely one month earlier on Thanksgiving Day.

The Elliotts had hosted the first of the federal court district's annual circuit of holiday cocktail soirees. It had been a shock to judges and staffers alike at the time; Randy Elliott's souse of a spouse to fire the first shot of the house party season? Most had attended with dread. And most like Livna Geller had been surprised—not to say, relieved, for poor Randy's sake—by the warm ambience of the affair, and by the grace with which Charlotte Elliott had comported herself as its hostess.

At Thanksgiving, only Liv among his colleagues had been aware of the difficult time that they'd had with their daughter. An apparent miscarried pregnancy. Diana's excessive drinking. Harsh words that Randy had confided he'd had. Words he regretted then and, as Liv imagined, even more terribly now. Still, at the time of the party, she had seen a softening in the public face of the Elliott's marriage. Perhaps there was even more to it, she'd wondered, dismissing out of hand a pang of what might have been jealousy?

New York's senior federal jurist picked absently at the raw silk sleeve of her black Lilli Ann business suit. She suddenly trembled, feeling the chill of a draft from the foyer. Liv rose and gave no second thought to starting a fire. One turn of a white lacquered knob, one flick of a switch, and the rough ceramic drift logs in the hearth's cold firebox were alight with a rosy gas flame.

She warmed herself for a moment before clacking self-consciously across an expanse of hardwood to the Christmas tree in the corner. Its manufactured white boughs spread an impressive twelve feet at the base, meticulously laden with sapphire blue bulbs and crystal white lights which remained unlit this morning. Beneath the tree was an assortment of presents, gaily wrapped in embossed Christmas paper and variously tied up with ribbons and bows. They completed a scene, Liv Geller thought, that might have jumped from a Norman Rockwell center spread in the New Yorker. The room, the tree, the precise arrangement of gifts. It was so damned heartbreaking! Her gaze was drawn to one on top of the pile, a flat clothing gift box wrapped in gold-colored foil, with a tag penned in a feminine hand: *'Welcome Home! Merry Christmas, Sweet Girl!'* Tears welled in her eyes.

So damned biblically tragic!

She welcomed the sudden distraction of voices behind her.

Liv sniffled and turned to see Randy in the foyer with the sergeant. They were with two men in plainclothes she assumed were detectives.

"Thank you, Judge, for your patience," said the younger of the investigators, speaking more formally than his skilled partner might have done.

"Everything seems to be fairly straightfo ..." he said, stopped cold by a sudden glare from the patrol sergeant. "I mean to say ... there should be no need from this point to trouble you further."

The older detective jumped in.

"Yes, Judge," he added. "It's sad that we've had to meet in these circumstances. If you have any questions or concerns, anything at all, you have Rick's and my cards."

"I do," Judge Elliott replied. "Thank you."

With that, the detectives donned their overcoats, nodded a solemn goodbye and disappeared through the front door.

Sgt. Hurley remained with the Judge for a moment and asked if there was any other assistance he could provide.

"What happens now?"

"Well, those two will be clearing their case with a simple report and your statement," Hurley replied. "There will be an autopsy, of course, that's just standard practice. I expect you'll hear from the M. E. by this time tomorrow."

"On a Saturday?" the Judge asked, surprised.

Hurley managed a smile.

"Westchester County," he said. "Not much of a workload this side of the city. Not this time of year."

"I see. And what then?"

"A certificate will be issued. It'll accompany Charlotte to a funeral home of your choice. You or your designate can instruct the M.E.'s office with that. Their front office gal, well, she's helpful as heck. Been around even longer than me."

"Thank you. I'm sorry, Ben, was it?"

"That's right," Sgt. Hurley replied.

"Now, I've made sure our people have tidied things up," he said, removing a business card from his breast pocket and pressing it into the Judge's hand.

"That's my card there, your Honor. If there's anything else we can do, don't bother with those two, call me. Fair enough?" Hurley nodded toward the lady who'd been patiently waiting in the adjacent room, and saw himself out.

Randolph Elliott watched the door as it closed. He cleared his throat and turned to face Liv, surprised to see the woman he had come to call Boss so visibly shaken. He remained stone-faced, of course, a Scots Presbyterian, whose range of demonstrative emotions ran from A clear through B. Randy Elliott had become legendary as a presiding judge as inscrutably deadpan.

Liv Geller embraced him and buried her face in his chest. How long had she known this lovely man? Five years as a close colleague? Ten at a distance and by reputation. The last few more dearly than she had ever let on.

She was calmed by his arms around her. She sniffled, stepped back, and wiped her eyes before getting the nerve to find his. "What can I say?" she asked bleakly.

"What can I?" he replied, lightly brushing her bangs and suddenly feeling awkward. They circled for a moment in front of the fire, uncertain of each other's personal space. She chose to cling to the nearest chair. He stood flatfooted at the mantle.

"I don't know what to think, Liv," he said. "First Diana. Now this? I ... She never gave me a clue. Twenty-nine years and I wouldn't have guessed it. Charlotte was ... self-absorbed, self-loathing, but not self-destructive. I never saw that."

"She was unbalanced, Randy," Liv countered.

It was a mistake.

"Unbalanced? Christ!" he swore, not in anger, distressed. "She was the most balanced person I've ever known! Balanced her demons on my damned cold shoulder. Failures against my successes. My ... heartlessness against her available options? Boozing to dull it. Anything just to get my attention. She never got it, and that's all on me! Don't dismiss her as unbalanced."

"I'm sorry, but you're wrong! She couldn't live up to her expectations, not yours. How many times did she disappoint you for spite? Just to shame you. Offend you in public. That was her and you know it. You're a pillar of strength that she chose not to cling to. A good man ..."

"Oh yes! And one hell of a father!" he shouted, slamming his fist on the mantle.

Liv sighed sadly, defeated.

It was nearly nine-thirty. She led Randy away to his study, where she poured him a stiff drink. And they talked.

He told her how, for the first time in recent years, he and Charlotte had been growing closer. Since Diana's miscarriage. His regrets, more deeply felt now than any agony he'd ever known. How Charlotte had harkened to that, coming to a realization they both had been driving their daughter away. He and Charlotte had talked and had hoped to resolve it; hoping to reconcile, at first with Diana, maybe next with each other. One day and one step at a time.

And then came the news she was lost.

Elliott stiffened. The Randy that Liv Geller knew.

"I'll need a couple of weeks," he said, rising and starting to pace as he spoke. "I'd appreciate it if you could arrange that."

She bit. "I can. Any idea of your plans?"

"I know Charlotte's wishes. She wanted to be buried in the family plot back in North Carolina," he said. "I'll arrange it with her family. Before the New Year, I suppose."

"And then there's Diana," he continued, struggling to maintain his composure. "No idea what that will involve. Might take me into January, and on the ninth we resume with Sorsheim and putting the case to the jury."

"We can postpone it."

"No," Elliott replied firmly. "I'll dispose of the case. There'll be no extended deliberation. The defendant clearly has lost."

"I see. You're an oracle now."

"Come on, Liv. Nazi plunder? Gursky has righteousness and the liberal media on her side. I would've guessed that you'd have seen that."

"What! Because I'm a Jew?" she blustered. "If you want to wrap this one up, fine. Go ahead. But after Sorsheim your calendar's cleared."

"No, Liv!" he protested. "I need to work. I need ..."

"No," she insisted, jabbing a finger into Elliott's shoulder. "You don't."

Liv's eyes softened. "Let's be realistic," she said. "You're off until I'm convinced you're okay. When things settle, think about taking a trip. A vacation. Spend some time at those damned ballgames you love."

Randy Elliott sighed. "I'm a Mets fan. It's baseball. There's a reason why they're called the Boys of Summer."

"Fine, smartass," she chided, her fingertips tracing the USMC on his chest. "But I'm still your boss. We'll work through this. One day at a time through the worst, and then we'll reassess where we stand. Agreed?"

He nodded.

But she knew they were swimming upstream.

LIV STAYED UNTIL ten o'clock. She would have remained except for an engagement with the U.S. Attorney for Manhattan, one which she could not have delayed if the morning's tragedies had been her own.

Randy made two telephone calls before she left. The first was to his sister Annabel, the medical doctor, whom Liv knew lived in Westchester County nearby.

What she heard had seemed surreal.

On connecting, Randy had barely got past hello before he was answering questions. They were all clearly about Diana and news of the crash, which he answered directly, not seeming inclined to control the conversation.

"Yes," he said. "No. I didn't know that. I haven't seen today's news. No, they haven't called. Yes, Belle, I have all the numbers."

Then when it seemed as if the call had run its course, Randy jumped in: "Belle, the thing of it is, Charlotte's dead. Yes. Suicide this morning. Pills. The police and the M.E. have been here and gone. Yes, of course, come by with Jim, I'd appreciate that. No, I'm okay. Of course. All right, Belle, I'll see you then."

His second call was to Charlotte's elder brother in Raleigh. So far no one on the Burke side of the family had been made aware of the news of Diana. Liv clearly heard the alarm and the sorrow in the voice buzzing in Randy's ear.

Liv thought he did very well.

"Colton? Randolph Elliott. I'm afraid I have terrible news. Last night we learned we lost Diana in an air crash overseas. Thank you, but it's worse. It was too much for Charlotte to bear and this morning she took her own life. No. No, I'm afraid that she's gone. An overdose. Her prescriptions it seems. No, I found her myself. It was. Well, I appreciate that. Colton, I'm counting on you to inform the others. Yes, as soon as I know anything further. I'll be with my sister's family, I think. I will call with that number. I know. Yes, she was that. I'll call you in a day or two. Yes, it is. Thank you for that sentiment, Colton. Goodbye."

Liv knew he'd get through this. She kissed him on the cheek and he walked her to her car—waiting a moment while her dutiful driver jogged down the drive from the gate.

As she left, Elliott followed her car to the street, mainly to thank and dismiss Hurley's men.

Officer Jenner protested. They had been assigned to assist him and, to be frank, Sgt. Hurley would be seriously pissed if they were derelict in that duty. Hurley, you see, had been a Marine in Korea. Semper Fi and all that. Judge Elliott assured him that his sergeant would understand they'd been given new orders, and Jenner and his partner begrudgingly left.

Belle and her husband arrived within the half hour. They stayed just long enough for Randy to pack a bag and lock up the house before they whisked him away. None of it had been discussed; in the Elliott way, the sensibility of it had been clear. And if a dozen words had been said the whole time, they would have been Jim's.

Chapter 8

BIG ROCKFISH PRESBYTERIAN Church in the town of Hope Mills, North Carolina, has a cemetery whose interred date to well before the South's War of Northern Aggression. It was there, Charlotte Burke had decreed, that one day she would be buried with kin. Five generations of the Burkes of Cumberland County had been laid to rest here since their people had settled this land in 1789. Moldering headstones marked 'BURKE' enjoyed the honor of occupying a cemetery named in the national register of historic places, and Charlotte's—a modest pink marble slab—would be distinct among them as the last it would ever receive.

Charlotte's body had been released on Christmas Eve by the Westchester County Medical Examiner's office, and Randolph Elliott had made arrangements for her to be transported to a Fayetteville funeral home. Its proprietor had initially balked at the interment plans—as Fayetteville had many more options to offer—until he confirmed that her plot at Big Rockfish Church had been purchased at birth. With that, he assured the bereaved that her homecoming would be as splendid, or as modest, as the family desired. Splendid but simple could be done very nicely, and so planning began.

Judge Elliott had left the details to his brother-in-law, Colton, a Raleigh land developer, who in turn left it all to his wife, which worked well for all concerned.

Charlotte's parents were dead. She had just three siblings: Colton, a year older, and two younger brothers—one, a lawyer in Savannah, the other a real estate agent in San Diego. All had received timely instructions. Travel was arranged for all to arrive in Fayetteville on the 28th, with a block of rooms booked in one of the city's better hotels. There would be a dinner meeting to review the details of the service and burial. Their party would number thirty, including children, all Burkes, all immediate family.

Dinner had been a somber reunion at first. Charlotte's family had never been close. Not to her, not to each other, and certainly not to the Yankee judge she'd been on the verge of divorcing for years. They had never shared so much as Christmas cards.

Elliott was surprised but found that he actually liked all the in-laws he met. Brothers-in-law he hadn't seen since his wedding. Their wives, the odd cousin, all saddened by his tragic loss—at losing Diana mostly, although they'd never known her—less so, it seemed, by Charlotte's suicide. It was as if they'd all expected as much. Since she was a girl, Charlotte had wrestled with demons that none of her family had quite understood. Still, it was clear to them all that her decision and passing had hit Elliott hard.

On the morning of the service, limousines collected them from the hotel and drove the family party the short ten miles from downtown Fayetteville to what once had been rural Hope Mills. It wasn't plantation land anymore. Dreary strip malls on the edge of the city's urban sprawl had taken over.

Perhaps two dozen more joined them at the church. Distant family choosing to pay their respects. The splendid but simple service included an organist and a local choir which sang beautifully. The pastor was a young woman who spoke about Charlotte as if she had been a beacon to southern women. She had done her research well, paying tribute to her accomplishments as a writer, a literate feminine voice of the South. There was a prayer for her salvation in the resurrection of Christ, and a final Presbyterian hymn: 'Lord of Living, We Praise Thee'.

Colton Burke gave his sister's eulogy. Five minutes, recounting her innocent heart as a child, her thirst for a writer's voice, and her giving in to addictions when she couldn't quite find it. He prayed for God's forgiveness in her succumbing to grief at the loss of her daughter.

At 1:15 p.m., her three brothers and three of their sons carried Charlotte's casket into the historic cemetery, and in the gray mist of a North Carolina winter's day, they laid her to rest. Earth to earth. Ashes to ashes. Her native soil was ice cold as Randy Elliott took the first handful and scattered it into her grave.

જ

"YOU READ TODAY'S news?" Colton Burke asked as he handed his brother-in-law a glass of bourbon. The men were standing together in the General Lee Room of the Fayetteville Sheraton Hotel.

Randolph Elliott hadn't.

"That Lockerbie crash was a terrorist bombing. It's all here," Colton said sadly, handing the Judge a copy of the New York Times. "The Arabs again. They're the bastards who killed your Diana. Drove our damned sister to suicide."

Judge Elliott took the newspaper and saw the headline: "Powerful bomb destroyed Pan Am jet over Scotland, British investigators find."

He read on. It was datelined London, December 28, 1988.

"A powerful plastic explosive device blew apart the Pan Am jumbo jet that crashed in Scotland last week, British investigators announced today," reported the Times. "The investigators said two parts of the framework of a luggage pallet, the metal rack in which luggage is stored, showed conclusive evidence of a detonating high explosive."

The article said it hadn't been established what sort of device was used, but that an explosion occurred at thirty-one thousand feet. It said the crash of Pan Am Flight 103 scattered wreckage in a wide arc up to eighty miles from the main impact in the country town of Lockerbie, killing all 259 people on the Boeing 747 and eleven more on the ground.

The report said Scotland Yard's anti-terrorist squad and the FBI would be taking part in a criminal investigation into the crash. Explosive residues recovered from the debris had been positively identified and were said to be "consistent with" the use of a high-performance plastic explosive—this, according to the Air Accidents Investigation Branch of the British Department of Transport.

The Times said speculation about who would want to plant a bomb aboard the plane included a wide range of terrorist groups. It said U.S. officials discounted a phone tip received by an American embassy in Finland on December 5th that a bomb attack would be carried out on a Pan Am flight from Frankfurt, West Germany, bound for the United States. Some of the passengers and luggage on Flight 103 had originated in Frankfurt, with the first leg of the flight on a smaller Boeing 727 aircraft.

Randolph Elliott was numb.

It was true. Diana hadn't been lost, she'd been taken.

JUDGE ELLIOTT RETURNED home to New York on a flight to Newark, New Jersey that arrived at 5:00 p.m. on New Year's Eve. He collected his bags and chose a limousine outside the domestic terminal entrance, instructing the driver to take him home to Port Chester. As they drove north on the Jersey Turnpike, he changed his mind as they approached Palisades Park. "Driver," he said, "take me into the city, to 137 East 117th Street."

They diverted, crossing on the George Washington Bridge and circling south onto the Henry Hudson Parkway before exiting onto West 125th to cross into Harlem. It was nearly 6:30 p.m. and dark when the Mercedes stopped in front of the walk-up apartment where Diana had lived. He took his bag but kept the car at the curb as he punched a buzzer marked 'Super: M. Cárdenas 101'.

Maria Cárdenas had just finished dinner.

The man outside said he was Diana Elliott's father and was asking if he could come in.

That lovely girl. She should have been home by now from her vacation to England. Now here was this man at the door.

"Can you show me some identification?" Maria asked, peering at him suspiciously through the barred glass.

The man showed her picture ID which indicated that he was a federal judge. Maria knew he must be telling the truth. Diana had told her that much about him.

"Miss Diana isn't home. She's away."

"May I come in?" the man replied, signaling to his driver to leave. "I do need to talk to you."

Señora Cárdenas hesitated but let the man in.

She invited him to come through the dimly lit hallway into her suite. The man set down his bag at the door and looked at her sadly. The Puerto Rican grandmother knew then that he'd be bearing bad news.

Maria was shattered and wailed when he told her Diana had died in that plane crash in Scotland. She didn't need proof, she could see the grief and the pain in his eyes.

Would she let him into Diana's suite?

Of course, she said, and she did.

Elliott was surprised by his daughter's apartment. The one-room suite was meager but clean and well organized. In one corner was a small well-stocked kitchen. There was little in her refrigerator, nothing at least that would spoil. There were two chairs at a round dining table. It had a checkered cloth and the obligatory Chianti bottle, coated in rivulets of candle wax.

Opposite the table was a double bed. It had no headboard or footboard, but it was neatly made with plumped-up pillows and an indigo Sashiko quilt. Her several book cases were filled with history texts, classic poetry, Dickens and light fiction, notably Joseph Wambaugh. French and German art posters hung on every wall. There was no television, but a small stereo sat amid a clutter of music cassettes. The Judge thumbed through them: opera classics, country and western, pop and blues. A frayed but elegant red velvet settee sat against the exterior wall, and on the fire escape window ledge behind it was a collection of liquor. Her glasses were crystal. Cutlery was mismatched but each piece was silver. The bathroom in the far corner had no door but a beaded curtain and drapes of dyed lace.

Maria stood by as he inspected his daughter's apartment, dabbing tears from her eyes.

He surprised her when he asked if she would join him for a glass of wine. She did, and over their glass of Merlot, he told her that he had also just buried his wife. Maria took that news even more poorly. This poor man! The grandmother crossed herself and whispered a prayer for his tortured soul.

In time, Elliott told her he wanted to stay overnight in his daughter's apartment. Maria understood. They agreed to meet again in the morning, and he spent the night on Diana's settee—listening to Turandot and Waylon Jennings and drinking Tromba Tequila Blanco until finally falling asleep.

New Year's Day 1989.

In the morning he ate a breakfast of rice, scrambled eggs and fried plantain at Maria's table. He wrote her a check for January's rent, which at first she refused but the Judge insisted. He asked her to pack up Diana's personal papers; he would arrange for them to be collected later. He invited Maria to keep whatever she wanted, and to give the remainder of Diana's things to any charity that she might choose.

Judge Elliott called his car service, and with that he and Maria said their goodbyes and he made his way home.

Chapter 9

Tuesday, January 3, 1989 – 7:10 a.m. GMT -1
Over Calvados, France

JAMES BRACE SHIFTED his linebacker's frame in the leather window seat of an Air France Boeing 747 as it began its descent toward Paris. Charles De Gaulle Airport was still twenty minutes away. The overnight flight from Washington-Dulles had been rough, with a succession of weather systems over the Atlantic making for turbulent air. But it had been sparsely seated, and like Brace, most of the business travelers and well-heeled tourists in the first class cabin had managed to doze.

Brace frowned as he noticed his dress shirt was creased and damp beneath his suspenders. He wouldn't have time to freshen up before his Paris meeting. Still, with these folks—none of whom he had met—perhaps the image of a rumpled American envoy would serve him better than superficial and starched.

At thirty-nine, the foreign affairs scholar from rural east Texas had no insecure angst over his own appearance. It was ego and self-confidence that, more than anything else, had propelled him so quickly through Washington's rarified air. First to the Jennings Institute for Strategic Studies as its policy whiz kid in the early Eighties, to the National Security Council under second-term Reagan, to his current post as the NSC point man on the transition team for George Herbert Walker Bush.

Still, image too was a matter for tactical self-promotion. That much he learned at the NSC under Frank Carlucci. In a town full of slick politicians, look like the smartest guy in the room and they'll think that you probably are. Hell, it worked for Colin Powell.

Brace took care as he sipped espresso from a china Air France demitasse—pinching its ridiculously ornamental handle between sausage-like digits while his other mitt balanced the saucer. Rumpled was fine; coffee-stained wouldn't do. It demanded enough of his concentration to clear his mind of the doubts he was having ever since he'd been ordered to Paris.

That call came early in the afternoon on New Year's Day. Brace had been at home, an apartment in the gentrified Old Town North section of Alexandria, nursing a hangover from an A list gala the previous night.

Gary Lindner. An outgoing NSC staffer and his immediate boss. "You've got a green light for Olympiad, buddy," he had said. Just like that. No fanfare. The overseas calls had been made. Buying in all around, just as Brace had predicted. A meeting in Paris had been arranged for 10:00 a.m. Tuesday. His flight had been booked. An NSC courier would meet him with the file in the Air France lounge at Dulles. That was pretty much it.

"I never figured they'd bite," Lindner had said. "But this Lockerbie thing? Hell, I'm just an old Cold War spook, what would I know? It's a new ballgame, pal. Just make sure that they know *we* are coaching the team."

Olympiad. It was an idea that Dr. James Brace had conceived in his first year at Jennings, an idea that had been killed shortly thereafter. Still, the grandest notions have multiple lives, and his had just been reborn with the incipient presidency of George H. W. Bush.

James Eldridge Brace had met him for the first time in 1977 at Rice University in Houston. The young Fulbright Scholar from Nacogdoches, East Texas had returned from a year's study at Trinity College, Dublin, to defend his doctoral thesis at Rice. Bush was into his brief stint as an adjunct professor at the university's Jones Business School, between his tenures as director of the CIA and chair of the Council on Foreign Relations.

Brace had admired the man for his hard-nosed public views on global terrorism. Bush had always been hawkish, raising the alarm on worldwide religious and nationalist tensions looming as America's preeminent threat. A voice in the wilderness amidst a whole generation preoccupied with the Cold War. He prophesied that there would soon come a time when terrorists, born of tensions abroad, would present a clear and present danger to the United States. Addressing that danger had been the chosen field of study for Dr. Brace, who—no surprise, had agreed with George Bush all along.

In 1983, as the institute's least senior research fellow, Brace had conjured the audacious idea of Olympiad. He produced a highly-classified working paper with the innocuous title: *"The New Face of War: A Proposal for International Cooperation in Direct Action against the Security Threat of Global Terrorism"*. It received good reviews but was shelved in short order, having no sex appeal in an era which saw Washington brass fixated on the Strategic Defense Initiative, Ronald Reagan's Star Wars.

Still, his ideas were sound.

Brace had based his proposal in an accepted tenet of international law known as *jus ad bellum*—the legal right of a sovereign nation to prosecute war against its aggressors. It had long been viewed as a right in the narrowest sense, of states making war against states, but he had argued that in the chaos of post-colonial nationalism, in the arbitrary nation making after both recent World Wars, strife had given rise to a new definition. More and more, rogue nations employed armed factions as proxies to achieve specific ends. Worse still were those whom Brace had dubbed "the spoiled children"—young European extremists with flexible loyalties and ideals, oblivious to borders, and with a seeming erotic addiction to death and destruction.

Terrorism was the new face of war.

In his paper, Brace maintained that *jus ad bellum* applied as clearly to terrorists bombing a plane as it did to the Japanese fleet sailing home from Pearl Harbor.

He pointed to a modern example of just that assertion. Few people knew at the time outside of the intelligence community, but it opened some Washington eyes. If only just briefly. After the 1972 Munich Olympics massacre, Israel formed a covert group to track down and kill the members of Black September, the Palestinian Fedayeen, who along with their international confederates, had been responsible for the attack. Over the course of three years, that team had quietly eliminated dozens who had planned or participated in the Munich operation.

Vengeful murder? Any blood shed in war is arguably murder; Israel had simply exercised sovereign rights. Retaliation is a right in the lawful prosecution of war, and Israel had been at war against terrorists since its inception in 1948. So had been the United States, Brace had suggested, since the Yom Kippur War of 1973—Israel's definitive victory over its neighboring Arab states—and Washington's policy of unswerving support.

He proposed an international effort to similarly act against global terrorist threats.

There were ticklish issues.

It could not involve the use of standing armed forces. The application of military force has strict limitations in the West, where it is invariably under the oversight and governance of elected legislatures. It is in the United States, in fact, where military might is wielded most freely. Under an executive order of the President, a military strike against any perceived aggressor could be legally ordered on an incidental basis. But any organized long-standing mission was constitutionally out of the question.

Nor could action involve the intelligence community, at least, not directly. The United States had a long and distasteful involvement in covert operations abroad. The CIA had a history of promoting coups in support of U.S. foreign policy, funding freedom fighters—terrorists by any other name—even conducting and contracting assassinations. Thanks to the Church Senate Committee of 1975, the U.S. intelligence services were out of that game forever.

Law Enforcement, Dr. Brace suggested, presented the only viable option. Police agencies act routinely across international borders. Cooperating in investigations; sharing intelligence; working together to enforce common laws—and the criminal aspects of terrorism had always been high on the list. Law enforcement activity is innocuous, respectable, and boringly pedestrian among legislators.

He proposed a covert force comprised of agents drawn from law enforcement and the security services of member nations. Such a force could be easily funded through existing programs and treaties. It would have, on its face, the mission of interdicting criminal terrorist threats: international arms dealing, conspiracy, cross-border flight to avoid prosecution, And, as required, such a force could be tasked with defeating a threat *ex-juris*. In the normal course of policing, suspects do sometimes die.

He called the force *Olympiad* with a nod to the slain Israelis at Munich. It was a brilliant plan, relegated to the past tense and the NSC archives until the bombing of Pan Am Flight 103.

PARIS HAD ALWAYS been central to the Olympiad plan. When the paper was first circulated, the three target partners—Great Britain, West Germany and France—had been quick to endorse it. France held the key to success. Its government oozed acquiescence. It had the most amenable laws to disguising and funding covert operations. And it was the host nation to Interpol, which since 1923 had coordinated cross-border law enforcement for member countries around the world. France was a perfect home for its headquarters.

When he had received his files at Dulles, Brace was surprised at the extensive preparations so far. Just weeks earlier, Olympiad had been on the NSC back burner. Britain had pressed for its formation since 1983 and the IRA bombing at Harrods in London. It had been steadily losing that war and sectarian extremists had only grown stronger, training beyond its reach in camps across North Africa. Bonn had been equally eager. Its resources strained against a tide of urban guerillas washing over its cities—finding support with homegrown German groups like the Red Army Faction, Baader-Meinhof, and the Anti-Imperialist International Brigade. The French were the least stressed of all, more aligned economically to the Arab world, and with only the crumbling remains of its African colonies left to police. Besides, its professional army could and would strike anywhere it was needed. France simply wished to be accommodating.

At just short of 10:00 a.m., James Brace arrived by taxi at 1701 Quai d'Orsay, Paris—the French Ministry of Foreign Affairs—and was quickly ushered to a small conference room overlooking the Seine.

He was met at the door by a uniformed Gendarme general, Hervé de Villiers, whose dossier was one of the four that he had reviewed through the night. De Villiers was a slight, convivial man—neat with receding dark hair and a thin, trimmed mustache. He had the handshake of a paratrooper, which he had been since joining the army at eighteen.

De Villiers led him into the room, where three other men in business suits stood chatting next to the boardroom table. They came over to greet him.

First was Sir Michael McPhail, CBE, deputy commissioner of the Metropolitan Police in London, a tall, gaunt blond man in his early fifties with an engaging smile.

Next was *Oberst* Jurgen Kleist, the former commander of West Germany's *Grenzshutzgruppe 9*, GSG 9, its elite counter-terrorism unit. Colonel Kleist, forty-five, had a squat muscular build, dark haired, dark complexioned with steel blue eyes and an earnest demeanor. He was a twenty-year veteran of the West German border police and now its national director of counter-terrorism in Bonn.

The last was the American, Deputy Commissioner Charles Watt of the New York Police Department.

At forty-eight, Charlie Watt was the first black NYPD officer to have risen through the ranks from patrolman to a leadership role at the top. The equivalent of a two-star general, Watt was responsible for intelligence and counter-terrorism liaison in a police department nearly thirty thousand strong.

Watt had been handpicked by the White House NSC oversight team. A quiet, intelligent man with no known personal or political agenda, he gained attention in 1986 when his name was put forward to lead an audit of FBI operations for the Senate Select Committee on Intelligence. It had come in the wake of disastrous revelations of leaks and criminal collusion with IRA supporters at its Boston field office. His report hadn't pulled any punches and it had left the Bureau red-faced.

Of the men in the room, Brace had been the last one informed of the Olympiad plan going forward. From the NSC file he knew that the White House had briefed Watt and sealed his appointment on December 26. The first of the five. Gary Lindner had penned in the margin: *"He was on our short list of one. Without Watt we're nowhere.—G.L."*

Charlie Watt shook Brace's hand and flashed a broad, genuine smile.

A young female stenographer in a plain business suit and skirt slipped into the room, closed the doors, and took a discreet seat by the window.

De Villiers invited Brace to sit opposite him, facing McPhail and Kleist, with Watt beside him at the table. He cordially offered coffee from a silver carafe and service that was set out between them.

"We are meeting today, Dr. Brace, at the behest of your government," De Villiers began. "And I want to say at the outset that France is pleased that Washington has finally come to its senses. If I might call you James? Since I first read your paper, six years ago now, I have been a strong supporter of your brilliant plan. Congratulations, my friend, on its present momentum."

Brace smiled.

"I must echo that, too," said McPhail. "You've had no stronger support than from those of us in the trenches at Whitehall. Kudos to you, James."

"This scheme *can* work," the Briton continued. "And frankly, Hervé, if your girl can take us off the record for a moment ... it is the only way we can think of to protect Her Majesty's government, and each of yours, I might add, from the necessary evils at hand."

"*D'accord*," De Villiers replied with a nod.

"Now then," he continued, "Our brief agenda today is to establish three things. Firstly, an agreement to develop and set in place an operational structure for Olympiad. I have taken the liberty of suggesting a basic formation. An initial estimation which, of course, is merely my own advice."

De Villiers sipped his coffee.

"Second comes the issue of funding. I have developed a cursory budget, based on the suggested organization outlined here. Four syndicates of twelve operators. One hundred million dollars a year. Overheads, travel, operating expenses. James, your government has agreed to fund half, less one percent, not wishing to have ultimate budget control."

Brace had read that in his briefing notes.

"And lastly," De Villiers concluded, "There is the matter of sanctioning targets. This is delicate for us all. We French have some experience in these matters, and I have included a proposal that might prove useful for consideration. It acknowledges as paramount the need to shelter our respective governments, measuring this against tactical imperatives and opportunities that will rise from time to time. I believe that, in every case, sanctioning decisions must be well-considered, supported by the case officers, with the ultimate decision made by we four of the executive. Sir Michael, Jurgen, Charlie and I, each man voting his conscience. What we don't want, of course, is a ... wild west show?"

"So then, let's get down to business."

The meeting lasted just over two hours.

Olympiad would proceed.

Its cover would be as an Interpol unit, gathering criminal intelligence about global arms dealing and terrorist activities. This it would undertake nominally.

It would have four initial stations—New York, London, Paris and Bonn. Each would be staffed by a dozen field operators at first, drawn from police forces and the security services of the host nation. Each station would operate independently, choosing missions, sharing intelligence. Station Paris would administrate overall and process any sanctions through the executive committee, if necessary by secure video conferencing. Funding was in place. Recruiting would start by mid-month. Operations to commence by April or June at the latest.

At the end of the meeting, the men chatted over coffee and Brace cornered Charlie Watt at the window.

"I'm an admirer, Commissioner," he said, as both men studied the waterfront view of the Seine. "Your work with the Senate committee? Not many men could take on the Bureau like that and survive."

"Call me Charlie," said Watt. "Tell me, one survivor to another, is this just a kneejerk reaction to Lockerbie? Because what we're starting here is going to take guts if we're going the distance. And from what I've seen of Washington, that's one thing we're short on."

"Honest answer? I don't know myself," Brace replied.

"Fair enough. Lemme buy you a beer when you do."

Chapter 10

Saturday, January 7, 1989 – 7:13 p.m. EST
151 Central Park West, New York, NY

"DAMMIT, LARRY!" BARKED Ted Bakker, pacing impatiently in the living room of his lavish Upper West Side apartment. "You gotta rein in those assholes! If the board thinks I'm gonna wear any of this, they're in for a fight!"

Laurence Sadler stared out a towering south facing window at the glittering skyline of midtown Manhattan and the traffic eight floors below navigating Central Park West. The lean sixty-year-old native New Yorker had been Ted Bakker's V.P. of Operations when he had been the Pan Am CEO. When Bakker left in July 1987, Sadler had been appointed Executive Vice-President and Secretary to the Pan Am board of directors—remaining an inside ear for his former boss ever since.

"The British investigation has already linked the device to checked baggage out of Frankfurt," Sadler said with a sigh.

"Well, there's a surprise!" snapped Bakker, clipping the tip from a nine-inch Nicaraguan Padron cigar. "It's right there in the anarchist whack-job handbook. 'Now that you've completed your bomb, make sure that you send it through Frankfurt!' Fuck!"

Bakker exhaled a blue haze of smoke that curled across the room. "What's our exposure here, Larry?"

"Ours, mine or yours?" the clear-eyed former airline captain responded without turning from the window.

"Oh, fucking humor me dammit!"

Sadler turned to face his longtime friend.

"Straight dope? We've been through this before. Tenerife, Louisiana, Karachi. This time it's two hundred and seventy dead. An entire college class from Syracuse, babes in arms, doctors and lawyers. We'll take a big insurance hit," he said. "But risk coverage isn't the issue, is it? Liability caps are out the window if negligence can be proved."

"And the board is suggesting there is?" Bakker sniffed.

Sadler bristled. "Well that's our exposure, isn't it? You took us out on a hell of a limb."

"Alert Management? Your no cost security option? The whole board bought in on that one. And it was your brainchild, son."

Arrogant bastard. Sadler grimaced, running his fingers over his face. Alert Management Systems Inc. had indeed been his baby. Created in 1985 as Pan American's answer to rising concerns about airline security, the company went into operation the next year as a Pan Am subsidiary. It was designed to deliver highly visible security at the airline's check-in counters, baggage handling centers and worldwide network of maintenance hubs. Physical security with a uniformed presence.

Larry Sadler's stroke of genius had been to capitalize the company with a five-dollar levy on all overseas tickets. That and to propose the contracting of its services to other airlines in the overseas market. It was a vision of Alert Management Systems as being uniquely self-sustaining, unheard of at a time when the entire industry was wringing its hands at the prospect of security costs. His no cost option was seen as a winner. And so was he. It was Bakker himself who had undone it all.

"It was supposed to pay for itself, Ted. Not become another damned revenue center," he replied. "Your interference turned it into a sham."

"Interference?" Bakker shot back.

"That's an interesting word," he continued, studying a growing cylinder of ash at the tip of his cigar. "I seem to remember the board calling it leadership!"

With a tap, the ash fell into a silver ashtray.

"We were bleeding money. Two years of negative earnings, one lousy quarter after another. The FAA and ICAO, croakin' like toads in a pond about passenger screening, hand checking bags, tracking and matching luggage to warm seats onboard. Chemical explosives sniffers? Fucking x-ray machines? Kinda blew your cost-modeling outta the water, didn't it?"

Sadler threw up his hands.

"You barely gave it three months, then you gutted the thing like a fish. Leadership? A good litigator might call it criminal misconduct."

"Austere business management," countered Bakker.

"Oh, please. That media event at Kennedy? Trotting out pet German Shepherds posing as bomb sniffing dogs? The half-day training courses for security staff?"

"Embroidery. Look confident coming out of the gate, then you can settle down to refining the process."

Sadler crossed the room and lit up a cigar of his own.

"I see, Mr. Bakker," he said in the tone of a courtroom attorney. "You're telling me that subsequent to this initial ... embroidery, Alert Management went on under your leadership to weave a strong and seamless security blanket?"

"I believe that would be a question for my former chief of operations, Mr. Laurence Sadler," Bakker replied.

"No." Sadler stabbed at the air with his cigar, punctuating his point. "No. You see, Ted, here's where they introduce their damning piece of inculpatory evidence. It's your signature on that memo, not mine."

Bakker glowered. His confidential cost cutting directive of May 5th, 1986 had been ill-advised and disastrously vague in its wording. Profits before safety. It had a long-term effect that both men would come to regret.

"That's the trouble with a shoot from the hip style, Teddy," Sadler said grimly. "Shooting yourself as well as everyone else in the foot."

Chapter 11

Monday, January 9, 1989 – 10:00 a.m. EST
United States Courthouse, 500 Pearl Street, New York, NY

"ALL RISE!" SAID a uniformed deputy in a commanding voice and the unexpectedly large gallery crowding the oak-paneled courtroom came to its feet. "The United States Court for the Southern District of New York is now in session, the Honorable Judge Randolph Owens Elliott presiding."

The courtroom went silent. Judge Elliott appeared through a doorway that opened in the wall at the left of the room. He made his way to the bench, looking tired, dressed in a white shirt, plain tie and dark suit pants beneath his black robes. He was carrying a large black binder under one arm. In place in his seat on the bench, he peered out over his reading glasses at the gallery and betrayed no reaction.

"Good morning," he said quietly to a murmured response from the attorneys and clerks.

"We are here in the matter of Gursky and Sorsheim et al, docket number 88-cv-01654," he began, looking up from the documents and directing his gaze to the six member civil jury—four women and two men in casual business clothes, seated in an elevated jury box at the right of the room.

He swiveled his chair slightly to face them.

"At this point in the process, ladies and gentlemen, we have heard the case for harm presented by the plaintiff, Ms. Gursky, and the response to her complaint by the defendants, Mr. Sorsheim and others," he said with an educational tone.

"The attorneys have made their closing arguments," he continued. "In summary, this has been a dispute between two parties over the rightful ownership of a property, a tangible object of value, a painting. The plaintiff, Ms. Gursky, maintains, and has presented evidence acceptable to this court, that she is the sole legal heir to its original owner, an uncle, deceased now some forty-six years, and who, having resided outside the United States in the pre-war nation of Poland, had ownership of the painting under the laws of that land at that time."

At the rear of the gallery, Chief Judge Liv Geller and more than a dozen of Elliott's friends and peers listened as intently as the curious public and the throng of reporters that sat sprinkled among them.

"Ms. Gursky maintains that the painting had been appropriated by persons unknown but acting for a sovereign state, Germany, which had occupied Poland at the time and under whose laws such appropriation had the color of right."

Elliott took a sip of water.

"As well, we have heard and accept Ms. Gursky's evidence that international courts of competent jurisdiction have ruled severally that such acts of plundering by an occupying power or its agents, is contemptuous of the most basic tenets of civilized common law. And is therefore illegal."

"Ms. Gursky maintains in her summation that, given these facts, her ownership of the painting is absolute. That it had never been legally excised from the estate of her uncle, and as the estate's sole legal heir, it is as much hers today as if had been given to her by her uncle in 1940. The year, in fact, of her birth."

Elliott pinched the bridge of his nose, rubbed his eyes, and turned a page in his binder.

"Mr. Sorsheim doesn't agree," he began. "His response to the complaint addresses two salient points. One is the ownership of property in the absence of a will. As we heard in evidence, it is a complex issue given the impact of history on this case. The second is the equally complex matter of the world trade in art and artifacts."

"Mr. Sorsheim argues," he continued, "and presents evidence this court accepts, that before its occupation by Germany in 1939, Poland had laws which provided that, in the absence of a will or a legal petition by heirs, such property would revert to the state. Ms. Gursky produced no such will. Nor did she produce any evidence that her parents had pursued a legal claim. This is, of course, complicated by uncertainty around the dates of actual death, with her uncle and her parents vanishing after 1941 into Nazi death camps. Nonetheless, it was argued that in the absence of supporting facts, a default to laws at the time should prevail."

Elliott studied the jury, expecting glazed boredom and was shocked to see two of the women red-eyed and sniffling into tissues. It was a case that could stir emotions. Perhaps a caution would be needed in his closing remarks.

He continued. "Mr. Sorsheim supports his contention in this regard with evidence of the fact that Ms. Gursky had made no claim to other property that might have belonged to her uncle. No real estate properties. No monies. Simply this painting, and on the evidence, only once it had appeared for sale in his gallery. If we are to accept this reasoning, then the painting might rightly belong to the people of Poland."

"Here, though," Elliott said, "I will instruct you on a matter of law. Without proof of a will, proof of death or of the intentions of individuals, you needn't consider any assertion or inference made in their regard. You are here to decide this case on the preponderance of the evidence you have heard. This means that if the largest portion of the evidence suggests a conclusion, you may make that conclusion. If, from an unfinished jigsaw puzzle, you see the face of the Mona Lisa, you may conclude it is her, even absent the pieces completing her smile."

Liv Geller grinned. The Mona Lisa jigsaw puzzle. She'd heard him charge civil juries with that metaphor. Brilliant. He was doing better than she had dared to expect.

"Then there's the matter of the traffic in art," he said. "Unlike homes and land, even items to which we can claim ownership by a registration or serial numbers, art can change hands with no requisite proof of transaction. As Mr. Sorsheim speculates, her uncle might have sold the painting to a Nazi on the faint hope of mercy. We can never know that. We do know that it was sold several times, even inventoried by dealers in Europe and itemized in receipts."

"Does this legitimize its eventual purchase and the claim of ownership by Mr. Sorsheim?" Judge Elliott paused to sip water again. "That's for you to decide."

"Finally, Mr. Sorsheim made much of the fact that a criminal complaint was initially made with respect to this painting, and that the United States Attorney had refused to prosecute him under the NSPA. This is the National Stolen Properties Act, which since 1932 has been the governing law in matters relating to stolen art and artifacts. I wish to be clear on this point. Whether the United States Attorney chooses to proceed or not to proceed with any criminal matter has no bearing here. Put this out of your mind, and do not consider this point in your deliberations."

Judge Elliott paused and sat upright. He scanned the jury again, troubled to see that the forewoman was still dabbing away at tears in her eyes.

He leaned forward, concerned. "Madam Forewoman? You seem distraught. Would you explain yourself?"

The clerk of the court motioned to the woman to rise. She was flustered, struggled to her feet, a florid and mildly obese redhead in her early forties.

The woman sniffled. "I'm sorry, your Honor. It has nothing to do with this case. I, well, actually there are several of us who just feel so sorry for you."

Elliott was alarmed.

"I mean, losing your daughter and wife. The story in this morning's Post. We …"

"Madam, I'll stop you right there!" the Judge said, blanching. Whispers and gasps rippled through the gallery.

Randolph Elliott paused for an eternity.

"Madam, please take your seat," he said calmly. "Clerk? Please note for the record that I thank this lady for her sympathy. But I must admonish the jury that this issue has no place in these proceedings. No place at all in this court. I, too, saw the Post article this morning, and regret that my personal life has been exploited in this public way."

Liv Geller's eyes moistened.

"I apologize to Ms. Gursky and to Mr. Sorsheim," he continued. "I don't believe this will impact the jury in their deliberations. However, at this point I'm inclined to call an adjournment. I'll see counsel in my chambers."

Court reconvened a half hour later. The packed room was silent, quietly coming to its feet as Judge Elliott entered and made his way to the bench. He looked solemnly at the gallery, his gaze moving from reporter to reporter, each of whom blushed or looked quickly away. When his eyes met Liv Geller's, he smiled weakly and nodded. Then he turned his attention to the jury.

"Ladies and gentlemen," he said, "before we resume, I want to thank you for your kind words of condolence. I am sorry, Madam Forewoman, if I seemed sharp with you earlier. I'm afraid that you simply caught me by surprise."

The jury forewoman shifted nervously in her seat, but returned his warm smile.

"You see," he continued, "we sometimes forget what makes this place a court of law. It's not the trappings or traditions of the court, not the case under contest or the obscure legal language we use. It's what makes a cathedral a church—the people who congregate here, brought together with one common purpose. Every one of us, warts and all."

A smattering of applause rolled through the gallery and Judge Elliott tapped his gavel. Again he addressed the jury.

"I have conferred with Mr. Solomon and Ms. Cartwright in chambers, and we agree that nothing in my personal circumstances would prejudice these matters here," he said.

"My charge to you stands. It has been my duty to outline the law as it applies to the arguments of the plaintiff and defendant. It is your duty now to consider these arguments and to decide solely on the ownership of the property at issue. The jury may withdraw. This court is adjourned."

Ninety minutes later the jury returned with its verdict. For Elliott it had never been in doubt. They found for Gursky.

Thursday, January 19, 1989 – 2:35 p.m. EST
First Presbyterian Church, New York, NY

FEDERAL MARSHALS, NEW York state and city police escorted the short funeral cortege from Randolph Elliott's Westchester home into the city and through Manhattan to the memorial service at First Presbyterian Church at Fifth Avenue and West 12th Street in Greenwich Village. It was a dull New York winter's day with an overcast sky delivering a trace of light snow and the temperature hovered just above freezing. Marked police cars with their red and blues flashing outnumbered the six black limousines that comprised the cortege, which was significantly lacking a hearse. Diana's remains had been released just a week earlier by the coroner's office in Scotland, barely twenty pounds of charred bone which had been cremated in Glasgow. Judge Elliott had chosen not to visit the Lockerbie crash site and had Diana's urn promptly flown back to the States. Today she had been cradled in her father's arms as the funeral procession made its way to the church.

Those few who met that morning for tea and sympathy at Randolph Elliott's home had included his sister Belle and husband, from East Fishkill; Colton Burke, his wife Janine and their family, up from Raleigh; the lieutenant governor of the State of New York; the deputy attorney general of the United States; the congressman from the 19th Congressional district of New York, which included Westchester; and the Honorable Livna Geller, chief judge of the Federal District Court for the Southern District of New York, along with their personal assistants or significant others.

United States senators for New York, Pat Moynihan and Alfonse D'Amato had been invited but had declined, both attending a memorial service that same day in Syracuse for thirty-five of its university students who perished aboard Pan Am Flight 103.

Neither Randolph nor Charlotte Elliott had come from particularly religious people. The Judge had Presbyterian roots among the small pockets of Scots who settled the lower Hudson River valley. The choice of the First Presbyterian Church in Manhattan for Diana's service had been made by the Judge for the more temporal reasons of its grandeur and logistical convenience. In fact, it had been Judge Elliott's law clerk, Andrew Connachie, who had made the suggestion. He and his wife had been married there three years earlier and the Judge had attended. It had been Andrew who had unselfishly shouldered the burden of making all the arrangements.

More than five hundred people filled the black walnut pews of the magnificent brownstone and Roman brick church, with its vaulted Gothic ceiling and soaring stained glass windows. The altar displayed a simple memorial for Diana—her plain silver urn flanked by candles, and a single framed photographic portrait of her smiling brightly at her degree convocation the previous summer. Again, Connachie had thoughtfully fussed over even these final details, invisibly and discreetly, before dutifully taking his place among the less-prominent mourners at the rear of the chapel.

Elliott himself had accepted the tearful plea of Professor Philippe Gaudreau to deliver the eulogy.

Gaudreau had been crushed by Diana's death. The aging bachelor had cried openly upon hearing the news, falling into a brandy-soaked misery which remained over Christmas and into the New Year. Barnard students and colleagues had been quick to dismiss his melancholy as typically Gallic. There had been whispers about a deeper, romantic attraction between them, and with Diana's reputation on campus, even gossip around paternity with the rumor that she had miscarried last fall. Nothing could have been further from the truth.

Of course Philippe Gaudreau had been physically drawn to Diana—few men who met her, no matter how briefly, had the will to dismiss a first erotic thought. But her academic advisor had always been a slave to his ethics, and in spite of her persistent flirtations, he always knew them for just what they were—simply Diana's way.

The memorial service had been short, lasting just thirty minutes. Verdi's Requiem had been sung by the choir during seating. An introduction and prayer was given by the Reverend Dr. Edward Neal, senior pastor of the church. Diana's aunt Belle and her uncle Colton briefly spoke for the family. Then Professor Philippe Gaudreau delivered his succinct eulogy.

"Diana was, more than anything else, an insatiable student of history," he began, unsteadily, his voice clear but filled with emotion. "And as it was the greatest of Diana's passions, I am certain she would forgive us our grief in her passing. As Nehru said on hearing of the death of Gandhi, 'The light has gone out of our lives and there is darkness everywhere.' Hers was no ordinary light. It continues to shine into each of our hearts, into all of our lives, and with each day that passes our pathways grow steadily brighter."

He recounted at appropriate length her brilliance as a student, her joie de vivre, her uncommon beauty, and what he had come to admire as a playfully audacious nature. He faltered, his voice breaking slightly, as he mourned the loss to the world of a promising scholar. Then he brightened in closing, recalling a paper she had written for one of his classes, in which she had convincingly argued that Winston Churchill was the greatest historian of the twentieth century.

"She had reasoned well, but sadly Diana was wrong," Gaudreau said with a quiet laugh. "The only truly great historian of the modern era is, of course, a Frenchman, my late friend and colleague, Fernand Braudel!"

A private joke among academics, but chuckles ran through the pews. "I will leave you with this piece of wisdom, words which I am certain our dear Diana would have embraced. They suit her so well. They are those of her beloved Winston, on the prospect of his own mortal passing."

Gaudreau smiled and his voice deepened to a gravelly imitation of Winston Churchill: "I am ready to meet my Maker. Whether my Maker is prepared for the great ordeal of meeting *me*, is another matter."

Chuckles became laughter. Anyone who had known Diana at all found the humor in that, and Philippe Gaudreau walked away from the pulpit an unburdened man.

Following the memorial service, just over one hundred who had made Andrew Connachie's guest list met at the Judge's retreat—The Yale Club, 50 Vanderbilt Avenue in midtown Manhattan opposite Grand Central Station.

The Library Room had been graciously offered. Bright and airy, plush with royal blue carpeting, alabaster walls lined with alcoves of books beneath a ceiling of carved blonde oak.

Guests gravitated into intimate groups to chat, catch up and release tension, even laugh. Gliding discreetly among them were uniformed servers, circulating with silver trays of canapés and sandwiches, wine in crystal glasses, or taking and quickly returning drink orders. Vivaldi's 'Four Seasons', Diana's favorite strings work, subtly filled the room. And tactfully from a corner, the Judge's doting clerk kept a dutiful eye, orchestrating it all.

He saw Liv Geller charming the deputy attorney general and the rest of the politicians. Cloistered together near the head of the room, the Judge and his family met and briefly greeted everyone in attendance. He thought he saw something in her furtive glances in that direction. She sipped wine between bright congenial smiles and polite conversation—distracted, it seemed, by Randy Elliott.

Connachie grinned. It was about goddamned time.

Chapter 12

"NO DIRTY WATER dog, eh Mac?" said a man who was blocking the sun over Randolph Elliott's shoulder.

The Judge had been about to bite into a hot dog when the cryptic comment surprised him.

"I beg your pardon?" he replied, looking up from his seat behind the Mets dugout. The man's figure was silhouetted against the bright Florida sun.

"Dirty water dog? *A cart dog?* You're a New Yorker, arn'cha?" asked the man, with an accent revealing that he clearly was.

"Oh. Right!" Elliott said with a grin. He remembered. A New York localism for street vendor hot dogs, coined for the cold water method of storing their stock.

"D'ya mind?" asked the stranger, gesturing toward the empty seat next to the Judge.

"No! Not at all," he answered cheerfully.

The man deftly changed rows with a beer and a hot dog in hand and took the unoccupied seat. There were plenty of empty seats in the stands at Tradition Field, a sparkling new 7,500-seat stadium in its second year playing host to the New York Mets for pre-season spring training. It was a clear afternoon with the temperature climbing into the high 80s and perhaps a thousand ardent fans sat scattered throughout the stands, awaiting the start of the 1:30 inter-squad game.

With nearly two weeks of workouts and trials behind them, the Mets wouldn't be facing other major league teams in Florida Spring Training Baseball for two more days. Even so, something as mundane as practice is heaven itself to those hardcore fans who flock south every year, and the stands at Tradition for the Mets versus Mets had a block party feel.

The stranger nestled into his seat. He was stocky, of average height and appeared to be in his early forties. Dark complexioned with dark curls rolling out from the back of his blue Mets ball cap to a denim shirt collar; a genial face with dark deep-set eyes, a long nose, thick lips and a Fu Manchu mustache framing his chin. A friendly enough looking fellow, thought the Judge and he offered his hand.

"Elliott's my name," he announced.

"Call me Sal," was the reply, and the men shook hands as they rose for the national anthem.

They sat as the upbeat announcer began to introduce the opposing line ups for the afternoon's game.

"Batting clean-up for the red squad today, the right fielder, number 18, *Da-r-r-r-y-l* Strawberry!" the public address system boomed. Most of the crowd cheered.

Sal cupped his hands to his mouth.

"Hey, Straw! You no-class overpaid mook, you ain't no Ted Williams!" he shouted, then grinned at the Judge as several nearby fans glowered at him and booed.

Elliott smiled and shook his head, amused.

"Seems they don't agree," he said. "But you can't really argue with thirty-nine homers and a one-oh-one RBI. The team leader across the board."

Sal stopped his rising beer cup short of his lips.

"Yeah, but for one-point-three freakin' mil?"

"Both Hernandez and Gooden make more," countered the Judge. "Carter twice as much."

"They're earners, my friend. Strawberry's a showboat. He's lazy and whines like a bitch. You watch. Give that *giamoke* a couple a years and he's in the Japanese League, pinch hittin' for tips."

Judge Elliott laughed, shrugged in half-hearted agreement and finally bit into his hot dog.

Sal Luongo studied the older man for a moment. There was something in the way he had laughed that seemed to have given him life.

"Know what? I friggin' knew that I knew you when you were at the concession, loading your dog."

"Knew me?" asked the Judge, clearing a crumb from the corner of his mouth.

"Yeah! Dry unsteamed bun. That got me thinkin'. Frank comes out. A line of onions, spread out real nice. Sauerkraut. Frank's back in. Three dabs a brown mustard. I seen that routine every Friday at noon for the past six friggin' years!"

Randolph Elliott turned in his seat, flipped up his clip-on shades and screwed his face into a perplexed squinting knot. In seconds it changed to surprise.

"Foley Square!" he said, flashing a smile. "Across from the courthouse. You're the Sabrett cart man! The hot dog vendor! Well, I'll ..."

"Friggin' eh!" Sal replied with a nod and hand flourish. "I always sucked at faces and names. Comes from growin' up on Mulberry at Kenmare. Nothin' but wops and chinamen, and we all look alike."

"But you remember routines."

"Like a freakin' elephant! Six years you come down to the square every Friday. Buy a dog. Load it up the same way every time. That's a ... whatchacallit, a quirk? In a good way, you know, like a habit. Twenty years I've been sellin' dogs in the square, April to November. Federal marshals? Sonsabitches have nearly paid for my condo in West Palm. Tourists? Tightwad court workers, no offense. And you? Yeah. Right there at the concession. Six years. Same routine every time."

Judge Elliott shook his head in amazement.

"Small world, isn't it Sal?" he said, offering his plastic beer cup in a toast.

"You said it, Mac. Salut!" Luongo replied with a grin, sloshing their lagers.

A loud *CRACK* resounded through the stands and both men quickly looked up at the field. Strawberry had hammered a fastball off David Cone high into left field with Lenny Dykstra advancing from second and Keith Hernandez sprinting from first.

"I think this one is *GONE* folks!" the announcer excitedly piped. "Yes? … Oh yeah! That's over left center. A three hundred and eighty yard three-run homer for the lanky leftie! Let's hear it folks for *Da-r-r-y-l-l* Strawberry! The red squad takes a three-run lead with one out in the top of the first."

The Judge and Sal the hot dog vendor looked at each other and fumed for a split second. Then they giggled like kids.

"Oh yeah, Sal. The Japanese Leagues," Elliott chided.

"*Mannaggia!* Friggin' Strawberry, he's still a bum."

Randy Elliott was enjoying himself in a carefree way he had almost forgotten. He was having fun. He held up two fingers after waving to get the attention of a strolling beer vendor. The girl came over, swapping two beer for a ten spot that gave her a three dollar tip, and the pair hunkered down to actually watch the game.

During the lulls in the action—there are plenty in baseball—they got to know each other, trading questions and answers.

Salvatore Giancarlo Luongo had been born in Hoboken, New Jersey, on December 24th, 1949—a month premature, while his folks, both second generation Sicilian-Americans, were visiting his mother's eldest sister for Christmas, and everything went for shit, obstetrically. *Mannaggia la miseria!* Premature labor brought on no doubt by his aunt Maria's manicotti, which his mother devoured by the pound. Gas? No, Maria, the baby!

He had grown up in Little Italy at a time when the old world Manhattan neighborhood was depopulating Italians to suburbs from Queens to Connecticut to Staten Island. Raised in a walk-up tenement in the 100 block of Mulberry Street. It was an Italian New York pedigree that even Elliott knew had juice.

Sal invoked the cliché that kids from his neighborhood became cops, priests or hoods. His only sibling, a brother two years younger named Vince, had gone into the Augustinian Order and was currently a parish priest in Yonkers. Sal didn't become a cop, which left, he confessed, becoming "associated" as a teen to the Genovese crime family, on a street crew under its big earner in the Sixties, Anthony "Fat Tony" Salerno. In Manhattan, the Genovese mob was into the traditional rackets of gambling, loan sharking, hijackings and labor union extortion in New York City's construction and trucking industries. Old school stuff.

In 1970, Sal had been sentenced to a nickel up at Dannemora for the gun-point hijacking of a load of Canadian furs coming down from Montreal. He was out in three, and as he told his new ballpark pal, he went straight and had been ever since. Single with no kids after a five-year marriage in his twenties. A nice seaside house in Midland Beach, Staten Island, an hour away from work in morning traffic with his Grand Cherokee towing his old Sabrett cart. A Florida condo in Spring Training country. What could be freakin' better?

"Don't knock the hot dog rackets!" Sal boasted. "Sixty G's a year for eight months work and I work for myself."

"So whaddabout you?" he asked, signaling the girl for more beer. "Your first time on the Grapefruit League circuit? A getaway from the wife and the screamin' grandkids?"

"My wife passed just before Christmas," Judge Elliott replied, surprising himself that the words came so easily.

Sal Luongo cringed, crossing himself.

"Oh, Jeez, Mac. I'm sorry! Now I feel like an asshole."

"Yeah," the Judge said, clapping his hand on Sal's on the arm of his seat. "Well, you get the next round and we're even."

Both men managed a smile and said nothing at all for a moment that seemed like an hour.

Sal scrutinized Elliott's face, then his eyes shot open wide.

"Sonofabitch. You're *that* judge! I read that thing they had in the Post. They ..."

He instantly wished he could take it all back.

Elliott bucked up in his seat, slapped his knees and responded, "Yeah, Sal, I am. But today I'm this guy who loves hot dogs and baseball. Let's say we just leave it at that."

Chapter 13

Saturday, March 4, 1989 – 3:37 p.m. CST
En route Houston, Texas

"I HAVE CONTROL," Stick Cunningham said from the right-hand seat of Gulfstream NG399X as it crossed the Louisiana border southbound over east Texas. As he did, Danny Halliday rose from the captain's seat on the left to trade places with Mr. Bakker, their boss.

A pilot with a lapsed airline transport rating, Bakker had spent the past half hour in the cockpit jump seat observing his crew. As agreed before leaving White Plains, Bakker would try his hand at a landing this trip if the weather in Houston was good. It was. The 3:00 p.m. ATIS—*Automated Terminal Information Service*—for their destination, Ellington Field on the southern outskirts of the city, indicated a fine flying day. Scattered altocumulus cloud around ten thousand feet, visibility twenty miles, winds fifteen knots from the northeast, and 64 degrees with the barometer steadily falling at 29.65 inches. Still good flying weather. In pre-flight they had been concerned by a cold front approaching Houston ahead of a deepening low to the west. Its passage was expected to plunge southeast Texas to near freezing with snowfall by early evening.

Bakker folded his lanky frame into the captain's seat, tweaked its adjustments and buckled in. Dressed down from his usual Hugo Boss style, he looked every bit the part of the millionaire jet set aviator: a custom kid leather flying jacket, yellow polo shirt with his corporate logo, pressed khaki cotton trousers, and brown Sperry yachting deck shoes, the latter being safer for flying than his standard Cuban-heeled cowboy boots. Ray Ban sunglasses with eighteen-carat gold frames. The only thing missing, Cunningham had silently mused, was a silk goddamned-scarf.

"Okay, Boss," Danny Halliday began, leaning forward from the jump seat behind Stick. "You heard the ATIS. We can expect an ILS approach to runway thirty-five left. So let's brief for that. We'll set up for the instrument approach but cancel to VFR when we can."

"Check," replied Bakker, attaching an approach plate detailing the instrument landing procedure to a clip in the middle of his control yoke.

Danny briefed the approach professionally, calling on his years of cockpit crew coordination in the Navy S3A Viking. He reviewed the ATC and navigational aid frequencies listed on the approach plate as Bakker dialed them in. Headings to steer, minimum safe altitudes, the decision height for aborting their landing—which Bakker set on the Grumman's radar altimeter, and the missed approach procedure.

"You'll have control but Stick's in command," he said in conclusion. "In the event of an emergency anywhere on approach, Stick will take over. Follow his commands. I'll be right here to assist. Should be no problem, Boss, on our last training ride you did great."

"Thank you, son," replied Bakker, limbering his fingers like a concert pianist getting ready to play.

"Anything to add, Skipper?" Danny asked.

"Nope." The Stick was a typical ex-fighter jock, a man of few words, used to flying alone.

"Okay! We're well into Texas, let's do it!"

"I have control," said Bakker.

"You have control," Cunningham replied.

Bakker pressed the mike button on his control yoke.

"Houston Approach, Gulfstream Three-Niner-Niner-Xray with you, out of flight level three-zero-zero for one-eight thousand, approaching VIERA," he said.

An approach controller in the Terminal Control Center at Houston Intercontinental Airport had been watching the computerized icon tracking inbound from the northeast on his screen.

"99 Xray, Houston Approach, good afternoon, squawk three-one-zero-one ident," he replied.

Bakker pressed the 'ident' button on the aircraft's transponder, causing their radar return on the controller's screen to momentarily flash.

"99 Xray, radar identified fifty-eight miles northeast of Houston. Continue your descent to one-eight thousand, the altimeter two-niner-six-five," the controller continued.

"99 Xray, roger, now through two-six thousand for eighteen, the altimeter two-niner-six-five," Bakker repeated.

"And 99 Xray, Houston, your wishes?"

"99 Xray, we'd like the ILS approach to runway thirty-five left at Ellington, thank you."

Danny Halliday was impressed by the Boss's flight deck confidence. Always had been. Mark of the man, he supposed. You don't get to the places that Bakker had been without a sure sense of self. And he was still a good pilot. Adept with his airmanship skills, if a little behind the technology curve.

Moments later, ATC cleared the flight for its instrument approach to Ellington Field, with Bakker advising their intention to cancel the instrument landing and join the VFR pattern when the airport was in sight. If good weather held, the switch to visual flight rules would be approved.

The Gulfstream smoothly altered course, banking slightly to the left and steadying on course. Child's play, the old stick-and-rudder man mused.

"Watch your descent rate, Boss." Danny Halliday's voice crackled in his ear. "Control airspeed with pitch, descent rate with thrust. That's it. Nudge it back to sixty-five percent. Trim your nose up a bit. Good. See? It's pegging on twelve hundred feet per minute descent and your speed's holding nicely at one sixty."

A walk in the park, Bakker thought, recalling his Korean War flying days, manhandling those temperamental machines around the sky, planes which in the best of conditions were constantly trying to kill you.

The sprawl of metropolitan Houston became clearer off their nose to the right. Its city center glittered in afternoon sunlight, spreading away to the west in a brown patchwork against the surrounding pale yellow of Texas winter grasslands. Off the left wing, the sparkling blue of the Gulf of Mexico ran to the horizon.

The Gulfstream shuddered as they slipped through a patch of altocumulus scud. The airport wasn't visible yet, laying off the nose somewhere around two o'clock. The instant it was, Bakker cancelled IFR with Houston ATC and was instructed to contact the tower.

Bakker was cleared to join a right-hand downwind for Runway 35 Left. Number three for landing, behind a pair of Air Guard F-4s at his ten o'clock position and a Lear 35 at eight miles on final. He acknowledged the instructions and saw the F-4s glint in the distance.

"Okay, Boss, let's fly this thing!" said Halliday.

Bakker switched off the flight director's automatic pilot and felt the pressure against his hands on the yoke and his feet on the rudder pedals. Much better. The actual feel of an aircraft in flight.

At ten miles northeast of the airport, they could see the sleek Lear on short final to Runway 35 Left and, above the field, two Texas Air National Guard F-4 Phantoms smoking their way to the "jet break". At the break, fifteen hundred feet above midfield, the fighters would bank hard to the left and settle into a landing pattern opposite to that of the civilian jet.

Bakker was thrilled to be back in the saddle.

Cunningham went through the pre-landing checklist as Bakker advised the tower that they were abeam the field.

"99 Xray, Ellington Tower, roger," the controller replied. "Number two for landing runway thirty-five left. Follow the pair of Phantoms turning final."

Bakker acknowledged, spotting the aging interceptors trailing exhaust onto final approach.

"Lone Star One-Five flight, Ellington tower, cleared to land runway thirty-five left. Departure end cable is up. Wind zero-one-zero at fifteen. Check gear down."

"One-Five Lead. Three green," replied the flight leader.

"One-Five Number Two, with the gear," said his wingman, and moments later the lead fighter settled onto the runway with Two a hundred yards behind him, off his right wing.

Leaving one thousand feet and about to turn the Gulfstream onto final approach, Bakker was set to key the mike when an urgent radio call got their attention.

"Two! Bad chute! Passing right!"

Halfway down the runway, the lead Phantom slowed as its drag chute caught air. Overtaking on the right side of the runway, Number Two cut away a tangled chute that hadn't fully deployed. The second F-4 shot past the first with its arrester hook down and trailing sparks.

"Two is taking the cable!" its pilot declared.

The Gulfstream crew craned to observe the emergency unfolding on the ground. Plumes of glycol and water shot into the air on both sides of the runway, the underground system providing hydraulic braking to the cable that had been caught by Phantom's arrester hook.

"99 Xray, landing runway is fouled," the controller said quickly. "Your intentions?"

Bakker pressed transmit without hesitating.

"Roger, tower," he began. "I think we'll extend our base leg here and, uh, swing around to the south to set up on final to zero-four. How's that?"

A thousand feet shorter, Runway 04/22 was the secondary jet runway at Ellington Field, crossing the main runway at a forty-five degree angle. It would be no problem, the Gulfstream pilots knew, to extend their flight to the west for a couple of miles, ply a gentle teardrop turn to the south, and come around with Runway 04 smack dab in their sights.

Simple as pie. It was exactly what Stick had decided, pissed that the Boss answered first.

"That'll give you a thirty degree left crosswind at fifteen knots," the controller responded. "Is that okay, 99 Xray?"

Simple math. Wind speed, angle, aircraft weight, runway length and width and its surface conditions. Cunningham and Halliday nodded as Bakker keyed the mike.

"We're good with that," Bakker reported.

"Roger, 99 Xray cleared to land runway zero-four. Wind zero-one-zero at fifteen and gusting. The departure end cable is up. Call me turning final for a wind check."

Bakker acknowledged and felt Stick's left hand on top of his right on the throttles. He was nudging them forward, applying thrust to stem their descent.

"What part of me having command wasn't clear?" asked Cunningham tersely.

"Watch your temper there, son," drawled Bakker. "Do you have control?"

"I have control," Stick confirmed, and Bakker slipped his hand off the throttle.

The former USAF fighter weapons instructor flew the Gulfstream through a perfect approach onto Runway 04, completing all of the flying duties himself—flaps, power, landing gear, radio calls. Danny Halliday bit his tongue and kept silent. The Boss sat back in the left-hand seat, arms folded across his chest and feet flat on the floor.

Cunningham taxied the Gulfstream to an assigned spot on the flight line in front of the fixed base operator's hangar on the southwest corner of the field. The three men said nothing to one another as Bakker left the cockpit for the cabin. Stick shut down the systems and engines. Danny popped the door and strode across the ramp toward the FBO's aircrew entrance.

Cunningham knew it was coming. When he left the cockpit he saw Bakker hanging up his satellite phone. The Boss had that look.

"You're a fine pilot, Rick," Bakker began. "But you don't know your place. I can't abide disrespect. Spud MacNeil is on his way down here tonight. He and young Halliday will fly me back tomorrow. Get all of your gear off my plane. You're fired. Make your way home on your company card."

ॐ

Saturday, March 4, 1989 – 8:43 p.m. CST
The Houston Club, 811 Rusk St., Houston, Texas

CIGAR SMOKE HAD begun to form a thin cloud in the corner of the Gulf Coast Room of the Houston Club, the city's most opulent haunt for the wealthy since 1894. Of the two hundred-odd invited guests who had been wined and dined on oilman Buck Peyton's nickel, it was mostly ladies and their insignificant others who remained at their tables for coffee, cognac and chatter. A platoon of uniformed staff had begun to bus tables as men in formal evening attire began making their way to the bar. Ice tinkled in glasses. The hum of bright conversation mixed with occasional backslapping laughter. A string quartet, which had entertained before dinner, resumed with a viola solo heralding Smetana's "From My Life" String Quartet No. 1 in E Minor. Not that this crowd of oilmen, bankers and spouses would have been moved; it might as well have been recorded elevator music. They had come to flaunt their social standing, being handpicked to dine on Texas quail and prime rib and to applaud Buck Peyton on his latest endeavor: a quarter billion dollar refinery expansion, set to break ground later this year. Fine wines had been drunk. Dinner had been eaten and two agreeably short speeches had been heard. And now, with the formal agenda concluded, the networking rituals of Houston's business elite could begin.

At the head of the room by soaring windows in the northeast corner, three men stood smoking together and were deferentially given a wide berth by anyone wandering near.

Ted Bakker was angry. Wordlessly fuming, forcing cigar smoke through his nostrils between quick puffs to inhale. His so-called friend Buck Peyton was attempting to sound conciliatory, coming off insincere with an inch-thick Honduran gran corona clenched in his teeth. And for his part, Sir Henry Cathcart, chairman of Albion Petroleum, Britain's largest oil conglomerate, smoked his own with aplomb.

"For chrissakes, Ted, it was a business announcement," groused Peyton. "Not the Oilers winning the damn Superbowl. I just wanted a plain, simple party. No fanfare, no marching bands. A few words to thank old Henry here for AP's long-term vision for the Gulf. I never meant to piss in your pickles, but the fact is, this is *my* party. I didn't mean to exclude you, you just weren't included."

"Don't goddamn patronize me!" Bakker hissed.

"Oh, get off your high horse. Peyton Oil is *my* company. Channelview Three is *my* refinery. AP is my customer, and it was my decision to ..."

"What? Ignore my contribution?"

Buck Peyton rolled his cigar between his teeth, his jaw getting tighter. His old friend was skirting a line that he never expected he'd cross. Well, fuck him.

"So AP's involvement was your idea," Peyton shot back. "That makes you an idea man, Teddy. I own plenty of those."

"Gentlemen, please!" Henry Cathcart interceded, clapping both men on the shoulder. "I am sorry, Ted, if you feel you've been slighted. Your role in this enterprise has been invaluable, clearly. It should have been recognized and it's a damned shame that it wasn't. Mea culpa, I'm afraid. Buck had included warm praise in the original draft of his speech. But, you see, I asked him to remove any reference to you and he kindly conceded."

Sir Henry had fallen on his own sword.

Ted Bakker blanched, choking for an instant on smoke.

"Remove any reference to me?" he sputtered.

The Brit, a balding, heavyset man with the look of a gout-stricken Dickensian aristocrat, peered at Bakker over his half-moon eyeglasses.

"Of course!" he replied, smiling broadly, exuding serene self-assurance. He lowered his voice. "Surely you realize, Ted, that these days you're persona non grata. Your leadership at Pan Am is being pilloried in the press. Cavalier handling of passenger safety. With the tabloids today, we're only as good as our last good decision, and as bad as the slightest mistake in our past."

An apprehensive young server handed each man a small ashtray and retreated as quickly as he had appeared.

Bakker and Peyton eyed each other stonily.

Sir Henry tapped loose an inch of ash and continued.

"That's business, my friend. Frankly, I have a board of obsequious toadies, so the decision to snub you was mine. I pride myself in my judgment of men, and believed, I still do, that a Texan like you could take one on the chin. I'm not wrong, am I?"

Bakker softened, slowly shaking his head, unsettled as much by his own egotistic display as he was by Buck Peyton's continuing glare.

Across the room, Ted Bakker's Number One Girl stood next to the bar, accepting a flute of cold Chardonnay from her gay shadow and escort, Mark Salzberg, Bakker's VP of money. She had been watching the Boss, biting her plump lower lip as she always did when she could tell he was angry.

At thirty-five, Penny Luscombe had the same figure and brunette country girl looks she'd had as Miss February 1980, a centerfold still adorning the office walls of service stations and plumbing contractors from Bremerton to Biscayne Bay.

Born in rural Miller County, Arkansas, just outside Texarkana, she grew up in a distinctly conservative hell that prized strong Baptist Church morals as much as its sexy cheerleaders. She had fallen from grace with the former as one of the latter. Pregnant at eighteen, she left home in disgrace for Los Angeles, where she boarded with a cousin whose life had followed a similar path. Had an abortion. Waited tables in Hollywood cocktail bars. Reached a low ebb in her life at age twenty and turned it around getting work as a stewardess with a west coast airline. Three years later, she caught the eye of a photographer who propelled her to centerfold fame in 1980. Even so, her fame was short lived and career wise produced nothing worthwhile until she met Ted Bakker, the president of Pan Am, in early 1983.

She had been meeting a friend from the flight sisterhood at the LAX Pan Am lounge. Bakker recalled her, as many men did. The pair got talking, one thing led to another and within a month she was on his payroll in New York and quickly a fixture in Ted Bakker's bed. When he left Pan Am in 1987, so did she, executive assistant to the president and CEO of Bakker Worldwide, Inc.

Men with a pulse were attracted to Penny. That's simple biology. Men who got the chance to engage her in conversation felt a deeper attraction. She had that Arkansas accent and pattern of feminine speech that completed nearly everything she said with a subtle question mark. "You're meeting with your lawyers at ten? I think I'll wear that black off-the-shoulder Prada? You're really a sonofabitch?"

She had the pouting wide-mouthed good looks of her favorite actress, Miss Linda Gray. The same cheekbones and eyes, but a better body. Anyone at Buck Peyton's party that night would have agreed that she was the most beautiful woman in the room, even dapper Mark Salzberg, whose three dollar bill tastes ran more to the muscular Latino bartender with whom he'd been trading glances all evening.

"The Boss really looks pissed," observed Salzberg between sips on a heavily-salted Margarita in his manicured grasp. "Yesterday, I caught him practicing a few words of humble thanks in his office like he had a lock on an Oscar or Tony. Hardly the butch Texan we all know and love."

Penny's eyes flashed. Mark was as quick with unflattering gossip as he was with fawning false praise.

"One day, Mark, your office girl side's gonna come back to bite you." she chided, pinching him on the ass hard enough that he slopped his cocktail. "Right where it hurts."

❧

SOFT BEDSIDE LAMPLIGHT and shadow played on the curves of Penelope Luscombe's body. Breasts rising gently between her arms as she steadied herself above Ted's grizzled chest. Freckle-dappled shoulders flexing as she arched her back. She and Bakker were not lovers. Not in the conventional sense that implied passion or anything mutually fulfilling beyond orgasm, which wasn't more often than not. Their regular coupling wasn't even 'sport sex', as modern partners liked to call purely physical relationships. That would have suggested play, something fun.

They might have dated in the beginning, but they were never a couple. She went onto his payroll as a personal assistant, paid to bring order to his disorderly life—which she did very well, more professionally than any personal assistant he'd ever had. Always discreetly detached. Rarely publicly on his arm. Separate rooms, sometimes even separate flights when they travelled. Still, sex was the one part of her job description that she'd understood from the start. From Arkansas cheerleader to centerfold, to downtown Manhattan and proximity to wealth, she had given up more for much less.

Penny knew when she left the oilman's party that Ted would expect her to come to his room, after six years she knew how to size up his moods. They had an understanding. She went to the functions Ted Bakker attended, usually with Mark or someone else in his entourage. If he was happy, getting into the bourbon, she knew right away to use her key to his room and lay there in waiting. If he was caught up with business or had an eye on somebody else, she could get a night's sleep. But if he was unhappy, she would tip the staff at the hotel to alert her when he returned. Tonight she left the Houston Club at eleven, having abandoned Mark Salzberg to drool at the bar, and it was just after one o'clock when the hotel concierge called.

Penny had waited half an hour and let herself into Ted Bakker's suite. She knew his routine. He had showered. She found him standing at the window in a white hotel bathrobe, looking out at snow falling lightly on Houston, smoking a cigar with a bourbon in hand. She knew not to speak. Her room, of course, was opposite his, and she slipped by in a robe over nothing at all. She wrapped her arms around him from behind, watching the wet snowflakes fall. He said nothing, which said plenty, and in a moment she led him to bed.

It wasn't working. She arched her back and rocked even harder, her fingernails scraping his chest.

"Stop!" Bakker grunted.

She bounced, squeezing her thighs.

"I said stop!" he wheezed, pushing her free and she rolled off beside him.

Penny caught her breath, lying beside him disheveled and plucking an errant lock of hair from her eyes. What the fuck is your problem? she might have asked, but she didn't. Instead she just lay there and softly exhaled.

"I c-can't," he stammered. "I can't do this right now."

What should I say? she wondered. Something coy and submissive? Tell him I don't give a shit?

"We could try something else if you like?"

"Just leave, dammit!" Bakker said, getting up from the bed and awkwardly pulling on his robe.

Bakker sat back down, swallowed a mouthful of bourbon and sucked at his cigar. It was dead. He got up in search of another. Penny rose, wrapped herself in her robe and quietly slipped away to the door.

"You know where I am," she said softly and left.

Chapter 14

Friday, March 31, 1989 – 8:55 a.m. EST
201 Varick Street, New York, NY

IT'S FUNNY HOW you get that déjà vu feeling about places you think you've never been. So thought Detective Jimmy Kenneally as he stepped from the cab. There was an article he'd once read in Scientific American—it explained how the brain stores our memory of specific locations, like the corner of Varick and West Houston in lower Manhattan. See that spot once and the brain triggers a single neuron with chemical orders to preserve the image—kinda like taking a snapshot—and, with that command, other neurons are assigned to preserving the image from every perspective. Coming at it along West Houston from Sixth, southbound down Varick to Charlton, every which way, even views from above and below. And the part that got Jimmy—if you haven't seen that spot from one of those angles, your brain will imagine that view on its own and create an impression. Amazing, really. Every place that we've been in our lives, all filed away like old holiday photos. Some in full color, vivid and clear; some grainy and barely imagined, and all of them getting a little bit clearer every time we return.

It's how humans are able to visualize journeys. Why some people can't navigate worth a damn, and how some can with an acute sense of spatial awareness. You know? Like Jimmy's brother Frank. Ask him at some backwater crossroads in Jersey, "Which way to Bayonne, Frankie?" and he'll say: "Turn left at the lights. That'll be south."

It's also why Jimmy got that déjà vu feeling this morning, in front of this south Manhattan address.

The twelve-story brick edifice took up half the block on the northwest corner of Varick and West Houston Street. It was one of those cookie-cutter federal office buildings they threw up everywhere back in the 1940s. Brown brick with rows upon rows of windows long since painted shut and a two-story granite façade at street level. Block-cut marble framed the main entrance, two steps up from the street to glass doors hung in brass. Its address outlined in gilt bold italics on glass below the Great Federal Seal.

201 Varick Street.

Visitors to its cavernous two-story lobby will find an expanse of green marble tile, stairwells in each corner, and two banks of twin elevators centered in the lobby on opposite sides of the room. Between each set of elevators is a building directory—1940's style glazed brass cases with neat rows of white plastic letters and numbers pressed into black velveteen. *United States Government Audit Office*—101. *Federal Aviation Authority, Flight Standards*—700. *The U.S. Job Corps*—910, and so on, a collection of federal agencies from the renowned to obscure.

Kenneally arrived just before nine o'clock. His instructions had been clear: Report to the National Archives and Records Administration, Northeast Region, 201 Varick Street. Enter through an unmarked brown metal door with a surveillance camera, around the corner on Houston. Use the key card provided for access. It would be down the block, next to an overhead door to a parking garage, just past the entrance to an office building at 246 West Houston Street.

That address too seemed familiar to Kenneally but he hadn't been able to place it. At least not until he walked to the corner of Houston and turned to look west.

Déjà vu.

It was an image that had lain dormant in his brain for nearly twenty-five years. White pin-striped signage on glass above the entrance to 246 West Houston Street: *'Department of Veterans Affairs, Manhattan Veterans Center'*. He'd gone through those doors often enough. Long ago, in another life.

THREE WEEKS EARLIER, Detective Kenneally had been listening in on an afternoon tryst between a *Russkaya Mafiya* gunman and a pair of exotic dancers when his pager vibrated a little too close to his crotch. He'd let out a yowl and sprang to his feet in a vacant, roach-ridden apartment in Brighton Beach, splashing coffee all over his partner, a brand new shield from the Brooklyn Six-Oh. Jimmy knew it would take ages to live that one down.

The page came from his boss, not the Brooklyn lieutenant in charge of the surveillance, but Captain Lou Passaglia at Technical Services, One Police Plaza. He had been summoned to headquarters, first thing in the morning.

Passaglia relayed a message that neither man understood or expected. Kenneally had been reassigned from the surveillance tech job he had held for six years. He was to clear his calendar and report by the end of the week to Deputy Commissioner Charles Watt, the mayor's point man on counter-terrorism. "Don't you and Watt have some kind of history together?" Passaglia asked.

"Yeah, we do," was all Jimmy said.

THE PARKING GARAGE off West Houston gave Kenneally an eerie feeling, as if it hadn't been used for years. His footsteps echoed as he descended one floor down the concrete ramp from the street. Ahead was a single unmarked elevator. The roadway itself took a turn to the right, opening into one parking level of perhaps fifty stalls, with only the first nearest three occupied.

His key card activated the elevator and in a moment its doors slowly opened. Inside was a scuffed tile floor and walls with an ancient coat of institutional green enamel. There was no floor indicator or buttons to press, simply a key card reader fitted to the right of the doors. A surveillance camera overhead had a small fisheye lens and a light that blinked red.

The elevator descended more deeply than Kenneally expected. When it stopped, its doors opened to a gentle rush of air and a small concrete lobby. It had the same pale floor tiles, two-tone walls with the same 1940's enamel, mint green below beige. It had fluorescent lighting recessed into the ceiling and a set of sturdy metal fire doors directly ahead. The doors had a card reader with a numeric keypad. He'd been given no code and smiled up at the surveillance eye.

The double doors opened outward, again with a rush of air, and he was met by an unsmiling black man about his own age. He was trim and athletically built, clean cut with short hair and a mustache, and casually dressed in a blue polo shirt and tan chinos. He extended his hand.

"Detective Kenneally," he said, with a forthright clip to his speech. "Come in. I'm Lincoln Coultart."

"Call me Jimmy," Kenneally replied.

Coultart led the way through the cavernous room beyond the self-closing doors. The place surprised Kenneally, not that he had really known what to expect. It was the size of a gymnasium and about as empty and uninviting. There were new office walls, some half completed, untended table saws, sawhorses and stacks of building material.

In a corner he noticed the only others apparently present. Two men in dark coveralls, one wearing headphones and slowly passing a wand over cardboard cartons of office equipment. Their role he knew: electronic eavesdropping countermeasures. Odd, thought Kenneally, they weren't locals, no one he recognized. Not feds. On a job like this feds would be wearing jackets and ties. Regardless, with a set up like this, these two would be around for a while.

As they walked toward a completed section of offices, Coultart stopped twice to explain where they were and what they were seeing. They were eighty feet below street level. He didn't know how many floors were above or below them, which was probably true. But at least, he said, they had their own secure entrance.

The place had been a federal government archive vault, designed to keep paper records in storage in a climate-controlled and pressurized environment, which explained the rush of air Kenneally felt leaving the elevator. It had nuclear attack survivability second only to NORAD and Washington operations, Coultart explained. And until recently it had stored volumes of once irreplaceable federal records, all now transferred to computer and microfiche. Renovations to suit its new purpose would be completed within a week.

Coultart led him to a glassed-in office that smelled of new broadloom and paint. It seemed as if he might have just been moving in as Kenneally arrived; there was nothing on the walls, nothing in the bookshelves, and nothing on his desk but a brown cardboard Bankers Box filled with what appeared to be personal knickknacks.

"I understand from Charlie Watt that you're not much for small talk or bullshit," Coultart began as they sat with coffee. Kenneally replied with a shrug.

Coultart smiled. "In our business, that's to your credit."

Our business? Jimmy wondered just what business that he and this stranger were in.

"Watt said you were surprised when he came to you with this. That you hadn't exactly kept in touch since the army. A few Christmas cards. Your wife's funeral in '76. Not much in the way of personal contact since?"

"That's correct," Kenneally replied. He noticed the look of regret that had quickly crossed Coultart's face. "The war was all we had in common."

"Ia Drang Valley, November 1965. You and Charlie served together in the 7th Cavalry. Custer's old regiment. I read your Silver Star citation. Took an NVA bayonet in the chest saving your wounded friend. I'm a little surprised that you haven't been closer."

Kenneally's mood darkened. "We became cops but our paths never crossed. I'm Brooklyn Irish. He's from Harlem and got educated. Worlds apart, we went on with our lives. Does that make a difference?"

Coultart said, "Thirty thousand cops on the job in New York. Why do you think he called you?"

"He didn't say and I didn't ask. Could be I'm someone he knows he can trust."

Right answer. Coultart had that look.

"Watt plays his cards close to his chest, doesn't he?"

"Always did when I knew him. Suppose he still does."

"Do you trust him?"

"Absolutely."

"Good," Coultart said. "So do I. And until two months ago, I didn't know him from Adam."

OVER THE COURSE of an hour, Jimmy Kenneally was brought up to speed on the business of Olympiad. The New York station had counterpart bureaus in Paris, London and Bonn. Coultart was the station chief and would administrate the station with a deputy and a single assistant. An intelligence and analysis cell of four, along with technical services, would support six teams of field operators, partnered in pairs. Each team would conduct individual or joint operations within their geographic region, or abroad in support of the overseas network.

The New York station had been established on paper in late January, with its chief selected from a very short list.

Linc Coultart had been one of the first black men to become a United States Treasury ATF agent. Raised in Arcadia, Bienville Parish in northwest Louisiana, he'd had Navy service as a demolitions diver before a Tulane commerce degree and a position with the Louisiana state attorney general's department. There his first major assignment had been to investigate fraud in the Gulf oil patch and the industry that supplied its explosives. His success had garnered a string of high profile convictions, and he had been riding the wave when, in 1972, the ATF hired him away. He quickly became its black market explosives guru, working his way through the ATF world, ending up as supervisory agent at its New York bureau in 1983—responsible for overseeing interagency task force operations on the entire east coast.

To his credit, Coultart's tenure in that New York post had avoided the taint of the *Valhalla* affair—the 1984 IRA gunrunning sting which had succeeded in netting arrests, but nearly brought down the entire alphabet of federal agencies involved when it was learned that FBI intelligence in Boston had been compromised. It was in the fallout of Valhalla and its subsequent broader investigation by Charles Watt that Coultart had caught the eye of his future boss.

Kenneally had been given only a high level peek at Olympiad by Watt, before a handshake had sealed his signing on. That and swearing a National Security secrecy oath. He knew it would be an international team, operating alone and covertly, with a mandate outside of the justice system. That suited the court-worn detective just fine.

"Interdiction is our business," said Coultart. "Targeting terrorist groups through their arms supply pipeline. Gathering intelligence to set up sting operations. Working them undercover. Breaking their supply chain and backs when we can. Since the Lockerbie bombing the gloves have come off."

"Charlie suggested as much," Kenneally said.

"We've got a good team in place," Coultart continued. "You've already seen two of the techs. Most of the operators are out of ATF and Drug Enforcement. That was my call. You and a cop out of Boston PD are the only ones who aren't feds on the team."

Coultart handed him a thin folder containing a photo and a two-page bio.

He said, "This is your partner. You don't know him, I checked. Go ahead and read that now. Not much on paper will ever be leaving this place."

Kevin Ahearn. An ATF agent. A tough looking ginger-haired Mick about Jimmy's own age, with a nose as visible proof that he could take a punch. Out of ... here's a surprise, South Boston. It took Kenneally just minutes to conclude that Ahearn had juice and that as a team they might be a good fit.

"Questions?" Coultart asked.

"When do we meet? How soon do we start?"

Coultart retrieved the dossier.

"Well, as a team you have already started. An arms sale interdiction that we've dubbed 'Operation Long Jump'. Ahearn is out of town working on setting it up. He'll brief you on the weekend. I understand you live on your boat out on Long Island? A thirty-six foot Grand Banks Sedan trawler?"

Kenneally chuckled. How to tell your new boss that he's wrong? You don't.

"Someone spoke to my sister, then?" he replied.

Since his wife Bernadette's death in 1976, Kenneally had lived above the boathouse on the property of his sister Sinead and her asshole husband, a Long Island dentist. They kept their own speedboat in the boathouse, his spent most of its time alongside their dock on lower Manhasset Bay. The only time Jimmy did live aboard 'Paddy' was when she was at anchor, or on the increasingly rare occasions that he came home too legless to make his own way up the stairs.

"Ahearn will be by on Sunday," Coultart said. "Introduce yourselves. He's your team leader, just take it from there."

Jimmy nodded. Entertaining aboard? He would need to clean up the boat.

Coultart's body language suggested that they were pretty much through. He pulled a slip of notepaper from a gummed pad and scratched a word on it in pen.

"The last thing I need to cover is your unique personal identifier," he said.

Oh, ho! Secret Squirrel shit.

"Not everyone in the organization has one. As a field operator, you do," Coultart continued. "It's yours alone. If you're ever contacted by anyone using your Olympiad codename, follow their instructions to the letter. If you need clarification? Contact me. You will be given the procedure in due course. Clear enough so far?"

"Yep," Kenneally replied.

Coultart sighed. "Someone in a higher pay grade liked codenames based on Olympic sports," he said. "Mine is Diver. Remember that. If and when anyone does contact you, they will indicate your association to Diver. If that doesn't happen? Again, contact me. Understood?"

Kenneally nodded.

Coultart pushed the slip of notepaper across his desk.

"This is you," he said.

Kenneally read the name.

He would have preferred something sexy like Gold Medalist or Downhill Racer.

Coultart took back the note and put it through his deskside paper shredder.

"Great!" he said, standing and offering Jimmy his hand.

"We're done. Welcome aboard."

Chapter 15

Sunday, April 2, 1989 – 10:35 a.m. EST
83 Shore Road, Manhasset, New York

THERE HADN'T BEEN a more glorious morning since spring had begun, or rather, since the long and exceptionally bitter winter had ended. It was warm, already pushing into the low fifties. The sky was bright blue, the air crisp and scrubbed clean by light easterly winds off the Atlantic, and sunlight bathed the stark stately elms lining Shore Road in Manhasset, Long Island, with a dazzling yellow hue.

Kevin Ahearn squinted against the sun, looking east as his truck rolled to a stop at the corner of Shore Road and Willow Court. Dammit! This was the third time that he'd cruised the length of the street with no Number 83 to be found. Helter-skelter bloody suburbs. He was about to swallow his pride and ask a lady who was approaching with a lapdog in tow, when he noticed a tree-sheltered lane ahead leading off to the west. Toward the water. The right direction at least for somebody who lives on a boat. He put the battered Ford F150 into gear and chugged away, leaving a Long Island matron and her frou-frou mutt in a cloud of blue smoke.

Number 83 it said on a brick lamppost halfway down the lane. Good luck ever getting your pizza.

Ahearn pulled into a short circle driveway in front of a sprawling brick rancher, stopping behind a landscaper's van that was blocking the way. He nodded hello to an old-timer in faded coveralls who was preparing a flowerbed next to the front entrance. A well-coiffed brunette in her early forties flashed really great teeth as she answered the bell. Soon she wasn't smiling at all, giving the shabby stranger the surly once over. "I told Hector there's a restroom out back in the boathouse," she sniffed.

"I appreciate that, ma'am," Ahearn said, "but my business is more with your brother, Detective Kenneally."

Sinead Dunleavy blushed and looked him over again. "That would've been my second guess."

The place had to be worth a million, Kevin thought as he made his way through a sprawling backyard toward a long weathered dock jutting into the tidal mud flats of Manhasset Bay. At the end of the dock, nearly aground at low tide, was a mid-fifties trawler style yacht—white hulled, with varnished wood gunwales and trim on its moss green cabin and wheelhouse. Nice boat.

Attached to the dock sat a two-story boathouse of about the same vintage. Whitewashed plank siding. Neatly shuttered windows on both levels. Clearly living quarters above, accessed by wooden stairs that led up from the dock to a landing and door on the shore-facing side.

"Jimmy *Ken-ay-lee?*" Ahearn called out as he stopped at the foot of the dock. He saw a broad-shouldered figure appear on the boat's quarterdeck, dressed in a wool sweater and jeans. With a watch cap and pipe, he might have been Ernest Hemingway.

Kenneally wiped his hands with a grease rag and called back, "Must be a Mick from South Boston, getting it right the first time."

A cocked turn of the head signaled to Ahearn to join him aboard, and he returned his attention to scrubbing a fouled fuel injector. Peering up from his work, he studied the man who was walking toward him. Steady on his feet. Like himself, about six-foot-two and in fairly good shape pushing fifty. A full head of ginger hair that wasn't nearly as gray, unkempt and over his ears in keeping with maybe a week's worth of beard. He was wearing work boots and jeans, a black gearhead t-shirt under a black nylon hunting vest, with his biceps and right forearm displaying faded mono-color tattoos.

Ahearn stepped aboard confidently and took a quick look around. "Nice boat," he said as he offered his hand. Kenneally wiped his hand on his sweater. Fair grip, they both thought.

"You know boats, then?" he asked.

Ahearn tapped his toe on the standing end of the stern mooring line, which Jimmy had neatly coiled flat on the deck in a tight concentric circle.

"I like that you cheese down your lines," he said, properly using a term so obscure that it reeked of old salt. "Mind if I look her over?"

"Fill yer boots," Kenneally agreed cheerfully, deciding to stow his troublesome fuel injector and step into the cabin to brew up some coffee while his new partner embarked on an inspection tour.

Ten minutes later, Ahearn thumped down the ladder from the flying bridge and pronounced his approval: "I'd love something as tiddly as this, but the wife keeps my balls in her purse." Now this was a partnership with potential.

INTRODUCTIONS CAME FIRST and Kenneally drew the short straw, expanding through conversation on the slim background brief that Ahearn had already read.

James Joseph Francis Kenneally. He had been born in 1942 on Abyssinia Street in the Catholic tenement slums of Falls Road, Belfast. Nearly four years of age before meeting his father, a merchant seaman whose ship had been sunk in Singapore harbor during its fall to the Japanese in February the year he was born. Joe Kenneally had been a skeletal shadow of his former self on repatriation after thirty-eight months of brutal internment. But the affable weekend footballer had quickly regained his outlook and nearly one hundred pounds before returning to his pre-war employment: stevedoring on the Port of Belfast docks.

Soon came two brothers and a younger sister for Jimmy. For some, the sectarian hate had abated during the war. But the long simmering hatred soon returned to Ulster, worse with postwar unemployment and labor discrimination hitting the minority Catholics hard. In the bleak summer of 1950, Joe and Caitlin Kenneally packed up their four children and emigrated to the United States.

They settled in the Irish Catholic neighborhood of Windsor Terrace in Brooklyn, with a spacious three-story townhouse on Seeley near the corner of 20th Avenue. New York was heaven on earth for the wide-eyed eight year old. His father quickly found work at the Brooklyn Navy Yard, where he became a crane operator and remained happily well-employed until his sudden fatal heart attack in 1979 at the age of sixty.

The Kenneally's had enjoyed a prosperous working-class American life, more than a world away from the grim Edwardian poverty and violent strife of a Belfast young Jimmy could scarcely remember.

He had excelled in sports at Brooklyn's Central Catholic High School, graduating a popular senior in June 1960. In May the next year he joined the United States Army. Earned Airborne and Ranger patches. Served with the 1st Cavalry Division in Vietnam. Wounded in action in 1965, a bayonet through his right lung.

He spent three months in a Navy hospital in Guam, and a year recuperating as an outpatient at the Brooklyn VA Hospital. It was there that he met and courted a leggy nurse named Bernadette Mary Catherine McMahon, second-generation Catholic Irish from Queens.

After six months of treadmills and long-distance running, he fully regained the lung capacity that he had lost, only to exhaust it by running his quarry to ground. They were married three years later in 1969, with the spectacular June wedding she wanted at Saint Augustine's Cathedral in Brooklyn. They settled into their first home together, a walk-up apartment on lower Dikeman in Red Hook. By then, Jimmy Kenneally had been a year on the job with NYPD, a beat cop in Brooklyn's 77th Precinct where he would serve another three.

February 1972 brought the birth of their son, Brendan Francis, whom his extended family adored and called "Wee Frankie"—on account of the fact that there were already two Brendan's and three males called Frankie among them. The same year saw them purchase their first home, a quaint moss green cottage, steps from the seashore in Gerritsen Beach, south Brooklyn.

The next summer, Jimmy was transferred to plainclothes duty in the street crime unit of the One-Four in midtown Manhattan. There he found his niche as a cop, becoming an expert in technical surveillance. Wiretaps. Long lens and low light photography, as well as the next great crime fighting tool: transistor closed circuit TV. Jimmy Kenneally found he was really good at it and "tech" soon became his career.

Bernie had become a surgery nurse. She made more than he did and their life together had become idyllic. Their boy. Their home. Money in the bank. Weekends away in the Catskills, and after one winter trip to Bermuda they were planning more. Then, in March 1976, it all came to an end when Wee Frankie suddenly died. An undiagnosed congenital heart condition. No one could have known, they said. Nobody's fault, bless him. Weeping grandmothers crossed themselves, it was God's will, they said. "Compassionate and loving God," they prayed at his funeral at Saint Augustine's. "Yours is the beauty of childhood and yours is the fullness of years. Comfort us in our sorrow, strengthen us with hope, and breathe peace into our troubled hearts."

Jimmy Kenneally couldn't accept it, he lost his faith completely when God took his boy. And Bernie would never recover. Eight months later she died alone in a fire that burned their home to the ground. Middle of a cold November night. Jimmy had been working a stakeout for two days. The fire marshal cited the most likely cause as toppled candles they'd found at her bedside, that and the empty whiskey bottle. Lesser men might have swirled down the bowl but Jimmy Kenneally soldiered on. Moving into his sister's boathouse. Devoting himself to his work and the Grand Banks Sedan he picked up for a song.

In 1981 he was seconded to a joint FBI-NYPD organized crime task force. Promoted to Detective-Investigator, mainly working wiretaps and surveillance on mafia operations across the five boroughs. After four years of that, another promotion—Sergeant Detective Supervisor, SDS, working in his current position out of Tech Services for the Chief of Detectives at One Police Plaza. Cops he worked with respected and liked him. Cool and calm and a leader, he was always the first guy on the team to go through the door.

His reliability profile had showed no relationship commitments. There was a friendship with a divorcee in her forties named Rhonda Ghiardelli, the bartender at the VFW post in nearby Mineola. She was a brassy, buxom gal, a raven-haired Dolly Parton with a Brooklyn accent instead of a country girl twang. It was a purely physical arrangement that they both could rely on when either was lonely.

No red flagged personal vices. An occasional penchant for a cheap Irish whiskey called Paddy, imported from County Cork. He had named his boat for it.

He had about $100,000 in a savings account. Another ten or fifteen in checking. No real surprise, with the insurance paid out on his home and late wife. Nothing excessive. Kenneally made a good living, forty grand a year before overtime and he lived cheaply enough at his sister's place.

Ahearn was a good judge of people and his first instincts were usually right. He could work with the guy.

ॐ

JIMMY KENNEALLY HAD never heard of Kevin Ahearn, and as the junior partner of their team, all he knew was what he had read in his brief two-page life story.

Kevin Riley Ahearn was born in May 1940 in Boston. He was the second of seven children to Aidan Thomas Ahearn— Tommy to his friends, a bus driver with the Boston Metropolitan Transit Authority—and his wife Aileen. Three brothers, three sisters. Third generation Irish, raised in a three-bedroom rental in a rough neighborhood in South Boston, around 7th and D Street.

Kevin graduated from South Boston High School in 1958 and worked for nearly five years on an uncle's scallop boat out of Gloucester, which was clearly the source of the brine in his veins. He married his high school sweetheart, Valerie Adamczyk, in August 1963, a week before entering the Massachusetts State Police Academy at Framingham. Twenty-six weeks of training, during which—in March 1964—his son Patrick was born.

His first posting as a trooper was to D2 Barracks in South Yarmouth, where he served four years patrolling sleepy Cape Cod. While posted there, twin daughters Fiona and Siobhan were born on the Fourth of July, 1966.

Kevin was transferred in 1969 to Troop F, the uniformed division of the Massachusetts Port Authority at Boston Logan Airport. After two years, he joined its intelligence section, investigating arms trafficking through the Port of Boston. It was work he enjoyed, and in May 1975, he left the State Police to join the Treasury Department's Bureau of Alcohol, Tobacco and Firearms as an ATF agent. He remained in the Boston area, spending four more years doing the same job with a different badge.

In 1981, after an administrative stint in the Boston regional office, Agent Ahearn moved to Washington, D.C. and a job in the ATF Office of the Deputy Director—responsible for liaison with the FBI, police and intelligence agencies on U.S.-based arms trafficking. It was during this time that he met Lincoln Coultart.

Coultart had an eye for individual talent. Those he met who showed real potential, he would earmark for some future project or personal team. One of these had been Kevin Ahearn. At a State Department cocktail party at the time, its deputy director of intelligence had cornered Coultart and quipped, "Next to me, the brightest light in this town is an agent of yours who's working for Bobby Pitcairn. Name of Kevin Ahearn. Smart, smart fella. You keep a short leash on that one, Mr. Lincoln, or I'm gonna hire him away."

In February 1986, Ahearn was seconded for six months to the State Department, operating out of the American Embassy in London, coordinating U.S. intelligence surrounding Libyan arms shipments to the IRA. He assisted in target location in Operation Eldorado Canyon—April 15, 1986—punitive U.S. airstrikes on Libya.

Three months later, Ahearn joined the ATF New York regional office as its intelligence section head. He and Valerie sold their Maryland home and bought a two-bedroom apartment on East 39th Street, off 2nd Avenue in the Manhattan neighborhood of Tudor City. And in January 1989, over a beer at Murphy's—Kevin Ahearn's local haunt, around the corner from his home on 2nd Avenue—Coultart asked if he was up for a change in career.

THE FADED GREEN tattoo on Ahearn's right forearm was a Celtic cross with the words 'Tiocfaidh ár lá' above it in an arc. Irish Gaelic: "Our day will come"—a Republican prayer for a united Ireland. It was a tattoo that could get you killed on Protestant Shankill Road in Belfast. The same slogan had been tattooed on Joseph Kenneally's shoulder, discreetly out of sight, but Jimmy had known as a child it was there.

"Tips your hand a little there, don't ya think?" observed Kenneally, sipping coffee across his galley table from Ahearn. It took a moment for his guest to catch what he meant.

"This?" asked Ahearn, rubbing his forearm. "The letters wear off in a couple of months. Neat trick though, barely skin deep. Looks as old as the cross, and I got that at eighteen."

"So this gimmick relates to the job we are on?"

Ahearn nodded. "You got any ink?"

"No," replied Kenneally firmly. "My mum would have strung me up. All I picked up was scars."

"They work just as well," Ahearn said, reaching down for the small shoulder bag that he'd brought aboard. He unzipped it and pulled out a Boston Police booking sheet, setting it on the table.

"Gino Testaverde. D'you know this mook?"

Kenneally had never heard the man's name. He studied the mugshot: beefy with a cartoonishly massive jaw, olive complexion, beady eyes, and hair slicked back in a 1950's pompadour. Might as well have had "goombah" stamped on his forehead.

"Never had the pleasure."

Ahearn stifled a yawn.

"Quite a mob pedigree, our Mr. Testaverde," he continued. "Born in Hoboken. Deep Genovese family ties on his mother's side. Heard of Fat Billy Grasso?"

Kenneally had. "Sure. Boston mob. The last intell I saw had him underboss to Ray Patriarca Junior."

Ahearn nodded.

"Grasso's a maternal uncle. Actually, his mother's first cousin. Anyway, he took a shine to the kid out of the army." He noticed an eyebrow rise.

He said, "I thought that might pique your interest. Gino likes to brag about his Green Beret service in Nam."

Kenneally grinned.

"He's that fuckin' guy?" he exclaimed, tapping the mugshot with his thick fingers. "I've heard of him. Makes out like he's John fuckin' Rambo, but his records show an I-Corps rear area tour. A file clerk or something like that."

"A supply technician," said Ahearn.

Kenneally rolled his eyes.

Ahearn went on. Testaverde had drifted a little after Vietnam. Hooked up with Uncle Billy up in Providence, where he's lived ever since. Made his bones on a Patriarca hijacking crew. Military supply service to his credit, he showed a real knack for precision and planning. Gathered intelligence well. Planned hijack jobs around customer orders and had an intrinsic knowledge of what might fly off the black market shelves. He knew how to get precise shipment information: loads, routes, timings. Planned the best interception sites, escape routes with back-ups, and stash locations. Even brokered the deals. He had more than sixty rip-offs to his credit, all without a single gunfight or anyone getting killed. Hell of an accomplishment, really. A good process model.

"So what's our interest in Testaverde?" Kenneally asked.

Ahearn stretched, cracking his knuckles, and stood to pour another cup of coffee.

"D'you smoke, Jimmy?" he asked.

"Nope. Never have," Kenneally replied.

"D'you mind?"

"Nope. Never did," he answered, seeing the relief on Kevin Ahearn's face as he scrambled to light up a butt. "Belfast working class roots, I suppose. My mum smoked while she was cookin' our dinner, and my dad would smoke while he ate it. Once knew a priest who smoked during confession."

Ahearn smiled and exhaled blissfully, plucking a strand of tobacco that had stuck to his dry lower lip.

"Back in November," he began, "NCIS at Naval Weapons Station Yorktown, down in Newport News, Virginia, alerted ATF and the FBI to a missing shipment of C4 plastic explosives. Nearly four tons worth."

Kenneally sucked in his breath.

"Exactly," Ahearn agreed. "An entire shipping container. Fifty eight-ounce sticks to a wooden crate. Three hundred crates to a forty-foot sea can. Seventy-five hundred pounds of C4. Enough to blow a helluva hole in somebody's world."

"So how does our navy lose four tons of plastic?"

"They never received it."

"Ah."

The shipment, Ahearn explained, had been one of twelve containers that left the manufacturer's plant in McEwen, Tennessee, back in November. A routine shipment into the military supply chain. Innocuous cargo containers, acquired randomly from the carrier's nationwide pool, each with the markings and livery of various rail and cargo shipping lines. Each container carried posted bar coded waybills and were marked to indicate hazardous cargo, but nothing beyond its HazMat content signage as high explosive to indicate the specific contents.

The twelve containers had proceeded by rail to nearby Nashville, where they were joined to a one hundred and fifty car freight that made its way via Knoxville to Roanoake, Virginia, north through West Virginia and Pennsylvania to Allentown, and finally to the Oak Island container terminal in Newark, New Jersey.

They spent two nights in Newark in a hazardous materials compound. On the third day, nine units proceeded to overseas shipping, and the three for Virginia joined a freight headed south. That night it sat unsecured in Wilmington, Delaware, and again overnight just down the road in Baltimore. Trouble with an engine. Finally, six days after leaving the Tennessee plant, the three cars ended up on a spur inside the secure confines of NWS Yorktown. Later that same day, the second sealed container was opened and, voila, nothing but rat shit and dust.

"It was Newark," said Kenneally.

"NCIS figures Wilmington," Ahearn countered. "ATF too. Overnight in the public railyard. No fencing, on a spur right next to an unlit side road. They're looking at one of the Wilmington yard crew as a likely suspect. Ties to some anti-taxation fringe group, and he's been AWOL ever since."

"They're wrong. It was Newark."

"Why?"

Jimmy Kenneally drummed his fingers on the table top.

"This would've been no random theft," he said. "They would have targeted this shipment right from the plant. Wilmington and Baltimore were unexpected stops, so unless you like these vigilantes for sabotaging the train, it was surgical all along. A military inside job or a high end custom theft. This was the mob. Tell me I'm wrong."

"Okay," Ahearn conceded. "But Newark? We're talking security up the kazoo. A secure flood-lit container yard. Armed patrols twenty-four-seven. A rip off there would take some kinda balls."

Kenneally continued. "Yeah, but the Port of Newark's been mobbed up forever. Security is only as good as who owns it. Get the right people to look the wrong way, all the hustle and bustle, gantry cranes zipping around? One zips in and picks up the container. Takes it away, maybe into a warehouse on site. A team of Guineas is waiting with transport. Unloads the C4, reseals the container and zips it right back to the line. Easy peasy and no one's the wiser."

Ahearn was truly amazed.

"Jesus, Kenneally, but you've got a criminal mind," he said with a broadening grin. "I like it. My own instinct's been Newark. With Testaverde behind it."

Ahearn pulled a photograph from his satchel, handing it to his partner as he lit a fresh smoke.

"Here's the guy I really like for the job."

The surveillance shot showed a male on a Manhattan street next to a Sabrett hotdog cart. Well fed, early forties, a wide smile framed by a drooping mustache. He was wearing an apron. The cart operator?

"Never seen him before," Kenneally said.

"We go back awhile," said Ahearn. "Meet Salvatore Luongo, another Hoboken boy made good. Connected to a Genovese crew, but has always stayed independent. Helluva hijacker back in the day. Had one job go sour back in the seventies and he did a few years upstate. Guess who's his cousin?"

"Lemme think," ventured Kenneally, rising to fix another pot of coffee. "Testaverde?"

"Right you are, Johnny!" his partner replied, mimicking Ed McMahon.

"So, we're going to set up on this hot dog vendor? Lougainis? Luongo. Find the navy's lost plastic?"

"No sir, we're not. We're through the looking glass now."

Kenneally looked confused. Surveillance on Luongo to track down the explosives seemed like the logical play.

"It's a brave new world, Jimmy Boy," said Ahearn. "Up is down. Black is white. Nothing's going to court out of this. Olympiad has a different agenda, and I have to tell you it's restored my faith in everything holy."

"About a month ago," he continued, "Olympiad got intell out of Britain that the Provisional IRA was onto an American source for C4. It's got to be Testaverde and Luongo. Everything fits. Paris figures there will be a buy offer in the next month to six weeks. Operation Long Jump. They want us all over Gino, and I've been working on that since the middle of March."

Jimmy Kenneally felt his pulse starting to race.

"Three weeks ago, Testaverde bought himself a yacht down in Fort Lauderdale. A seventy-eight foot Hatteras blue water cruiser. One beautiful boat. Paid a half million cash."

Jimmy whistled.

"This Friday," Ahearn said, "the boat and a delivery crew will be making its way up the coast. It's heading for a refit at A&J Marine in Providence. Which is where I've got a job, and where you start in ten days when the boat's alongside."

"You're joking."

"I am not. A&J has a long, sketchy history of hiring ex-cons. Part of a Prison Fellowship helping hands program. How about that for pure bullshit luck."

Ahearn handed Kenneally an envelope.

"Here's your new identity," he said, exhaling smoke. "All our background's been set up in depth. I'm ex-navy. Kevin

O'Leary, a New Bedford boy, by way of Leavenworth. A hull tech and carpenter, which works with my skills. And you? A real asshole, I'm afraid."

Kenneally studied the Florida driver's license and his state parolee card, each with ID pictures of himself from recent NYPD undercover operations. James Peter Rafferty, 2135 Sea Coast Court, Pensacola, Florida. Parolee ID 539398U.

"How big an asshole?" Jimmy asked.

"A disappointment to your poor fictitious mother, bless her," Ahearn said. "Once a longliner out of Pensacola, and a hard drinking thug since your teens in New York. Raped that poor girl in Key West in 1978. Saved her own life, shanking you like she did. You just finished ten years of a fifteen-year bit at Homestead CI in Florida City, south of Miami. Learned a new trade, marine electronics. Stayed clear of all that Aryan-Black and Cubano gang shit, mostly cuz you're such a tough guy and loner."

"I see. So why then am I allowed out of state?"

"A&J gave you a helping hands job in your field."

"Am I grateful?"

"Not really," replied Ahearn.

"So, here's the thing," he said soberly. "Coultart figures Gino will cut his own deal if the IRA bites. These days he's a mob man of leisure. But since Valhalla, he's been paranoid about surveillance. This new boat is ..."

"A tech's dream if we get our hands on it first!" interrupted Kenneally, with a smile from ear to ear.

"Listen," Ahearn said, butting his smoke. "You're the genius here. Get down to Florida to get a peek at the boat and to work on your cover. We've got plenty of money. Get Coultart moving on equipment acquisition. We've gotta have a plan and all the widgets by the time you show up in Rhode Island. Ten days gonna do it?"

"Ten days will be plenty."

Chapter 16

Tuesday, April 4, 1989 – 9:52 a.m. EST
United States Courthouse, 500 Pearl St., New York, NY

"BLOOD PRESSURE 120 over 80, the same as your right, and completely normal," said the Fire Department paramedic as he released the cuff on Randolph Elliott's left bicep. "In fact ... How old are you, Judge?"

"I'll be fifty-nine on the tenth of May." The commotion had subsided at the door to his chambers. Andy Connachie fretted next to Liv Geller, who stood dressed in her judicial robes, her arms crossed, glaring at Elliott.

"Pretty fit for any age. Whaddya do? Racquetball? Tennis?" asked the paramedic as he began to pack up his gear.

"I run," Elliott said, wearily rubbing the bridge of his nose.

"No prescribed medications," the paramedic continued, recapping the notes he had made. "No recent head injury. No cardiovascular issues or history of diabetes. Your blood sugars this morning are normal. Vital signs fine. Cincinnati Stroke Scale indicia are negative, all completely normal. Have you ever had an episode like this before?"

Episode?

The *episode* had occurred not twenty minutes earlier, just after the judge had taken his seat on the bench. It was Elliott's first day back after three months of compassionate leave. A simple motion hearing on an upcoming criminal case. Only lawyers, courtroom staff and a handful of people in the public gallery had been present, and after the assistant United States attorney had spoken to the motion, the Judge simply didn't reply. He just sat there, his gaze fixed on the back of the room, responding to no one and nothing at all. Alarmed, the staff had promptly called 911 and helped him, still in a daze, to his chambers, everybody convinced he was having a stroke.

"Episode?" Judge Elliott replied, irritated. "As I don't recall it, I really can't say!"

He sighed heavily. "Look, I'm sorry. I've been a bit tired lately. Sometimes I suppose I nod off. But like this? No, not before, not that I'm aware of."

The paramedic nodded to his partner to seal up their crash bags. No transport this time. They were done here and dispatch was crackling radio orders.

"Well, your Honor," he said. "You seem fine now and it's clear that you haven't suffered a stroke. I strongly suggest you get in to see your family doctor. Get a full neurological check-up. There could be all kinds of reasons for something like this. Okay? Anyway, we've got another call. You take care, sir."

In a moment the paramedics were gone and Liv Geller shooed Connachie from the room. She closed the door behind him and turned to Elliott, red in the face.

"What the hell was that, Randy?" she shouted. "*Sometimes I nod off*? I was there! I looked in on you on the bench. You were goddamned catatonic. Scared the shit out of everyone here. Especially me!"

Elliott closed his eyes and rocked gently in his chair.

"Liv, I ..." he began, quietly.

The Chief Judge stormed across the room and stood in front of his desk. She pounded it hard with the palms of her hands. "You said . . . You *fucking promised* that you were okay!" she ranted, quickly checking herself and lowering her voice. She took a deep breath.

"If I'd thought for one second that you weren't ... that you hadn't completely recovered, I'd never have let you return. No damned way."

She released breath and frustrations in an exhausted gasp and sat—a controlled collapse, into a deep leather seat.

Her eyes glistened.

"What happened?" she asked.

Elliott rubbed his temples.

"I don't know, Liv. I remember sitting there, listening to Walker drone on. Then, it was like ... tunnel vision? I drifted. Unfocused. Thinking about Charlotte. About Diana. And the next thing I knew, we were here. The paramedics. For chrissakes, I don't know."

"I knew you weren't ready."

"Really? Doctor Geller?"

"Don't you patronize me!"

"I'm sorry," Elliott sighed.

"No, Randy," she said, clearing her throat. "I'm sorry. I'm sorry I let you return."

"What are you saying?" he asked, suddenly much more lucid. Liv stood and wiped her eyes.

"I have a session in recess, I've got to get back," she said, mustering strength in her voice and demeanor.

"Consider yourself on an indefinite suspension, as of right now. I have no other choice," she said. "You understand."

Liv Geller, for all her aloof chairman of the board wiles, all the strength and savvy that had gotten her to this place in her life, she couldn't quite pull it off.

"Don't you?" she asked softly, almost childlike.

Randy Elliott felt a burden release from his shoulders. He nodded and smiled at this woman he loved and admired.

"Actually, Livvy, I do."

Tuesday, April 4, 1989 – 11:53 a.m. EST
Foley Square, Pearl and Centre Streets, New York, NY

"ASSHOLE!" SHOUTED SAL Luongo as he stumbled backward on the pavement of Foley Square. He struggled to regain his balance. The cyclist, as they always do, had come out of nowhere. A blur he hadn't noticed until the last moment, bearing down on him on Centre Street before doing that thing—tugging up on the handle bars and bouncing airborne over the curb. Young guy in a suit and a rocket man helmet, with a bike that was probably worth more than most cars. Cyclists everywhere. Breaking every law on the books. Traffic. Common courtesy. Physics.

"You're all assholes!" Luongo cursed.

Returning to his cart, Sal adjusted the gas on the grill, added a dozen wieners, some smokies and bratwurst. He stirred a pot of simmering onions. It was nearly noon. Time to get ready for the lunchtime rush.

"Two dirty water dogs. Dry buns, please," a voice said politely. Sal hadn't seen the man step up to the cart. He looked up and recognized him.

"Hey!" Luongo said, smiling. "Judge! Sal Luongo, remember? How the hell are ya?"

"I have been better," Elliott replied.

"Good to see ya, my friend!" Sal said genuinely. He handed the Judge two unsteamed buns to get ready. Sure enough, he went through his routine of lining them with onions and sauerkraut, spread out real nice.

"It's my first day back in business this year," Sal said, laying two perfect franks into place with his tongs. "I woulda got started last week, but I've been having trouble getting motivated. Know what I mean?"

"I do," the Judge said, squirting three dabs of brown mustard onto each dog. "Today was my first day back as well. It will probably be my last."

Sal screwed up his face. "Whaddya mean?"

"I'm thinking about quitting, Sal. I'm on an indefinite leave of absence as it is. Might as well make it official."

"Quit? Get the fuck out! Judges don't freakin' quit. Aren't you, like, appointed for life?"

"True," Elliott replied, taking a bite of his first dog.

"But, the thing is," he said, munching. "I'm the one who decides when it ends. Maybe it's time to retire." Then he wiped his chin.

"With the hand you been dealt? I would a put in my papers a long time ago," said Luongo, conveying genuine admiration.

Lunch customers from the courthouse and the federal marshal's service had begun to queue up to the cart. Elliott stepped to the side in the square to enjoy his hotdogs.

Ten minutes later, the first rush having subsided, Sal rejoined his friend.

"You make it to the season opener yesterday?"

"No," Elliott replied. "I had other commitments."

Luongo smiled. "I'll tell ya, it was freakin' amazing! Beat the Cards eight to four. You probably heard all about it."

"Only the score."

"Gooden was a friggin' machine! Pitched five hits into the eighth inning. Strawberry goes three-for-three with two doubles, a single and a walk. Knocked in two runs and stole two bases. And Hojo? Two singles and a homer, drove in three runs. You should a been there, Judge. It was great!"

"I can imagine it was," Judge Elliott said, as Sal returned to his cart to serve up more dogs.

"Say," Sal mused. "If you're gonna be off work for a while, maybe we could catch a few games. You know? Together? My sister's boy Tony looks after the cart during day games. Tomorrow afternoon? The Cards at one-thirty?"

"I don't know," Elliott replied. Baseball hadn't been on his mind since he'd returned from Florida. Still ...

"C'mon! You and me! I've got a two-seat box behind the Mets dugout. They're the sweetest seats in the park. Ojeda's starting. Whaddya say?"

Elliott hadn't been to an afternoon game since he was a kid. What the hell. "All right Sal, you're on," he replied with a grin. "If you promise to just call me Randy. Why don't you give me your address and I'll send my driver around."

"Your friggin' driver? Whoa, Randy! This could be the start of a beautiful thing."

❧

RANDOLPH ELLIOTT TOSSED Andy Connachie's legal brief onto his desk and sighed. What was the point of pursuing Pan Am in the courts? Dozens of suits had already been filed in the New York Eastern District federal court—and as Andy had noted, much was being made in the press of an impediment to litigation in this case. The Warsaw Convention of 1929, governing international air travel, effectively barred punitive damages in air accident suits. Under the treaty, only *compensatory* damages could be sought by the families of air crash victims. And a limiting cap of seventy-five thousand U.S. dollars on awards for each victim had been agreed to by members of the International Civil Aviation Organization at its Montreal conference in 1966.

Several suits sought to challenge the treaty on this issue, which Connachie asserted would fail, as the United States Supreme Court had already ruled that the courts cannot alter the intended legal effect of international treaties. Only 'willful misconduct' on the part of the airline would remove the award dollar cap and leave it open to unlimited liability for compensation damages. It would have to be conduct so egregious that it verged on criminal negligence—and as both men knew, it would have to be proved to the legal standard of nothing less than a formal inquiry. Which was unlikely to happen, Connachie had astutely concluded, in spite of the media frenzy currently surrounding the crash. At the end of the day, Lockerbie was clearly a terrorist act. There's your willful misconduct.

Judge Elliott rose and poured himself a brandy.

It had been pouring buckets all day. Game Two of the Met's season had been rained out, and he and his new-found baseball buddy had decided early to give it a pass. But they had made a date for the next home game, April 17th, an evening match up against the Phillies. It astonished him that life takes the pivotal turns that it does. Six months ago, hell, all of his smug adult life, he wouldn't have given invisible people like street hot dog vendors the time of day. Now here he was, laboring the same way against labels, ones we whisper and use to exclude. Grieving parent. Widower. Worse, a widower to suicide. A victim. A terrorist victim. Sad case, once a federal judge. As he sipped his brandy, Randy Elliott realized that just to be someone's baseball buddy felt good.

The house felt less empty than it had since Christmas. He had thought about selling it, now he wasn't sure. Charlotte had owned it free and clear and she'd willed it to him. Her remaining wealth, nearly twelve million in cash and investments, had been set aside for Diana—and with their daughter intestate, that along with Diana's sizeable trust fund had come back to him. And it wasn't as if he had been a pauper. There was no Elliott family money, but he'd earned and had invested well from his practice of law, and on the federal district court bench, he had made a good living at about $125,000 a year. His net worth today, he had been told, was in the neighborhood of fifteen million exclusive of personal income or pension. At age fifty-eight, tragedy had left him substantially wealthy.

His first act, once the estates had been settled, had been to fund a one million dollar scholastic endowment in Diana's name. His second had been a spontaneous gift of $100,000 to Maria Cárdenas, Diana's apartment super and friend, who had also agreed to an offer of employment as a live-in housekeeper. The Puerto Rican widow moved into the guest suite at the beginning of March and had been doting on him ever since.

Today, however, Elliott was alone in his home. Maria had been away in the city since Monday, supporting a son and his wife whose youngest girl was bedridden with measles.

Randy Elliott paced in his study, found Dutch courage in a mouthful of brandy, and picked up the phone.

He dialed Liv Geller's personal office line, hoping that she might still be in chambers. It just rang. His heart sank. He searched his desk anxiously for that brown metal Bates pop-up address book that he'd had since college. It was in his center drawer. He slid the pointer to "G" and Liv Geller's contacts appeared at the top of the list.

He tried her car number.

It rang twice and she answered.

His heart was pounding and his throat was dry. He hadn't spoken to her since he'd stormed out of the courthouse, just before noon yesterday.

"Liv? Where are you?" he asked.

"Stuck in midtown traffic. It's ridiculous."

What the hell am I thinking? he thought, now even more anxious. "Liv, what would you think about coming up here?" he asked hoarsely.

Stuck in traffic that was inching toward the Midtown Tunnel, Liv Geller smiled.

"For the night?" she asked coyly.

"If you can," was all Randy could muster.

"I could get to Grand Central, get the train and a cab," she said. "Do we need to talk?"

"I'm not sure. Maybe we should ... maybe later."

"I can be there in an hour."

Chapter 17

Sunday, April 9, 1989 – 7:01 a.m. EST
Escambia County Jail, 1700 W. Leonard Street, Pensacola, FL

"STEP UP, PRISONER, and give me your name," squawked the florid jail sergeant from behind bulletproof glass.

"James Peter Rafferty, boss," Jimmy croaked, shuffling into a yellow bordered rectangle on the floor of the county jail's prisoner processing room. The 'National Geographic' square presented a two-foot by three-foot refuge from getting tasered or taken down hard. The room stank of urine and the cloying pine scent of aerosol disinfectant being spritzed on a timer from canisters above its entry and exit doors. Angry voices and the metallic bang of cell doors being kicked resonated sharply through the jail.

Jimmy looked like the personification of drunk and disorderly, eight hours past tense. He had a black eye that was swelling bright purple—thanks to a metro Pensacola cop who hadn't liked his body language when he'd arrested Jimmy the night before. His black KISS t-shirt was flecked with stale vomit and torn wide open across his chest, exposing the puncture scar above his right breast. The rip was thanks to the cop's female partner. With one painful fingernail clutch and a leg sweep, the perky pony-tailed blonde had taken him to the floor of a seedy bar on West Main.

"Public intoxication," squawked the sergeant. "There's a fifty dollar municipal fine. I see from your property that you can pay it today. Or do you want to contest it?"

"Pay it today, boss," Jimmy mumbled.

"Smart choice. You'll be escorted to the cashier."

A metal chute clanged open.

"Here's the shit you came in with. One sandal, black. One belt, webbed. One watch, Casio, broken bezel. One motel room key. One wallet, single fold, brown leather. Your driver's license. A state parole card, no fucking surprise. You're lucky we're not pushing for a breach charge. Two hundred and four dollars cash."

The sergeant pushed paperwork and a ballpoint pen through the slot. "Step forward, Rafferty, and sign for your property where indicated."

Jimmy took one pace forward, smartly, as if a military drill movement, signed the form and stepped back.

"Good," said the Sergeant. "Think about taking the high road, convict, and get the fuck out of town."

"I plan to," he muttered. "Thank you, boss."

Jimmy Kenneally found he could not catch a taxi in front of the county jail, nor anywhere else down the street, with one bare foot, a ripped t-shirt, and looking as if he had just spent the night in the Pensacola drunk tank. He tossed his one good sandal into a trash bin and sauntered the mile to the Buena Vista motel.

He showered, shaved, and felt human again. He neatly placed his shredded t-shirt and urine soaked jeans into the motel room's waste basket, and grinned at himself in the mirror as he dressed in clean clothing. The past week had gone precisely as planned.

He had spent Monday and Tuesday at Olympiad in Manhattan, working on technical details. Coultart had issued him one thousand dollars in pocket money and an American Express card in his operative name—risky, Jimmy had said, being an unemployed convict with credit. Plastic was a necessary evil for travel these days, Coultart had countered, and easy to discard and replace if you have to.

On Wednesday, he had flown on an Eastern Airlines shuttle from La Guardia to Fort Lauderdale. That afternoon, with his stubble trimmed neatly and decked out in the pastel cotton, he had nosed around the slips at Bimini Yacht Sales, off Portside Drive in Lauderdale Harbor. There he found 'Mysty Mae'—a seventy-eight foot Hatteras CPMY cruiser, built in 1982 and glistening white. A pair of dock boys were scrubbing her up for a delivery cruise on the weekend.

Sadly, the salesman had told him, she had just been sold to a businessman up in Rhode Island. But, he said, they had another just like her. A year older but a real cherry, if he'd like a tour. What the hell, Jimmy told him, he had a reprieve from the wife.

Kenneally spent long enough aboard Mysty Mae's sister to gather the details he needed. He expressed interest in the ease of upgrading its entertainment and communications fit. The salesman had been only too happy to provide a Xeroxed copy of the boat's electrical and engineering diagrams, impressed to encounter such a knowledgeable potential buyer. He had invited him for a drink. Perhaps talk financing over a Bahama Mama or beer? Jimmy declined, but he took the man's card with a promise to call him again.

Kenneally drove to Miami on Thursday. There he took a good look around the sites that he needed to know. First, the State Parole and Probation Office, downtown on Biscayne Boulevard. It was in a glass high-rise complex. Miami's elevated commuter rail service ran past it, above broad palm-lined downtown sidewalks crowded with tourists. Next, Homestead Correctional Institution, HCI, twenty-five miles south of the city. The prison was as he expected, a drab institutional complex, set on a featureless stretch of coastal plain as barren as prairie. It occupied maybe a square mile of land, and might have been a school or an auto parts plant if it weren't for the successive ranges of fencing topped with razor wire that stretched to the horizon around it.

In both places he absorbed the sights, smells and sounds, and surveyed the lay of the land. *Undercover 101.* Know more than your background story. Get a feel for it. The waiting room at the fifth-floor parole office had two dozen chairs, three information wickets, and was standing room only. Its air conditioning was too cold, still the room stank with sweat. The roads around the prison were drifted with dust, which would have been as pervasive as the buzz of cicadas and the sickly sweet smell of the surrounding saltwater marshland. You could hear the sound of jets at nearby Homestead Air Force Base. You'd have gone to sleep in your cell to the all-night drone of eighteen-wheelers on the Ingraham Highway.

On Friday, he flew up to Pensacola on the Gulf panhandle bordering Louisiana. There, his first order of business had been to check out his most recent address, 2135 Sea Coast Court, a fleabag complex of a dozen clapboard shacks nestled between West Navy Boulevard and the rail yard. The manager of the wartime collection of former holiday cabins was a grizzled alcoholic named Rusty, who informed Jimmy that there were no vacancies now, but to give it a couple of days, as Fat Nellie and her Old Man in Cabin 6 had been arrested the previous night after another domestic. This time, shots fired. The address worked for his cover. If you flopped at 2135 Sea Coast Court, Pensacola, local cops would mark your booking sheet: NFA—of No Fixed Address.

When Jimmy checked into the Buena Vista Motel, a mile down the road from the jail, it had been with a plan to get noticed. As Ahearn had suggested. *Undercover 102.* Check in with the local cops. Get your name on the books. Get drunk and stupid and get arrested. No big deal. The trick is to do it still reasonably sober.

On Friday, he had found the perfect bar. Big Bad John's was a strip mall dive on West Main Street, just south of the downtown core. A genial haunt for hardcore local boozers, with an attempt at a nautical theme to its décor. He sat there alone for a couple of hours on Friday night, knocking back Jack and checking out the clientele before retiring to the motel to work on his preparations.

It takes skill to come off as a seasoned street drunk. You need to actually stink, stale booze sweating out through your pores. Jimmy had spent the remainder of Friday night in his room, watching TV, drinking an entire fifth of Jack Daniel's over an eight-hour span, cutting it with aspirin and tepid tap water. Delicate work. A less experienced man might get hammered and would therefore be useless the following day. But Jimmy could handle his drink. He stayed lucid enough to stick to the plan.

Still, he had a bad temple headache when he awoke at mid-afternoon on Saturday. A job hazard. More aspirin and Bromo-Seltzer took care of that. He didn't change his clothes or freshen up and returned to Big Bad John's around seven.

By nine p.m., having nursed four Jacks and water, he began to beak off at the crusty locals seated beside him. That was all that it took for a fight to ensue. Jimmy rose to his feet and dry heaved whiskey and spittle onto his first challenger. Fists flew and he took one in the gut, ungracefully folding as the bartender was onto the cops. A pair of Pensacola's finest arrived to roughly fit Jimmy with cuffs, getting in a jab or two for "resisting" before hauling his sorry ass to the tank.

Mission accomplished.

ঙ

Tuesday, April 11, 1989 – 8:27 p.m. EST
201 Varick Street, New York, NY

JIMMY KENNEALLY TILTED the magnifying goggles up from his eyes and blew away a wisp of smoke that rose from the circuit board. "There," he said, setting down the soldering iron. "That should pretty much do it."

The tech lab at Olympiad Manhattan's headquarters was so new that its doors hadn't even been hung. It was destined to become a state of the art lair for Coultart's handpicked tech wizards—Ray Morgan, ex-ATF, and his younger sidekick Steve Smith, formerly Drug Enforcement. For an hour the two had stood like parentheses around Kenneally, peering in on his work before Coultart and Ahearn arrived for the show.

Arrayed on the workbench were the solid state entrails of an eavesdropping package that he himself had designed. At its heart were two electronic 'black boxes' which were actually gray and bore the Westinghouse logo. One was the size of a shoe box, which Kenneally had disassembled to accept the board he had just modified. The other was slimmer, sprouting wires that trailed away to pairs of miniature electronic devices, one set laid out at each end of the bench. These were easily recognized as audio video receptors. The remaining components baffled even Morgan and Smith.

The first was an antenna about the size and shape of a road safety cone, with four squared sides tapering to the top and made of white fiberglass. It was connected to a spool of coaxial cable.

Second was a bright yellow clamshell case, polycarbonate plastic, three feet by two feet by ten inches high, marked 'EPIRB'—an emergency position indicating radio beacon for seagoing vessels.

Last was the disassembled workings of what appeared to be an advanced sort of telephone handset, also Westinghouse. It lay neatly in pieces.

"Let's get started," Kenneally said.

"Mobile venues are always a problem. Access. Placement. Service limitations like power and transmitting distance. Now, a boat, and one with a two thousand mile range? That's a challenge. Still, get a job on board fitting new electronics? Kinda washes your troubles away."

Kenneally beamed like a kid at the state science fair.

"Plain sight works to our advantage," he continued. "The controls for this surveillance suite will be sealed in that EPIRB case, which I will be installing aft of the boat's flying bridge. Connect it to shipboard power, run a few cables ... Emergency gear won't attract uninvited attention. It's sacred. It's perfect."

He moved on to the sensor sets. At the end of each pair of twinned wires was a tiny circuit board with a black plastic disk the size of a dime.

"This is the Panasonic pinhole wide angle video chipset," he announced. "Latest in black and white television imaging.

A one-twenty degree field of view. Operates in low light to a value of zero-point-five lux."

Steve Smith whistled. At thirty-five, the athletic, balding engineer looked more like a high school gym teacher than a former Special Forces officer who, during his DEA years, had bugged the bedrooms of Columbian drug lords.

"I'm guessing that's good," said Ahearn.

Smith explained, "It's a unit of illumination, like decibels are to sound. The light in this room is, say, three hundred and fifty lux. A sunny day? Ten thousand lux. Zero-point-five? Well, that's an overcast moonless night."

Kenneally continued.

"This is a probe contact mike," he said, tapping the audio sensor paired with the camera. It looked like a blank dollar slug on the end of a wire. "Attach these with acoustical putty to a resonating surface, like a bulkhead on a boat, and the whole structure acts as a sound receptor. Ray's idea."

Ray Morgan was a lanky MIT grad, fifty-five years of age. With his rumpled western shirts, blue jeans, unkempt gray hair and mustache, Ray came across more like a McMurtry cowboy than a genius I.Q. engineer. He hand rolled cigarettes and never said much unless there was something to say; and when impressed, he would pluck at his whiskers and nod, as he had been doing all evening.

"What about range?" asked Coultart. "We're talking a boat here. What happens when he goes to sea? How close do we have to follow?"

Morgan chuckled. He knew.

Steve Smith scratched his head. He didn't.

Kenneally replied, "I think we've got that covered. Ray, would you mind hanging here?"

"Nope," Morgan said, smiling.

Kenneally led the group to Coultart's office on the opposite end of the "gymnasium" floor. He placed a heavy tote bag on the credenza, producing a twelve-inch monitor he attached to a component that looked like a cassette player. He plugged them in and the monitor came alive with rolling bars of black and white static.

"Okay," Kenneally began proudly. "Here we are, in some distant corner of the world. Where doesn't matter. Wonder what's happening on our bad guy's yacht?"

Opening the component's cover revealed the receiver of a communications modem. He picked up Coultart's phone, dialed eleven digits and seated the handset.

"Abracadabra." The display shimmered and came into focus with a black and white view of the lab. Wide angle and clear. Ray Morgan was idly pacing.

"What?" Ahearn looked puzzled. "How the ... ? "

Jimmy selected a second phone line, switched to speaker and dialed the lab's extension. The workbench phone rang through the monitor's speakers. Morgan strolled over and answered.

"Ray's Bar and Grill," his on screen image announced.

"Morgan?" Kenneally snickered, "Come here, I need you."

"You're fucking hilarious," he replied, hanging up the receiver and waving as he walked off camera.

Coultart and the others stared at the televised image, dumbfounded, muttering together until Morgan arrived.

Ray entered the office and saw the video image. He smiled and shook his head. "Have to tell you, Jimmy, that's a good one. Kinda figured that daughter-board was the guts of a satellite phone. Beautiful. What's the data rate of the modem? Twenty-four hundred baud?"

"Fifty-six."

Coultart fiddled with the monitor's volume. He could hear their voices being captured more than one hundred feet away. "If you techies are through jerking off, can anyone tell me just what we've got here?"

"This," Morgan said, "is the future of bloody surveillance. Passive receptors, installed, powered and accessible anywhere in the world. Anywhere there's a phone."

"Bullshit!" Ahearn touched the screen.

Kenneally continued.

"At the other end is Westinghouse gear they call a 'portable satellite voice data ground terminal'. Basically a satellite phone, but cutting-edge stuff, maybe five years ahead of commercial use. I got three from a buddy at State. Office of Diplomatic Telecommunications. They started limited trials this spring, as did CIA. It uses a new set of Air Force satellites. Low earth orbit. The only commercial option right now is Inmarsat, and their surface gear needs an antenna the size of a Volkswagen. Five or ten years? This will be handheld technology like the cellular phone. Except coverage is global."

"So," Coultart began slowly, "we fit this equipment on Testaverde's boat. Then, anytime we like, from wherever we like, we dial up this unit and *bingo* ... real time sound and video as good as this?"

"Yep," Ray Morgan confirmed.

"By moonlight," added Smith.

Kenneally practically blushed.

Chapter 18

"YOU GET A two-week probation here, fella!" shouted Vince Playsted as he led the new hire away from the firm's dockside office. "That's it! No second chances!"

The scrawny hawk-featured foreman was competing to be heard over the refit yard noise: a cacophony of droning diesels, metal banging on metal, whistles, the warning bells of traveling cranes, and the screech of circling gulls.

"You're not gonna be a pain in the ass, are you, fella? Cuz, showing up late your first day? I'm thinking, this one's gonna be trouble!"

Playsted stopped abruptly as they approached the end of the weathered gray two-story structure. His arm came up quickly and stopped Jimmy from passing as a massive Caterpillar loader lurched past, only inches away with a spool of steel cable in its bucket. It belched diesel exhaust and chugged off down the dock.

"No, boss!" Jimmy shouted, removing his battered blue hardhat for a moment to adjust its fit.

The foreman signaled to Jimmy to keep up and continued his march across the concrete deep water jetty. It stretched nearly a thousand feet along Providence Harbor's waterfront just south of downtown and Collier Park.

"And don't call me boss! You're not in stir now!" he barked, with Jimmy skipping along beside him in new work boots.

In a moment they reached their destination, an elevated industrial trailer that served as the yard foreman's office. Inside, Playsted motioned to Jimmy to take a seat next to his cluttered desk. He sat for a moment and rocked in an ancient wooden office chair as he sized up the new man.

"How old are you, Rafferty?"

"Forty-six."

"How long were you in the slam?"

"This last stretch? A ten spot down in Miami."

"General manager tells me that you raped some gal?"

"So *she* said!" Jimmy countered. "I was in Key West and drunk. This dolly picks me up in a bar. Next thing I know, I'm waking up in the hospital, stabbed in the chest and the broad's crying rape. I'm no fucking skinner! If you think ..."

"Whoa! Settle down!" Playsted interrupted, waving off the new man's rising ire. "Thing is, see, we don't get many cons with that tag. Gotta think of my workforce. Our deal with these Prison Fellowship folks has been a good one so far, and I wanna keep it that way. Clear enough for you, fella?"

Jimmy nodded.

The foreman twirled a pencil.

"Six-thirty in the morning means clocked in and ready for orders by six-twenty-nine. Now, is *that* clear enough?"

"Yes, sir."

"You a problem drinker, Rafferty? An addict?"

"No, sir."

"Well, see, they did one last NCIC check before sending you over. You got drunk and disorderly in Pensacola before heading up here," the foreman said, grinning. "Never guessed we knew that! Did ya, fella?"

Jeez, Jimmy thought, this guy's fucking brutal! *Call me fella one more time* ... "No, sir." he replied. "Just blowin' off steam."

"Yeah. Right out of stir," Playsted said, exhaling and laying down his pencil. "Well, I'm required to give you a two-week trial. But I'll be honest. I never much liked your kind. Don't go making long-term plans, cuz I'm gonna have my eye on you."

The ground rules were set. The foreman picked up a work ticket and studied the details.

"Tell me about your experience, Rafferty. I hear you were a long-liner down in the Gulf. The boss is a Gloucesterman, see. He likes you long-liners."

"Been on the boats since my teens," Jimmy said. "Mate and mechanic. Looked after the engines, the jenny and capstans. Ice plant and refrigeration. Stood wheelhouse watches."

"The electronics training you took in stir. Learn anything?"

"Yeah. Radar. Radio installations. Satellite navigation. It was good hands on stuff. They had a lab ..."

The foreman cut him off.

"Fine, fine." he said without looking up from the paper. "We had a seventy-eight foot Hatteras come in yesterday. *Mysty Mae*, up from Florida for some fat cat new owner. She's being re-registered as the *Salacious II* out of Newport. Requires radio upgrades and some kinda fancy entertainment package for the main salon. Your pal O'Leary says you could handle a job like that on your own. What'd you think?"

"Yeah, boss. I'd like it."

"Good." Playsted got up and beckoned Jimmy to a window overlooking the north end of the dock.

"See that *Travelift* making her way down the jetty?"

Jimmy nodded. The massive blue crane, shaped like a hollow four-story building on wheels, rolled slowly along the dock with safety walkers at each wheel. It was the source of the persistent bell sound he'd been hearing.

"Follow it. Find the lead hand, Phil Goyette. Red hardhat, redder nose. Their next haul is going to be Mysty Mae, she's alongside at the lift point. Got it?"

In a second he clapped his hands briskly.

"Come on, fella! Let's go! Get a move on!"

KEVIN HAD RESERVED Jimmy a room in the same cheap motel where he had been living since early March. It was off the I-95 in Cranston, just a few miles south of Providence and less than fifteen minutes to the gates of A&J Marine.

Day One was under their belt.

After the Mysty Mae had been plucked from the water, Kevin and Jimmy had spent the rest of the day working on prepping the hull. Getting it ready for paint would take at least two more days, but beyond touch ups on the stern for renaming, there was no further hull work in Mysty Mae's plan. With luck, Jimmy's work on the electronics could begin early the following week. Fingers crossed.

Ahearn dug into a carton of chicken lo mein while Kenneally cracked open a beer.

"How about that Playsted?" said Jimmy, wiping foam from his lips with the back of his hand. "What a piece of work."

Ahearn fumbled with his chopsticks, giving up in despair and grabbing a plastic fork.

"Did fifteen years up at Walpole for felony murder," he said, slurping up noodles.

"Really?" said Jimmy, surprised, digging in to the takeout.

"Yeah. Back in the fifties. Had just turned eighteen. Beat an uncle to death with a pipe."

"Really!"

"Some suggestion he'd been kiddy diddled."

"Really."

Kevin spat out a chunk of gristly chicken. "My thoughts exactly. Explains a whole lot."

WITH MYSTY MAE on dry land up on blocks, the shoring timbers and scaffolding around her made it hard for a big man like Kevin to squeeze in down by its keel. He knelt at the stern to check the shaft and rudder seals on her fiberglass hull. The port shaft was encrusted with barnacles and sea weed, so he pulled a rubber mallet from his tool belt and began pounding away.

"Buddy!" someone barked from nearby in a deep gravelly voice. "Hey you! Fuckin' goof with the hammer!"

Ahearn strained to turn in the tight spot, and from an uncomfortable crouch he looked up to see three men standing near the stern.

"You break it, you buy it!" the man warned with a chuckle.

Ahearn peered up into the bright morning sunlight.

Gino Testaverde.

"No problem, Mac!" he replied, pounding the steel toe of his boot. "See? It's rubber."

"Yeah? Fuckin' whatever," Testaverde said dismissively and the trio moved on.

Kevin's pulse was racing as he resumed his uncomfortable crouch. Testaverde in the flesh. Bigger and badder than his mugs and surveillance shots had suggested. Going a bit grey and still sporting the same slicked-back pompadour. He was dressed in maybe two grand's worth of calf leather jacket, silk shirt and suit pants, and at least five times that price tag in solid gold bracelets and chains.

With Testaverde was one of his goons. Faces flickered through Ahearn's mind but he was drawing a blank. It wasn't his long-time bodyguard and driver, Benny Dofasco, a big bald sonofabitch who looked like Telly Savalas. But judging by his cheap windbreaker, no one of particular rank. The third figure was Playsted, who was squiring the customer around.

Their conversation dwelled on the painting timetable. Testaverde had his own artist lined up to apply her new name and home port details on Sunday. It had better be ready, he warned, because this guy was tougher to book than a tee time at Winged Foot—not that Playsted had a clue what that actually meant, but he promised that the boat would be ready for his artist on time.

Kevin scrambled out from under the keel and made his way forward to the starboard bow. Above him on the gleaming white upper deck, Jimmy sat straddling the stainless steel vertical capstan that he'd disassembled to clean.

"Jimmy!" Ahearn called in a loud anxious whisper. "Hey, Jimmy! Goddammit, down here!"

Jimmy's face appeared over the side of the bow.

"What?"

"The owner is here and he's coming aboard. The *owner*, Jimmy! Get your mask on if you've got it!"

Kevin disappeared back under the bow.

As Jimmy returned to sit at the capstan, he saw three figures watching him through the spotless bridge windows that he had just cleaned. He acknowledged them with a friendly wave. Casually he pulled up the fabric dust mask that had been draped around his throat all morning, and resumed buffing the capstan components with an emery cloth.

That was too close. Men like Testaverde have an uncanny knack for connecting people to places. Faces to events and occasions. Get yourself associated to work on his boat? He'll recall that in a future encounter. And buddy? When he does, all the pieces had better add up.

Testaverde and his companion left fifteen minutes later, just as the yard's noon horn was sounding. Kevin and Jimmy sat together on the scaffolding with their lunch buckets. From now on, they agreed, they would have to be much more alert. This time it had been bullshit luck.

Chapter 19

THE DOCTOR'S FINGERS trembled as he lit a cigarette on his oceanfront terrace, an elegant narrow portico of white columns and terracotta tile. The night breeze off the Mediterranean was soothing and carried the scent of lavender that flowered among the clumped fescue grasses on his beachfront foreshore. His cigarette glowed in the darkness. It was moonless tonight. The sea spread away to every horizon but south, a millpond of ink against a star studded sky, with only the gentle rush of the surf betraying its presence just fifty meters away.

His night vision returned. He saw headlights approaching along the coastal highway, promising pinpricks of light making their way from Tripoli, a low orange glow twenty-five kilometers to the east. But the vehicle, now clearly a diesel transport, wasn't making the turn to his seaside estate. He heard its engine brake bark through successive downshifts as it lumbered westward past the nearby village of Al Mayah.

The slight, balding man was growing increasingly anxious and checked his gold Rolex. It was 10:38. The Irishman was more than a half hour late.

Mohamed Shakir al-Warid had good reason to be nervous. His decision of conscience today contemplated high treason. Punishable on suspicion alone by summary execution, which he knew would be certain if he was found out. He would be given no quarter; not for his wealth, his contribution to Libya and its people, nor for the favor he held among the elite of the ruling Gadhafi regime. No trial, only merciless torture—as much to punish as to extract information—which would inescapably end with his public garroting.

He could stop and undo what he'd already done. Contacting the Irishman as he had that afternoon? They were well acquainted after all, and even if there had been listeners taking note, there was no conspiracy here. Not yet.

Hand-made Italian loafers clacked as he paced on the terrace. He flicked cigarette ash from the sleeve of his white cotton *galabeya*—a calf-length, open-necked robe he wore with his Armani trousers. The doctor was a cosmopolitan man, of the new breed of secular pan-Arabian Muslims.

Born to wealth in pre-war Tripoli, Shakir al-Warid was educated as a physician in Cairo, as a surgeon in London and as an urbane Sixties sophisticate at gaming tables and cocktail parties from Beirut to Monaco.

Doctor al-Warid had been the chief of cardiology at Tripoli's modern Tajura National Heart Center since the hospital opened in 1976. He was an esteemed voice in the medical world, published widely in international journals as an early proponent of angioplasty over invasive open-heart bypass surgery; the toast of Tripoli society and around the Arab world. More importantly, he had gained the trust of Moammar Gadhafi's corrupt and petroleum-rich inner circle—and it was the latter which precipitated the fateful choices that he made today.

Another set of lights approached on the highway. His heart began to pound. Another damned lorry! He fretted. What if the Irishman didn't come? What then?

The physician had met him by chance four years earlier.

Tajura Hospital was located in the eastern outskirts of sprawling Tripoli, just across the Second Ring Road motorway from the capital's largest army installation, Tajura Barracks. It was from the army compound that, on the morning of Friday, December 13th, 1985, an ambulance rushed a heart attack victim to the hospital's emergency room.

Doctor al-Warid had been called away from his morning rounds to attend. The patient was a young foreigner, thirty-one years of age, who had arrived with a swarm of concerned high-ranking officials. The man had been lecturing at the army's engineering school, where he had suddenly developed a racing heartbeat and fainted. Tests would reveal that the attack had simply been heatstroke—exacerbated, the doctor would caution, by the man's wanton abuse of his liver. His patient was the celebrated IRA bomber, Martin Quinn, a guest in Libya since he had fled Britain the previous year.

Quinn had hardly gone underground as an exile. Libya's warm welcome had afforded him a luxurious flat in Tripoli. He routinely appeared at the best dinner parties. Had money to spend. Beautiful girls on his arm. He and the nation's leading cardiac surgeon, himself a widower, often left social engagements together with an entourage. In this nation of extreme contradictions—poverty and concentrated wealth, devout Islam and hedonistic western excesses—it surprised no one that the genial doctor and the charismatic young Irishman had become personal friends.

Another of Shakir's patients was Musa Ibrahim Mansour, unquestionably the second most powerful man in Libya. The former artillery officer had joined Colonel Gadhafi in 1969 when he seized power in a military coup d'etat. And since 1982, Mansour had been at the leader's right hand as the director of *Haiat amn al Jamahiriya*, JSO, the Libyan security-intelligence organization.

Now sixty, he was a fat, alcoholic, paranoid schizophrenic with a pathological interest in pubescent boys. His catered tastes were an official Libyan state secret, and the only desire that trumped his perversity was an unswerving need to impress his leader Gadhafi.

Musa Mansour had acute coronary artery disease, and in the past five years, Dr. al-Warid had performed three procedures to clear blocked cardiac arteries, the most recent having been just two nights before. The man flatly refused to adhere to a diet or drug regimen. It would kill him, he had often been warned, it was a medical certainty and only a matter of time. There were many who privately hoped that it would be sooner than later.

Now 10:45 p.m. Al-Warid lit another cigarette.

On the previous morning, Dr. Shakir al-Warid had completed his ward rounds and found himself stalling to avoid his last post-operative patient, Musa Mansour. He had received an angioplasty that Sunday evening, and with the doctor's approval, would be discharged on Monday at noon. Shakir had approached the security chief's private room, pausing for a moment to wash his hands in the bathroom it shared with the vacant adjacent suite. The bathroom door into Mansour's room was slightly ajar and as he lathered his hands, the doctor heard voices. It was Mansour berating Jamil al-Salabay, the man Shakir knew to be the head of security for the Libyan national airline.

"Lockerbie wasn't enough!" Mansour barked. "We must hit them again and again! Show me a plan within a week, Jamil, or by God, you will find yourself in Abu Salim at our pleasure. Chained naked, face first to a wall!"

Abu Salim, the regime's darkest prison. Shakir had cringed, quietly backing away as al-Salabay was dismissed. The pair passed each other in the hall, al-Salabay sweating and white as a sheet. A moment later, forcing a smile, Shakir calmly entered Mansour's suite and greeted his patient— followed seconds later by the man's deputy at JSO, Malik Abu-Asara, who had arrived to collect his leader. With Mansour pronounced fit, the pair quickly departed and Shakir had to cancel the rest of his day.

What he heard had appalled him. Lockerbie? Libya had been making strides toward acceptance and normalcy. Why such evil? For what noble purpose? This corrupt, perverse regime would forever relegate the entire nation to the status of pariah, cast out from the civilized world.

By that evening he had decided the world had to know. He would leave Libya and get to the West. Overland to Cairo? A flight to Riyadh? That would take weeks just to concoct an excuse and months to get an exit visa approved. These days, he and every other Libyan was as much a prisoner of his own state as banned by the United Nations from international travel. As much a prisoner of this damned country as ... the Irishman Quinn!

Yes! Martin once had drunkenly bragged of escaping by boat. Twice, he'd said, slipping away to Italy to indulge his 'God given right' to an Irishman's vices. Yes. Shakir knew Martin would help.

It was 11:00 p.m. when a pair of approaching headlights slowed and turned onto his road. A Renault cabriolet wound its way up the gravel path and came to a stop outside his darkened beach house.

Shakir walked warily to the car, relieved finally to see the Irishman's face.

"Thank God! Come in!" he said, leading Martin inside.

His sitting room was richly austere—leather settees, sandalwood tables, modern art on the barren white walls. Shakir went to his bar and poured them both a glass of his favorite whiskey. He downed his own quickly and refilled it before he said another word.

"I called," he began nervously, "because we are friends, Martin, and I trust you completely. What I must ask doesn't come easily."

The Irishman smiled broadly.

"We're brothers, Shakir!" he replied in his Ulster brogue. "We've shared women. Your liquor. But you look like a man who's renouncing his faith."

"No. Perhaps worse. Renouncing one's country."

"About time, so it is!" Quinn joked. "You said it yourself. You're a nation of cutthroat goat fuckers. No offense to your livestock, of course."

Shakir didn't laugh. "I am serious, Martin."

Quinn sat and took a sip of whiskey.

"All right, then," he said in a comforting tone. "Your call sounded urgent, now how can I help you?"

The doctor paced.

"I need to leave Libya. You say you have ways."

Martin blanched and quickly sprang from his chair. He glared at Shakir and grabbed him, roughly patting him down.

"Outside! *Now!*" the Irishman growled.

Quinn pushed him out through the terrace and onto the beach. "If you are fitting me up," he hissed, "friends or not, I will fuckin' kill you!"

"No!" Shakir protested. "If anything, I risked my *own* life calling you! I must leave Libya, Martin. I need you to help me! Please, we should go back inside."

"No chance!" snapped Quinn. "Whatever you have to say, you can say it out here. Start talking, Shakir."

The men walked together on hard-packed sand at the tide line, Shakir's voice scarcely audible above the rush of the surf. He nervously recounted the episode in Mansour's hospital room. His dismay at what he had heard.

"Did you know about Lockerbie, Martin?"

It was an unwise, very dangerous question.

"Of course not!" the Irishman said. "I am a freedom fighter, remember? We target the forces of occupation, not innocent people."

And that much was basically true.

"Tell me what Musa said," he asked.

The doctor stopped and thought for a moment in anguish.

"He said Lockerbie wasn't enough! That we must hit them again and again! He demanded that Jamil devise *another* plan. Within a week or risk the consequences."

Martin's eyes widened.

"Jamil al-Salabay?"

"Yes," Shakir answered matter-of-factly. "The director of security for Libyan Airlines. I must say, I wondered why he ..."

Quinn cut him short. "Your decision to leave. Down to shame, is it then? Or fear for your life, being privy to this?"

"Both!" the doctor said, suddenly haughty. "I have the same chauvinism as you. A love for my country. Pride in my heritage, not this evil regime. They impugn us all with these terrorist acts. I must leave Libya now. I have no choice!"

"Of course. And where to, Shakir? Monte Carlo?"

Shakir flustered.

"You *mock* me?"

Martin patted his shoulder.

"Calm yourself down," Martin said. "It's me, so it is, you have been talking to! I know your vanity. Where do you think you can get to, Shakir? With what kind of foolhardy plan?"

"To Sicily!" sputtered the doctor. "You said it is easy to travel from there. I have access to plenty of money outside of the country. That might take time, but I could make it to Rome. Go straight to the Americans. No ... to the British. They would listen! Accept the evidence I could provide against Mansour and Gadhafi. Warn that they're planning more bombings. The British would give me sanctuary."

"Oh, aye," Martin agreed.

Now it was the Irishman's mind that was racing. "That they quite likely would. The right information in just the right ear and the world is your oyster."

The doctor smiled uneasily.

"Then you will help me?"

A rising tide began to lap at their feet.

"Aye," Martin replied, steering Shakir toward the glow of his beach house. "How long will you need to get your affairs in order?"

"I—I am not certain. Two weeks?"

Only now had the reality of it begun to sink in. He would be leaving his whole life behind. Except for the two properties that he owned, liquidating his assets on Tripoli's thriving black market would be easy, but at a punishing loss. Still, most of his family wealth had been stashed overseas before Gadhafi took power.

The Irishman chewed on his lip, engrossed for a moment in thought. Any Tuesday. Only Tuesdays. Karim would need a few days to arrange it. And the quicker we get underway ...

"It will need to be less," Martin said firmly. "One week and no later. Discreetly now, mind, but be ready to leave next Monday at midnight. No more than the bags you can carry. Leave this to me. I'll be in contact when everything's set."

Chapter 20

Friday, April 21, 1989 – 2:37 p.m. EST
A&J Marine Services, Providence, RI

JIMMY RELEASED HIS grip on the needle gun scaler and stood flexing his fingers to relieve the numbness. Ten minute cycles, they said. Yeah, right, if you wanna end up an arthritic cripple. Except for their half hour lunch break, he and Kevin had been squeezing a needle-gun trigger since seven that morning, when they were assigned to the refit of an old Navy messing barge. A month-long project, according to Playsted and his almighty work order. And they got the honor of doing the needle-gun work—wielding the handheld jackhammers to strip away forty years' worth of paint, rust, and painted-over rust from YRBM-48, a floating two-story barracks half the size of a football field. It had just been towed down from the Navy's mothball fleet up in Boston to be refurbished for use as fleet accommodations out in Pearl Harbor.

Jimmy massaged his right hand. The ten-pound pneumatic needle gun drove a dozen steel chisel tips at five thousand beats per minute with its trigger fully depressed. It scaled off layers of enamel and rust down to bare metal. Scaling was hard, dirty work that strained Kenneally's once-athletic frame. Its numbing vibration blurred his vision and rattled his teeth. Ten minute cycles? Bullshit.

He was about to get right back to work on the bows of the barge when he heard a distant bell.

Jimmy wiggled a fingertip in his right ear, forcing a yawn to try to pop it. But the ringing wasn't coming from inside his head. He knew that sound. The Travelift crane. He wiped dust from his goggles and about a hundred yards down the jetty he saw the wheeled crane with the yacht Salacious II slung in its belly. The familiar ding-ding-ding-ding was now clear enough over the crane's diesel roar. It was inching its way down the sloped concrete ways, returning the boat to the water.

Jimmy turned and looked around quickly. He spotted Kevin scaling away with his needle-gun on a railing two decks above him.

"Kev! Kevin!" he shouted several times before getting his partner's attention.

Jimmy gestured in the direction of the Travelift.

Kevin looked down the jetty and beckoned to him to come up. Jimmy scrambled up two sets of ladders and joined him for the sight that had captured his interest.

There on the jetty, next to the slipway, was a small group of men looking on. Prominent among them was one in a camelhair overcoat. Testaverde. No doubt about it. With him was a handful of well-dressed goombahs, the thug in the windbreaker who came along on his previous visit, and two others—the yard's general manager and Vince Playsted, in his white "I'm in charge" hardhat.

Neither Kevin nor Jimmy spoke; they observed, trying hard to identify faces. Both quickly concluded that the big man with Testaverde was Fat Billy Grasso, his uncle. And to his left, in the charcoal gray raincoat, none other than Ray Patriarca Jr., the Boston-Providence mafia boss.

The ringing stopped as the Travelift came to a halt in the waters of Providence Harbor. The yacht hadn't yet floated free. Indistinct orders were shouted. In a moment, straps were released on the yacht's port side and fell away into the water. Salacious II bobbed for a moment and slid gently astern, suddenly fully afloat on the tide. Its engines roared to life and a coxswain from Phil Goyette's boat handling crew reversed the motor cruiser into the river before turning and coming alongside the jetty. A crewman on the boat helped a pair on the dock to secure her, running a gangway up onto her deck.

Kevin and Jimmy watched as the group boarded the yacht and disappeared into the cockpit lounge.

For ten minutes the pair pretended to work; Kevin zapping rust with needle gun bursts, while Jimmy wiped the same patch of rail with a rag. Soon they saw movement on board. The coxswain and crewman left over the gangway, followed by the yard's general manager and foreman. The shore crew pulled in the gangway, let go the mooring lines and the yacht nosed away from the jetty. She slowly made her way into the harbor, headed south toward Newport.

As she passed the bow of YRBM-48, Testaverde and the mob chieftains moved into the main cabin. Kevin and Jimmy were startled, suddenly trading stares with a man who remained on the stern. Cheap Windbreaker. Unblinking as the yacht squatted into its wake and powered away.

IT HAD TAKEN Jimmy three days to complete his work aboard Salacious II. Monday saw him devoting his time to the pilot house upgrades. His first task had been the satellite navigation bridge repeater. It was a "black box" device with a face about the size of a brick, which displayed latitude and longitude in orange digital numerals. Next was a plain Jane set of digital VHF radios to replace the boat's crystal sets. That had taken the rest of the day, with the new radios being one-third of the size of the original gear. Playsted had been impressed with Jimmy's cabinetry innovation. Good attention to detail. The fella might have a future in this line of work.

Tuesday should have been a piece of cake, upgrades to entertainment electronics in the yacht's main salon and the master stateroom directly below. Replacement of televisions and stereo equipment in their existing consoles. Delicate cabinetry work would be necessary to accommodate fit.

"This is teak, Rafferty," Playsted had noted, caressing its sensual grain. "Ever work with teak?"

"Not much aboard fish boats," Jimmy replied.

"Well, you did good work on the bridge," the foreman had said. Then the other shoe dropped. "But any dockyard matey with a man's growth a whiskers can work with sheet metal and wood grain veneer."

Playsted snuffled a highbrow little snort, putting on airs.

"Our customers always come first," he droned. "And Mr. Testaverde, well, I don't think we'd want him unhappy. My first inclination is to bring on a shipwright, someone whose skills I can trust. What do you say, fella? Should I pull you off this job? Keep you on? Pull you off? I dunno, I'm undecided."

"You're the boss, but I'd like the chance to complete it."

Playsted's eyes narrowed in pretentious deliberation.

Jimmy wanted to smack him.

"Okay fella, it's yours!" the foreman declared, "Do it first class and we might just keep you around."

With that, Jimmy made some quick calculations and headed off to the shipwright's shop for material.

"Don't be wasting teak, Rafferty!" hollered the foreman. "We plan to make some good coin on this job!"

By the coffee break whistle on Tuesday morning, Jimmy had completed the installation. Kevin had stopped by with his thermos bottle. They toured the strangely empty salon, which had been stripped bare over the weekend by an outfitting contractor. Over coffee, the pair had reviewed the decorator's plans and sketches.

Kevin held up a dry-mounted sketch and stood eyeballing the empty salon.

"See this one?" he'd asked, as Jimmy took measurements at the television console. "It's gonna look like a whorehouse."

"This from a Southie who'd know," his partner replied with a nail in his mouth, not looking up from his work.

"Come on!" Kevin countered. "I mean, *really*. Red and gold? Black lacquer this, marble that? All that's missing is a stripper pole in the middle."

"Yeah, well I like the layout," Jimmy said, moving to the rear of the salon and standing between its doors.

"Inside conversation concentrated right here," he said, gesturing with his arms at the salon's imagined seating.

He turned and motioned outside to the cockpit, shown in the designer's drawings with deck chair seating for ten.

"Outdoor chitchats down there."

Then Jimmy patted the bulkhead above the cockpit doors.

"Here's the resonating surface we're after. Complete coverage for both areas, all concentrated in one six-inch spot."

Kevin grinned. The man knows his business.

Jimmy tapped the deckhead ceiling. "I'll mount the control unit on the upperdeck, over an exterior electrical outlet that's right about here."

"Candy from a baby!" said Kevin, with a sly smile.

"Fish in a barrel," his partner agreed.

That night they tested their work from Kevin's motel room. Jimmy dialed up the satellite unit, and in the low light of dusk over Providence Harbor, *Channel A* showed an image of the bare main lounge aboard Salacious II. A crisp wide angle view of the entire room from the stern. Switching to *Channel B*, there was the cockpit lounge. It was just as clear and with audio set to three on the scale, they could hear the night sounds of the port and the city. *Fuckin' eh!*

That left Wednesday, working around a crew that would spend two days outfitting the main salon. Jimmy completed the dummy EPIRB installation just aft of the mast, snaked wires, made electrical connections and installed the antenna on the boat's rakish mast. It had been just short of 4:00 p.m. that afternoon when Jimmy climbed down from the yacht and returned a ladder to the tool crib on the dock. *Done.* Job completed, right down to the last tucked wire, vacuumed curl of hand-chiseled teak and ticked checkbox on Playsted's work order. It was then that the foreman dropped by.

Playsted spent half an hour scrutinizing the vessel and Jimmy's work. It had passed muster; the asshole actually smiled. And why not? The most delicate and expensive aspects of the job had been handled by a convict on the state's minimum wage.

"Good job, fella!" he said. "You might pass your probation."

❧

FRIDAY AFTERNOON'S COFFEE break horn sounded across the dock and could be heard echoing throughout downtown Providence. Jimmy and Kevin paused on the bow of the barge before heading down to the jetty. They watched as other workers made their way to the 'Roach Coach', a catering truck that arrived three times daily with sandwiches, coffee and pop.

"Well," Kevin asked, eyebrows rising. "Are we on?"

Jimmy had been having second thoughts. He didn't completely agree with the plan. It might be too soon; too close to completing their work on the boat.

Kevin had been working at A&J for nearly six weeks, but Jimmy had been there just one. That dickhead Playsted was even beginning to like him. There might be complications, leaving so soon after just the one job. It could come back to bite them in time. But Kevin was senior, and he did press the point. Then again, there was all that needle-gun work. Which sucked, absolutely.

Fuck it.

Jimmy nodded.

Kevin reached into his lunchbox and pulled out a pint of Old Turkey bourbon. They each gargled half of the bottle. Kevin put the empty flask in his pocket and they made their way to the group surrounding the catering truck.

Perfect timing. Playsted was there, buying a coffee.

As they closed in, Kevin started.

"You're a hang down and a wank, motherfucker!" he said loudly. "I been carrying your lazy ass since you started!"

"Fuck you!" Jimmy snarled, shoving him hard.

Punches were thrown. The pair wrestled to the ground. Out popped the whiskey flask, smashing on the jetty at Playsted's feet, with a crowd of hooting A&J workers closing around them. Co-workers pulled them apart.

Playsted got into their faces and winced, smelling the booze. "Drinking on the job?" He smiled smugly. "Oh, you two, you're done!"

He looked Kevin in the eye. "I knew since day one that you were a goof and a loser! You're fired, fella! How about that?"

"Fine by me, fucko!"

Hoots and catcalls rang through the assembled crowd. The foreman ignored it. Then he faced Jimmy and frowned.

"But you, Rafferty? You disappoint me," he said, quickly grinning again. "I thought you showed promise."

Playsted looked Jimmy over as two burly men held him. "Fucking skinners. Never pays to give rapists a break."

Jimmy spat at him and missed.

Playsted threw a dismissive wave. He ordered them from the yard and their handlers began to escort them away.

"And fellas?" he called after the pair with a smirk. "Don't hold your breath waiting on paychecks!"

Chapter 21

Thursday, April 27, 1989 – 4:22 a.m. GMT +2
The Mediterranean, ten miles off Porto Empedocle, Sicily

THE RUST-STREAKED bows of the trawler *Isabella IV* rose and fell slowly as she hove to on a swell that was rolling offshore. The dark outline of a small coastal seiner closed silently on her starboard quarter. Both vessels had been running with their navigation lights off, and with dawn a pink line on the horizon, the seiner thudded against Isabella's jute fenders and quickly came to a stop. Lines were exchanged and men traded greetings in whispers. All knew that on this windless sea, their voices could carry for miles.

Isabella's mate stepped onto the deck of the anchovy boat and was met by its master, a round grizzled man with an impatient scowl. Their exchange became agitated, if only briefly, and a second man crossed onto the seiner's bow. He interrupted in broken Italian: "*Scusilo, capitano, due passageri? Ora soltano uno. Pago entrambi.*" Excuse me, captain, two passengers? Now only one. I pay for both.

The seiner's captain groused. He had been a border runner for years and the change in their plans hadn't sat with him well. Still, he offered the stranger his hand. Martin Quinn shook it. He pulled a roll of American cash from his jeans and thumbed-off two thousand dollars—two full fares for this, the final leg of his journey. A bargain. He had come five hundred miles in fifty-two hours and now, with his destination in sight, he pressed the money into the man's weathered hand. Then he counted out five hundred more.

"*Per la vostre difficolta,*" he said. For your troubles.

The Sicilian fisherman smiled broadly, saluting Quinn with a knuckle tap to the brim of his salt-crusted cap.

With that, he ordered his crew of three to cast off from the trawler. His men busied themselves with the lines and soon the tiny white and blue wooden craft heeled away as both vessels rang on their engines—Isabella returning to her fishing zone west of Malta, and the seiner back home to Porto Empedocle, a string of twinkling lights ten miles to the north.

Martin stood on the bow of the anchovy boat as it bucked through the swells, sea spray feeling good in his face.

He had made this trip twice before, each time aboard Isabella, arriving in Porto Empedocle as a crewman on a local boat. Round trip journeys, but this sailing was not. Both fares this time had been booked one way.

The Irishman slipped away from Libya in the dark of the night. Just after one in the morning on Tuesday, a full hour late, and again from the tiny port of Sidi Balal on the western outskirts of Tripoli. Karim the boatman had pressed for their midnight departure. The trip had been meticulously planned, tight connections at sea, delay could put the entire journey at risk. Martin had prevailed—but one hour passed with no sign of Shakir, and he sailed with that single regret.

As before, Karim Samnani had rowed Martin to sea in his skiff; out past the breakwater to his thirty-foot fishing yawl, riding at anchor off Sidi Balal. Once aboard, Karim had hauled up his sails and his boat glided silently into the night and away from the Libyan shore. With five miles behind them, he had started his engine, motoring directly north into the open Mediterranean.

Forty miles offshore they met a coastal steamer, making its scheduled way from Famagusta, Cyprus to the Tunisian port of Sidi-bou-Said. It diverted to a point just east of the island of Malta, when at nightfall on Tuesday, Isabella IV accepted her lone passenger. Two days more brought Martin to this dawn rendezvous one last time.

The seiner chugged past an ancient stone breakwater that protected Porto Empedocle, as morning broke with a bright cloudless sky. As she came to rest, Martin busied himself with the nets on her bow. Dressed in a worn leather coat, jeans and a woolen watch cap, he looked for all the world like one of its Sicilian crew; and after an hour of effort unloading its bounty, he stepped off the seiner and disappeared into the town.

Once again, Martin was free; this time, for good.

Ten hours later, Quinn stepped from a bus in Messina, a bustling city on Sicily's northeastern coast and a short ferry ride from the mainland. He caught the last sailing to Reggio di Calabria, on the toe of the Italian boot, where he settled into a two star tourist hotel with plans to catch the first train the next morning for Rome. Free after five years as a prisoner of the Gadhafi regime.

MARTIN QUINN was born on December 4, 1954 in Newry, County Armagh, on the Northern Ireland border with the Irish Republic. He was the son of pacifist Catholic farmers whose family had resisted the violence that swirled around them for three generations.

He was in his second year of electronics technology at college in Dublin when, in 1974, Martin had lost so many friends to the Troubles that he returned to the North and joined the Provisional IRA.

Quinn became a bomb maker. Their best, a wizard with timers. Conscientious, insisting that his devices target just the oppressors—the Brits, soldiers of the English occupation; the Royal Ulster Constabulary, police who supported Unionist rule; and, whenever they got the chance, the protestant paramilitaries.

His bombs were art, with his signature: delicate timers, as was advance warning to minimize loss of life. Even so, Quinn was the chief suspect in an August 1979 bombing that killed the Queen's cousin, Lord Louis Mountbatten—without warning—aboard his yacht off Mullaghmore, County Sligo, in the Irish Republic. It had never been proved, but the best minds in counter-terrorism had no doubt it was him.

Martin fell off the radar in the early 1980s after a series of his trademark bombings in England. Intelligence at the time suggested he had left Ireland and was hiding in North Africa. The truth was that for nearly a year he had been holed up in the south, in a thatched cottage just north of Killarney in County Kerry. A dispute between the Belfast Provos and the IRA leadership in Dublin had kept their prized asset on ice. Martin stewed in Killarney and wasn't surprised, in 1984, as Moammar Gadhafi invited terrorists to join a global struggle, that feuding IRA leaders fobbed him off to the Libyan leader.

Quinn left Ireland that June to become Colonel Gadhafi's prize pig, trotted out to instruct and inspire every anarchist revolutionary the regime would support. In the end, he lent his expertise to their JSO, the Libyan security intelligence service. To devastating effect, he realized, with news of the Lockerbie bomb. Quinn had been shocked when Musa Mansour thanked him personally for his contribution to Gadhafi's jihad. It was then that he knew he must leave, and soon, and then that Shakir al-Warid had called. It's a curious thing, life taking turns as it does.

MARTIN SAT ALONE in the sidewalk café outside his hotel, enjoyed a bowl of gnocchi and guzzled a liter of wine. When he finished his meal, he strolled inside and approached the comely young clerk at the desk. The doe-eyed Calabrian beauty was in her mid-twenties, demure in a starched blouse and plain uniform blazer that strained to contain her bosom. She smiled at him warmly.

"Might I have an overseas line, darlin'?" he asked.

"Of course, *signore*," she replied, pointing to the lobby phone in an old-fashioned booth near the lift before retreating into the office.

Seconds later, she returned to announce that the line was connected. Martin blew her a kiss as he ambled away.

He opened the accordion door to the phone booth and its interior light came on. He entered. It stank of cigarette smoke and he sat on its worn wooden bench. Martin closed the door and picked up an olive green handset. Hearing a faint dial tone, he fingered the rotary dial—a number he had committed to memory five years before.

Martin checked his watch. Eleven-twenty. Two hours earlier in London. The line hissed and rang twice at the receiving end. A male voice answered crisply: "Good evening, Argyll and Sutherland Tartans."

"Is the proprietor in?" Martin asked.

"Possibly, sir. May I know who is calling?"

A bemused look spread across Martin's face.

"Catesby. Bob Catesby."

It was a codename that Martin had chosen himself. Robert Catesby, an English nobleman who plotted in 1605 to kill King James I and restore a Catholic monarch to the English throne. It was Catesby who contracted Guy Fawkes to blow up Parliament—the infamous 'Gunpowder Plot', remembered every November 5th in Britain as Guy Fawkes Day.

There was a two-minute wait.

Over the hiss of the long distance connection came a sudden shrill whine and the line became clearer, with a faint background tone, a chimed note every fifteen seconds.

"Martin?"

It was him, Martin knew. Jamie Mayhew himself, deputy-director of the British Security Service, MI5.

"Mayhew, y'old bastard, how are ya?"

"Martin. How nice."

And so it began.

Chapter 22

Saturday, April 29, 1989 – 9:02 p.m. GMT
Hertford College, Oxford, England

THOMAS HOBBES NIGHT isn't celebrated by all who attend Hertford College, Oxford, where the 17th century philosopher laid the foundation for modern political thought—his notion of a natural equality between men, and that legitimate power must come from the people. Hobbes was hated, of course, by nobility at the time, but for scholars and students who loved the man later, his birth in April 1588 was as good a reason as any to piss it up. And for the Hertford graduating class of 1979, Thomas Hobbes Night became an excuse for their ten-year reunion.

Having a party in the 'great room' at Magdalen Hall was like holding a disco night at Westminster Abbey. It had tremendous acoustics but the place had the chill of a tomb.

"I can see your nipples, Nick!" sniggered Trevor Pembroke, who was already drunk. No surprise. The haystack of a man, heir to a construction fortune, hadn't drawn a sober breath during his Oxford days. Now richer and even more idle, why change? "Wanna see my willie? It's getting hard too!"

Nicola Fry took a sip of champagne.

"No, thank you," she replied, smiling. "You did show me once, you'll recall, and I'm still in a therapist's care."

Pembroke guffawed loudly and staggered away in search of more wine.

Nikki had enjoyed the formal dinner. Now, though, she wasn't so certain that she would stay. There hadn't been a single member of her Hertford class whom she'd been that happy to see. Few former close friends. None of her former lovers, of which there had been remarkably few. She had hoped she'd see Peter, but hadn't.

She had just turned thirty-four and still had her girlhood athletic good looks. Blue eyes and sharp facial features that hinted at distant Nordic blood. She was tall but not imposing at five-ten in heels, and her once mousey blonde hair was now paper white, in a short Euro-cut that was stylishly edgy. Nikki was turning heads. Men were looking her over. And, with the absolute exception of Trevor, she began to think that might be good.

Nicola Jeannine Fry, of Bishopsbourne, Canterbury, was the only child of Detective Superintendent James Beckwith Fry, of the Kent Constabulary CID, and his wife Alicia, a school teacher, both happily retired.

Academically gifted as a teen, she attended Hertford College from 1976 through 1979, earning her degree reading PPE: Philosophy, Politics and Economics. After university she went directly into the Security Service, MI5, as an intelligence officer. She trained in counter-terrorism operations, serving two tours in Northern Ireland, her first as an undercover operator, enticing young IRA men into making bad choices, and her second as an interrogator. It was an experience which, in a significant way, left Nikki with scars. She left her Irish nightmare behind in 1984, briefly landing on the counter-terrorism desk in London before a posting to Britain's security contingent at the European Parliament in Brussels.

Nikki brushed a drop of champagne from the bodice of her strapless black dress. Trevor Pembroke had been right, her nipples were showing.

"Nicola?" The voice came from behind her.

"Peter?" She spun and flushed with excitement to see he had come after all.

He smiled, speechless to be facing the girl he remembered, his arms opened wide. She threw her own tightly around him.

Peter's smile was as broad and as warm and engaging as when Nikki first met him. Love's faces fade. They say scent, singular moments of pleasure, even turns of a phrase remain with us through time. But as hearts and affections move on, the faces we swear we will cherish forever ... fade.

"I'm so ..." they blurted together and laughed.

"Happy to see you!" said Peter, completing his greeting.

"Surprised at how little you've changed!" Nikki declared.

His smile lit up his face. A great face, at once boyish and manly: clear hazel eyes, a rugby nose, bronze stubble on wind-burned cheeks and his chin. Nikki remembered every contour and line, freckle and scar. His was a face she still cherished.

"Look at you!" she marveled.

Peter de Chastelaine had his flowing dark hair knotted back in American Indian braids. He wore 'white tie' with a black formal waistcoat, denim jeans and suede desert boots that had long been his trademark.

"What?" He self-consciously brushed his lapels.

Trevor Pembroke wobbled up beside Nikki, taking a moment to recognize Peter.

"Peter de-fucking Chastelaine!" he slobbered. "You've gone native! *Heh, heh*, it suits you. May I present the lovely Nicola? Oh, that's right, you knew her years ago."

"Hello, Trevor. I see you've been eating well."

Pembroke fumbled to light a cigarette with a wine glass in one fat fist and a plastic lighter in the other. Eyes alternating between squinting and bulging wide open. He sucked hard to inhale from a butt he lit halfway along. Depth perception had failed him.

"Oh, do us a favor!" he groaned, handing the lighter to Peter. In a moment he exhaled luxuriously and was able to focus again.

"Yes, thank you, life *has* been treating me well. Money, money, money, money." Then he winked. An exaggerated, pantomime wink. "Pussy, pussy, pussy, pussy."

Trevor grinned, rocking on his heels.

Peter caught him by surprise with a feint punch toward his elliptical midriff.

"Pembroke, you haven't changed one iota! I've known all along that you wouldn't. Don't you agree, Nicola?"

"Yes!" she agreed sweetly, planting a kiss on Trevor's cheek. "Dear old predictable Trev."

For a moment their silence was awkward.

Trevor brightened.

"Lord Linford ..." he said with droll deference, "Regale us with your adventures since Uni. More to life, eh, than noblesse oblige and beating your indentured peasants?"

Nikki was rolling her eyes and they sparkled.

"Quite right, Pembroke!" Peter replied stuffily. "I exempted myself from the House of Lords when father died. All those appointed life peers? Puffed up commoners. Fuck 'em, I said, the Ninth Earl of Linford would do with his life what he pleased. Academia. Traveling the world, conjuring anthropological theories. Chasing grass-skirted natives. You know, Trevor? Study, study, study, study. Rumpy, pumpy, pumpy, pumpy."

"Too right!" Trevor snorted. "We're the same, you and me. *Usque'quaque frater in dilgenter.* Brothers in earnest forever. You said that, don't you remember? First time we met. I drank you under the table."

Trevor wobbled and threw a beefy arm around Nicola's shoulder. "And what about our d-darling girl?" he hiccupped, eyes again straining to focus together. "Has it been ten years as well for you, m'lord?"

He gave her a wet smooch on the cheek.

"I'll have you know, Linford, that I have it on g-good authority, that our lovely Nicola has become a spook!"

Peter's amiable gaze quickly hardened.

"The best authority, I hasten to add. Highly placed." Trevor continued, lowering his voice to what he thought was a whisper. "MI5! Maybe six, seven, or e-eight."

"I think that's enough, Trevor," Nikki said.

"No, tell me, Nicola," he persisted, his eyes bulging wider. "Surely when you were vetted, you told them all about

Oxford? Fucking the son of a left-leaning lord? Perhaps you were a spook even then!"

In a blink of an eye, Nikki had removed Pembroke's arm from her shoulder, leaving him to drunkenly wonder why it suddenly ached at his side.

Peter drew close and gripped his other arm at the bicep, squeezing hard. "In either case," he said in a whisper, "if she is, or she was, I shouldn't think she would want it so freely announced."

"N-No! You're right," Trevor groaned. "Apologies, Nick. I should freshen my drink and leave you two alone for a mo."

Pembroke retreated into the crowd, working out painful kinks in both arms.

Nikki was smiling, unflustered.

"Not to worry," she said. "I'll have him killed."

They laughed, genuinely, heartily. She took Peter's arm and they went with champagne in hand into the night air on the quadrangle outside the hall.

Ten years. They caught each other up in ten minutes. She couldn't discuss much of her own life, which Peter of course understood. Instead they concentrated on generalities which might have been banter had they not been so deeply connected. They had both remained single; neither so much as engaged, no relationships which had stood the test of time. Her work was interesting, at times tedious, other times exhilarating. She traveled. Recently lived in Brussels. Still painted the odd watercolor and read. How incredibly uninteresting I've become, Nicola thought.

Peter had continued his studies in anthropology, gaining a doctorate in Canada at McGill University in Montreal—studying aboriginal peoples, the struggle to maintain their vanishing cultures. He was considering a research fellowship at Columbia in New York, and had in fact just returned from a four-month field trip to the high Sonoran desert of New Mexico, hence his sunbaked tan and unusual choice in coiffure.

The braids suited, Nikki had decided the instant she saw him. These things were no gimmick with Peter, he had always been guileless. Once on an undergrad visit to Papua-New Guinea, he'd had his nose pierced through the septum with a six-inch crescent of wood. After all, he had reasoned, to understand the angst of the boys of the *Kombai* tree people as they approached ritual manhood, it would be useful to feel something of it himself. Still, it had been to his great relief at the time that at birth he had been circumcised, as the Kombai used ceremonial knives of sharpened bamboo.

"Do you find your work satisfying?" Nicola asked, shivering a little in the night air.

Peter draped his jacket over her shoulders.

"Actually, yes!" he replied cheerfully. "After four years of lecturing in Edinburgh, it's good to be back in the field. Gathering data... well, supervising the lackeys who gather the data, while I sample the local cervezas and sit on my fat pompous ass."

"It's not really that fat."

"You're too kind," he grinned. "I remember a girl who was much more acerbic in dealings with men. Completely castrating at times. The Conference of Colleges Ball? I'd be surprised if, even today, poor Trevor could father a child."

"Poor Trevor?" Nicola protested. "In my defense, his was an unnatural act. Even for Oxford, and that says a lot."

They giggled. Peter closed his arms around her.

"Tell me," he asked, kissing her on the forehead. "Did you think about us over the years? I did love you, you know."

Nikki nestled her face into his chest. Heard his heart beating. They had been here before, and this was what she remembered when she did think about them as *us*. "No, you loved being Lord Linford. You changed when your father died. Assuming that onerous mantle. You became ..."

"An ass? I remember."

"I would have called it self-absorbed."

It would have been an honest assessment. Peter had been iconic in his own right, again, even for Oxford. Handsome, bright, noble peer and the master of all he surveyed. The problem for Nicola, then, was that in his dominion were women. They were destined to part and when she moved on, she did find herself stronger for it.

Nicola shivered.

"Shall we go back in?" Peter asked.

"I'd rather we left."

He brightened. "Do you have somewhere in town? I don't."

"I do. But do you have a car? I came from London by train."

"No," he said. "I came by helicopter."

"Helicopter!"

"It was a commercial shuttle!" he protested. "Heathrow to Oxford for two hundred pounds! My flight arrived late. I needed to get here!"

In that instant they kissed. It had been too long in coming.

"I'll find us a taxi," he said, once he caught his breath.

TWENTY MINUTES LATER, they entered Nicola's room at a luxury hotel on the High Street. They were barely seconds inside before clothing began to be eagerly shed—and with all the groping and groaning, they never got close to their pillow-topped bed. When Nicola eventually rose and excused herself to the bath, Peter sat naked against the foot of the bed, attempting to muster the energy to rise and locate the convenience bar.

It was 11:37 p.m. when Nikki emerged from the bathroom wrapped in a thick terrycloth hotel robe. Peter was softly snoring in bed, with the top linens draped discreetly across him and CNN soundlessly on the telly. She found the remote and had just switched it off when she noticed the flashing light on the phone.

The desk clerk relayed a message marked urgent. Would she call her service in London? The message was marked as having been received at 10:40 that night.

Nikki dialed the number and punched in the code.

"Dancer, it's Gymnast," intoned a familiar voice. "Your Irishman called and we're a little alarmed. Can you return to London by midday tomorrow?"

She slumped in the chair when she hung up the phone. Her first Olympiad call and she shuddered to think what it meant. She would leave for London at daybreak. But for now, she slipped into bed beside Peter. Where she had always belonged.

Chapter 23

Sunday, April 30, 1989 – 12:17 p.m. GMT
Lancaster House, Stable Yard Road, London, England

NICOLA FRY ARRIVED by taxi at Lancaster House—a massive four-story stone mansion just north of The Mall behind Buckingham Palace—and passed quickly through its plainclothes security. It was signed as 'The Commonwealth Office' although its entire top floor had recently been assigned to support the British contingent at the European Parliament. Or so the bureaucrats in the rest of the building had been told, and had no reason to question. It was the UK headquarters of Olympiad.

She had taken the first train to London from Oxford, stopping by her flat on Reeves Mews in nearby Belgravia just long enough to change clothes. When she entered the office of the station chief, Jamie Mayhew, an aging Cold Warrior also from MI5, there was another man in the room. Mayhew introduced him: Sir Michael McPhail, Deputy Commissioner of the London Met.

They moved to settees in the corner of Mayhew's cluttered office, where Mayhew kissed Nikki hello as they sat down to business and tea.

"Thursday evening, we received a rather startling call from Martin Quinn," he began. "In Italy again. I told Sir Michael of the significance of your relationship over the years."

Their relationship? Nicola cringed.

Quinn. Back to haunt her.

During her first tour in Ulster, Martin Quinn had risen to the top of the Britain's Most Wanted list. The proverbial "invisible man"—seen everywhere and nowhere, rumored to be behind every bombing attack, yet tied with evidence to few. It was during her second tour in 1983 that she spent days interrogating a young man who was Martin's first cousin. The boy broke, eventually hanging himself in his cell, but not before Nikki had learned of Martin's Libyan exile and overseas movements.

Her last active case as an MI5 agent had been to track Martin down. She found him in Rome in June 1984, enticing him to inform. Quinn had been given absolution for his sins, with the understanding that he would keep Britain informed of any serious risks to the realm. But that deal fell apart in April 1986 with *Operation Eldorado Canyon*, Ronald Reagan's decision to bomb Libya in response to a plague of terrorist bombings in Europe. Quinn had gone underground and hadn't been heard from since.

"I suppose it would be best," Mayhew said, "to simply hear the recording." He pressed play on the cassette machine on the coffee table between them.

There was a hiss, a poor connection.

"Mayhew, y'old bastard, how are ya?"

"Martin. How nice."

"Sorry we've not kept in touch. Got a bit of a shock, so I did, when your man Reagan dropped bombs in my garden. Spent two months with a leg up in plaster. You weren't targeting me now, were you?"

"No, Martin. That's the last thing ..."

"Aye, sure it is, we'll let bygones be bygones. I have some information I'm thinking you'd like. Serious information, if you're inclined to be negotiating."

"I'm listening."

"That Pan American Lockerbie crash. Brought down, so they say, by our Palestinian brothers-in-arms."

"Yes?"

"Well, it wasn't."

"How do you mean?" Mayhew asked.

"I read that your boffins have found some bomb fragments. Any truth to that is there, Jamie?"

"What do you know?"

"Did they find anything of the timer?" Quinn asked. "If they did, or they do, it'll be something they've not seen before. A computer chip."

"We've had thousands of tips. We heard that one before."

"Aye, but I know that it was for a fact. A timer made by the Swiss. Cutting edge gear, not at all like that Dusseldorf crap. Palestinians ... Theirs would've been barometric."

Silence.

"I'll take that then as your confirmation."

"Your handiwork, Martin?"

No! Nikki shuddered. There was a pause and she thought she heard Martin snicker.

"No, Jamie mate. I'm not that bad a bastard. Retired to teaching, I am, and you can't blame the master for sins of the pupil."

"You said you had serious information. Give us a taste."

Martin laughed. "A taste? I'd need one hundred grand."

"I beg your pardon?"

"For this next bit alone, one hundred thousand. Our Swiss account's nearly into the red and I'm needing some scratch for expenses. Pounds sterling will do."

"Agreed."

There was a pregnant pause.

"You can forget about Abu Nidal. He threw in his sorry lot with those Germans. No, Lockerbie's right down to Daddy Gadhafi."

"What's your proof?"

"Eighteen months ago, I was researching digital timers. Passed on what I learned to his JSO monkeys. Two months later, they sent me to Zurich with a shopping list. Got the royal tour, so I did. And came back with twenty of those beauties at ten thousand American dollars apiece."

Mayhew's surprise was audible on the tape.

"We need more than your word."

There was a rustling sound.

"What's this, then? A Meister-et-Bollier bill of sale? Right here in my hand! Let me see now, *Vendu a* ... that's French for 'sold to'... *The Great Socialist People's Libyan Arab Jamahiriya, Ministry of Science and Technology.* Twenty chips, listed right here with their serial numbers. Not a photostat but an original copy. The pink one, part three."

Silence.

"Done," Mayhew said. "What else can you give us?"

"You'll get this much on credit. The orders came from Gadhafi's own lips. That would be hearsay, I reckon, but I heard it from Musa Mansour."

"The JSO director-general?"

"The organ grinder himself."

"Mansour's dead," Mayhew said drolly. "Didn't you know? Please assure me you have more than that."

Nikki thought she heard Martin gasp.

"Dead? When?"

"Monday morning. Assassinated in his doctor's office. We're told it was a bodyguard gone berserk. Killed Mansour and everyone else in the room before he was shot dead by Mansour's deputy, Malik Abu-Asara. He's now in charge."

Dead silence.

"Killed his doctor as well?"

"That is our information. A fellow named al-Warid."

Martin sighed.

"Sad, so it is, the man was a mate. Still, it was Mansour who Gadhafi directed to work out a bombing campaign."

"A campaign? Then Lockerbie isn't the end?"

"Not likely," said Martin.

"I see. How might we get together?"

Martin suddenly sounded brighter.

"Send Nikki to meet me in Rome."

"Nicola Fry? I'm sorry," Mayhew said. "She's left the service. It would be difficult to ..."

"No!" Martin snapped. "You're not listening. Send me Nikki or naught. It's what you might call a condition. Nikki and nobody else."

"I'll see what I can do."

"Cheerio then, Jamie. You've plenty to do. It's been grand talkin' to ya."

The tape ended.

Nicola winced, massaging the strain from her temples.

"Anything to substantiate his claims?" she asked.

Mayhew retrieved a thin file from his desk. It was marked 'Department of Transport—Aircraft Accidents Investigation Branch—Secret'.

He handed her an AAIB forensics photograph. It showed a nondescript piece of burnt plastic against an L-shaped metric ruler. Barely three centimeters square. It had the letters M-E-B-O clearly imprinted.

"This is the timer recovered from Lockerbie," Mayhew said solemnly. "MEBO is the mark of the Swiss firm of Meister-et-Bollier. AAIB says it's a digital timer chip."

"Then he *does* know," Nikki said grimly.

"Evidently."

"So where do we stand?"

Sir Michael sat forward, pressing his fingertips together, studying the young woman's face.

"The Home Office is interested in anything this man can tell us," he began. "Anything of evidentiary value. If this was a Libyan operation, we need verifiable information. Anything of use in the international arena. Names, dates and details of involvement all the way down the chain."

He sipped cold tea from his china cup.

"Olympiad, however, has other interests. Jamie?"

Mayhew picked at the tweed weave of his jacket cuff. He smiled that professorial smile that Nicola had always found so endearing.

"What do you remember, Nikki, of Stakeknife?" he asked.

She pursed her lips, wondering whether Sir Michael had the requisite clearance.

"Stakeknife," she began. "Code name for our ... for MI5's high-level mole in the Provisional IRA. Army's Force Research ran him. Cost dearly in lives, protecting a single informant."

Mayhew stuffed aromatic cherry tobacco into the bowl of his calabash pipe.

"What of him?" she asked.

"Stakeknife has alerted the service to something big," he said, sucking on the stem, drawing flame from his lighter. "We got this through the back door."

Mayhew went on to outline what they knew.

The Derry Brigade of the Provos had recently broken with Belfast and Dublin. They had gone directly to American sources for funding and arms. This in itself, Nicola realized, was exploitable, an opportunity to further divide the IRA leadership trinity.

Derry, he said, had secured an American source for plastic explosives. Tons of it. There was some suggestion as well of ground-to-air missiles, Angolan war surplus, likely through Cuba. Plans were being made for shipment to Ulster by sea.

"Olympiad hopes to interdict this shipment," Mayhew said, exhaling a blue haze of smoke. "Send our opponents a message, if you like. Sir Michael?"

The London cop stroked his long nose.

"I understand you developed a close relationship with this Irishman Quinn."

Her face hardened.

"Remarkably close, considering I had someone he loved like a brother tortured to death. And for no greater purpose than to learn his whereabouts."

"A raw nerve there?"

Mayhew started to speak and Nicola waved him off.

"Only perhaps when it's touched on so lightly," she said.

Sir Michael apologized. He poured himself a fresh cup of tea and the others declined.

"Quinn," he continued. "Once an IRA die hard. Now his motives seem entirely mercenary. Is that your sense of the man?"

Nikki nodded. She brushed her bangs from her eyes.

"We *own* him," she said. "His republican loyalties had been typically youthful. In time, he came to see the Dublin mob for the self-serving politicians that they had become. Felt abandoned by comrades in Ulster. We flipped him for financial gain. And he said it himself. 'Even whores can recover their virtue. But grass once for money? Your soul's lost forever. You can't get it back.'"

"A philosophical terrorist bomber," said McPhail. "Morals aside, what of his ... reliability? Soulless mercenaries have been known to work both sides of the ledger."

"Veracity won't be an issue," Nikki said confidently. "I've no doubt of that. He may mete out the truth, bit by bit, to get the best possible price."

"To be expected," acknowledged McPhail. "The Home Office assures we have limitless resources on the Lockerbie matter. Still, let's not grab our ankles too tightly too long? Agreed?"

Mayhew nodded.

"As for Olympiad's interests," said Sir Michael. "Do you think, Ms. Fry, that this man could be turned as an *agent provocateur*? An operative on our side?"

Her eyes narrowed.

"I have cleared this with Paris and my counterpart in New York," McPhail continued. "In our interdiction scenario, Quinn could have use in New York as a controllable asset. Not completely disclosed, but he would need to be on board. Would he bite?"

Nikki began to chuckle.

"Let me provide some perspective," Mayhew quickly cut in. "Five years ago, when we turned him in Rome, Nikki implored me for any option that would land him in the States. He was embittered by his impending Libyan exile. Prepared to undertake any assignment. Even an offer of wet work, anything so long as it got him across the pond. It was an intriguing offer. But there was no way to accommodate him. Our American partners were in turmoil and, well, Whitehall would hear nothing of it. They preferred that he languish at yon flyblown wadi to twist in the wind for his crimes."

"I see," said McPhail. "Now after five penitent years, his appetite for ... *apple pie* ... might be easily whetted. That's good."

The Met bureaucrat plucked up the knees of his trousers and prepared to stand. They would move ahead with their plans. He instructed Nikki to get whatever she could on the Lockerbie bombing and Quinn's allegation of Libyan ties.

"As for our own agenda? Sell him on the American Dream," he said. "With the requisite carrot and stick. But we want this Fenian bastard on side."

Chapter 24

Monday, May 1, 1989 – 8:29 p.m. CEST
Mecenato Palace Hotel, 3 Via Carlo Alberto, Rome

MARTIN KNEW SHE would be meeting him here. Not simply at this boutique hotel in the touristy Esquiline Hill district of central Rome, but precisely here, at the bar on its sixth-floor rooftop terrace. It was here they first met nearly five years earlier—strangers, it seemed, among a handful of the bar's patrons who had risen to marvel at the coming sunset. The view from the terrace at the Mecenato Palace is always impressive, looking out as it does over one of Rome's most magnificent landmarks, the Basilica di Santa Maria Maggiore. But on clear days at dusk, the ancient Byzantine church will glow dazzling amber as daylight retreats across its broad square, giving way to the velvet embrace of the Eternal City at night.

On that June evening in 1984, Martin had been at the terrace rail with the others, enthralled by the sight, when a feminine voice from behind him had cautioned: "Sir? Pardon me, but you're spilling your beer."

Martin had glanced down and, indeed, Peroni lager was lapping out of the canted beer glass in his hand.

"Ta, darlin'," he replied, lifting the glass for a sip as he turned to meet her, suddenly stopping, agog at the sight of the beauty who had sidled beside him.

He had been instantly smitten. Bright-eyed lass with that look of the devil about her. A Brit he surmised from her speech, and not a tourist, from her chic business attire and self-confident air. He had kept his eyes on her as he downed a mouthful of beer, wiping his lips with the back of his hand and nodding a thank you. She held her ground at an intimate distance, a coy smile in response to an impish grin.

"Do us a favor and pinch me," he said, turning an ear lobe her way. "Come on now, luv, just a wee pinch right here!"

Nicola chuckled and obliged, tweaking it firmly.

"Ouch!" he exclaimed with a grimace.

"Cheers, now I know I'm not dreaming!" he said. "I'm blessed, so I am. Sunset on the Church of the Virgin, and now you as well? Two visions of heaven, one right after another."

"Blasphemy!" she gasped, feigning shock with fingertips pressed to her lips. "What will the children think when they ask us how Mummy met Daddy?"

They shared laughter at the terrace rail. It continued at a table for two, quickly becoming the timeless two-step of a holiday fling between strangers. A light dinner. More wine. The attractive Irishman said he called Dublin home, an engineer, enjoying a short vacation before a dreaded North African contract. *Poor you!* The winsome blonde was from County Kent, a civil servant on a brief secondment to the British embassy in Rome. He found her refined and refreshing. She thought he was cute, charismatic in spite of his blarney. They enjoyed each other, sharing signals and lies on the terrace before retiring to his ground floor garden suite and both of them getting eagerly into his bed.

It hadn't been the first time that Nicola Fry had given herself to the job.

Her entire first tour in Northern Ireland had been as MI5 honey pot bait, meeting IRA lads and fucking them silly until lust or misguided emotions became their undoing. It was a legitimate counterinsurgency role and one of its most dangerous, producing more and better outcomes than any other coercion technique. More than bribery or extortion. A damned sight more than interrogation. It was a job, simply that, with not much of an upside for the operator beyond its proven results for the Crown.

And it was a job that Nicola Fry had done especially well; an actor, living her roles when she played them, and neatly divorcing them all from her personal life. But in time she discovered it came with regrets that she hadn't expected. Targeted lovers paid dearly for Nikki's attentions. Some with their lives. Some whom she had come to care for. Betrayal, she learned, is a singularly painful act and one with no reasonable prospect of solace.

It wasn't duty that night that had drawn her to Martin. He was handsome, well spoken and funny. She was a lonely traveler, swept off her feet after one bar encounter visiting Rome. How can such a thing happen?

When she appeared the next morning with coffee as promised, Martin's hope for an early romp were dashed when she flashed her credentials—along with the silenced Sig Sauer she had drawn from the embassy's stores.

"Martin Quinn? MI5," she announced to her crestfallen lover. "You're nicked."

His brief custody in Rome proved cathartic, a memory he took fondly into five years of exile. And for Nicola Fry, an odd sense of closure, a cleansing that let her move on.

"SLAINTE!" THE IRISH toast came from behind Martin as he stood again at the bar's terrace rail—*'Slan-shuh!'*—in the voice he'd been waiting to hear. A smile came to him as he watched vestiges of sunlight waning on the Basilica's plaza. He turned to see Nikki, as lovely as he remembered the last time he had seen her, precisely here. More comely. More stylish. That paper white hair. Dark suit and a navy silk blouse that plunged deeply. Glossed lips and sparkling eyes. Saluting him with a glass of white wine.

"Nikki, luv!" he said happily. "A day or two sooner than I had expected." He kissed her on the cheek.

"You look grand," he said. "Tell me you're not here to kill me and you'll make my day."

"The night's early," she said.

Nikki joined him at the rail. Below them, five lanes of traffic hurtled around the vast plaza, a cacophony of motors and horns. Sirens wailed. And with night quickly falling, the broad avenues transformed into rivers of light—red, white, flashing amber, and the revolving blue of ambulances and the Carabinieri.

Martin cupped a palm to light a cigarette in the warm evening breeze. "Last night," he said, exhaling, "I watched the sunset from down on the street."

"Really? From where?" she asked, embracing his shoulder.

He pointed to a spot at the base of the Marian column, towering one hundred and eighty feet at the southernmost point of the plaza.

"Right down there," he said. "More splendid a sight than this evening. I wished you were with me."

"I am now," she said.

An hour later they were in Martin's room, much like the room they had shared years before. It was small with a twelve-foot sculpted ceiling, white walls and floors of pale marble, and a raised queen-sized bed draped in a down duvet. Its French doors opened onto a compact but lush courtyard.

It wasn't the end to the evening that Martin expected.

Nicola took a seat at a table by the courtyard doors and produced a microcassette recorder. He faced her from the foot of his bed. "So we're all business, then? Fine. What's on offer?" he asked.

Nikki switched on the recorder.

"Show me the receipt," she said.

He presented her with a creased sheet of pink NCR paper.

She studied it closely. It seemed genuine. A Meister-et-Bollier receipt which listed twenty serial numbers for MST-13 timer chips, along with their pricing and the purchaser's details. Just as he had said. She checked the serial numbers and found the one she'd committed to memory in London. Damning evidence. She tucked it away.

Martin grinned. "And the money?"

"By noon in your Zurich account. Now tell us everything else that you know."

"So we're on a new chit?"

"I am authorized to spend more."

"All right, then," he began. "The Lockerbie bomb was fitted into a Toshiba cassette stereo. The particular model, a Bombeat, was chosen for its ample void space inside. A flash bit of gear, oversized to attract the young buyer. Thing is it's practically hollow."

Nicola scribbled a note.

"It would've been packed in a suitcase, checked in Malta but tagged to New York through Frankfurt and Heathrow. It was unaccompanied baggage from Germany on."

Nikki looked up, startled.

"You see, that's the chink in their armor," he said. "There's a great hue and cry around matching bags to filled seats on board. But it's a costly endeavor. Few airlines keep at it, not beyond a wee spot check here and there. They know it's their weakness. So do we. And Pan Am at Frankfurt? There's your worst offender."

Her troubled look turned to dread.

"These are disturbing details, Martin," she said.

He recognized her dismay.

"No! I lectured on airline security measures," he explained ruefully. "Cited practical ways to defeat them. Well before Lockerbie and in the most general terms."

"Lockerbie, was it your plan?" she asked bluntly.

Martin grimaced. "No! Fucksakes, I had no part in that! None of this is at all down to me!"

She stared at him icily.

"Let's presume for a moment you're telling the truth," she said. "What we want to know, more to the point, what we might pay for are tangible, verifiable details about the Pan American bombing. The names and roles of anyone associated or directly involved. Any ... future terrorist plans you know of directly ... And you as the guiltless, detached pedagogue? I get it, Martin. Let's move this along."

Quinn rose and anxiously started to pace. He poured himself a large whiskey at his bedside table. Nikki declined.

He began.

This much he knew second hand: as JSO director-general, Mansour had received a verbal directive from Gadhafi himself. Early spring 1987. Hurt the Americans. Hit them hard. He relayed the order to his deputy, Malik Abu-Asara, this time in writing: put together an operations team from within the JSO, get technical support from the science ministry and have a plan in place by summer that year. In broad strokes, the mission was to direct bombing attacks at American or America-bound airliners.

"They'd buggered around with various digital timers," Quinn continued. "These and barometric triggers. Both fine if you're off to meet *Allah* and boarding your target flight. But stowed luggage? Rough handling, two or more feeder hops? Clock and altimeter triggers are *shite*."

He said he had been researching the problem in the summer of 1987, when an engineering article about computer clock chips got his attention. Programmable read only memory. Shock-proof chips with a binary clock that can be programmed to control an electronic or mechanical sequence. Accurate to milliseconds. Open a valve inside a nuclear reactor. Turn an antenna array on an orbiting satellite. Or deliver a low voltage charge to an electrical detonator. Within a week he had a technical model on paper. Within a month he proved that the process would work, igniting a detonator through the low-voltage bus of a clone desktop computer.

"I demonstrated my findings in September to Malik Abu-Asara in person," Martin said. "And, on October 12, I was off to Zurich, back in four days with their order. We trialed our first device with an MEBO chip a fortnight later, at a desert airfield south of Bani Waled. Blew an old air force drone from the sky with two pounds of Semtex, detonating at precisely the time we programmed into the chip. To the split second. Fuckin' amazing it was."

Martin regretted boasting the instant he did.

Nikki looked up from scribbling notes. He expected distain, but that wasn't the look. Curiosity better described it.

"And what of your further involvement?"

"I had none. Nikki, you have to believe me. After Bani Waled, they seized all my notes. All my gear. From then on, I was out of the picture completely. A tribal lot, so they are. Anything of importance or secret they keep in the family. A queer duck from the science ministry ... Doctor Aziz? He took over the technical side."

"Who was the operational authority? The leader?"

"Abu-Asara. He had overall control. Under him, the hands on planner, the details man, would have been Jamil al-Salabay. Heard of him, have you?"

She hadn't.

"He's married to Mansour's niece and a distant relation to Colonel Gadhafi. Appointed to rank in the JSO, chief of security for the Libyan national airline. No background for it. A right little weasel. He'd know it all chapter and verse, with Lockerbie or anything else up their sleeves."

Nicola reviewed her notes.

"Twenty chips," she said. "What of their disposition?"

Martin sat close at the foot of his bed.

"Half lost to bench tests. Two in airborne trials that I know of. Lockerbie, another. I'd reckon there's no more than seven outstanding."

Seven more Lockerbie bombs.

She chewed on her lower lip. Carrot and stick.

Nicola rose to stretch and looked out into the courtyard. It was moonlit and empty, ornamental cypress and lemon trees rustled in a gentle breeze.

She said, "I'll consult with London tonight. We'll need detailed specifics. But for this information? If Mayhew agrees? A half a million."

"He'd go double that," Quinn ventured, his relief evident in a lopsided grin.

"Not fucking likely! But then, I'm just the monkey."

Nikki smiled wearily and massaged the back of her neck.

"One million pounds? I could retire with that, invested wisely. What would be your plan moving on? You love it here. Italy could be arranged easily."

"You know what I've always been after," Martin pleaded. "Nikki, champion me! I'm giving you plenty. Mayhew has pull. Get me to the States!"

"There is *no* chance of that!" she howled. "The Americans would shit. Forget that right now. Look at your options. Footloose with dosh and a clean British passport? For God's sake, Martin, get under the radar and on with your life."

"No!" he shot back. "Get me across the pond! I'd have value there, so I would!"

"Value? How exactly? I can't see it."

"As their operator! I know the funding network from Ulster to Boston. The dealers in arms. Their names and their faces. I made the offer before and it stands."

"So not simply a snout but a collaborator?"

Martin sighed.

"I'm already a traitor, I was from the moment I took Mayhew's money. Dublin knows, surely, but why waste a bullet when Libyan exile is worse."

Nicola took his face in her hands. She kissed his forehead lightly and returned to her seat. He looked lost.

"The Yanks would never agree," she said sadly. "They don't play as dirty as we do. Not anymore. And even should they let you in? Work our side of the street and in no time at all you'd be grassed. The Provos would find you and kill you. Make no mistake about that."

Martin sipped from an empty glass.

"You *do* love me, Nikki, don't you?"

She had him. "Enough that I'd rather you lived! If that matters, then do it for me. Live here! Pickle yourself on Chianti and die an old man. Get shot by a jealous husband at ninety. Forget the damned States."

❧

CHARLIE WATT DECLINED the offer of coffee or anything stronger. It surprised him that Coultart kept a desk drawer bottle, not so much that James Brace had accepted a drink. The big man looked haggard. No surprise there, the deputy National Security Advisor had just flown to and from London in less than a day. He had called Charlie from a westbound British Airways Concorde four hours earlier and asked him to set up this meeting. Even then he had sounded exhausted.

Watt knew what was coming and studied Linc Coultart. The man's instincts since March had been right on the mark. London confirmed that the IRA was in the final stages of planning its purchase. A ship had been found to transport the contraband this summer from an American port. Shades of the Valhalla affair.

It had been Coultart who proposed two risky objectives for the operation. First, to let the IRA make its purchase and take the explosives offshore, thus relieving its coffers of funds. What the hell, they should let the mob keep it. Windfall profits fuel greed, greed fuels predictability, and in this game that's useful. Then, to interdict the shipment at the point of delivery with lethal force. Blow it up as they get their hands on it. Send a message. No one denied the merits of that, but the mechanics of making it happen had been hotly debated. As had been the pitfalls of failure.

Coultart's team had devised a plan to locate the shipment in the States and covertly place a bomb aboard. Ray Morgan, his resident genius, had proposed Kenneally's clever use of the satellite phone for their purpose. With deep-cell battery technology, he found that one configured to power such a device could keep its charge for three weeks. Long enough for a trans-Atlantic voyage. But there were too many 'ifs' in the plan. *If* the shipment could be located in time. *If* a device could be stealthily planted. *If* the technology worked.

In the end, it was vetoed in favor of London's solution: a force of ex-SAS contractors taking it out during a ship to boat transfer off Ireland. One well-placed anti-tank missile would likely suffice.

"Linc, I'll cut to the chase," Brace said in his east Texas drawl. "Something's come up that could impact your Long Jump operation. Charlie figured it needed a buy in at the national level. As usual, he was right."

Coultart looked puzzled.

"Seems London has had an IRA turncoat fall into their lap," Brace continued. "Trading credible information on the Lockerbie bombing for a deal to land him over here. A new life in the States. In return he'd be willing to work for us off the books. Washington gets complete deniability."

"High value?" asked Coultart.

"None higher," he said. "A bomb wizard. Disenchanted. Disaffected. On the Brit payroll since the IRA exiled him to Libya five years ago. We think he might give your bomb option a chance. Thing is, Linc, it shifts control of the whole enterprise to our side of the Atlantic."

"Any chance he's a double?"

"The Brits insist he's been turned. Regardless, he's taken their money, so in IRA terms, his card has already been marked. It's your decision, Linc. You're the one who'll have to run him. Ultimately it's your ass on the line, but you'll get all the support you might need from Charlie and me."

Coultart cracked his knuckles and exhaled.

"When do we meet this *disaffected* Irishman?"

Watt and Brace traded glances.

"Can't really say," Brace replied. "That's up to London."

Chapter 25

THE WOMAN HOLDING the small silver bullhorn gave it a sharp rap with the palm of her hand. It squawked, emitted a feeble electronic bleat and went silent. Unperturbed, she returned it to her Pan Am shoulder bag and turned to the small group of protesters who had assembled with her at the corner of Park Avenue and East 54th Street. She was about to speak when it occurred to her that she had forgotten the handouts. His picture. The one she had photocopied the night before and planned to pass out as leaflets today. The stout, graying grandmother rummaged through her bag, producing a sheaf of paper and a yellow glue stick. Now she was ready.

"This is the man!" she declared, holding up the handful of paper for all to see. Each sheet bore the glowering face of a man, reproduced from a newspaper photo, bearing a bold overprinted label: CRIMINAL!

"Theodore Rumsfeld Bakker!" she said loudly. "The former president of Pan Am! The criminal whose lax security let terrorists murder our children, our friends and our loved ones! This place is his corporate hideout, and we're here to tell him today that he won't escape justice!"

The crowd of about two dozen men and women echoed her disdain, in turn taking and pasting Bakker's image to the placards they carried—hand-printed signs denouncing Pan Am for the Lockerbie tragedy.

Under their leader's guidance, they started to march in a revolving queue at the edge of the sidewalk, taking care not to impede the pedestrian flow. It was an orderly information picket, as the NYPD had prescribed for the daily vigil the group had been holding for months in front of the Pan Am Building, which loomed just eight blocks to the south.

It had been by chance that Randolph Elliott had met the demonstrators that morning. At 11:30, he had been en route by cab to the Yale Club for an early lunch. He had become accustomed to their poignant presence, picketing every day in front of Pan Am headquarters, just a block from the club. But today they had been on the move, passing in front of his taxi at East 45th, heading north with their placards past Grand Central Station. He abandoned his lunch plans and had quickly caught up with the procession on foot.

He trailed them to this office tower at 399 Park Avenue, unaware of the significance of the address until the woman made her proclamation and distributed Bakker's picture.

"This man is a criminal!" she said as she handed copies to passersby. "His policies at Pan Am killed innocent people! Ted Bakker! Remember his name!"

A handful of pedestrians had begun to linger at the scene of the protest. Some applauding the group, some stopping to study the leaflet their leader provided. As she handed one to a bystander—a tall older man, casually dressed and wearing a Mets baseball cap—her mantra stopped in mid-sentence and she gave him a quizzical look.

"Do I know you?" she asked.

"No, I don't think we've met," Randolph Elliott replied.

She smiled bleakly. Then she straightened her shoulders, returning to duty.

"Remember this man!" she beseeched all within earshot.

The media had begun to arrive. Television news vans from WABC Channel 7, WNBC News 4 and others. Print reporters and photographers too, joining a scrum that grew around the group's polished spokeswoman. As floodlights came on and video began to roll at the entrance to 399 Park Avenue, Elliott slowly withdrew into the burgeoning crowd looking on.

The workings of television news had never ceased to amaze him. The technicality of it. The theatrics. The sham. As cameras captured a flurry of questions and answers, well away from the scrum, a line of 'talking heads' faced producers and their cameramen, either on-the-air live or being directed through B-roll segments for editing later. They presented expressions on cue: nods suggesting a deep comprehension; a look of commiseration; even re-asking questions to better suit answers they already had in the can.

Twenty feet from where Elliott was standing, a pretty brunette and her crew had set up with the building's entrance and address as a backdrop. They counted down to a live feed for their station's noon news. The reporter glanced at the notes her producer had hastily scribbled, took a deep breath, and faced the lens in the glare of the lights with a look that suggested astuteness. Her producer's upheld hand closed from four fingers to three, to two ... and she paused, nodding twice before speaking.

"That's right, John," she began. "You may remember Sonja Grossman. She's the sixty-five year old Prospect Heights grandmother who, for the past three months, has been leading a daily protest vigil in front of the Pan Am Building in midtown ... Protesting what she and others claim is the airline's complicity in the loss of Pan Am Flight 103, brought down by a terrorist bomb over Lockerbie, Scotland, last December. Tragically, Mrs. Grossman lost her son, a London-based banker, his wife and their two teenaged children. She is one of some thirty families from the tri-state area who have filed suit against the airline in Eastern District Federal Court, suits alleging that lax passenger security on the part of Pan Am directly enabled terrorists to target and bring down the jumbo jet. John?"

The reporter paused and nodded again.

"Today, Sonja Grossman and her Pan Am protesters have taken their vigil uptown. Here, to this Park Avenue address, where, on the thirtieth floor, are the offices of *this* man, millionaire deal maker and former Pan Am CEO, Ted Bakker, on whose watch, according to documents filed in federal court, cost cutting measures he personally ordered led to significant lapses in passenger security. Sources say Bakker is meeting today with his attorneys, with a deadline looming Monday for filing an answer to the first of these lawsuits. Bakker has been keeping a low public profile and it's not known whether he will confront or avoid demonstrators today. For News Nine at Noon, I'm Veronica Gamble."

"Okay, Ronnie, we're clear," announced her producer, a young woman in an NYU sweatshirt and jeans. "Now, let's see if you and Lennie can squeeze through for some one on one facials with the old lady."

Before she could acknowledge, there was a commotion in the midst of the crowd around Sonja Grossman. Few had noticed the Mercedes limousine that had quietly come to a stop at the curb behind them. Angry voices were shouting: "Criminal!" and the protesters surged from their orderly line on the sidewalk toward the building's entrance.

Elliott could see what had aroused the crowd's interest. Inside the glazed lobby was the Criminal! himself, standing just back from the doors with a small entourage. So this was Bakker. Tall, tanned, silver-gray hair and sunglasses, wearing an olive green seersucker suit that shimmered in sunlight. On his arm was an attractive woman who seemed agitated, pulling away. Clearly she had decided that if he chose to leave by this exit, she wouldn't be coming along. The others gesticulated misgivings, three men in more conservative business dress. Lawyers, Elliott knew intuitively; two clearly junior. On the briefcase scale: the more heavily burdened, the lighter their fighting weight. The one carrying nothing at all was Chet Randall, the fixer at Easton and Meares. Strategic defense at six hundred and fifty an hour.

Uniformed cops suddenly appeared from thin air. That would've been Randall. But they weren't really needed.

"Ladies! Gentlemen, please!" Sonja Grossman pleaded. "Remember our pledge. Dignity! We're not here to lower ourselves to his level. Make way! Make room! Our actions speak louder than words!"

The placard-carrying protestors fell quietly back into line, parting without the intervention of New York's finest, clearing a path from the doors to 399 Park Avenue to the limousine parked at the curb.

The group fell silent and the onlookers and media followed suit. Eventually. Bakker chose his moment, left the building with his lawyers and strode to the car.

"Shame!" Grossman sniffled.

"Shame!" her fellow protestors began to chant.

Bakker brought it all on himself. Just steps from the curb, he stopped and swore when he noticed the placards with his face and the Criminal! label. "Goddamned slander!" he growled. "You're all gonna be sued!"

With blood in the water, the media swarmed and the Brooklyn grandmother's best attempt at a dignified protest became chaos. Reporters verbally trampled each other with inane questions: "Mr. Bakker, how do you feel being labeled a criminal?" ... "Are you responsible for these deaths?" ... "Was it the Iranians?" ... "Who was that woman you left in the lobby?"

Bakker and his lawyers escaped, quickly speeding away.

Randolph Elliott watched it all in dismay. The man clearly could not have cared less. Completely aloof and unapologetic. And that, to the seasoned jurist, *was* criminal.

Friday, May 12, 1989 – 8:05 p.m. EST
Shea Stadium, Brooklyn, NY

IT WAS THE first of a three-game home stand against the San Diego Padres, and if the first inning was anything to go by, 32,000 Mets fans were in for a long and miserable night. Dwight Gooden faced six Padres batters in the top of the first and they'd been getting a piece of everything he'd been throwing their way. First at bat, "Mr. Padre" himself, center fielder Tony Gwynn, singled a line drive to short left field on a 1-0 pitch. A sacrifice bunt by left fielder Marvell Wynne on the very next pitch moved Gwynn to second. And, sure as shit, after Gooden walks right fielder Jack Clark, Gwynn is stealing third as Gooden's throw to Hojo goes wild and Mr. Padre sails home to score. One-zip with one out and Roberto friggin' Alomar coming up in the middle of the Padres batting order. Gooden managed to knock off 4-5-6 in a row without much more mayhem. But at bat in the bottom of the first, the Mets managed no offense at all.

Top of the second inning, Padres at bat, and Gooden is dragging his toes on the mound. Blows into his fingers. It's a cool night. Maybe that's been his problem. Sizes up Padres catcher Benito Santiago at the plate. Gets a fastball signal from Barry Lyons and thinks about blowing it off. Nope. There's the windup and pitch. *CRACK!*

"Aw, goddammit!" yelped Sal Luongo, jumping to his feet from his Row 12 seat just above the Mets dugout. His ire dissipated as the big Puerto Rican grounded out between second and first.

"I dunno," Sal groaned, returning to his seat. "Gooden's been feeding 'em nothing but fastballs. He's gotta start mixing it up." He swigged a mouthful of beer as he looked over at Randy, who continued to stare off into space.

"Hello-o-o-o," he droned, snapping his fingers in front of the Judge's face. That got his friend's attention.

"Sorry," Elliott replied. "Miles away. Fastballs? You're right. Gooden's all over the zone when he tries to throw heat. Damp tonight. He needs to warm up."

"Then you are paying attention! Something on your mind tonight, Randy? Don't think you've said a dozen words since we sat down."

The Judge sipped his beer.

"You're an observant man, Sal."

The PA announcer introduced the next batter. Number eight in the Padres batting order, shortstop Garry Templeton.

Luongo groaned. "Templeton's batting left against him. One down the pipe and it's out of the park."

"Gooden will switch it up. You'll see," Elliott countered. He was right. Two curve balls, three sliders and he struck him out looking.

Next up at the bottom of the order was Bruce Hurst, the pitcher. Eight pitches and the goat of the 1986 World Series couldn't keep fouling them off. Three up, three down. This was more like it.

"So are you gonna tell me what's up?" asked Sal. "The long face. That thousand-yard stare?"

Elliott's sullen gaze didn't shift from his beer. "Ever want to kill somebody, Sal? I mean, actually close your fingers around someone's throat and just choke them to death."

Luongo wiped foam from his moustache.

"Eh, Judge! Gooden'll pull up his socks!"

Randy Elliott laughed.

"No. But I mean it."

"Serious? You're asking a goombah like me if I ever wanted to kill somebody. What, you wearing a wire? Kill somebody? I've wanted to, plenty. But actually did? Sorry, buddy, I'm taking the fifth." They both chuckled.

Bottom of the second inning and Mets second baseman Timmy Teufel strikes out with Hurst throwing heat. Keith Hernandez gets the crowd to its feet when he connects with a 3-2 fastball and it looks like it's into the left field stands, but Marvell Wynne makes a diving catch at the wall. *Out.*

"Friggin' hell!" Sal grumbled as they returned to their seats. "So what gets you thinking about giving somebody the chop?" he asked, signaling to a passing vendor for beer.

Elliott sighed. "You know that protest vigil in front of the Pan Am building?"

"No. Hardly ever get that far up town."

The Judge explained who they were and their purpose, and how he had connected with them earlier in the day. He described Sonja Grossman, her own loss and his empathy with her. Bakker and his role in it all. The media frenzy. How seeing Bakker for the first time in person cut him to the core. Sal understood.

"I felt ... I don't know. *Fury?*" Elliott continued, struggling for words. The man's fucking aloofness. The sneer on his face. "Not enough it was clear that he couldn't care less, you could see his confidence. The smug certainty that he *is* going to beat this. And you know, Sal? He will."

Luongo sympathized and shook his head sadly.

"I guess if anyone knows ..." he began, unable to finish. His heart sank for his friend.

The inning closed with the Mets catcher, Barry Lyons, taking a walk, and the shortstop, Kevin Elster, popping up to his opposite number. It was becoming a defensive game.

"I could've killed him, Sal," Elliott said sadly.

"Nah, Randy, you couldn't. You know how they wrote 'We the People' in the constitution? Wanting a more perfect union, justice and freakin' tranquility? *You're* the people they meant. Me? With what you've been through? I'd gut the sonofabitch like a fish. Which is why the rest of the people need people like you."

The Judge chuckled. "I think that's the best constitutional reference I've ever heard argued."

"Yeah? Maybe I'm in the wrong line of work."

Top of the third. Padres batting, ahead 1-0, with Gooden facing the top of the batting order again.

"Still, I wanted him dead," Elliott muttered, sipping flat lager beer from a plastic cup. "Know what I mean, Sal? In my heart. Fucking dead."

The game would run nearly four hours, a pitching duel with the Padres tying it up 2-2 in the top of the ninth. The Mets pulled Gooden with reliever Randy Myers taking the mound for one-and-a-half innings before bringing in Roger McDowell to face Alomar. He gave up two runs in the top of the twelfth and Mets responded with a single by pinch hitter Mark Carreon that scored Keith Hernandez.

Not enough, the Mets lose 4-3.

THEY ARRIVED IN America on a nine-hour Alitalia flight that had followed the dawn from Rome to Newark, New Jersey. Miss Nicola Fry, on a British diplomatic passport for a short weekend stay, and Martin Robert Catesby, an Irish engineer with a London address, on a six-month tourist visa.

They had shadows: two West Germans, man and wife, on a week-long vacation to New York City. The four were the last passengers to be delivered by the Blue Bus Airporter Service on its midtown route to the Essex House Hotel. They checked in together at noon and seemed to desk staff to know one another. Three separate parties, three separate rooms. The German couple went straight up, bidding '*auf weidersehen*' to their friends with a promise to meet later that day for a drink.

The bellman took Miss Fry's and Mr. Catesby's luggage to their suites on the seventeenth floor—1702 and 1707—and got the impression, based on decades of discreet observation, that these two would be sweating the sheets before long. They would be good tippers, too.

The bellman had barely returned to the elevator when Nicola corralled Martin and led him away. He had hoped there'd be time to freshen up, perhaps have a wee nip, but no. On to business.

They were met at the door to Suite 1730 by a redheaded woman in her early thirties. Muscular, unsmiling; attractive in an Amazon way, and so much a copper that Martin could just imagine her slapping on cuffs. Likely had one of those .357 Magnum cannons these Americans carry, right there in a shoulder holster under that loose-fitting suit. Right there next to that rocket left tit.

She escorted them into the suite. It was identical to Martin's own—a small foyer opened into a large central parlor; well furnished, with a wall of windows looking out over Central Park, and open double doors to the left revealing the bedroom.

There were two men in the suite. One black, about fifty and trim, wearing a dark polo shirt and cotton trousers. He was standing in the middle of the room and welcomed Nicola with a smile. The other was white, middle-aged as well, and imposing; he wore a blazer and slacks and sat in a chair by the windows. He didn't get up. He simply sat there with a cup of coffee, sizing up Martin like beef on a hook.

"You can call me Diver," the black man said by way of introduction as he shook hands with Nikki.

"Nicola Fry," she replied. "It's the name that he knows. May I present Martin Quinn, here under the name of Martin Robert Catesby."

"Mr. Diver, how are ya?" said Martin.

The pair shook hands.

"I'm well, thank you," Lincoln Coultart replied.

"Who's he?" Martin asked without skipping a beat.

"Him? He's happy to meet you. May we take a seat?"

Martin studied the man and smiled at Coultart.

"I'm sorry, Mr. Diver. I'm not ordinarily testy, but I knew too many men like our friend here in Ulster. I'll feel much safer once we're introduced."

Coultart grinned. "Not to worry. I am your handler, you'll answer to me. You'll meet the rest of the team in due course."

Martin's smile evaporated.

"No. I need Mr. Happy to say a few words. Now, before we carry on. Humor me, would you? Anything. A nursery rhyme. Fuckin' read from the telephone book."

For a moment the room went uncomfortably quiet.

"Little Boy Blue come blow your horn," Mr. Happy began. "The sheep's in the meadow, the cow's in the corn. But where's the boy looking after the sheep? He's under a haystack and fast asleep. Will you wake him? No, not I. For if I do, he is certain to cry."

A chill went down Nicola's spine.

Martin's smile slowly returned. "You're American."

"You're a genius," Mr. Happy replied.

"Irish American. Sorry, mate, I just needed to know you're not recently landed. There's plenty who'd follow me here. And apart from fair Nikki, I'm trusting no one. Not fuckin' yet."

Mr. Happy glowered at Martin.

"Diver I get, but what about *this* one?" He gestured toward his redheaded colleague. "What, no dancing a jig? No belting out a rendition of Danny Boy?"

"Eagle tattoo," Martin replied. "Inside left wrist."

The redhead blushed self-consciously. All, including Coultart, strained to catch a glimpse.

"It's Polish."

Mr. Happy grinned. One-nothing, visitors.

"Well, isn't this nice!" Coultart said, a little unsettled. "Now we're all warm and fuzzy, lets get down to business."

Coultart explained their circumstances and outlined the rules. Martin had a clean INS entry on a tourist visa. Six months; a probationary period, if you like. This would be reviewed in time to extend it or change Martin's status. They had found him a furnished apartment in lower Manhattan, as requested through London. Little Italy. Apartment 3C, 174 Hester Street. He could move in tomorrow; it would be subject to routine surveillance and unannounced checks.

He had a Citibank account and credit card established in the name of Martin Robert Catesby with his Manhattan address. It drew on his own Zurich funds. He was banned from unapproved travel outside of the metropolitan New York area. He would be issued a cellular telephone. It would always be with him. He would meet Diver or another team member at least once every three days, and under no circumstances would he go more than seventy-two hours without face to face contact.

He was not to make or to have, and was to immediately report, any unapproved contacts with any persons or organizations, foreign or domestic, known to be associated to the Irish Republican Army, any known terrorist or criminal group, government agency ... peddler, hooker, canvassing Mormon or Jehovah's Witness. No one in the least dodgy. Martin got it. Unapproved being the operative word.

He was not to operate any motor vehicle, aircraft or vessel, nor to possess any firearm or prohibited weapons. He was not to engage in any criminal activity, use illicit drugs, or bring himself into negative contact with law enforcement. When requested and briefed, he would assist his hosts in classified operations, activities including the design, construction and positioning of improvised explosive devices.

"If you breach any of these conditions at any time," said Coultart in conclusion, "you may be subject to penalties, including summary expulsion from the United States. Are we good?" They were. Nicola signaled that London concurred.

"Show me where to sign," Martin said glibly. "I got pretty much the same deal from Gadhafi."

Chapter 26

WITHIN FIVE MINUTES of arriving at the dock in Vineyard Haven, the ferry *MV Eagle* had discharged the light load that boarded her 5:00 p.m. sailing from Woods Hole. Soon this would be the busiest of the hourly crossings to Martha's Vineyard, but with the tourist season still a few weeks away, the majority of the 238 passengers this time were islanders commuting home for the weekend from jobs in and around Boston. Most marched directly to their vehicles in the nearby lot, or into the arms of family gathered outside the Water Street ticket office. Visitors tended to saunter—milling around near the sightseeing buses or racks of brochures, getting their bearings, devising a plan. There were fewer of these than usual for a late Friday sailing, and the two men among them who looked like tourists, but moved with a purpose, were conspicuous as a result.

"I have eyes on Doherty and Moran," Magda Wojcik said, transmitting with a button mike clipped to her bra.

The redheaded former Boston cop stood astride a mountain bike at the foot of Union Street, watching the pair through a camera lens as they moved along the passenger walk from the dock to the rear of the terminal building.

"Doherty, tall, sunglasses, sky blue jacket and jeans. Moran on his left, chunky with a dark brush cut, khaki shirt, carrying a yellow sweater," she continued. "Heading southeast toward the main drag, Water Street."

"Copy. I'm still on John Doe," her partner replied, his voice clear in the Walkman headphones she wore. "Still westbound on Beach Road, coming up on the bike rental place at the ...

uh, five-way corner. He's removing his windbreaker ... Now in a bright red t-shirt and jeans. Water Street in thirty seconds."

"10-4, Tinker. My guys are just about there."

Wojcik and her partner Gerry Bell had arrived at Martha's Vineyard by helicopter barely an hour before. With information from Boston and the team in Newport, they had spotted the yacht Salacious II abeam Cuttyhunk Island, heading northeast into Vineyard Sound. Its destination had been the last missing piece of an intelligence puzzle that had taken shape over less than a week. And when it tied up at Tisbury Wharf, a half mile east of the ferry dock in Vineyard Haven, the two were deposited at the nearby airport and made their way into the quaint seaport town.

LONDON HAD GOT its break only six days earlier. A wiretap on the IRA's arms middleman in Dublin, in conversation with Testaverde's lieutenant, Benny Dofasco. The meet was arranged for Friday, June 3rd in the States. All would enjoy a short cruise. "Tell them to wear deck shoes and bring Dramamine," Dofasco had said.

New York had cheered at the news.

Next came informant intell out of Ulster the following day. The principals in the plan, Kieran Doherty, tactical commander of the Londonderry Brigade of the Provisional IRA, along with its intelligence chief, Jackie Moran, would fly out of Paris on Friday morning for the United States. This was all that they had. Linc Coultart had argued for concentrating on Testaverde and his boat, although he had to admit that the man himself had been off their radar for more than a week. Frankly, New York had had no clue where he actually was. And what if plans for a cruise had an alternate meaning?

Jamie Mayhew made the decision to trail the Irishmen just to be safe. It was known that they would smuggle themselves separately into France. Olympiad would gamble on casting its net at the Paris airports: Orly and Charles de Gaulle, with three teams each from London and Paris. The plan worked. At 8:35 Paris time Friday morning—2:35 a.m. in New York—a French team signaled that Doherty and Moran, on fake Irish passports, had left Charles de Gaulle. Air France Flight 664 for Chicago, arriving at 10:35 a.m. local time.

Chicago? Coultart scrambled, getting a team to Chicago O'Hare airport with an hour to spare. He was spread thin. Two teams in Newport, close surveillance all week on Benny Dofasco and the boat. One in place at Boston Logan airport, where they all had expected the pair to arrive. Maggie and Tinker standing by there with a helicopter. Ahearn and Kenneally? Down the hall with the techs in Manhattan, monitoring the yacht's electronics. One team had been all he'd had left and by mid-morning he was chewing antacids.

Still, Chicago made sense. You don't leave from Ireland. You don't enter the States near your real destination.

Relief came at just before noon in New York, when the Chicago team called in with eyes on their targets.

Doherty and Moran had cleared immigration and were met at arrivals by a limousine driver displaying a card with their traveling names. All he did, the team reported, was hand Doherty an envelope and leave. The pair had a quick kiosk breakfast and proceeded to American Airlines domestic departures, boarding an 11:35 a.m. flight to Boston Logan. It would be arriving at 2:30 p.m. Eastern time.

Chicago reported that Doherty and Moran had presented Illinois driver's licenses as identification at the American Airlines ticket counter. Now they were locals, traveling freely within the United States. They knew their business.

An hour later, the Newport boat team reported activity aboard Salacious II. Its crew of three had arrived and was making ready the yacht for departure. In Manhattan, they saw and heard it all on projection TVs.

Shortly after two o'clock, a limousine arrived at the Newport yacht club where the Salacious II was berthed. Down the dock had come Benny Dofasco, Paulie 'Cheeks'

Benafaci—a button man in the Patriarca mob—three women who looked like lap dancers, and the man they all knew as John Doe.

John Doe. He was the stranger Ahearn and Kenneally had spotted twice at the boatyard. Husky white male, maybe thirty-five, always wore a windbreaker. All research on him had drawn a blank. He was somebody no one in the world seemed to know.

For a week there had been no sign of Gino Testaverde, a fact that worried Lincoln Coultart when the yacht slipped its moorings at 2:20 p.m. and headed to sea.

Doherty and Moran arrived in Boston on time. The team at Logan spotted them at the arrivals gate, where they were followed to an airporter bus for Woods Hole. They would be making for Martha's Vineyard, Coultart agreed, and the news was relayed to Maggie and Tinker in the helicopter—which had already moved on to Newport and was tracking the yacht into Vineyard Sound.

"CONTACT!" MAGGIE WOJCIK said. "My targets have met your guy at the corner of Water and Union."

"Seen," Bell replied. "Jeez, Mags, they're hugging like brothers! Hold on a minute, he *knows* these guys. Maybe we all got it wrong about Johnny. Could be he's no goombah at all … I'm thinking he's *Irish.*"

"That'd shock them in Manhattan."

The three turned down Beach Road and it was clear they were making their way to the yacht.

"I'm hanging here at the bike rental shop," said Bell. "Meet up, you can dump that thing and we'll follow on foot."

"10-4. There in two minutes."

They followed the trio a half mile to the entrance to Tisbury Wharf, watching from the street as they boarded the yacht, tied up alone at the end of a commercial quay.

A hundred yards farther down the road was a fuel farm with four rust-flecked tanks the size of small houses. On the waterfront side of its graveled lot, Gerry spotted an office shed with road dust caked on its windows. Moments later, he and Maggie were set up inside. She had fresh coffee in her thermos, he had a half-pack of smokes, and they settled in with a view of the boat.

Electronic surveillance gave up nothing important. The Irishmen came aboard with John Doe and were greeted by Benny. After a brief tour of the yacht, they left to staterooms below for a nap. The three women drank cocktails on the stern, flirting with Paulie Cheeks while Benny spent most of his time on the flying bridge with the skipper.

The real shock came at dusk, when a taxi appeared at the dock and, as Maggie reported by cellular phone to Manhattan, Gino Testaverde arrived on his own. The Manhattan team could exhale. No one knew at the time that he had just flown in on a chartered Lear from Las Vegas.

Everything changed with the big man aboard. The skipper received his orders, and at 9:30 p.m. precisely, the Salacious II slipped from the dock, made its way north past the harbor's breakwater and turned westward into Vineyard Sound.

Benny had the steward rouse the Irishmen from their nap. Doherty and Moran appeared refreshed when they arrived in the main lounge a few moments later. John Doe was absent, up on the bridge. Benny had sent Paulie Cheeks below with the three female guests. "Entertain yourselves. Just stay the fuck outta Gino's stateroom!" were his only instructions.

Gino Testaverde was in his throne, a leather recliner, port side aft in the yacht's main salon. He was finishing a thick tuna sandwich on rye, sitting back with a linen napkin stuffed into the open neck of his black silk shirt, a goblet of red wine on the table beside him.

Benny offered the Irish guests any snack they desired. Gino's Filipino steward didn't speak real good English, but the fuckin' guy was an artist with food. They declined. But they did accept his offer of whiskey.

The pair were presented to Gino, who remained seated and munching, as if this were an audience with the Pope.

"Make yourselves comfortable, fellas," Gino said cordially, brushing crumbs from his lip. "Benny's been looking after you? That's good. Glad you could finally make it."

It was dark now, clear, with a star-studded sky and a light offshore wind from the north. Salacious II cut through a low swell off her port bow, her engines droning effortlessly at twenty-two knots on a course that would take her south of Long Island. And in Manhattan, two hundred miles distant, a crystal clear image of the yacht's main salon was monitored and recorded, along with every word that was said.

Pleasantries were brief. They got right down to business.

On offer was military-spec C4 plastic explosives. Three hundred crates, army field use standard, each of fifty-eight ounce sticks. Seventy-five hundred pounds. Transportable in one forty-foot sea shipping container.

Jackie Moran whistled.

"That's more than we thought or expected," Kieran Doherty said, surprised. "You told our man a ton, maybe a ton and a half."

Testaverde smiled. "First thought I might parcel it out. Maximize earnings. But if you boys can handle the lot? I could cut you a deal if your bosses agree."

Moran scowled.

"There's been a wee change, so there has, since our people first spoke," Doherty said. "We two are the bosses now. You'll be dealing directly with Jackie and me."

"I deal with who pays."

"That's fine, then. You're looking at us."

They talked price. Testaverde had heard that they'd paid as much as $500 U.S. for a pound for plastic explosives. One-off deals, Moran quickly countered. British Army C4, smuggled off the range or from quartermaster stores by opportunists. They bought Semtex from Libyan vendors for $200 a pound, but Czech plastic was shit. One-third the detonation effect of its NATO counterpart. Nearly four tons of C4 would be by far the largest purchase they'd ever recorded. Twice the total of all of the plastic explosives the IRA had acquired since the start of The Troubles.

"Make it one-fifty a pound," Testaverde suggested.

"A million-one?" protested Doherty. "For the lot, we'd be wanting a volume discount."

"It's top flight C4, not some cheap Czech plasticene."

"Not enough of a bargain," Doherty replied. "Would you consider this? We'll give you one million even. One quarter tomorrow in cash, the remainder into any account on delivery, FOB to a ship we'll have here in the States. I'll even throw in ten cases of Jameson whiskey to sweeten the deal. Limited Reserve. Eighteen years old."

Gino settled back in his chair. A million dollars. It wasn't as if he had been saddled with cost. What? A hundred grand in expenses to pull it all off? Not too bad a return on his money. "Done," he said decisively and offered his hand.

Doherty took it and shook. Moran smiled.

"But if you're gonna throw in some whiskey, make it Bushmills. You know, the good stuff."

The Irishmen blanched.

"No," Doherty said. "I'm afraid that's a deal breaker. If you're wanting Bushmills, we're back to square one."

Testaverde was confused.

"Bushmills," said Doherty, straight-faced, "is a Unionist whiskey. It's Republican drink or we're walking away."

Saturday, June 4, 1989 – 12:12 p.m. EST
Pier 59 Marina, West 18th Street, Manhattan, NY

SALACIOUS II ARRIVED at the Pier 59 marina on Manhattan's West Side at eight o'clock in the morning. She cruised through the night to the entrance into New York harbor. Verrazano Narrows at the turn of the tide, and on into the Upper Bay and the Hudson River. Shipping details were discussed over an open-air breakfast on the stern, just as they were passing Liberty Island. Gino's guests had needed a moment to admire the view.

The shipment would leave the United States on July 8th, aboard the *MV Procyon* from Port Fourchon, Louisiana. The offshore supply vessel, which had been supporting oil platforms in the Gulf of Mexico, had been sold to an Irish buyer and was being readied for service in the North Sea. The container was to be delivered by flatbed truck to the High-Seas Logistics company wharf at Port Fourchon, in the Mississippi delta south of New Orleans. Its contents were to be labeled on waybills as drilling equipment, and it was to arrive at precisely 5:00 p.m. on Friday, July 7th, the day before sailing. No further details were discussed.

An hour after they had arrived in Manhattan, Jackie Moran and John Doe went ashore and left by taxi into the city. They returned at ten past noon, along with a battered van with the markings of a Midtown liquor store.

"What the fuck is this?" wondered Benny Dofasco aloud as the pair led its driver, manhandling a dolly, up the gangway and onto the yacht.

"Whiskey," replied Moran, crossing onto the stern. "Ten cases, as agreed. Where would you be wanting it stowed?"

"There. And watch the fuckin' woodwork!" Benny said to the kid who was hauling the first five cartons aboard.

John Doe had a sports bag in hand and said nothing as he carried on through into the main salon. He waited dutifully just inside for a signal from Kieran Doherty, who was lunching on crab with their host at the dining table.

"Your money," said Doherty.

"Bring it here," Testaverde replied, wiping his fingers and chin with a linen napkin, and indicating a spot on the table beside him. Doherty nodded and his comrade complied before silently leaving the cabin.

Testaverde picked at a strand of crabmeat in his teeth as he peered into the unzipped nylon bag. Bundles of cash, circulated fifties. The bulk seemed about right.

"A quarter million," Doherty said, sipping Budweiser from a bottle. "Count 'er up, if you like."

Gino smiled. "My line of work? No one ever fucks me," he said, cracking another crab leg. "Never had, *whatchacallit*, trust issues. Know what I mean?"

He signaled to Benny, who quickly removed the bag and disappeared down the spiral staircase into Gino's stateroom.

John Doe and Moran joined them at the table for cracked crab and beer. Paulie Cheeks and the trio of tittering girls had gone ashore early, not to return. It became clear the previous evening that his services would not be required—and theirs had been well employed through the night.

Details and commitments reaffirmed, the Irishmen left at 2:00 p.m. with undisclosed plans. The three would remain in Manhattan until Monday, taking a bite of the Big Apple before parting ways—Doherty and Moran on an Alitalia flight out of Newark to Rome, and their quiet comrade on a flight back to Boston.

TWO HOURS LATER, Sal Luongo arrived at Pier 59 as Benny Dofasco instructed that morning. So this was Gino's new toy. Fuckin' guy loves to splash it around. Shiny suits, fancy cars, and now this. Old school he is not. But he's always been a real earner, and in the rackets it excuses a lot.

Benny met him on the gangway with a hug and a kiss on the cheek. "Been too long, Sally! How's the hot dog business?"

"Keeps me in Mets season tickets and outta the slam," Sal replied. He had always liked Benny, the fat Neapolitan fuck. He got the nickel tour and was shown into the lavish main salon, where some little brown guy appeared out of nowhere, all freakin' smiles, and asked if he wished a refreshment. Wished a what? Oh. Hey, what the hell, he would have a beer. It promptly arrived on a silver tray in a frosted Pilsner glass with a napkin folded, Japanese origami-like, around it.

A couple of sips and Gino appeared, rising from a spiral stairwell in the corner, dressed for golf, complete with the plaid dress pants and pastel sweater.

"Sally! C'mere!" he roared, embracing his cousin. "Last time I seen you was Tia Paulina's funeral. You gotta come up the parkway more often. Sit! Sit! Aquilino, a sparkling water!"

They didn't spend long catching up.

"That navy job, Sal? We're in business," Gino began.

Luongo had figured as much.

"Go on, whaddya need?"

"I need you to do a road trip. Jersey down to a Gulf port just outta New Orleans. First week of July. You still got your air brake license?"

"Yeah. Why?" Sal's eyes narrowed. "How much are we talking about?"

"The whole fucking thing, cugino!"

At that they popped open wide.

"One buyer, Sally! They want it all, so I want you to haul it yourself. Rent one of those Penske rigs and a highboy. The load's gotta transport legit, with interstate papers for oilfield equipment. Benny's got all the details."

Luongo's mind was racing. Interstate transport of stolen government explosives. Minimum forty years federal time.

"So what's my end?" he asked.

Testaverde peered into his Perrier bottle.

"You and me, Sal? We're getting long in the tooth for the rackets. Know what I mean? Done any retirement planning? Money in mutual funds? Florida condos?"

Sal exhaled. No, not really. It's the downside of going pretty much straight: working to live, covering your bills, and pinning your retirement to a social security check.

"What's my end, Gino?" he persisted.

A strange and unsettling look had begun to spread across his cousin's face.

"We're blood and I love you. But you know that, doncha Sal?" Gino said, signaling to Benny with a sideways glance.

Dofasco rose and disappeared down the stairwell.

Sal checked around for a plastic sheet on the floor.

"This navy thing?" Testaverde continued. "One great friggin' score, and we wouldn't a got to square one without you. Taking care of the whole Jersey end? Thing a beauty. Seven months and still the feds have their thumb up their ass! All thanks to you. Anyways, I talked to Junior. You deserve a cut, not just a payday. Just do this last thing and wrap it all up nice and neat."

Benny reappeared with a blue Puma sports bag and sat next to Gino, stone faced.

"There's a hundred G's in that bag."

Luongo's eyes went even wider.

Gino smiled. "Another two hundred when you make the drop and the customer pays."

Sal was dumbfounded.

"Get the fuck outta here! Three hundred grand?"

He had figured fifty, tops.

"You deserve every penny, but this thing has to keep going smooth. I'm trusting you, Sally. No slip ups! I did this ... *We* did this one on spec and my neck's out a mile. Could bring down plenty of heat, this thing goes off the rails. Anything does and Junior has Paulie Cheeks can us for dog food—and you know he'd do it without thinking twice."

Chapter 27

Monday, June 12, 1989 – 10:48 a.m. EST
174 Hester Street, New York, NY

MARTIN GLANCED IMPATIENTLY at his watch. Nearly ten to eleven. He sighed and lit another cigarette on the butt of the first. He was standing in front of the Hester Street tenement where he had lived for a month; outside Rudy's Pizza and Restaurant, which occupied its narrow street level frontage. '*Hot and Cold Heroes*' the broad green awning announced. Martin sniffed. Truth in that, so there is.

He had been told to be out front at 10:30. It was the rest of the message that had left him a little unnerved. "You might want to ditch the blonde with the swallow tattoo on her throat. She went through your things when you were asleep." Thing is, he had only just met her the previous evening.

Late morning and the streets of Little Italy were starting to bustle with tourists. It had been thirty days since Martin had arrived in New York. Nikki had left him after just two. No rekindling of passions, merely a peck on the cheek, a stern warning to keep his nose clean, and adieu. You'd have sworn she had somebody else.

The Irishman had quickly become focused on great big embraceable New York City—enjoying himself with some dosh in his pockets, living his scripted life as an engineer between overseas contracts. His flat turned out to be less than he had hoped for, but it was comfortable and sufficient. Tripoli's had been grander, but this was Manhattan.

He walked its streets every day and could never go far without being enthralled, as he had been, finding himself at the foot of the World Trade Center towers, a mere ten minutes away. It was there, on his first day on his own, that he'd had a Guinness in '*The Greatest Bar on Earth*' on the 107th floor of its North Tower. Who'd have believed it back home in the hayfields of County Armagh.

Two weeks in the neighborhood and he had become pals with Johnny Maccio, the crowd puller at Puglia's, across the street from his building. Every day from noon until nine, Johnny would stand outside the iconic restaurant, dressed in a tuxedo, wooing potential patrons from the tourist tide sweeping by. He was a skinny kid, maybe twenty-two, a young Frank Sinatra, charming the crowds with old standards like 'Three Coins in the Fountain'.

Fast friends, Wops and Micks, with generally two things in common: the supremacy of the Roman Church, and of technically virginal Catholic girls. Okay, *three* things: their passion for both and for late boozy nights on the town. Young Maccio, he quickly discovered, had impressive credentials with the latter two. It was in fact the ever smooth Johnny who, on the previous night, introduced Martin to Shelley—the blonde showgirl whose tattoo was less an ornithological tribute than an advertised talent.

Martin had just lit his second cigarette when a van with darkened windows pulled up in front of Rudy's.

"Get in!" was all he heard as the side door slid open.

When he did, he was manhandled into the middle of a bench seat and a black canvas bag was slipped over his head. Well, isn't this shades of home! In Belfast, the next and likely the last thing he'd see would be an alley off Shankill Road. Martin relaxed. He knew he wouldn't be coming to harm.

The van came to a halt fifteen minutes later, after driving a circuitous route through Manhattan, stopping and starting and slowly descending a ramp. He was removed from the van with a guiding hand on each arm. Their footsteps echoed and there was a faint smell of damp. They entered an elevator. It went down. Now carpeting beneath his feet. A rush of air brought the scent of fresh paint. Air conditioning hummed. Doors opened and closed. Finally he was seated and the bag was removed.

Quinn found himself in a darkened room with large video screens on the wall above banks of blinking electronics. Two men were seated at consoles, backs to him, and two others took shape in the gloom.

"Morning, Martin."

He recognized the voice to his right. It was the man whom he'd come to know as Boxer. "Want a coffee?" he asked.

"No, ta," Martin replied. "I'm a little hung over."

The other he soon identified as the black guy who called himself Diver, who nodded hello before he leaned away to confer with the seated technicians.

Boxer sat down beside him.

"A bit of telly, this morning?" Martin asked brightly. "I'm hoping there's nothing that's starring yours truly, at least not last night in my flat."

"Wow!" he gasped, as the wall ahead suddenly brightened with two separate images, each six-foot-by-eight and clear. Elevated sound levels. A slight background hiss. Indistinct murmured voices, and the throb of a diesel engine?

It took a moment for the images to make sense. Two views aboard a yacht at sea at night. On the screen labeled "1" on the left: from the yacht looking aft, empty deck chairs around tables and its wake streaming silvery-white into blackness. Screen "2" on the right: a richly-appointed ship's lounge, well-lit and well furnished. There was a man in an armchair eating a sandwich. He had the look of somebody in charge.

Soon three figures appeared at the front of the cabin. They spoke for a moment; a fat bald guy poured drinks, and then they approached the seated man, looming larger and clearer on screen. The fat bald guy sits left. The other two settle in on a leather sofa, camera-right. The video image froze.

Martin was smiling.

"Do you know these men?" Coultart asked.

"I do, surely," he replied. "Derry boys, and I've known them for years."

"Continue."

"Ginger lad on the left, that's Kieran Doherty. Thug beside him is Jackie Moran. Both born and bred in the Bogside. Kieran's the bright one, their planner. Jackie? The security chief, or so we like to call it. His job is to investigate rumors and ferret out traitors. Dirty business. But the thing about Jackie, he's always found it good *craic*. Enjoys it a little too much for my liking."

"How do you mean?"

Martin studied Moran's stony face. It had been eight years since he'd seen him and it hadn't changed.

"Over here you might call him a serial killer. I reckon Jackie's dispatched more than two dozen people himself. Irishmen. Irishwomen. In the Cause, our tradition for traitors has been a merciful bullet. Not with Jackie Moran. With our Jackie, you're punished, and in some unholy terrible ways. Enjoys power tools, so he does."

The Americans winced.

For twenty minutes, Martin watched and listened as details of the explosives purchase unfolded. Nearly four tons of C4 plastic? What he could have done with even a quarter of that! And a million dollars? How the hell could two paupers from Derry come up with that kind of scratch? Fat prideful Yanks and their donation jars, he surmised.

New video rolled on Screen 1 on the left. Morning and breakfast enjoyed on the yacht's open air cockpit deck. The Statue of Liberty passed in the distance. Doherty and Moran stood and gawked with the same obvious awe that Martin had felt the first time he had seen it. Then it was breakfast again and their discussion of plans to ship from a seaport in Louisiana. Briefly a figure appeared on the screen to the left. A man moving from the starboard walkway and stepping inside through the doors to the main lounge.

"Hold up! Hold on there a minute!" Martin said, suddenly agitated. "Run that one back a tick!"

Screen 1 video stopped and slowly scrolled back, freezing on the face all Olympiad knew as John Doe.

"Jesus Christ!" Martin muttered.

He stood and looked at the face long and hard.

"It can't be. He's dead!"

"Do you recognize this man?" Coultart asked.

Martin stared, squinted and focused.

"Can you run it again?"

The video segment was repeated in slow motion: the right profile to a frontal view of the man's face, then freezing again.

Martin went pale.

"His name's Eddie Darragh. You'll not have heard of him, I'm guessing."

He paused, clearly in shock.

"Would you know the name Michael McGuigan?"

There was tapping on keyboards. A technician at the console held a low conversation through his headset mike. A moment later, Steve Smith turned in his seat. "London says Sir Michael McGuigan is one of the richest men in Northern Ireland. Owns a chain of breweries throughout Britain."

Martin nodded agreement.

"Seven years ago," he said, "February of '82, his teenage daughter was kidnapped from their vacation estate in the Algarve. A seaside villa near Tavira on Portugal's southern coast. McGuigan paid ten million pounds sterling to recover his daughter unharmed. All without the involvement of the local coppers. It was all down to Eddie Darragh. It was his undertaking."

"How would you know about that?"

"Because I was there and took part," Martin replied. "A few bombs for diversion when we snatched the girl from their chauffeured Bentley. In the end, it was the snapshot of a Semtex necklace around her wee neck that convinced the bugger to pay."

The room went silent.

"I wouldn't have hurt her! It was faked!"

Still, Coultart adopted a cooler demeanor.

"You said you thought he was dead."

Martin shook his head in dismay.

"Saw it with my own eyes! I was to make my way home on my own. Eddie and the three others sped off from McGuigan's dock. A mile out to sea and their speedboat exploded. Lost with the money and all hands aboard. The affair's the main reason I fell from grace back in Dublin. Getting taken in by a mate. None of it had ever been for the Cause, it was all just a criminal plot and one that went pear-shaped."

"So this Darragh's alive after all," said Coultart.

Martin studied the face on the screen. It was Eddie Darragh, sure enough. As lads back in Newry, they had been joined at the hip. And he'd mourned him sorely these past seven years. Crafty bastard! Now the whole bloody scheme had begun to make sense.

FOLLOWING THE VIDEO show, Martin was ushered into an adjoining conference room. It was narrow; three walls lined with shuttered whiteboards and one at the end with its shutters open. Facing it from the center of an elliptical conference table was a carousel slide projector. Next to that, an arrangement of items hidden under a cotton drop cloth. The table had seating for twelve. Martin was directed to a seat alone on one side. He sat facing Diver and Boxer and a third man who had joined them from the Ops Room, gangly with a mustache and shock of grey hair.

"So which one are you?" Martin asked the man glibly. "Dasher, Prancer or Vixen?"

Ray Morgan glowered. "My name's Ray," he said, with a tone that suggested the joking stopped here.

Coultart fixed on Quinn with an unblinking stare.

"I'm told you're enjoying the city," he said. "All settled in nicely? Not getting too bored?"

Martin smiled. "Settled in, aye. Bored, never, not me."

"It's time then we put you to work."

For the record, Coultart restated Martin's commitment to work with his hosts. Wasn't it *carte blanche* services that he had offered? Did this recent twist, the resurrection of Darragh, change his outlook at all?

"No. But for argument's sake, what if it did?"

"We'd reunite you with Jackie Moran."

Martin had no doubt they would.

"What's the craic, then? You've got my attention."

"Pull back that cloth and tell Ray what you see."

He did, uncovering an array of electronic components and hardware; some familiar, some not. Martin stood and studied it thoughtfully for a moment.

"Your handiwork, Ray?" he asked.

The dour man simply nodded.

On the table were a pair of grey component boxes. The first one, clearly the controller, had a telephone handset attached. The back panel was removed and wiring led to a plain cardboard carton the size of a pound of butter. The control unit was connected by a data cable to the second, smaller solid state device which, in turn, had a co-axial connection to a strange looking antenna—a folding flat panel an inch thick, opened and about four feet square. Lastly, a DC power supply that powered both was connected to a battery slightly smaller than automotive.

"If that's a radiophone, it's surely the strangest one I've ever seen," Martin observed rhetorically.

"I'm presuming you've disabled the ringer," he continued, running his fingers along the wires from the handset to the small cardboard box.

"Ah!" It was as he expected. The wires terminated in a standard electrical detonator, seated in the contents of what he guessed was modeling clay.

"I'd have done it just the same way."

Next he studied the power supply and attached battery.

"A deep cell battery? Low cranking amps, extended life. I don't know the brand. Marine use?"

Ray Morgan plucked at his mustache. Not bad.

"A golf cart," he replied.

Martin smirked. He studied the array for a moment, took a breath and began to detail what he'd learned.

"A neat set-place device," he began. "But with this high-priced gear, the actual charge would be bigger, I'm guessing. Interesting, the radiophone. Ring it up, Bob's your uncle. But with that antenna? If that's UHF, there won't be much range from your trigger device. Still, I like what you've done with your power source. Not much amperage drain from a phone switched to standby. A deep cell battery. Fully charged, you'd be getting, what? Two weeks of life?"

"Closer to three," Ray replied.

Martin sat and smiled. "So have I passed my A levels?"

Morgan picked up the remote for the projector. It whirred to life and shone a bright blank square against the far wall.

"Not quite," he said. "But that's not your fault."

He clicked the remote and a brightly-colored slide was projected—a Mercator map of the world, overlaid with a peeled orange representation of satellite signal coverage.

It took a moment for that to sink in.

Martin's smile faded. He studied the components again.

"That's no radiophone, is it?"

"No. Satellite. Trigger range is worldwide."

Martin's eyes widened.

"You'll be rigging that shipment to blow!"

Coultart beamed.

"Nearly full marks," he said smugly.

"We're not going to be rigging that shipment. *You* are."

Chapter 28

Wednesday, July 5, 1989 — 6:23 a.m. EST
Hudson Iron & Scrap, 155 East 7th St., Paterson, NJ

"THEY JUST FINISHED loading up the container," reported Gerry Bell from a grimy line of poplars across the tracks from the scrap yard's back gate. He swatted at a cloud of bluebottle flies that had annoyed him since taking up station at a quarter-to-six. East fucking Jersey. Must be a body dumped somewhere nearby.

"Copy," Maggie acknowledged from her cover position a block to the north.

"Still have eyes on the subject?" crackled Kevin Ahearn in his earpiece.

"Negative," Bell replied. "He's under the trailer. Probably checking the air. Now the crane is moving away. Okay, there he is. He's with the bug-eyed toad from the office. Toad has the paperwork. Subject is looking it over. He's nodding. 'Thanks for the fake manifest, Thyroid Tony!' *Fuggetaboutit!*"

"Cut the shit, Tinker," said Ahearn. "How are we looking for notice to move?"

Bell adjusted the focus on his binoculars. Luongo and the Toad were standing in front of the rented Penske semi, a bright yellow cab-over Freightliner with no sleeper.

"Close," he replied. "Subject's climbing into the cab. Truck's fired up. He's got air. A little wave to his wiseguy buddies. Gates coming open. We've got forward motion."

"10-4," Ahearn answered. "Maggie, watch for the gates to close behind him. If they don't? Take it slow going by. But we want to hit him on Wait before River."

"Copy. What's your 20?"

"In position at Putnam and River, under the rail overpass." She acknowledged.

As they briefed before sunrise, if he kept to River Street, he would be making for the westbound I-80 and the slow road south through the Appalachians. Should he veer onto Straight Street at Putnam—signed as Passaic County 647—then it's eastbound to the I-95, the coast road through the Carolinas. Two weeks of surveillance and Luongo had scouted both of these routes out of central New Jersey. Either way, with the set up today they were covered.

"Big yellow truck coming out. Turning south, and they're closing the gates," Bell reported.

A block north, Maggie punched the gas on the unit's stock Chev Caprice. It fishtailed away from the gravel shoulder of the industrial Jersey backstreet. She closed quickly on the ass end of the trailer, with its blue Hanjin Lines container riding high. A stop sign at Putnam was one block ahead. She swerved across the double line, passing the rig and careening back in before braking hard. There was a blast from the Freightliner's air horn and she watched the truck shake and shudder behind her.

"What the fuck is this!" spat Sal Luongo, locking up all eighteen wheels. His heart thumped in his chest. He glared from the cab at the redheaded bitch who had just cut him off. A black four-door Caprice. Shit! A police interceptor? Now some dude getting out on the passenger side? Feds! He was done. He was *freakin'* done.

Sal frantically checked his mirrors, expecting a swarm of Caprices and big ass Crown Vics closing in from all sides. Nothing. Just this fuckin' guy with a backpack walking toward him from the redhead's car.

Martin Quinn clambered up the right side of the cab and opened the door.

"Mornin' Sal!" he said brightly, climbing right in. "How the hell are ya?" Luongo was stunned, staring back at him slack-jawed.

"Mind the road, Sally boy," said the stranger, gesturing ahead to the Caprice, which was accelerating away. A delivery van behind them was impatiently honking its horn.

Sal put the Freightliner into gear and chugged through the intersection, slowly picking up speed. His pulse pounded. How many times had he hijacked dumb bastards exactly like this? Although this guy hadn't shoved a gun in his face.

"Who the hell are you?" he demanded, giving the man an anxious glance as he double clutched into third.

"I'd be your swamper, boy-o!" Martin replied, smiling as he settled in. "You didn't think you'd be making this wee trip alone? That's our million dollars you're hauling behind us."

Sal's composure returned and his heart rate began to settle as the rig picked up speed, keeping to the right along River Street. The westbound I-80, the inland route.

"Nobody told me!" he protested.

"Nor did we tell Cousin Gino," Martin countered, as scripted. "Or his man Benny. A secretive lot, so we are."

Sal fumed. Fourteen hundred miles; three days ahead that were scary enough. And now this? He concentrated on remembering how to drive a tractor trailer.

The Freightliner lumbered along narrow River Street, through a shadow-dappled canyon of warehouses, overgrown vacant lots and the darkened storefronts of a tired city that was still mostly asleep. Traffic was starting to build, mainly commercial at this early hour, as horizontal rays of blinding sunlight and sapphire blue overhead held out the promise of a fine summer day.

One block behind, Ahearn with Kenneally at the wheel kept pace in a gutless Reliant K family sedan. Four door, silver-blue. Maggie had circled back to collect Tinker, caught up quickly, and fell into position two blocks in trail. Together they wove their way in a conga line around the city core, following an oxbow of the listless Passaic River toward the elevated freeway that filled the horizon.

Luongo deftly maneuvered the rig through one tight turn after another, finally mounting the Grant Street on ramp to the westbound I-80. Merging continually left, he settled into the right-hand truck lane of the broad interstate, cruising toward Parsippany.

"Fair motoring skills you're displaying for a hot dog vendor," the stranger said, agreeably.

Sal bristled. "Oh right!" he groused. "You know everything about me. Bet you didn't know *this!*"

With one hand, he drew a soft pack of Marlboros from a breast pocket, tapped up a single cigarette and plucked it out with his lips—then, with a book of matches from the same pocket, he curled one to the striker and snapped his fingers to produce a flame. Sal inhaled and coughed lightly, pointing to the large *No Smoking* roundel on the dashboard.

"Yeah! That's right! A no smoking rental. Big deposit for that. And guess what? I'm a rebel, I don't friggin' care!"

Martin chuckled. It grew into a laugh. He accepted a cigarette and the pair began smoking like fiends, even though Sal had been off tobacco for years.

"What should I call *you?*" Sal asked, keenly watching the signs for the I-287 exit to Morristown.

"Well, as we're getting so friendly, the name's Martin. My mother, bless her, called me after the saint. It's our way, isn't it, Salvatore?"

Sal nodded slowly and actually smiled.

They drove on.

Since they hit the freeway, Martin had been glancing from one mirror to the elaborate other, with an eye out for Boxer, his shadow. He soon realized that every other car on the interstate was a boxy sedan, silver blue or blue gray. Sneaky fuckers. He promptly quit looking.

"Okay, I gotta know," Sal asked naively as they rolled along, "Are you real IRA? I mean, from over there? Not just some wannabe out of Boston?"

Martin grinned. "Are you real Mafiosi? A gangster? Cross you and I sleep with the fishes?"

Sal chuckled. *Touché.*

"Yeah, Sally, I am. A dyed in the wool IRA volunteer. And I'll tell you, mate, if I'd had half the plastic we're hauling? We'd have had the Brits to the peace table ten years ago now."

That was that. Sal was intrigued by the Irishman who'd hijacked him so boldly. He enjoyed his company.

They soon left I-80 onto I-287, taking them through Morristown into Pennsylvania and their first weigh scale station. No problems, and at noon it was I-78 through the verdant Appalachians, on to the I-81 across West Virginia. By the end of the day, they'd been driving for nine hours straight, five hundred and fifty miles, stopping for the night at a truck stop motel near Wytheville, Virginia.

Martin found the day's travels exhilarating, a road trip through an America he had never begun to imagine. Ahearn and Kenneally were never more than a half mile ahead, with Maggie and Tinker behind them, their subjects not once out of sight the whole way.

Friday, July 7, 1989 – 1:02 a.m. CST
Roadside Inn, 4320 Skyland Blvd E., Tuscaloosa, AL

AFTER FIVE YEARS in the Libyan desert, Martin Quinn thought he knew about heat. Once down in Bani Waled, well away from the moderating influence of the Mediterranean, he saw the mercury rise past 130 degrees Fahrenheit. It was a dry heat, as if that cliché made it sufferable. But he had never been to Alabama, let alone in July. One o'clock in the morning and the thermometer outside the office at the Roadside Inn had its pointer pegged at 90 degrees. That day, according to the local television news, Tuscaloosa had set a record of 114 degrees. OOO-WEEE! the weathercaster had chirped, it had indeed been a hot one! Wet heat, Martin now understood, was unspeakably worse than dry.

He swabbed rivers of sweat from his eyes with the sleeve of his t-shirt, gasping to breathe in the close humid air. Outdoors it might have been 90, but inside the container the heat of the day had remained amplified and likely closer to a stifling 120. It's a good thing C4 plastic explosive is stable. Soldiers sometimes even burn it for kindling and the fact is, without a concussive detonation, the explosive itself is nearly as inert as clay. Which, of course, Martin knew. And kept reminding himself.

The Roadside Inn was an aging two-story cinderblock motel off I-59 just south of the city of Tuscaloosa. It was favored by truckers for its easy service road access and acres of parking, set up with lanes reserved for tractor trailers. There could have been no better choice for this phase of the Long Jump operation. Luongo had parked his rig in the farthest, darkest part of the lot—a naïve nod to his dangerous cargo—although it was the cluster of gasoline and propane tankers parked around it that, in themselves, made the parking lot a blast hazard.

Boxer had knocked at the door to Martin's motel room at midnight-thirty. He brought the device in a red nylon kit bag: the satellite phone assembly, its folding flat panel antenna, and the fully-charged deep cell battery—all connected, tested and ready for installation. Across the service road from the motel, Maggie and Tinker were in the Caprice with eyes on Luongo's room, observing through night vision goggles. There had been pizza and television with Quinn until about ten. Lights out at 10:30 p.m. Some residual light from the TV for maybe ten minutes more, and no movement at all ever since.

Access to the container had been simple enough. Its lock had been dealt with the previous night. Tinker had done a reconnaissance during a lunch stop in Virginia: three lock positions on the swing-arm locking bar for its double doors. Only one lock was fitted, an American Master Series 7300, stainless steel, a big sucker that no tool could easily cut. By the day's end in Wytheville, Martin received a replacement.

And that evening, when he'd asked to inspect the cargo, he swapped it and the keys on the ring that Sal handed over. Simple as that.

Inside the container were three hundred wooden crates of C4 plastic explosives, stacked fifteen deep, five across, wall to wall, and four high—leaving four feet of free floor-space inside the doors, and the same in headroom along its forty-foot length. Martin was to crawl two-thirds of the way along the top of the stack, open a crate and remove enough of the C4 to make room for the device and the battery. Then he was to do what he did best: assemble and arm a viable bomb.

Easier said than done in the darkness and unbearable heat. To avoid attracting attention, Boxer had quietly closed the container door behind him, and all Martin had inside for light was a strap on caver's headlamp.

He inched along on the top of the crates on his hands and knees, shoving aside empty pallets that had been thrown up on top, and picking up splinters from rough-hewn pine. Every few feet he'd drag forward the kit bag beside him.

About thirty feet in, Martin stopped and strained to catch his breath. Sweat dropped like rain on the crate at his elbow, and he decided this would be the one. He quickly opened the lid with the small crowbar he'd hauled with his gear. Inside were the cylindrical tops of fifty half-pound sticks of plastic explosive, wrapped tightly in brown waxed paper. He removed twenty and set them aside.

First to be installed was the battery, half the size of automotive though it seemed twice as heavy. He used a wrench to ensure its post connections were cinched tight, lest motion at sea jar them loose. Next, he placed the stripped satellite phone unit into the crate, breaking open a few sticks of C4 for use as putty to secure it snugly in place. Same treatment for the battery leads and the wiring to the electrical detonator, which he inserted into a stick in the middle of the remaining lot. More C4 as putty to tidy things up. Confirm power to the telephone unit in standby mode, replace the lid, then lay out the antenna array on top of the crates, hiding that from view with one of the pallets. Done. Elapsed time: thirty-five minutes.

Martin loaded the remaining dozen sticks of C4 into the bag with the tools, cleared up pieces of wrapper and took a look back as he made his way out. Perfect. Nothing looked out of place. No hint he had ever been there.

Boxer felt a rush of hot air like he'd opened an oven when he answered the Irishman's knock from inside.

"Jesus, man!" he whispered as Martin emerged. "You look like you've been swimming."

Quinn shivered in the night's gentle breeze. After what he'd endured, even 90 degrees was a relief. With the container secured, the pair jumped down from the trailer and made their way quietly to the motel. In the room, he draped himself in cold wet towels and gulped room temperature beer. He noticed the surprised look on Boxer's face.

"Bedouin wisdom," he explained. "The colder the drink when you're overheated, the quicker it's straight out your arse. Cramps and all. It's all about balance." Made sense.

Boxer sat on the opposite bed and debriefed him on setting the bomb. Most importantly, was the antenna laid out on top, flat and facing skyward? It was.

"Then we're in business," he said. "I will call you just north of New Orleans. Convince him that there's been a change of plan, and that no one's to know that you tagged along. Keep it simple. Then pick a drop spot once we're into the city, an exit that won't hold him up. One of us will be tailing and we'll collect you. Any questions?"

Martin had none. Now he was ready for a cold beer.

"Get some sleep," Boxer said as he was leaving. "And don't suck back too many of those."

Martin toweled off at the room's dressing table, and was surprised when he noticed that Boxer's kit bag was just where he left it beside the door.

Chapter 29

Friday, July 7, 1989 – 1:29 p.m. CST
Interstate 10 Causeway, Lake Pontchartrain, LA

"SO, YOU'RE SAYING the whole bloody thing is infested with alligators?" asked Martin skeptically, marveling at the expanse of Lake Pontchartrain, a silver sea spreading away to the western horizon.

"Not the whole lake itself, I suppose," Sal replied, guiding the Freightliner southward down the Interstate 10 causeway, twenty miles north of New Orleans.

"I got a cousin, Paulie, who's lived down here for years," he said, as the rig bounced rhythmically along the tar-beaded blond concrete highway.

The Irishman smirked. "Another cousin."

"Hey, I got *dozens* of cousins! Anyway, New Orleans Paulie got outta the rackets and became *whatchacallit*, a blue ribbon chef. Five star? No! A chef de cuisine. Has his own restaurant in the French Quarter. A highbrow kind a place. And their big ticket item? *Alligator.* Alligator gumbo. Alligator steak. Deep fried alligator. Says they got more gators down this way than Brooklyn's got rats."

Martin laughed. "You nearly had me thinking I'd try it."

He felt great. It was a beautiful day, if not a bit hot for his liking. They left Tuscaloosa at seven that morning, winding their way down I-59 through Meridian and Hattiesburg, Mississippi, crossing into Louisiana south of Picayune. Three hundred more miles of scenic splendor that Quinn found astounding.

The I-10 causeway seemed endless, a four-lane ribbon of concrete that appeared to be floating on water. The sky was a bright robin's egg blue with a line of billowing white thunderheads scudding eastward in the distance. What might have been a drift log on the lake's silver surface got their attention as the truck rumbled past.

"Think that was a gator?" Martin asked excitedly, craning to look back for a fleeting glimpse.

"I think it was!" chirped Luongo. "I saw friggin' teeth!"

The causeway came to an end and the truck lumbered onto a broad divided highway, running through a prairie-like expanse of delta lowland, dotted with thickets of stunted trees. If New Orleans was somewhere in the distance, you couldn't see it.

A telephone rang. Its ringer was muffled.

Martin fumbled through the overstuffed backpack that lay at his feet. He pulled out a clunky Motorola cellular phone and punched at its buttons.

Sal glanced over, surprised. Friggin' cellular phones. It was strange Martin had one and hadn't flaunted the fact. More for ego than communication. Pretentious yuppies strutting around with those chunks to their ears. Holding loud street corner conversations. Never: "Yes, honey! I'll bring home some milk." Always self-important bullshit: "Tell the mayor that I won't do the deal!" "Wake my people in Paris!" or "Buy!" "Sell!" or "Merge!"

The Irishman said hello and listened.

"That's bloody ridiculous!" he muttered.

Then: "Right you are. If you think it's best."

And: "Aye. Yes, of course I will tell him."

Closing with: "I'll stop in New Orleans and take in the sights. All right, then, cheerio, bye."

He pressed a button and returned the phone to his bag.

Neither man said a word for a moment.

Martin seemed incensed.

"You got one of those mobile phones," Sal said.

"Ball and chain, so they are. Technology's shit. You can never get a damned signal when you need one, but the last place you want one? It comes through five square."

"Bad news?" asked Luongo.

"A wee change in the plan," Martin said. "The ship that we're meeting? We can't confirm the loyalty of all of its crew. I can't risk showing my face, so we'll need to part ways in New Orleans."

Sal looked stricken. "Do I have a problem?"

"No," Quinn assured him. "The problem is me. The Brits have a price on my head, dead or alive, and dead is always the preference. This face is well known, and in our mob there's plenty a rascals who'd do me like that for the prize."

"But the deal's still on, right?" Sal persisted.

"Yes, for fucksakes, but no one can know I was riding along. These boys aren't fond of surprises. You made this trip alone. Just come and go clean, Sally boy, you'll be fine."

Fifteen minutes later, Sal eased the Freightliner off the I-10 service road at Bullard Avenue in north New Orleans and pulled into a busy Chevron truck stop. They stepped down from the cab and shook hands. Best of luck was offered both ways, with the hope that someday they might meet again. It was unlikely, but hoped all the same. Sal and the rig quickly disappeared back onto the highway, with Port Fourchon still more than two hours away at the southernmost tip of the Mississippi delta.

Martin had barely shouldered his backpack when a new Ford F250 crew cab pickup pulled up nearby. Boxer. He beckoned to him to come over and the driver's window whirred down.

"All good?" Boxer asked.

"Aye, Sal's on board and no wiser," Martin replied. "I expected Red and that wanker she rides with. Change of wheels, so I see. What's the craic?"

"Diver's giving you a break. The concession you wanted."

Quinn beamed.

"Five days. That's it. And next Thursday morning you're back in Manhattan, back on the choke chain again."

"That's brilliant!" Martin said happily. "Five days, aye. You can trust me on that."

"Don't fuck up, Martin!" the American warned. "I mean it. No second chances. By the way, you still have my kit bag."

Martin's smile melted. He unzipped his backpack and produced it, complete with caver's lamp, crowbar and tools. He handed the bag through the window.

"Sentimental value?"

"Something like that," Boxer said. "Now, go on. And don't make me come after you. That would be a mistake."

The Irishman tapped a knuckle to his brow in salute and was beaming again.

❧

Friday, July 7, 1989 – 4:58 p.m. CST
352 A. J. Estay Road, Port Fourchon, LA

THE WHITE FORD pickup came to a stop in the parking lot of Halliburton Services on A. J. Estay Road, at the south end of Port Fourchon. It had come down from New Orleans, winding along State Highway 1 through the featureless delta of the Mississippi to this place where the river meets the Gulf of Mexico.

Port Fourchon proved to be as dreary and confusing as the delta itself. A dredged network of deepwater docks spreading like cul-de-sacs from a single channel that led to the sea. This, amid a tangle of bayou waterways, overlaid on reclaimed land by its roads and structures. Winding dusty avenues lined with wire-fenced compounds, tank farms, and low metal buildings housing oilpatch and marine industries. Here and there were rows of prefab dormitories for offshore oil workers, along with the barest of amenities: long-term parking, gas stations and the odd cocktail bar. Port Fourchon had a frontier feel.

Ahearn and Kenneally had followed the Freightliner to its destination, 352 A. J. Estay Road, a fenced compound signed: High Seas Logistics, Inc. It had a small metal-clad office in a yard dotted with warehouses and stacks of drilling pipe. Fifty yards down its entrance road was a pole barrier which its minder, who waddled out of the office, lifted after checking Sal Luongo's paperwork.

They watched the transport continue another hundred yards before turning alongside an orange-hulled ship with a beige upper structure, port-side-to at the dock.

"MV Procyon. Aberdeen, Scotland," radioed Maggie. She and Tinker were observing a quarter of a mile further ahead to the west, with a view of the ship from the stern.

Ahearn simply nodded. He didn't acknowledge.

"Odd looking ship, don't you think, boss?" she continued. "Looks like a big old flatbed truck."

She was right. It did.

Procyon was an offshore supply vessel, an OSV, a rugged class of ocean going workhorse designed to support offshore drilling platforms. She was named for the brightest star in the constellation *Canus Minor*. The 1,000-ton ship had three story accommodations forward, leaving two-thirds of its 190 foot length as an open cargo deck. It had a range of 15,000 miles at a speed of twelve knots, and a crew of seven: the master, two watch officers, two engineers for its diesel engines, and two deck hands, one being a cook. Built in Lauzon, Quebec in 1973, she had spent fifteen years in the Gulf of Mexico before being bought by an Irish consortium out of Cork, for service in the North Sea oil patch. This would be her first voyage under new ownership and with her Irish crew.

"You're not going to believe what they've got on deck," squawked Tinker. "Two, four ... *a* half dozen cargo Zodiacs, twin-outboards, all battened down. And what looks like a wartime landing craft."

"10-4," acknowledged Ahearn.

Smart. Less risk of a transfer at sea going wrong if you can land all your cargo yourself.

The mast of a one hundred-foot heavy lift crane got their attention as it began to move along the dock. It crawled steadily toward the High Seas compound and MV Procyon.

Cameras whirred from the pickup and the Caprice down the road. It was in place at exactly ten after five.

Men scrambled onto the Hanjin container and connected leads from the crane's hook to its corners. Then in one easy lift it was hoisted aboard. Sal was seen shaking hands with a crewman before driving away from the dock. The rig and trailer rumbled back toward the street, stopping briefly as the guard raised the barrier and gave Sal a friendly wave. Seconds later it disappeared down A. J. Estay Road, back through Port Fourchon the way that it came.

Three hours later, Ahearn and Kenneally were at the Delta Airlines counter at New Orleans airport with tickets to La Guardia on a flight that would land after midnight. Maggie and Tinker continued on, planning to overnight in Picayune, where the truck had been rented, before setting out on the long drive home with both cars.

Martin completed a chore before making his way into the heart of the city. A cab had whisked him to a strip mall UPS outlet where he prepared a package addressed to himself in New York. Eight pounds, packed tightly in complimentary Styrofoam popcorn. Ground transport would be fine, he told the clerk. It would arrive in five business days.

It was nearly 9:30 p.m. when he left the hotel on Saint Louis Street in the French Quarter. The concierge had been helpful: two blocks up to Bourbon Street, turn right, five blocks to Dumaine, turn left, and it will be half way down the street on the right. And, yes, it would be worth his while.

The bistro was bigger than its entrance suggested, but crowded, with a Zydeco band just starting its set as Martin arrived. He was shown to a small table near the bar and was about to order dinner when a familiar voice interrupted the server: "Set another place, sweetheart, and tell the chef he's got two special guests who are both having gator!"

Sonofabitch. It was Sal.

Chapter 30

Thursday, July 13, 1989 – 3:56 p.m. EST
201 Varick Street, New York, NY

"JESUS!" LINCOLN COULTART was startled to see his own face become a six-by-eight foot image on the Ops Room wall. He fiddled with the joystick on the controller that Steve Smith had placed on the desk. The image drew back to show him seated with Charlie Watt at his side. In shadows behind them sat Ahearn, Kenneally and Morgan. The Long Jump team leaders, as London had requested.

At 4:00 p.m., their image flickered and was replaced by a similar view of three men in a darkened room across the Atlantic. Two were familiar to Coultart and Watt—the professorial Jamie Mayhew in the middle, and Sir Michael McPhail on the right of the screen. The third man, well-groomed and a boyish forty, was unknown to them all.

"Good evening from London," Mayhew began, facing the New York team with a camera and screens in the same configuration. Greetings were exchanged.

Mayhew continued, "With us is Geoffrey Dalgliesh. He is our operations officer, formerly Royal Navy. Geoff put this briefing together, so without further ado, I'll turn things over to him."

"Thank you, sir," Dalgliesh said. He tapped on a keyboard and the second screen came to life in New York. It displayed a navy blue slide with 'Operation Long Jump' centered in bold white letters above a smaller one-line security caveat: 'Top Secret – Olympiad Eyes Only'.

Next appeared an aerial close quarters picture of MV Procyon at sea, taken from its recent listing for sale. Dalgliesh briefly reviewed the ship's history and characteristics as images from the Port Fourchon surveillance were shown.

A Mercator projection map of the Atlantic north of the equator then appeared on the screen. Highlighted locations were Port Fourchon and Aberdeen, Scotland. Dalgliesh tapped his keyboard and a track appeared as a yellow line overlaid on the map. It showed a sailing route out of the Gulf of Mexico, up the eastern seaboard of the United States, crossing the Atlantic south of Nova Scotia on a track to the north coast of Ireland. It then continued north around Scotland and down to the port of Aberdeen.

"This track represents an economical passage for a ship like Procyon, transiting the Atlantic to her new home," Dalgliesh said. Details on the screen indicated a distance of 5002 nautical miles, representing a voyage of seventeen days, nine hours at an average speed of twelve knots.

"Procyon departed Port Fourchon at 0700 hours local time on Saturday, 8 July," he continued. "1200 hours Zulu. As of 1800 hours Zulu today, two hours ago, her progress over the past five days should have placed her about *here* ..."

A quarter of the yellow track's length turned green.

"Roughly abeam Richmond, Virginia, in a northbound traffic lane, eighty to a hundred nautical miles offshore. Fortunately, we have an intelligence source in the Aberdeen office of her owner's agent. Procyon is reporting her progress four times daily by radio teletype, and her latest position report puts her *here* ..."

The green track drew back to a point in the Bahamas Channel off the Florida coast, turning dramatically eastward into the Atlantic to a new position just south of Bermuda.

"Interesting," said Coultart. "What do you make of that?"

"Well, it was a bit of a puzzler when we first noticed her change in course," Mayhew said. "Until last night."

The display changed to a photograph of a cargo ship alongside a dock. It was a black-hulled freighter with white upper structures and towering yellow deck cranes.

"This is the MV Arroban Prince," Dalgliesh continued. "An eighteen thousand ton general cargo freighter under the

Liberian flag. Her owners are a syndicate out of Beirut. She has a somewhat checkered history. Hauling arms to Angola, Nigeria, running the South African embargo and the like."

A series of images showed the vessel loading cargo.

"These were taken three days ago in Benghazi, Libya," he said. "For two months, Bonn has been running an operation in the Middle East, following a West German-based Palestinian group with plans to acquire *these* ..."

A close-up photograph of cargo on the dock showed wooden crates with markings in Arabic, as well as Russian Cyrillic. Lincoln Coultart's jaw tightened. He knew neither language, but the letters stenciled in Russian told him all he needed to know.

"Strela-3s," he said grimly.

"That's quite right," said Mayhew. "The Strela-3, second-generation Russian MANPADS. Man-portable air defense systems. NATO designation, the SA-14 Gremlin. Similar to our Blowpipe and your Stinger missiles. Introduced in the mid-seventies. Superseded in operational use by newer technology, but still very deadly."

Both Ops Rooms fell silent for a moment.

Dalgliesh said an estimated sixty Strela-3s had been loaded aboard Arroban Prince in Benghazi. Bonn had learned that they were surplus Angolan arms, part of a shipment the Libyans were returning to Cuba.

The North Atlantic map returned to the screen. Now a red track extended from Benghazi, west through the Straits of Gibraltar, past the Azores into the Atlantic, ending in Havana.

"Arroban Prince left Benghazi yesterday morning," he said. The red track retreated from Havana to a point marked X, just south of the Azores Islands. "At standard speed, she should arrive at *this* point at around 2100 hours on 20 July. Next Thursday evening."

The green track, which had ended just south of Bermuda, now inched across the screen on an unaltered heading, intercepting the red track at point X.

"As will Procyon, projecting her current course and speed. Both ships arriving at the same point, on the same day, almost to the hour," Dalgliesh said.

"Quite a coincidence," remarked Coultart.

"We thought so," Mayhew replied. "This next bit, as you Americans say, really clinches the deal. Bonn's people took these prior to her leaving Benghazi."

The first images were of figures on the dock, mounting the gangway, standing on deck. A single frame appeared in close-up, a head and shoulders shot of two men in civilian clothing with a ship's officer.

"Oh shit!" muttered Kevin Ahearn in New York.

"Exactly," Mayhew said. "Our friends, Messrs Doherty and Moran. Gentlemen, I believe we have some late nights ahead."

Thursday, July 20, 1989 – 9:05 p.m. GMT
Atlantic Ocean, 65 NM south of Ilha das Flores, the Azores

"WELL, PILOT, DO you reckon our villains had planned for this weather?" asked Commander Tony Boyle, Royal Navy, of his navigator. The two men stood hunched over a tiny chart table in the control room of *HMS Saracen*, a British Swiftsure-class nuclear fast attack submarine.

"Not likely, sir," the young lieutenant replied. He tapped a finger on the bold "H" on the surface weather plot he had just pulled from the signal room fax.

"This high hadn't figured at all in the long-range forecast," he continued. "It's pushed rapidly east, now centered three hundred miles north of our present position. It's drawing northward this tropical low, spinning off from Cape Verde. Hurricane season now, and that low is deepening fast."

Lieutenant Bevan Deverell scratched at his sparse blond beard. At twenty-nine, the young Cornishman had been a naval officer for ten years; five now in submarines, and one year in Saracen's ships company. This was his first cruise as

Bugsy Boyle's "pilot", the Royal Navy's traditional title for a warship's navigator, the all-seeing, all-knowing vizier of things celestial and temporal. It was an onerous mantle that still made him nervous.

At nine o'clock, he had taken a quick surface observation with Saracen at periscope depth. There was already a stratus overcast, growing steadily thicker and lower. Sea State 4, a moderate sea with six-foot waves on a long swell running from the northeast. Winds were a strong breeze from the north at twenty-five knots. This would freshen to gale force with rain squalls and twenty-foot seas by midnight. Dirty weather. If I were planning a cargo transfer tonight, Deverell ventured, I'd not want to dawdle.

"What time is sunset?" asked Boyle.

"2113 hours," the Pilot replied promptly. "Seven minutes from now. We have twenty minutes of twilight at these latitudes. Less tonight. There's no moon and that stratus layer is growing opaque."

"Right!" Boyle said cheerily. "Time we earned our keep."

HMS SARACEN HAD received its emergency tasking order from the Admiralty four days earlier. She had been exercising with the U.S. Sixth Fleet off Corsica in the Mediterranean when Boyle had received his encrypted instructions. Saracen was to detach from exercise duties to intercept and shadow the MV Arroban Prince, a freighter out of Benghazi, making its way through the Med for the open Atlantic and Cuba. Intelligence indicated that she would rendezvous on the evening of 20 July, just south of the Azores, with an OSV, the MV Procyon, out of Louisiana.

It was believed Arroban Prince intended to transfer cargo to Procyon, including Strela-3 missiles destined for Ulster and the IRA. Saracen was to covertly observe the rendezvous and any such transfer, and transmit real time imagery by satellite uplink to CINCFLEET Operations, Northwood. She would await further orders, depending on the "dynamics of the situation". It was this bit that made the Falklands veteran uneasy. The last time CINCFLEET Ops had its fingers *this* deep in the pie, his own had sent two Mark 8 torpedoes into the Argentine cruiser General Belgrano. It sank with the loss of 323 lives. But that had been a shooting war.

The beefy forty-six year old Captain moved to the conning position between the attack and search periscopes. Boyle squeezed past his Officer of the Watch, who had the conn, and picked up the broadcast system microphone.

"All positions, Captain, mission briefing," he said.

"It is coming on 2109 hours, just shy of nautical sunset on top. Skunk 31, the Arroban Prince, is twelve hundred yards off our starboard quarter, hove to with her engines rung off. Skunk 32, as you know, was identified on our last run as the OSV MV Procyon. She is presently maneuvering into the lee of the freighter's port side. We believe the two will shortly begin a transfer of illegal arms destined for Ulster. Saracen will position to observe undetected and transmit imagery in real time to Northwood."

"Starboard fifteen!" called the OOW, making a course adjustment. "Midships, steer one-eight-zero."

"Steady on course one-eight-zero," replied the helmsman.

"Very good."

The Captain continued. He intended to maneuver to a loitering station two *cables*, twelve hundred yards, off the port beam of Arroban Prince. This would put Saracen against the darkening eastern sky, reducing the chances of her periscope and surveillance masts becoming visible in silhouette. Her sound signature wasn't at issue, but he would call for quiet on station. Saracen would effectively hover in a mile-long box parallel to the Arroban Prince, dead slow, conducting teardrop turns to remain in the box. Her computerized imaging suite, infrared and low light television, would lock-on target independently of maneuvering. Lastly, in the event of an emergency or discovery, she would bail out on a heading of 180 degrees at full ahead, make their depth five hundred feet, and open their distance to five nautical miles before evaluating the situation. He was in command. Lieutenant Waring, the OOW, had the conn. Pilot, as attack coordinator, would supervise the surveillance suite. Any questions? There were none.

"Very good," he said. "Mister Waring, get me on a station."

"Aye, sir. Port thirty! Make my depth forty-five feet."

"Port thirty, aye!" replied the helmsman.

"Ten degrees up on the bow planes!" barked the boat's quartermaster.

"Up ten degrees, aye!" the planesman replied.

"Very good," said the OOW. "Midships, steer zero-three-five. Slow ahead, revolutions two-zero."

"Rudder's amidships, steering zero-three-five, revolutions two-zero rung on, sir."

"Very good."

❧

Thursday, July 20, 1989 – 9:18 p.m. GMT
Royal Navy CINCFLEET Operations, Northwood, England

AS LONDON'S NUMBER two policeman, Michael McPhail joined the Met right out of university at Cambridge. He had never served in the military let alone the Royal Navy. Mayhew hadn't always been a spook. He had served in the territorial reserves as an army intelligence officer, and deployed once overseas during the Suez Crisis of 1956. Hardly military service at all. His only experience with the navy was its wardroom cocktail party circuit. Fortunately, Commander Geoff Dalgliesh had enough for all three, as they'd been abandoned on the hangar-like floor of the Royal Navy's CINCFLEET operations center at Northwood.

Called simply "Fleet Ops", the facility had the look and feel of a NORAD command center. Three giant screens, each the size of barn wall, presented a numbing array of video and satellite images, providing a real time overview of worldwide Royal Navy operations. Before them were a dozen rows of computer workstations occupied by officers and enlisted ratings, each monitoring their "part ship" in Royal Navy-speak. From NATO anti-submarine patrols in the arctic, to spotting and tracking Britain's Trident nuclear fleet, to world news and weather.

A Royal Navy lieutenant-commander invited the three to join him at his station.

"I'm Dave Bown, Sub Ops 3. I understand that you lot are behind Saracen's tasking in the Azores," he said, scanning their Visitor ID tags.

"We've just made contact on Spike, our UHF intelligence broadcast service, satellite uplinked and fed to me here," he said, pointing to his computer monitor.

There was an infrared image on his screen. It glowed green, dark background, sea against sky, with the pale green "hot" image of the two vessels together. Bown sat and tweaked the image with keyboard inputs. What his observers were seeing was plain. The smaller Procyon was alongside Arroban Prince, and the vessels were being secured with hawsers and lines. He tapped the keyboard again and the picture switched to live color video. It was dark. He increased his manual gains. The low light television imaging from Saracen was impressive. Crisp and clear, right down to the rust-streaked sides of the freighter and the bright orange gunwales of the smaller OSV.

"Real time?" asked Dalgliesh.

"That's correct, sir. Real time," Bown said.

He explained that the sub was on a loitering surveillance station, and that the image would degrade every fifteen minutes or so as the boat maneuvered in a racetrack turn to maintain its optimum distance. The image flickered.

"She's about to turn now," Bown said. "Cameras in her surveillance mast stay fixed on target, computer-controlled, gyro-stabilized. But the technology isn't perfect. The sub loiters but creeps out of the optimum box. As she breaks station, she'll do a teardrop turn to return to a reciprocal course. The image skips. See that flutter there? It's Saracen turning away."

Bown was distracted by a voice in his headset.

"Aye aye, sir. I'll bring it up in a moment on 'One'," he replied, and clacked at his keyboard again.

"That was the C-IN-C, Admiral Braithwaite," he said, gesturing with his thumb over his shoulder to the glassed-in mezzanine that overlooked the Ops floor. The trio looked back toward it. A room full of gold braid.

"The Old Man is apparently interested in your game," Bown added. As he spoke, the middle Ops Room screen flashed to life with a forty-foot image of Saracen's view of their surveillance target. Arroban Prince crewmen could be seen on deck, scrambling to break out its midships cargo crane, preparing to transfer goods in a purse net to Procyon's open deck. The video was mesmerizing.

"Does he have contact with the submarine?" Mayhew asked Dalgliesh in a whisper.

"Yes," he replied. "Voice and text in the datalink with a VLF radio backup."

Mayhew turned to his host.

"Dave, is it possible to have Saracen focus more closely on the cargo being transferred? Image detail is the main thing that we're after."

"Aye, sir," Bown replied. He pushed a button on his console and spoke into his spaghetti mike.

"Tommy Boy, Tommy Boy, Pole Star, over," he said.

A speaker squawked at his workstation.

"Tommy Boy, send, over."

"Tommy Boy, Pole Star. Increase image magnification on your next inbound run. We need cargo detail, over."

"Tommy Boy, roger."

On the next run, it was clear that crates containing the Libyan Strela-3s were being swung onto Procyon's deck.

Mayhew stoked his chin. "Commander, may I have access to an outside line?"

"Certainly," Bown replied, pointing to the vacant console beside him. "Outside unencrypted? Dial nine, then another nine to get out. Listen for the dial tone before you punch in the numbers. Otherwise the damn thing rings through to the Hertfordshire police 9-9-9 center."

"Good to know," Mayhew replied. "Thank you."

Images of Procyon loading amazed the naval brass. Were they getting this on video tape? Was there potential for its admissibility in criminal court? The Admiral was enthused.

Mayhew picked up the handset and punched in a long distance number, taking care to listen for dial tones as Bown had instructed.

"Paris," Hervé De Villiers answered.

"Do we have agreement?" Mayhew asked.

"Yes. We are unanimous," replied the Frenchman.

"Thank you, Paris. Goodbye," said Mayhew, disconnecting the call. He pressed 9 again, then 9 and got a dial tone.

Mayhew retrieved a slip of paper from a pocket in his suit jacket. On the big screen he saw the image from Saracen beginning to flutter. He dialed the ten numbers in sequence.

He was told that he would hear a series of strange clicks followed by a hollow echo. It would sound like a telephone off the hook down a well. He was to press the pound key twice. If it didn't work, he'd know soon enough.

Mayhew heard the echo and pressed the key as instructed. Five seconds passed and there was a brilliant flash on the main screen at Northwood. It went blank and displayed a computer message: 'Signal Lost'.

All hell broke loose in Dave Bown's corner of Ops. He punched a button and his voice link with Saracen went to speaker, filling the room with audible chaos.

"Pole Star, Tommy Boy! Bailing out to the south!" It was the anxious voice of the submarine's navigator. Conning orders were being shouted in the background. Saracen had gone to collision stations and an alarm claxon was wailing.

Bown jumped in, his voice filled the room.

"Tommy Boy, Pole Star! Send Sitrep, over!"

He repeated the request for a situation report three times. The entire Ops Room at Northwood went silent.

"Pole Star, Tommy Boy!" finally came their reply.

Saracen's pilot was breathless. "There's been a massive explosion! We were two thousand yards off their port bow. The concussion caught us broadside and we rolled thirty degrees! Maneuvering now to return to the box. Standby for data handshake."

"Tommy Boy, Pole Star, roger. Say your damage state."

Bown's tone was anxious.

Amplified static filled the Ops center for five long seconds. Hearts pounded.

"Pole Star, Tommy Boy," another voice boomed. "Boyle, here. That was one hell of a detonation. No damage reported aboard, save a few bloodied noses. We're back into the box and you should be receiving our transmissions now."

Screen One came to life at Ops with a horrific image that compelled audible gasps in the room. Procyon had vanished completely. The blazing stern of Arroban Prince stood upright in the water and was rapidly sinking straight down. In less than ten seconds, she too was gone.

"We're switching to infrared," Saracen's captain said.

The image on the screen glowed eerily green, revealing the choppy surface of the cold Atlantic against the warmer cloud-laden sky. Here and there, spots of flame flickered bright white and slowly extinguished. Within a minute there was no visible evidence that either vessel had ever been there.

"What's your sense of this, Tony?" asked Admiral Braithwaite on speaker, on his feet in the mezzanine.

"Well, sir, somebody had their thumb up it," Boyle's voice replied. "And that was a damned sight more than a shipment of Strelas. No cascading or residual detonations, just one ruddy great bang. Concentrated high explosives. Several tons of a plastic like Semtex, if I had to venture a guess."

"Survivors?" asked Braithwaite.

"Not likely. Our IR can detect a lone man's body heat on the surface. Even in this sea state. But we're not seeing a thing. Not so much as flotsam, just a hole in the ocean that opened and closed."

"Any surface contacts nearby?"

"Standby," Boyle replied. A moment later he reported that there was nothing on radar to a distance of one hundred and twenty miles.

"Thank you, Tony," said Braithwaite. "I'll look forward to your after action report."

❧

TWO DAYS LATER, newspapers carried a minor wire service story that contact had been lost with the oilfield supply vessel, MV Procyon, on a voyage from New Orleans to her new home in Aberdeen, Scotland. According to the ship's owners, the Procyon, with a crew of seven, gave its last reported position as four hundred miles east of Bermuda. There were no reports of the loss of a Liberian flagged freighter out of Benghazi.

Chapter 31

Wednesday, July 26, 1989 – 8:22 a.m. EST
201 Varick Street, New York, NY

"WELL DONE, NEW York!" said Jamie Mayhew, beaming from the London feed on the video screen. "Brilliant news. I doubted that Darragh would ever resurface, let alone wriggle back onto the hook."

Linc Coultart smiled, as did Charlie Watt, seated beside him in the New York operations room.

"The credit goes to Kevin Ahearn, our Long Jump team leader," he replied. "His gut instincts, not mine. I was ready to call it a day after Procyon sailed, but he pressed for increased surveillance on Testaverde. Got taps on his landlines. He knew more was in play than just the one deal. Now we know he was right all along."

On the second video screen in New York was the Paris feed, with Hervé de Villiers and Britain's Sir Michael McPhail seated side by side.

"We read the transcript you sent us this morning," de Villiers said. He picked up a sheet of paper and peered at it over his reading glasses.

He said, "Darragh, speaking at line twenty-seven, says and I quote: 'Those fucking Libyans! Poncy ship, poncy crew. I warned Kieran and Jackie to take it more slowly. Now they're fucking dead. Both shipments are gone and I'm out two bloody million!' Clearly unsettled by what has transpired."

De Villiers took a sip from a crystal glass.

"Still, it seems he attributes the loss to a mishap at sea," he continued, with nods from Mayhew and McPhail. "Jamie, you say there's been no press in Britain to suggest misadventure? *Agence France Presse* has carried only the original UPI snippet reporting lost contact with Procyon."

"Indeed," Mayhew replied. "Nothing at all on the Arroban Prince. It was as if she never existed. As for Procyon, minor headlines today in the Aberdeen Citizen and the Scottish Sun. She's now officially overdue, having been scheduled to arrive in Scotland last night. Missing northeast of Bermuda. Apprehension, hopes fading, et cetera. No search with so little to go on. A 'Notice to Mariners' has been issued for North Atlantic traffic to be on the lookout for any trace of the ship."

Mayhew sucked on his pipe.

"Intell out of Aberdeen is much more telling," he said. "Our contact in her agent's office reports that on Thursday evening they received the prearranged signal that she'd made her Azores rendezvous. A one-line teletype message stating service had been restored to her backup generator. After that? Silence. Nothing heard from her since. Caused quite a kafuffle among those in the know; frantic telephone calls by the night supervisor, uncertain to whom. Then, on Saturday morning, much buzz about Arroban Prince going missing as well. The betting line, says our contact, is even odds on a catastrophe whilst transferring cargo."

There were smiles on both sides of the Atlantic.

"That's the official conclusion of the Admiralty, as well," added Michael McPhail. "I've read a synopsis. No hint at all over Procyon's role beyond her receiving the shipment of missiles. The magnitude of the explosion is being attributed to unknown stores aboard the Libyan vessel."

Charlie Watt nodded.

"The CIA received that brief," he said. "The summary they circulated faults our domestic intell. An American connection flying under the radar. ATF and the FBI take a hit."

It was almost comical, he added. The FBI had issued an advisory on Tuesday to East Coast regional offices, warning that stolen Navy C4 might ship through an Atlantic port.

De Villiers looked pleased.

"Then the success of your Long Jump operation has been complete," he said, raising his water glass in a toast. It was afternoon in Paris. It might have been wine.

"We missed a chance to make our presence felt," he continued. "But, in the end, it is to our advantage. It seems this man Darragh is inclined to move quickly. Is that your sense of it, Lincoln?"

"A qualified yes," Coultart replied.

Uncovering Darragh as the IRA money man had been an opportunity Coultart let slip through their fingers. Manpower had been the issue. It had taken all of his people to follow the explosives trail, imperative at the time. Darragh got away after New York, but Ahearn's gut told him he would soon reconnect with the source he had been courting. And he did. One four-minute telephone call came through on Monday just before midnight. Darragh's tone had seemed anxious, not desperate, indicating he'd be back in touch. There was one reference to another deal and it was game-on again.

"At this point," Coultart said, "all we do have to go on is Darragh's location. The call he made to Testaverde was from a resort hotel in Nassau. I have Ahearn and his partner heading to the Bahamas today. Darragh has a real bankroll. Getting on him is key. The rest are on Testaverde twenty-four-seven. Whatever this other deal might be, we'll work it out."

"Very good," de Villiers replied. "Now to weekly reports. On behalf of Bonn station, I can report that they continue to pursue a Libyan link to their Palestinian cells. Semtex and Strelas remain high on their shopping list. In France, we are concentrating on an internal concern. An anarchist group, one that has been a thorn in my side for some time, has made threats regarding a nuclear power facility at Saint Alban. It is possible that they are attempting to secure fissile material from Pakistan. Perhaps for a so-called 'dirty bomb' with an aim to discredit our nuclear program. We are working on that. London?"

Mayhew clapped his jowls and thought for a moment.

"Still focused on Lockerbie," he said. "Following up on the information that Gadhafi's people in Malta were the point of the spear. We have names. We've developed a plan. I will call you offline after this with a point or two to discuss."

Mayhew fumbled through some notes.

"Oh, and Lincoln?" he asked. "In that vein, how is our Irishman faring?"

"Just back from a furlough on his own," Coultart replied. "He did a good job for us on Long Jump, had the Mafia's driver eating out of his hand. My plan going forward is to use him again. When we nail down his friend Darragh, we could tap into a whole range of options."

"Watch him, Lincoln," Mayhew warned.

"We are," Coultart replied. "Is there a specific concern?"

Jamie Mayhew grimaced.

"It's ... well, the bugger's smitten with one of my people. His original handler. You met her. A strain of the Stockholm Syndrome, I shouldn't wonder. Just keep a wary eye on the man. He has money now. Newfound freedoms. I'm worried that he might be inclined to bolt. And with him on the loose, we'd all have a problem."

"Okay, Jamie," said Coultart. "We will. But by all reports, he's getting all kinds of lovin' right here in New York."

"Fine, fine," Mayhew said. "I've nothing further."

"Then we're concluded, gentlemen?" de Villiers asked.

Going once, going twice.

"Right. We will talk again Monday. *Bonsoir,*" he said and screens from New York to Paris went blank.

MOMENTS AFTER THE video conference ended, Mayhew had Paris on a secure telephone line. He relit his calabash pipe, having the call up on speaker.

"Hervé, I trust Sir Michael has you up to speed on our Maltese adventure?"

"Yes," de Villiers replied. "I must say I'm surprised that you're moving so quickly. Long Jump has been a distraction from Lockerbie, and I understand the pressure you're under to act on this front. But this Libyan, al-Salabay, you believe that he warrants our direct attention?"

"Absolutely," said Mayhew. "My best operator has been in Valletta and the man's shadow for nearly three weeks. I trust her assessments. She says he's weak. Physically, mentally and morally. Clearly involved in the Lockerbie planning and no doubt any broader campaign. As such, his capture and rendition from Malta for interrogation is a priority now. I'm seeking approval to plan it."

In his office in Paris, Hervé de Villiers looked grim. He glanced at McPhail, who simply shrugged. The lifelong London cop knew little of dark and despicable things.

"How soon?" de Villiers asked.

"Late August at the earliest. Middle of September?"

"Rendition is out of the question."

Mayhew rhythmically rapped fingertips on his desktop.

"I see," he said.

"It would involve outside resources," de Villiers explained. "France would be the only option. We have a place in the south, near Avignon, but the DGSE would in the least need to be advised,. if not to participate fully. No. Long Jump shows we've succeeded in remaining hidden. Now isn't the time to step into the light."

Mayhew acquiesced. "Yes, you're right. Then we will need to stay local. Find a place in Malta to conduct our business. That introduces another layer of risk, but we'll work it out."

How quickly could London provide a timetable?

Mayhew said he could by the end of the week.

"I presume you'll be seeking a sanction on al-Salabay? On successful conclusion or otherwise?"

"I reckon that goes without saying."

"You will have my support," de Villiers promised.

Friday, July 28, 1989 – 6:14 p.m. EST
21 Rye Road, Port Chester, New York

"OH, MISTER SAL, please come in!" cried Maria Cárdenas at the front door. "I am so glad you came! His Honor has locked himself in his study for nearly two days. *¡Él está loco con tristeza!* He has been crazy with sadness!"

It was the second time Sal Luongo had been to Elliott's home; the second time he had met his housekeeper Maria, and the Puerto Rican grandmother was distraught.

Wednesday, July 26th, had marked the birthday of the Judge's late daughter Diana. Maria had accompanied him to the cemetery where her cremated remains had been laid to rest. Her Honor, Miss Livna, had planned to join them, but had been called away to Florida where her aging mother had suffered a stroke. Since that afternoon, his door had been locked and he refused to answer. He had his bathroom, a sofa to sleep on, but *Dios mio*, he'd been acting crazy!

Crazy with sadness.

A week earlier, Sal and the Judge had agreed on a road trip together, a three-game series in Chicago for the Mets against the Cubs. Friday through Sunday. Wrigley Field. The will call tickets had been purchased; airline and hotel reservations had been made. As Sal had been ready to leave for the airport, there was a strange message from Randy on his machine. It simply stated he wouldn't be coming and asked Sal to stop by. Maria took him to the door to the study and dabbed at tears as she discreetly disappeared.

"Come in, Sal, it's unlocked," Elliott said from inside.

Luongo found the Judge seated at his desk, unkempt in a wrinkled grey USMC sweat suit and three days' worth of whiskers. His eyes were red-rimmed. The room smelled of sweat, scotch and stale pipe tobacco smoke.

"You look like shit, my friend," observed Sal.

Elliott managed a smile. He rose and turned to the credenza behind him, filling his glass and another with scotch from a crystal decanter.

"Do you know," he began evenly, stopping for a moment with the glasses in hand, "that in the past forty-eight hours, I've gone through all of the whiskey I have in the house. This is the *absolute* last."

He set Sal's drink within reach, stood erect again and continued that thought. "I had to do a little recon last night after Maria turned in. Found a bottle of *anCnoc* single malt in the kitchen pantry. Good stuff. A gift."

He had a sip before resuming his seat.

"Habits are strange, don't you think? Right away, I came back and filled that decanter with it. Without thinking, you know? And just as I'd done with the others. All the empties are here," he said, his toe tapping a wastebasket that clinked.

"Charlotte always said it was crass to serve liquor from anything but your best crystal decanter. Especially if you are entertaining. Naturally, in these matters, I always deferred to her expertise."

"O-o-o-kay," Sal began in response, "now I can see why your housekeeper's freaked out."

Elliott smiled.

"Maria? Bless her Latina heart. Me? I come from a long tradition of Scots Presbyterian maternal warmth. Know what I mean? It's a wonder that, even today, I can work up the courage to slouch in a chair."

Sal chuckled. Randy was alright.

"I'm glad you came, Sal. Sorry about the last minute change in our plans. I hope that wasn't too disappointing."

"Nah," Luongo said. "But I got a good feeling. Three wins over Atlanta, three losses to Pittsburg. They're due."

The pair sipped a mutual toast to the Mets.

"So, my friend, why am I here?"

Sal could see the tremor in Randy Elliott's hands.

"What I need to ask could wreck a friendship I've come to rely on. Come to cherish. Believe me, I've wrestled with this."

"Then it's Bakker. You want the guy dead."

Sal saw the look of despair.

"You *know* people," Elliott pleaded.

"And you think you know me?" Sal shot back.

For a moment both men simply stared at each other.

"I'm a *goombah*, I fuckin' get it! People like me settle scores in the alley with two in the pumpkin. *Right?* Bam! Bam! Behind the ear, just like that! *You think you know me, Randy?* I sell hot dogs. Love baseball. Done things I'm not really proud of, but I *never* had a guy whacked!"

Sal gulped a mouthful of whiskey.

"You know, when we became friends, became actual pals, I asked myself, *Sal? What's his angle?* Freakin' judges don't hang out with street corner hawkers like me. You've got your club, uptown friends, a pedigree ... Sometimes friends in low places come in handy. Is that it? You don't fuckin' know me!"

Tears welled in Randy Elliott's eyes.

"Sal, I'm sorry, I ..."

Luongo stood and handed his empty glass to the Judge.

"Sorry I had the temerity ..."

"Jesus, you and your ten dollar words. Am I good for a refill or what?"

Sal smiled. "Look," he said as he returned to his seat, his glass half full again, "what you're asking, my friend, is serious shit. Go down this road and there's no going back."

"It's a risk that I'm willing to take."

"No, goddammit, it's not about risk! Crossing the fuckin' street is a risk. And, by the way, it's a risk we'd *both* be taking. It's about losing your soul. Do this and you're changed forever, there's no going back to the person you were."

"Don't you get it?" the Judge implored. "The sonofabitch took *my* life when he took Diana and Charlotte. *My life, Sal!* The person I once was is already gone. I need to do this to move on."

Neither man said a word for an eternity.

"I *do* know people. But it'll cost."

"I've got millions."

Sal snickered. "Holy cow, you're a sap! You don't play much poker, do you? If I wasn't such a stand-up guy, I'd shake you down to your last dollar myself. You don't need millions. I know guys who would do this thing clean for the price of an '89 Buick."

"Then you'll do it?" Randy asked, eyes as wide as a deer's on the freeway.

"Did you think I wouldn't?"

Judge Elliott exhaled slowly and color returned to his face. "Sal, I really don't care what it costs. And unless it offends, I'll ensure you're looked after."

"I'm not offended so easy," Luongo said, smiling. "Leave this to me, I'll arrange it."

Glasses clinked, sealing the deal, sealing mutual trust and their fate. The relief both men felt was palpable. Judge Elliott lit his pipe and savored sweet smoke, drawn deep, sweeter in its easy release.

"I want him to feel fear," he said, words that escaped on a smoke ring that lingered.

"Don't go there, Randy," Sal cautioned, feeling an instant sense of foreboding. "You'll just torture yourself."

"No. I have this recurring dream. A nightmare. Diana's fear when that airplane exploded. The terror that she must have felt. That they all must have felt. Inescapable death, hurtling to the ground. He has his own plane. I want him to feel that."

"You want him to die? *Fine!* We can do fear really cheap. But you'll go fuckin' crazy if you think you're gonna get more than that. Listen to yourself, for Chrissakes! Bomb a plane just to punish one guy? The man flies with innocent people! You're not that cold blooded."

Randy Elliott sagged in his chair.

"No, you're right." Then he straightened.

"Look, I've got a lot of money now, plenty offshore, thanks to my accountant. On Monday, I'm going to give you two hundred thousand in cash. Spend what you need. Two in the pumpkin? That works for me. And if you can get that done for the price of a Buick? Go ahead, pocket the rest."

Luongo's jaw dropped. "That's too much," he said, quickly wishing he'd bitten his tongue.

The Judge looked him in the eye.

"But Sal ... If you can find another way? Punishment that fits the man's crime? I'll see you walk away a millionaire."

Chapter 32

Saturday, August 5, 1989 – 4:46 p.m. EST
Lyford Cay, New Providence Island, The Bahamas

"TAXI JUST TURNED onto Bayswater Lane," Maggie Wojcik reported, her voice crackling from the handheld radio on a glass-topped table next to Ahearn. "Two minutes out."

"Copy," Kevin replied. They were ready.

Two teams had been in the Bahamas just over a week, having arrived in Nassau on the afternoon of July 28th. Eddie Darragh's call to Testaverde had been traced to the Brittania Beach Hotel on Paradise Island, a narrow, resort-studded slip of land protecting the north side of the capital's harbor. They found him in its lavish casino the very first night. The man they'd once known by his trademark windbreaker had been in classic black tie, blending in well at the baccarat table—unfazed, so it seemed, by the losses he'd suffered at sea.

Darragh had been an easy subject to shadow. For two days he lounged at the hotel. Morning jogs on the crushed coral beach. Late lunches at its Café Martinique, which continued to promote its cameo as a location in the 1965 filming of James Bond's *Thunderball.* Evenings, of course, on the casino floor. Maggie and Tinker Bell had fitted in well at each of these venues as doting American newlyweds.

On the third day, they followed Darragh to a storefront business on Bay Street in downtown Nassau.

New Providence Vacations rented private homes and estates across the island for periods as short as a week and as long as six months. Waiting in the office, the honeymoon couple overheard the Irish tourist's selection—a luxury three-bedroom beachfront home, pool and twice weekly maid service, in exclusive Lyford Cay on the island's west end. Two weeks until the middle of August? Done. Two thousand

Bahamian dollars, paid in full by Mr. Edward Duggan with a draft on his Union Bank of Switzerland checking account. It was available now, and he could move in tomorrow if it suited. Would he be requiring guest privileges at the Lyford Cay Golf and Country Club, only minutes away from his vacation home? Yes, the Irishman quickly agreed. He had guests coming who might.

The American couple who next joined the agent confessed that they'd heard Mr. Duggan's details. Did she have anything similar to let? Why yes, Dolly Atherton had replied. Both of the adjoining properties were available as it happened. To the west, a stunning five-bedroom home on an acre of beachfront, steel and glass, the design of a Miami architect. It was a named estate: Windward Reach, and came with a price tag of $1,500 a week. To the east, on the right, was a three-bedroom home in the art deco style. Much more modest. Cozier for a honeymoon couple, with a surrounding copse of Caribbean Pine among palms on three sides. Just vacated and a real bargain at $750 U.S. weekly.

They chose the larger estate without blinking. Family and friends would be coming to visit. They too would move in tomorrow. The term? Open-ended. Week to week would be fine. It was available until November. The newlywed groom didn't flinch, handing over his American Express. He took the golf option too. Pure profit, that. Dolly had been so pleased with the afternoon's business, she closed up shop as soon as the couple left.

☙

"YELLOW TAXI PULLING into the driveway," the radio squawked. "Seen," Kevin replied. Maggie's rental Toyota continued along Bayswater Lane, turning onto the crushed coral driveway of the adjacent estate and disappearing into a three-car garage.

Windward Reach was a two-story home of 4,400 square feet, excluding the attached garage and an architecturally congruent stand-alone cottage for guests. It was stylishly furnished. Nearly all of its exterior walls were glass, mirrored with blue sun-reflecting Mylar. It stood amid elegant palms with manicured lawns to the sugar-white beach, and though rarely was heard a disparaging word, its mistress loathed the invasive view of their neighbor. The boor, a Minnesota car dealer, had cleared out the pine to the property line and extended his concrete pool apron to mere inches from it. Day or night, those in her finest guest bedroom had a ringside seat for the neighbor's pool parties—and a view into his living room that was appallingly unobstructed.

Kevin Ahearn watched from the second floor bedroom at Windward Reach as the taxi arrived. It was one hundred and fifty feet across the pool apron to the bungalow's entrance, and he recognized Testaverde as he emerged from the cab. Ahearn smiled. They were in business.

Darragh greeted Testaverde and whisked him inside.

Next door, Jimmy Kenneally raised a pair of red plastic goggles to his face. He pressed the 'Test' button on a solid state unit in an aluminum case that sat between him and Ahearn. He watched a red dot flicker on the middle pane of the living room windows next door. It was too low. He peered through the viewfinder of a camera on a tripod between his feet. With subtle adjustments, the red dot climbed to the top of the glass panel. Well above eye level. Then he turned a knob on the transmitting unit, marked 'Gain'. Instantly through his headset, he heard Darragh's voice in his foyer, instructing the taxi driver to place the luggage and golf clubs in the first room on the left down the hall. Laser audio surveillance—picking up voices from sound frequencies resonating on glass.

Darragh and Testaverde settled in the living room and had drinks. Pleasantries were exchanged and soon they were onto the topic of Procyon's loss. Both sounded certain an accident must have occurred, a collision perhaps. Darragh was angry that Doherty and Moran had included the Libyans in their plan—overreaching themselves, adding dangerous factors without consultation. Well, they had paid for it dearly.

And then they talked golf. Testaverde had been a fanatic for years, a six-handicap and on the list for a membership at Winged Foot in Mamaroneck, New York. Darragh was more of a duffer, but he had consistently broken 90 since taking up the game after he'd arrived in the States. In fact, he and Testaverde had met a year earlier when a mutual friend had invited him into their foursome at elite Baltusrol, one of America's oldest courses, in Springfield, New Jersey.

Darragh booked an 8:05 tee time the next morning at the Lyford Cay country club down the road. Then the men dressed for dinner and left by taxi back into Nassau with Maggie and Tinker in tow.

The pair returned to Windward Reach with nothing exceptional to report, except that the conch and sherry chowder at the Graycliff restaurant *was*—and that one little bottle of Pouilly-Fuisse could cost forty-five dollars.

It was just after 10:30 when Darragh poured Testaverde a nightcap. They stood in the living room of his vacation rental, unaware of the intrusive neighbors.

"Is your Colombian mate standing firm on October?" the Irishman asked, adding ice to his guest's glass of whiskey. "No chance at all of advancing the date?"

"What's the rush?" asked Testaverde.

Darragh looked pained.

"Derry's been thrown into turmoil, as you can imagine," he said. "They'll sort themselves out, but my reputation as their benefactor isn't gaining much traction."

"And that matters?"

"It fuckin' matters to me!"

Eddie Darragh chose not to explain. His criminal windfall had nearly been perfect, until two years earlier when the Dublin general IRA council learned he was alive. Living the high life in the Caribbean, with nearly eighteen million dollars U.S. tucked away in banks in Switzerland and the Caymans.

Banking secrecy saved his life, and he had agreed at gunpoint on St. Barts to contribute half to The Cause—not including a million dollar contribution to the IRA leadership's so-called retirement fund.

The Azores loss would come out of his pocket, because, as Dublin had promptly asserted, nothing had landed in Ulster. Testaverde had gotten his money, so had Gadhafi, and Eddie would suck up the hit. *That* mattered. Next time, he resolved, he would make the transport arrangements.

"You're not his only customer. We're still looking at the middle of October," Testaverde said, adding that he was sorry, he'd already checked.

"We stick to your original order?" asked Gino.

"Aye," Darragh replied. "And I've warmed to the notion of shipment by air."

He recited the order from memory. Forty-eight M-72 light anti-tank rockets; $10,000 apiece, twelve cases of four. One hundred and twenty M-61 fragmentation hand grenades; thirty to a case, four cases at $15,000 each. Sixty M-18 Claymore anti-personnel mines; ten cases of six, at $20,000 a case. One $740,000 cash sale.

Next door at Windward Reach, Kevin Ahearn whistled through his teeth as he scribbled notes in the surveillance log. One hell of a shopping list.

"Tinker," he said, "get onto Coultart. I-and-A needs to work on any Colombian connection to Testaverde or the Patriarcas. We need a name. C'mon, son, get at it!"

A Nikon camera whirred and clicked on its tripod as Testaverde crossed the living room to the windows. He plucked at his mustache, staring outside, unfocused.

"He has your order," said Testaverde. "No change. Maybe if we sweeten the deal, you can jump to the head the line."

"Sweeten the deal?" Darragh complained. "*Fuckin' we?* So far it's been *my* sugar bowl you have all been depleting!"

The American turned from the window.

"Okay, you took a hit. Throw in twenty-five grand and I'll match it. Call it goodwill. That should move things up to the end of September, and that works with your airmail option. Or work out the transport yourself. You choose."

Darragh glowered, nibbling from a bowl of pistachios.

He clapped the nut dust from his fingers.

"I'll give you the cash tomorrow," he replied. "Now tell me again about his pilot, the Canadian."

"Peterborough Pete?" Testaverde crossed the room to the bar and helped himself to another whiskey.

"Funny guy. Doesn't drink, doesn't smoke, doesn't swear. Works out of Cartegena. He's been flying in the Colombian jungle for maybe ten years. Started out hauling in bibles. Got hooked up with the North Coast Cartel and for the last six or seven, he's been flying coke into the southern gulf States. Helluva pilot, they say. Used to water bomb forest fires and likes to fly low."

Testaverde strolled into the room's conversation pit.

"A year ago I hear he's getting out of the business," he continued. "Finally pulling the pin. Buying Catalina flying boats from the Argentinian Navy. Anyway, for a hundred grand he can stretch his final flight all the way to the Ireland coast. He'll just need a few weeks heads up."

"When?"

"There's a two-week window at the end of September. You fix the date and make the arrangements on the Irish end. I'll do the rest."

Darragh grinned. "Done! Go ahead, make the deal. And Gino? You don't want to fuck me."

Sunday, August 6, 1989 – 12:35 p.m. EST
171 Hester Street, New York, NY

JOHNNY MACCIO MAINTAINED his composure as cameras flashed in his face and an obese grandmother with withering halitosis planted a slobbery kiss on his cheek. He drew back discreetly and continued to croon.

"Volare, oh oh, e contare, oh oh oh oh... No wonder my happy heart sings... Your love has given me wings... Nel blu, dipinto di blu ... Felice di stare lassu ..." He concluded the Dean Martin version of the old standard with a hand flourish and brilliant smile.

"Thank you, ladies, you're too kind!" he gushed, midday heat beading sweat on his brow.

His performance for the twittering flock *of* Bespectacled Midwest Bluehairs had paid off. A dozen old gals, just discharged from a Gray Line Tours bus on the corner, giggled and fussed as they trotted into Puglia's for a meal. Johnny stepped back from the restaurant's entrance and lit a smoke. Twelve lunch covers? He'd rake in a good tip.

Hester Street was awash with tourists. Maccio eyeballed every mini-skirted thigh and jiggling bosom that passed by, blowing smoke rings and mentally undressing them all. There was worse work than this.

"You Johnny Maccio?" asked some guy who suddenly stepped up beside him. A New Yorker. A Wop.

"Depends who's asking?" he replied, exhaling smoke. "You a jealous husband or a talent agent?"

"Nah, maybe a cousin," the man said. Looked friendly enough. "You got an Uncle Carlo? Drove truck? Lived on Mott at Kenmare?"

Maccio's eyes narrowed. Who's this fuckin' *giamoke*?

"Yeah," he said. "Died in '85."

"It was August '86. Service at St. Mark's in the Bowery."

"So, what's this? We're family?"

"Nah," the man replied. "He used to deliver produce to my old man."

The stranger smiled and extended his hand.

"Sal Luongo," he said. "From the neighborhood, years ago, hundred block a Mulberry."

Maccio shook his hand. Looked him over.

"And what can I do for you, Sal Luongo?" he said flatly, blowing another smoke ring and winking at a pair of cute girls passing by arm in arm.

"I'm looking for a guy who told me he knows you. An Irishman. Just moved onto the street. Name's Martin, you know him?"

Johnny's eyes narrowed again.

"I know lots of Micks. What's your angle?"

"No angle. Might have a job for him, is all."

"Yeah? How about this," Johnny began, drawing a last hit of smoke before crushing the butt with the toe of a gleaming patent leather shoe. "How about I go inside and give him a call. Stay put and I'll let you know if there's a message."

"Fair enough."

Barely three drags into a Marlboro and Sal heard a familiar voice at the restaurant's door.

"Salvatore! As I live and breathe!"

He turned quickly to see Martin grinning and clearly happy to see him again.

"I was wondering if you'd track me down!" Martin said as they shared a slap on the shoulder hug.

"Glad you did, mate!" he continued. "Can you join me for lunch or a beer?"

Sal said he could, if they could talk business.

Business? Now, what could that mean?

Martin took a good long look at the crush of passersby on Hester Street. No faces that he recognized.

"Let's go inside and catch up. I'm all ears."

Chapter 33

Monday, August 14, 1989 – 11:31 a.m. EST
399 Park Avenue, New York, NY

"SIX GODDAMNED-FIFTY an hour and your best advice is I'd come off as petty and vindictive? Well, here's some news for you, counselor, I *am* petty and vindictive!" Ted Bakker said as he stood at the glazed wall of his private office, staring down thirty floors onto Park Avenue. "You don't get here by being Mister fucking Congeniality. Or don't they teach that at Harvard?"

Chester P. Randall smiled and brushed at a hand-painted silk tie, preening wearable art that likely cost him at least ninety minutes of billable time.

"Clearly you're not," he replied. "And no, Ted, they don't. Perhaps over the river in Allston, but I studied law. We can go from selfless to vengeful on cue, and with me it's a gift. You, on the other hand, can't afford to seem callous. Not now."

Bakker returned to his glass-topped ebony desk, stopping and drumming his fingers on an antique humidor, considering whether he needed a smoke.

"So you're saying no injunction."

"That's my advice."

"What she's doing is harassment! That picket for weeks now, day in and day out. The court wouldn't see that?"

The natty middle-aged lawyer pursed his lips.

"Oh, you'd get your injunction, but you'd be crucified in the press. Grieving widows and orphans? Let them vent. It's not as if they've been costing you business. Once these cases commence, the airline itself will be back in the headlines. That'll shift their attention from you and it all becomes moot."

"Fine," Bakker conceded, lighting up a Padron that he knew he'd only waste. Randall declined the offer, which was fine too. At fifty bucks a pop, the senior litigating partner at Easton and Meares could afford his own hand-rolled cigars.

It had been twenty minutes since Bakker's attorney had arrived early for their business lunch. It was important, he'd said, that they review his file.

To date there were thirty-three civil suits pending before the federal court naming Bakker among the defendants in the wrongful death of particular victims of the Lockerbie crash. And this, Randall noted, was just the thin edge of the wedge. Dozens more, maybe hundreds, were awaiting the outcome of pre-trial motions that Randall and others had filed. Most attacked the court's jurisdiction. His, importantly, sought to remove Bakker—the person—from the defendant list, arguing that decisions he made as Pan Am chief executive were those of an agent of its Board and the body corporate, and he was therefore indemnified from personal liability. The argument was unlikely to succeed, still it would tie up the process, and prove forceful when played out in front of the jury. As for this woman and her irritating campaign? Let it pass.

"For the time being," Randall continued, "it would be better for you to disappear into a hole."

Bakker rolled his eyes and rocked back in his chair.

"Day after tomorrow, Buck Peyton breaks ground in Houston on his Channelview Number Three refinery," he said slowly, evenly, through his teeth. "A quarter of a billion dollar deal that I put together. I intend to be there with a hand on the shovel. Gripping and grinning, chrome hard hat and all."

"I don't ..." Chet Randall began, before Bakker cut him short with a single raised finger.

"A week Friday, we're announcing a new subdivision out in Chandler, Arizona. Six hundred new homes. Nearly two hundred million in development costs and I have a one quarter ownership stake. It's going to make the next cover of Business Week."

Bakker raised his finger again.

"Next month, Bermuda. A golf resort and marina."

He sucked on his cigar and exhaled.

"And you're telling me to crawl into a hole?"

"My turn?" Randall asked patiently.

"Your turn."

"Two things have come up," the attorney began. "One, on or by September 15th, the FAA is going to release its formal report on security issues around Flight 103. Specifically, Pan Am baggage checking at Frankfurt and Heathrow. You're aware of the preliminary findings ..."

"Yes, yes," Bakker replied. "Larry Sadler's been keeping me up to speed. There'll be the FAA's standard equivocal slap on the wrist. A ream of compliance orders and some shrill calls from the Hill to overhaul the entire system. None of that concerns me."

"Really? I've learned that its draft report was as you suggest, vintage FAA vacillation. Then, just ten days ago, Transportation had it yanked from the agency's hands for review. I'm told there's been a rewrite, faulting the airline completely and calling for millions in fines. The revised final report hit Skinner's desk on Thursday morning."

Bakker's eyes widened.

"Secretary Sam Skinner?"

"None other."

"You've got some kinda sources."

Randall smiled.

"Well, we're not quite Yale Bonesmen, but the Harvard network is nearly as tight."

"So the airline is going to be savaged. Again, that's not my concern."

"It should be," Randall continued. "So long as you remain named in these actions, you *are* Pan Am. Worse, at the defendant's table, you are the face of its leadership before the bombing. Its failings are *your* failings. Its lapses in judgment, *your own*. Particularly in light of your regrettable memo, which has yet to be disclosed in the civil arena. For now it's protected. In the hands of criminal investigators. When it does become public, depending on timing, your jeopardy could be huge."

"You're saying when and not if," observed Bakker.

His lawyer went on.

"Two," he continued laconically. "Executive Order 12686, announced August 5th. I have a copy of its terms of reference."

He rose and handed Bakker a file.

The Presidential Commission on Aviation Security and Terrorism, ordered ten days earlier by President Bush, had caught many observers flat-footed. Coming amid ongoing criminal and aviation safety investigations on both sides of the Atlantic, the announcement of a blue ribbon inquiry by Congress had seemed ill-timed at best, or, at worst, politics to redress the President's media label of "wimp".

"At first glance," Russell said as he returned to his seat, "its mandate seems innocuous enough … 'To review and evaluate policy options in connection with aviation security.' It's the adjoined caveat that's concerning: 'With particular reference to the destruction on December 21, 1988, of Pan American World Airways Flight 103.' I can assure you that this will be its sole unswerving focus. The administrative section of the order gives the Commission its teeth. There, where it says: 'the heads of executive departments, agencies, and independent instrumentalities shall provide the Commission, upon request, with such information …' and so on. That's their right to subpoena anything in the least evidentiary, and to call anybody it chooses to testify under oath. *Anybody.*"

"I see. And what's your assessment?" asked Bakker.

The lawyer tucked the papers back into his briefcase and stood, taking a moment to straighten his tie.

"I'm told he'll be appointing Ann McLaughlin as the Commission chair," he said.

Bakker's shoulders sagged.

"Reagan's Labor Secretary."

"She's a tiger," cautioned Randall. "A digger, completely tenacious. Any bone in her teeth will get chewed."

"So I'm fucked."

"Not to put too fine a point on it, yes."

"What's your advice, then, counselor?" Bakker asked, collecting himself as he rose from his desk. They had reservations for lunch at Delmonico's in twenty minutes.

Randall grinned. "Off the record? In your shoes, Ted, I'd start moving my assets offshore and fake my own death."

THE INTERCOM BUZZED on Penny Luscombe's desk in the outer office. Bakker's voice clearly rang through.

"I'm leaving for lunch with Chet Randall. Have Miguel bring the car to the express elevator on P-3."

Penny frowned.

"Sir, your 11:15 is still here. Mr. Quigley. You spoke yesterday. He called about leasing your jet."

Silence. Then Bakker again.

"We can't meet, not today. Halliday can deal with it. He knows our schedule and rates. Refer Mr. Quigley to him. I will be back at two."

"Yes sir, Mr. Bakker," Penny replied.

"My car, Penny."

"Yes sir, Mr. Bakker."

She knew he was already gone. Coming and going through his private entrance was becoming his habit these days. That insufferable woman and her damned picket line.

Penny looked across at the Irishman, Quigley, who had politely occupied himself for the past half hour with a copy of Fortune magazine. An attractive man. Boglioli suit. She'd seen the glances directed his way through the glass from the girls in accounting—steaming the glass, more like—and as she ruled the roost on the executive floor, it was incumbent on her to warn each of them off with a tested and true icy glare.

She was about to offer an apologetic explanation when Mr. Quigley put the magazine down and flashed her a smile.

"All the same, bosses, eh?" he said warmly, with that accent that made her heart flutter. "Not so much as a please, lass, or thank you, or kiss my imperial arse. You've got my sympathies, darlin'."

Penny brightened.

"I am sorry, Mr. Quigley," she replied, as the Irishman picked up a worn leather satchel and rose to his feet. "Shall I book another time? I'm afraid, however, that the rest of this week doesn't look good at all."

He shrugged amiably. "No? Well, then, if you could turn me in the direction of this fella, Halliday? Perhaps we needn't bother his lordship again."

Penny Luscombe's green eyes broke their lock for an instant to narrow and flash at the girls through the glass. Just as quickly, they returned to meet his and twinkled again.

"Oh, right, Danny Halliday? Do you have a car, Mr. Quigley?" she asked, tapping a pen to a full lower lip that was blossoming into a pout.

The Irishman looked surprised, expecting directions to a subordinate's office somewhere down the hall.

"Back in Dublin, a new Beemer, yeah."

Penny giggled.

"Ah, you meant here and now. No, I'm legging it, darlin'. Just how far away are you planning to send me?"

"Out to White Plains airport," she explained. "That's where we keep our aircraft. It's up in Westchester County, about an hour by taxi. Or I could call up our service? It's expensive, but quicker. You'd get there in style."

The Irishman nodded agreeably and Penny started to pick up the phone. He waved her off, checking his watch.

"It's gone nearly twelve," he said, lightly setting his satchel down onto her desk. "After lunch would be better. One-thirty, let's say? That is, if there's somewhere nearby that you'd fancy?"

Penny beamed.

"Are you asking me out to lunch, Mr. Quigley?" she asked coyly, and loudly enough to be heard all the way down to Receivables.

The Irishman squared his jaw, playing the part.

"I am. I've been so sorely slighted, it only seems fair. A concession, we'll call it."

She sparkled, and punched a button on her intercom. "Lisa? Cover my desk until maybe one-thirty? I'm going to be out."

Monday, August 14, 1989 – 2:45 p.m. EST
White Plains Airport, Westchester County, NY

"MR. QUIGLEY? I'M Danny Halliday. Pleased to meet you, come in," said the young man in a Navy flight jacket. Quigley, whom the Dixon Flight Services front office girl had brought in, shook his hand firmly and took a seat facing his desk.

"How can I help you?" asked Halliday, glancing at the man's business card. Martin Quigley, P.Eng, it announced. Managing Director, Tech-Eireann, with a Dublin, Ireland address, and a New York cellular telephone number.

"I was admiring your Gulfstream, that tan beauty out on the ramp," Mr. Quigley said. "A first class machine, and available for private charter? I'm here to enquire about that."

"Yes sir, on both counts, she is!" Halliday replied proudly.

It had been only a month since Danny Halliday had been made the manager of flight operations for Ted Bakker's latest endeavor, Bakker Aviation. It was to be the start of a fleet of luxury executive aircraft, with his Gulfstream starting to pay for its keep. Halliday's own incentive was a ten percent commission on any charter the business brought in. It surprised him that one ad in Aviation Week had already brought interest from the likes of this businessman Quigley.

"What do you have in mind?" Danny asked.

"A fair bit of business, I'd venture," the Irishman replied.

Tech-Eireann, he explained, was an Irish technology company with contracts to develop the country's mobile telephone infrastructure. His firm was considering American suppliers, and within a month he would be needing to transport VIPs, including potential investors, to various venues around the United States. To Virginia and Georgia from New York. San Jose in the Silicon Valley. Passenger loads from one through seven or eight. Same day return on the eastern seaboard, possibly overnighters out west. Perhaps a half dozen flights a month? Would Bakker Aviation be able to support such a plan?

"We are a can do operation, Mr. Quigley," assured Halliday. "Your particular requirements would dovetail very nicely with our own operations."

He turned their attention to a whiteboard on the wall of his cluttered office. It was a six-month calendar outlining the disposition of Bakker's aircraft, numbering just two at present—NG399X, the Grumman G3, and NC214T, a Cessna Conquest twin-engine turboprop.

Halliday explained the color code.

Red dates indicated scheduled use by their owner, Mr. Bakker. Blue dates? Maintenance down time. Those in green were dates available for charter. And in black, charters already booked. There were just two with black information penned in. Otherwise, red and green seemed the dominant colors.

"Do you see anything there that might work?" he asked.

The Irishman scanned the wall.

"First few weeks of September look good," Mr. Quigley replied. "One thing I'm needing to ask. I understand that your Grumman has a satellite phone?"

"Latest technology," Halliday said. "Mr. Bakker demands it. Both his aircraft have the antenna fit. The phone units themselves are portable. Plug and play."

"Both aircraft?"

"Of course! Both the Grumman and his turboprop Conquest. He needs to keep in touch with his clients, worldwide. I presume that's important to you?"

It could make all the difference, he said.

And the rates? The young aviator gave him a brochure. They seemed fair, and the Irishman made a substantial deposit with a certified draft on a Swiss bank account. Their signatures clinched the deal.

"For starters, then," Quigley said as he studied the board. "Tomorrow morning to Roanoke, Virginia, for a meeting at noon. Return to New York maybe three hours later? Your turboprop Cessna? One passenger, me."

"That would be no problem at all, Mr. Quigley," Halliday replied. "I'd be happy to fly you myself. On the ramp at, let's say, nine sharp?"

Chapter 34

Friday, August 19, 1989 – 4:01 p.m. EST
201 Varick Street, New York, NY

LINC COULTART PEERED at the briefing notes through his brand new eyeglasses, with their progressive lenses correcting his vision but making him queasy. It takes time to adjust, he'd been told. What, adjusting to constantly wanting to puke? Screw that. He took a shallow breath, returned them to his breast pocket and transitioned back to a squint.

"Let's get this thing started," he said, more upbeat than his ashen pallor suggested.

Steve Smith sat at the head of the conference room table, Linc and Ray Morgan to his left, Ahearn and Kenneally to his right. All eyes turned to the viewing screen as the projector at mid-table whirred to life.

Smith clicked the remote and flashed up the first slide. It was a surveillance photograph of a neatly-bearded Latino male in his mid-forties, arms crossed imperiously, proudly standing in front of a stretched white Rolls-Royce. In the background was an elegant two-story villa on manicured grounds. The image was stamped: *'COE/PNC—Comando de Operaciones Especiales/Policia Nacional de Colombia'*—the Special Operations Command of the Colombian National Police.

"Linc asked me to brief this segment, as I spent nearly five years down there with Army Delta and DEA," he began.

"This murdering sack of shit is Carlos Perez-Garcia, Testaverde's Colombian friend. Not Colombian, actually, but Uruguayan. Ex of their Air Force military police. He trained up here at Benning, the Army's School of the Americas on a six-month course back in '74. After marrying a Colombian national in 1978, he got into the cocaine business, rising quickly through the ranks of the North Coast Cartel, operating out of Barranquilla. A multi-millionaire in his own right. As security chief for cartel boss Alberto Orlandez-Gamboa, his primary duty is to identify and eliminate threats to the cartel leadership and its trafficking network. He is very good at his job."

Next up was a slide of a smiling Perez-Garcia, posing with a pair of uniformed guards in the open doorway of a vast warehouse of arms and ammunition. It appeared to be on a tropical marsh waterfront with a wooden deepwater dock.

"Here we have our friend mugging for a personal photo. This was uncovered recently among snaps of his tenth wedding anniversary, a film his wife's sister dropped off at a Barranquilla Foto-Mat."

There were quiet chuckles at that.

The next slide was an enlargement drawn from the same photograph. It was an enhanced close-up of a taxi idling at the side of the warehouse.

"And here, gentlemen, we learn why nobody down there has been able to smoke out his armaments sideline. The license plate on that taxi is Venezuelan. Note the state marking, Zulia. Estado Zulia borders Colombia on the Caribbean Gulf of Venezuela, just south of Aruba, and contains oil-rich Lake Maracaibo. The guys over at State believe the location in this photo is a petroleum storage site just northwest of a village called San Rafael de El Mojan, shown here."

The screen displayed a map of Zulia state in northern Venezuela. An arrow pointed to a speck on an inland lagoon at the seaward entrance to the lake.

"San Rafael de El Mojan is conveniently located about twenty-five miles north of the bustling state capital of Maracaibo. It is forty miles by road from the Colombian border ... Features direct access to the Caribbean sea, as well as to a hundred square miles of protected saltwater lagoon ... Both suitable for conducting seaplane operations."

The silence in the room was telling.

The next slide showed a grinning party of sports fishermen holding up lunker Lake Trout on a north woods dock, standing in front of the red and blue fuselage of a float-equipped Twin Otter marked La Ronge Aviation. To their right, standing near the floatplane's cockpit door, was a lanky, baby-faced pilot in his late twenties, wearing jeans, a denim jacket and aviator sunglasses.

Smith continued.

"This, Larry in I-and-A says, is the only known photo of the pilot Testaverde refers to as 'Peterborough Pete'. The photo is about ten years old, taken in northern Saskatchewan, Canada, where Pete made his name in the bush. His real name is Thomas Alistair Edward Collins, originally from Peterborough, Ontario, where he adopted the name of his hometown hockey team as his preferred nom-de-guerre."

He glanced at his briefing notes.

"DEA Bogota says he's living in a modest beachfront apartment off the Boca Grande in Cartagena, although he's rarely there. Collins maintains his front, flying for 'Bibles for Missions', an organization that takes medicine, food relief, and the Lord Jesus into the Amazon basin. On the side, he flies cocaine north to market. Has a fifty mission cap, and has never had so much as one DEA bird on his tail. The friggin' guy is a ghost."

The screen then displayed a photograph of an aging PBY Catalina in the markings of the Argentinian Navy.

"I spoke on Wednesday with Abby Caldwell, the DEA intelligence lead in Colombia since my time down there. She says Collins has business smarts. Three years ago, he set up a Canadian company, Fast Attack Aviation, with himself as paid CEO and a minor shareholder. Its majority shares are owned by an offshore Caymans syndicate, which we're guessing is Collins as well. So far, Fast Attack has bought and imported seven PBY Catalinas from Argentina. He flies them up to Montreal, they get refurbished as water bombers, and he contracts them with crews to forestry services from

California to northern Labrador. Revenues in the millions. As we speak, he's flying one like this one up the east coast back home. Alone. Long haul tanks, Buenos Aires with hops to Miami, overnighting tomorrow, then non-stop to Montreal. There's one more purchase set up. Late September. Then, Bogota's sense of it is, he's out, going straight."

"Any plans for arrest or prosecution?" asked Ahearn.

"Nope," Smith replied. "Pilots are too low on the narco food chain. If they don't catch pilots transporting cocaine they get away clean. The protocol's simple as that."

Smith relaxed and the room lights went up. "Anyway, boss, that's me."

"Thank you, Steve. Discussion?" asked Coultart.

Kevin Ahearn chewed on his pen.

"Let's see that map slide again."

With a click it appeared on the screen. Northeastern Colombia, Venezuela and the southern Caribbean.

"DEA and the Coast Guard try to interdict flights into the southern States," Ahearn wondered aloud. "Across the west, through the Yucatan, north of Cuba, checking routes into Gulf states and the Glades. But there's nothing covering the east? Out into the lesser Antilles?"

"That's correct," Smith replied. "No one has the resources. Few cartel fliers have the range to try that kind of end run. But I suppose it does happen."

"Right," Ahearn said. "And if you were planning a trip into the north Atlantic ... Wanted to avoid our airborne early warning ... heading up from just south of Aruba would be perfect. I mean, look. Venezuela, straight northeast, through the Virgin Islands, and you're good to go. Next landfall? The British Isles."

Heads were nodding.

"This Collins is smart," said Ahearn. "If he agrees to the job on his last ferry flight, he'll push to pick up at the warehouse. Right there in ... San Rafael de los Ammo."

The station chief snickered. They all did. It made sense.

"I agree," Coultart said. "So does Paris. We briefed them this morning. We're being tasked to interdict this at the source, San Rafael. To take out Perez-Garcia's operation. Take out Darragh's shipment. Bomb them into the Stone Age with Quinn's assistance."

Kenneally fumed.

"Mount our own operation? Why not just hand it off to DEA? They could send in a whole team of grunts and raze it all to the ground. We're cops, for fucksakes! Why us? What's the point?"

"DEA can't cross that border!" Steve Smith quickly asserted. "No chance. You know fucking borders are sacred."

"Right," spat Kenneally. "Like Cambodia? I bled in sight of a border that we couldn't cross!"

Coultart slapped the tabletop.

"Enough!" he said. "The point is they can't and we can. Remember your high school English and Frost? We're working that forest that's lovely and deep. Promises to keep. Miles to go before we can sleep? Paris expects us to do this and do it alone. Do we have a problem with that?"

"No, boss," said Kenneally.

"Good. Now, Kevin, tell us all about Darragh."

Kevin Ahearn opened his own set of notes.

"As you know, we decided to set up on Darragh after the meeting in Nassau. Testaverde's like nailing down Jell-O unless we catch him on his boat. As well, he's got so many deals on the go, we'd spend hours just sorting them out. Darragh's only got one, so we're all over him."

Ahearn explained that after a week in Lyford Cay, Tink and Maggie followed the man to the French Island of Saint Barthelemy in the Lesser Antilles, east of Puerto Rico.

"He's living on a leased hundred-foot yacht. In St. Barts that's what you'd call a low profile. You've got to admire the guy. He's got three identities under valid Irish passports. Uses them to travel unhindered around the Caribbean and back and forth into the States. Enjoys the high life with money to burn. Anyway, along with Foley and Granger—who, I have to tell you, pass way too easily for a gay couple—our team is on him twenty-four-seven. They're eating up our budget, but when Testaverde makes contact again, we'll know."

"And what about Quinn?" asked Coultart.

Kenneally studied his fingertips for a moment.

"If the Brits think he's planning on bolting, they're wrong," he said. "The guy loves Manhattan. Does the tours like old ladies in town from Dubuque. Hits the hot spots at night. I show up in his shadow every couple of days, and he nearly shits when I do. He's on the straight and narrow and wondering what's coming next. There's no problem with him."

Coultart collected his thoughts.

"All right, gentlemen. Operation Spring Board. Take notes."

❧

Friday, August 19, 1989 – 3:57 p.m. EST
Battery Park, New York, NY

"I'LL HAVE A bratwurst and a Coca-Cola," Quinn told the hot dog man at the State and Bridge Street entrance to Battery Park.

"Six-fifty, pal," the vendor replied. Martin handed the man a ten spot and told him to keep the change. He bit into his snack and strolled to a bench just inside the park.

It had been two hours since Quinn had returned from his second flight to Virginia. Today it had been to Richmond, again aboard Bakker Aviation's Cessna Conquest, although this time with another pilot, a fireplug of a man in his forties, called Spud MacNeil. Aptly named. The man had the wit and the charm of a russet potato. Halliday, he had been told, was flying his boss back from Texas.

A plan and its pieces were coming together. His first flight, on Tuesday to Roanoke, had been for no other reason than Martin inspecting the plane. A destination that he'd picked at random. Martin had found Virginia and the Blue Mountains particularly appealing on his road trip down south. Roanoke. Name kinda rolls off your tongue.

His flight to Richmond, on the other hand, had had a definite purpose. There were as yet few suppliers of satellite telephone technology to the aviation industry, according to the edifying young Danny Halliday. The model that Bakker had chosen had a sole authorized retailer on the eastern seaboard, Spartan Avionics, at Richmond International Airport. It was there that, today, Mr. Quigley had made his own purchase, a base unit alone, plug and play. Just short of nine thousand dollars with taxes. It was activated to Tech-Eireann with an Inmarsat 811 virtual country code and ten-digit number.

On his return to White Plains, Martin had been waiting patiently for the day's invoice in Halliday's office, when he noticed that the scheduling board had substantially changed. Red dates replaced nearly half the available green for the coming weeks into September—most, to his surprise, noted Ted Bakker himself as flying his turboprop Cessna.

When MacNeil had finally appeared to settle the day's business, he explained the changes.

"The boss needs to recertify his instrument rating to fly in command of the jet," he said. "You wouldn't figure a guy like him has the time. But they're his planes. He sets the schedule."

The September 1st flight? A night instrument solo, White Plains to Charleston, South Carolina, over to Bermuda, returning to White Plains before midnight.

"Bermuda? Yeah, that is a bit off the wall. Over water like that for an IFR ride. But he's into some kinda resort over there. Gonna be dropping in plenty with the Grumman, so, what the hell? The guy's got balls and a Distinguished Flying Cross. Anyway, got your next booking dates figured out?"

Martin had. There was just one for now.

Thursday, August 31st, if the Cessna was available. It was. A breakfast departure, Charlotte, North Carolina, return early in the afternoon. Just one passenger again, him. Done deal. Spud MacNeil penciled it in.

QUINN WIPED MUSTARD from his lip and flicked the remnants of his bratwurst bun toward a collection of pigeons that had staked out their turf at his feet.

"Don't feed those fuckin' things!" admonished a voice drawing near. "Flyin' freakin' rats!"

Sal Luongo appeared next to the bench. "You know? On my corner? Foley Square, twenty years now, I've been telling mugs like you to not feed the pigeons. Does anyone listen? You try dodging those shit hawks all day."

Martin looked up and smiled. Then he belched and tossed his empty pop can into a wastebasket. Ten feet, a rim shot.

"What a prince!" Luongo chuckled. "Every day, more and more a New Yorker."

"Good to see you, too, mate. Sorry about the short notice, I'm glad you could make it."

"I'm four blocks that way. Not such a big deal."

Martin rose and clapped his friend on the shoulder. He gestured with a nod down the promenade, and the pair walked slowly together toward the Castle Clinton monument.

"You got some news?" Sal quietly asked, eyeballing their distance to the nearest stranger. It was the end of the day and the tourist crowd in Battery Park was rapidly thinning.

"Aye. You can tell your man that he's getting his wish."

Sal stopped in his tracks.

"Get the fuck out!" he yelped, quickly catching up and lowering his voice to an excited whisper: "Are you shitting me? Get the fuck out!"

Martin stopped and grinned. "Friday, September 1st. He's flying his Cessna propjet on a round trip to Bermuda. Alone. A training flight. Practice he needs for his certification. Your man says the word and he won't be making it all the way home."

"Jesus!" Sal needed a moment to breathe.

Martin canted his head and looked him in the eye.

"Don't stroke out on me, Sally! C'mon, exhale ..."

He did and stood clapping his cheeks.

"Whew! It's just, well, you said you'd know either way pretty quickly. This is real fuckin' quick!"

"It's a window of opportunity, Sal. And not one that's likely to open again. I thought ..."

"No, we do it!" Luongo said without hesitating.

"You don't need to ... ?"

"No! He's in. We're all in. You surprised me, is all. Got it into my head that, you know, planning these things would take time. But what the fuck do I know?"

The pair started strolling again.

"We proceed then?"

"Oh yeah!" Luongo replied. "I'll give him the good news tonight. How much detail should I tell him?"

"Just tell him the date's firm. And the fact that our man will be flying alone. I know that might've been a deal breaker."

"You don't know the half of it, pal."

Martin stopped and fished a pack of cigarettes from his suit pocket. Sal took and lit one as well.

"Everything set? Money holding out?"

Martin exhaled. Fifty thousand up front had been for expenses but his either way, still the project had racked up a sizeable tab—business cards to business suits, aircraft rentals to satellite telephone hardware. His spending had been a bit lavish, but why the hell not? There would be two hundred grand more on completion, and today he could smell it.

"Money's good. Plan's in place and I've got half the hardware," he began. "Would you know anyone in the construction business?"

Luongo snickered. It was contagious.

"Silly me, what was I thinkin'?" Martin said.

He produced a pen, tore the top of the box from his cigarette package, and scribbled.

"Here," he said, passing the scrap to Luongo. "It's the specification for an electrical detonator, a blasting cap. Standard across the whole industry, these. I'd like a couple or three, but I don't have the license to buy them myself."

"I got a cousin."

"You're kidding."

"Just these caps? You got everything else?" Sal asked, surprised, as the pair turned back toward the park entrance.

"We're good," Martin assured him. "Get those to me in no more than a week and we're away to the races."

"No problem. You interested in grabbing a beer?"

Quinn checked his watch. Nearly half four.

"Maybe one, mate, then I have to beg off. I'm taking a darlin' to dinner."

Chapter 35

Wednesday, August 30, 1989 – 4:35 p.m. VET
Highway 6, North of Maracaibo, Venezuela

DRIVING IN LATIN American cities like Maracaibo, with its population of nearly two million, requires nerves of steel and a certain degree of panache. Rules of the Road? Articles of War. Traffic control signals and signage are simply suggestions. And "Yield!" as a concept, as well as a word, doesn't translate in Spanish at all. Foot to the floor and a palm on the horn, drivers stand their ground proudly, pressing ahead and defying all comers with an indecent gesture and a hurled epithet: *"Hejo de Puta!"*

Steve Smith arrived in Maracaibo that afternoon aboard a storm-delayed flight from Bogota. Two hours late. He skipped checking in at the Hotel Presidente, which would have had him navigating the city core, and took his rental car directly to the main interstate highway and north toward San Rafael de El Mojan.

Good thing he drove like a local.

He drew on machismo he quickly acquired during his five years in Colombia. Not as a Special Forces operator or DEA agent, arguably licensed to kill, but as a licensed driver—which, in Latin America, is pretty much the same thing.

And it helped that he was so effortlessly fluent in Spanish. Steve Smith could hurl epithets with the best.

GROWING UP IN La Jolla, the native Californian had been educated in Spanish immersion from kindergarten through his high school senior year. It secured him a scholarship and a bilingual undergrad degree in Electronics and Computer Engineering at UC San Diego, where he went Army through

ROTC. His linguistic abilities were further enhanced at the Defense Language Institute at the Presidio in San Francisco. It was there that he came to think and to dream in Spanish, a degree of fluency that would serve him well in his chosen profession. He developed a distinct Colombian accent. Born and bred, many locals surmised. If not Bogota, then elsewhere in the province of Cundinamarca, surely!

He was traveling on an American passport in the name of Esteban Santos Torres, a naturalized U.S. citizen born in Colombia. Steve Santos, a satellite communications engineer with Conoco, the Continental Oil Company, out of Houston.

There were two important reasons why Linc Coultart had chosen him to command. Soldiering experience, first of all. Unmatched on Olympiad's New York roll. Six years airborne Rangers and two Delta Force. This would be a paramilitary operation. Military weapons and explosives, cam-stick darkened faces, humping through the jungle—the whole nine yards, and it was all second nature to Steve. Kevin Ahearn? He was smart and a leader, a consummate Fed. Booze-Smokes-and-Guns to the core. He knew organized crime and could master a sting, but this would be night and day different.

The second reason for choosing Smith was even plainer.

Regional operational knowledge—the sum total of everything he had learned and had been until now. And all of it down to a doting mother, who decided back in 1961 that her little Stevie would get a leg up learning Spanish.

And Smith's other choice for the team? Jimmy Kenneally was a Vietnam vet with the Silver Star and two Purple Hearts. He still had the mettle for it, if not the knees. More importantly, though, he had the leash on Quinn, the only wild card they'd drawn from the deck. Spring Board needed Kenneally.

WHEN HE ARRIVED in Bogota on August 22nd, the first thing he'd done had been to reconnect with Abby Caldwell.

He had worked closely with the DEA mission's intelligence chief for nearly three years. Steve in the field, a specialist in covert surveillance; Abigail Caldwell in their Bogota compound, analyzing the data his kind generated. The former Justice Department lawyer had fled D.C. for a frontline adrenaline rush and she had quickly found it in Colombia. The two had connected as colleagues and briefly as lovers, an intimacy which had come to an amicable close with his departure in February.

Steve's new post in New York was, as Abby understood it, gathering intelligence on arms traffickers, with the sexy ring of 'Interpol' to the job. After his pointed enquiries around Carlos Perez-Garcia, it hadn't really surprised her to see Steve grinning again at her door.

Bogota had more recent intell on the activities and movements of both his subjects.

Collins, she reported, was closing the Colombian chapter of his charmed life. He had given notice on his Cartagena apartment, as well as at his job with Bibles for Missions, both effective September 1st. He was seen closing his accounts at Banco de Occidente. He had booked a one-way flight for Tuesday, September 12th: Avianca from Cartagena to Caracas, Venezuela, connecting that same afternoon on an Aerolineas Argentinas flight to Buenos Aires. Goodbye, Peterborough Pete. Good riddance, Abby had added. The DEA wouldn't miss him at all.

Carlos Perez-Garcia had been busy as well. On the previous Friday, he had flown with his wife to Cartagena, returning home to Barranquilla the same evening. He rarely flew with Margita but had been known to indulge her addiction to emeralds. It wasn't certain, but it was suspected that, while Margita was out maxing her Platinum card, he'd had a brief meeting with Collins.

"These two together is new," Caldwell had said. "A line pilot, high value but still rank-and-file, getting face time with a *jefe* like Carlos? That's like ... *Jack Lawn* flying down for a coffee with me."

The forty-two year old brunette, who still cut a hell of a figure in a satin blouse and a suit, had been batting her eyelashes at him. We *are* still partners, aren't we?

"Lawn might if you were retiring," Steve countered. "Jet down from D.C.? Extend the best wishes of the President and a grateful nation. Palm off a gold watch?"

"Yeah, right!" she scoffed. And Smith understood. The DEA Administrator, a former FBI man who had led the Bureau's internal affairs division, had all the endearing qualities of J. Edgar Hoover.

"But Carlos? No way, not his style. Head office is looking for answers. So c'mon, Stevie, what's up?"

"I can give you this much," he obliged.

He said Interpol had an active investigation into Perez-Garcia's arms dealing. So far it had been continental. Shining Path in Peru. The *Ejército de Liberación Nacional* in Bolivia, wiped out with Che Guevara in '67, was rebuilding, thanks mainly to Carlos. Paraguay. Even right-wing Chileans. But their biggest concern at the moment was with the *Macheteros*.

"Puerto Rico?" Abby Caldwell was surprised.

"That's right, on American soil. They've been two-bit Marxist insurgents until now. Poorly led, poorly armed. We think Carlos and this Canadian pilot have struck a deal for transporting a shipment by air. Paris thinks ..."

"*Oooh*, Paris!" she cooed. "Now you're place-dropping."

Smith slowly shook his head. She had gotten enough for head office. And again with the batting eyelashes.

"There's enough to it to warrant attention."

"Get there a lot?" Abby enquired wistfully. "I mean, to places like Paris? To locations actually in the First World?"

"No chance," he replied, smiling. "At my pay grade, I get to come back to places like this. Maybe if I'd learned French ..."

❧

THE GUTLESS FORD Fiesta protested with a tinny whine as Steve Smith downshifted and stamped on the gas. This was his chance to pass the smoking oil tanker he'd been trapped behind for half an hour and barely five miles. He crossed the double line on the two-lane highway and accelerated slowly past the lumbering rig.

"Come on! Come on!" he groaned, bucking forward and back in his seat like a jockey whipping his mount.

Oncoming traffic was looming. A multi-colored old bus led the endless procession that hurtled toward him. Its headlights flashed and he could hear its air horn, which blared 'La Cucaracha'. Seconds from inevitable impact, he yanked the wheel to the right and the Ford swerved to safety ahead of the tanker. The trucker hadn't backed off an inch.

"*Cago en tu leche!*" Steve swore over his shoulder. 'I shit in your milk!' never really caught on as an insult in English.

San Rafael de El Mojan was ten miles ahead on Highway 6, which wound north along the western reaches of Lake Maracaibo. Steve cursed again as he checked his watch. It was already 4:35. Traffic was thinning a little, with the ramshackle barrios on the city's outskirts behind him at last. Only two hours left until sunset and night fell like a curtain at these latitudes. Daylight, then darkness. And he would need more than a little of both.

Time was becoming a critical factor.

Coultart had reached him on Friday with news.

Testaverde had been contacted in Providence by Perez-Garcia. A brief, cryptic conversation late Thursday evening, acknowledging the sale of their interest in a Venezuelan racehorse, now set for Thursday, September 21st. Would he relay the news to their partner and confirm the air cargo arrangements? He would.

He did. Tinker and Maggie reported Darragh's delight in St. Barts after receiving an overseas telephone call. The substance of that conversation was unknown, but it had quickly been traced to a Providence, Rhode Island number.

And, the next morning, there were outgoing calls from his yacht to banks in Zurich and the Caymans.

Spring Board was on.

SMITH REACHED HIS destination with an hour of daylight remaining. A white-gloved traffic cop on the outskirts of San Rafael de El Mojan had been obliging. An oilfield warehouse with a wooden dock on the river? Yes, six miles west on the highway. It was a place known to locals as Puerto Mara. If you reach the bridge, the cop said, you have missed it.

He didn't. Along the short stretch of Highway 6 leading to the bridge over the Rio Limon was a single exit to the right. Puerto Mara. He left the highway and followed a narrow paved road for a quarter mile to a dead end at a locked gate in wire perimeter fencing.

Steve stopped the car at the side of the road. His heart thumped in his chest. This was the place.

Puerto Mara was all of two graveled acres of cleared Mangrove jungle. It had two nondescript buildings. On the right: a prefab office trailer with CITGO Petroleum signage and a massive multi-colored cache of fifty-five gallon drums in its yard. To the left: a rust-streaked, single-story metal warehouse with a hundred foot frontage. It had *Petroleos Vargas* in plain black lettering above its closed double doors. From where he was standing, it was exactly the view from the Colombian intell photograph.

He quickly withdrew, returned to the highway and parked the Fiesta just west of the Puerto Mara exit.

It was 6:05 p.m.

He took his rucksack from the trunk of the car and made his way back through the sandy Mangrove and Buttonwood forest to the compound's fence line. There he sat, taking photographs and making notes. The warehouse had a single "man door" to the right of its vehicle doors. Every fifteen minutes, an armed guard would emerge through it and spend ten walking the yard before disappearing back inside. There was no video surveillance. No dogs or apparent alarms.

Steve noted that the CITGO fuel cache was stacked against the east wall of the warehouse. Hundreds of drums. Focusing more closely, he saw their markings: AVGAS 100-130. High octane aviation fuel, each drum with a sheen at its bolt ring seal and pressing heavily into the gravel. They were not empty, but full.

As he rose from his crouch, draped in the thin filigree of a camouflage scarf, Smith noticed movement fifteen feet to his left. A six-foot Bushmaster dangled then dropped from the Mangrove canopy. The snake darted its tongue his way before slithering off through the leaf litter and compacted sand. He grinned. Ahearn and Kenneally are gonna *love* this place.

IT WAS DARK by seven o'clock. There is no twilight to speak of so near the equator. The sun sets, slipping below the horizon and that's all she wrote. Sudden darkness that's deep. The sky remains midnight blue overhead, briefly brightened by oblique rays of sunlight that cant off into space on the earth's atmosphere. And then it's pitch dark. Water will shimmer silver with a wind breaking its surface. Otherwise, it lays black and flat and imperceptible to the human eye.

Man-made light broke the darkness at Puerto Mara.

Incandescent roadway lights glowed like a loose string of pearls along the length of the bridge over the Rio Limon. Around its footings and at its abutments on both sides of the river, there was the cheerful glimmer of gas lamps from the dozens of fishermen's shanties, boats and barges, floating nested together beneath the bridge.

Eight o'clock. Steve Smith drifted with the river's current back toward Puerto Mara.

At sunset, he had driven away from the compound on the south side of the river, crossed the bridge and descended its embankment to a parking lot at the river's edge. The lot was crowded with vehicles belonging to its resident fishermen, and downriver were dozens of their *piragua*—thirty-foot, flat-bottomed fishing canoes—beached above the tide line of the estuary. They were crawling with rats. At the water's edge, there was occasional violent thrashing as a caiman, six-foot-long river kin to the crocodile, seized a black rat as a meal. He spanked the gunwales of a canoe with a paddle, scattering rats to their fate, and had stolen away from the shore.

Smith paddled silently into mid-channel and grounded the canoe on an island a hundred yards north of the lit compound at Puerto Mara and a mile downstream from the bridge. Here he had a direct line of sight to the target.

Through night vision goggles he observed the dock at the rear of the warehouse. It was constructed of creosote-treated pilings and timbers, and extended about fifty feet into the river, with a tethered barge as a permanent dockside float. It could easily handle an aircraft the size of a Catalina. He took high speed infrared photographs. Made notes.

By nine o'clock, he returned to the north shore, fighting off caimans in their rat-feeding frenzy as he beached the canoe.

It would be dead simple, he thought, grinning as he made his way south along Highway 6 to Maracaibo and his hotel. Almost too easy.

Friday, September 1, 1989 – 1:48 p.m. EST
White Plains Airport, Westchester County, NY

MARTIN QUINN STOOD and sipped a foamed café latte on the second-floor observation deck at the Dixon Flight Services hangar. Below on the ramp, a crew with an Exxon fuel bowser was topping the tanks of Bakker Aviation's Cessna Conquest, NC214T.

Just two days earlier, Martin had received the detonators that Sal had promised to source—cutting it too bloody close—and that night he constructed his bomb. Although he was certain that his Hester Street flat wasn't wired as had been implied, he took the precaution of assembling the device in the bathroom. One stick of the C4 he kept from the container job, wired up inside the guts of the telephone unit he had purchased in Richmond. He used the same circuit-bypass technique that Diver's man Ray had shown him. It would trigger detonation on receipt of two 'pound sign' tones from the phone of a connected caller.

On Thursday, Martin had taken his charter flight to North Carolina with Spud MacNeil as his pilot. The Cessna had executive seating for eight in the back: two facing forward behind the cockpit bulkhead, four face-to-face, then two more facing ahead at the rear. Out and back, Martin occupied the port side forward-facing club seat, which placed its "plug and play" satellite telephone unit on the fuselage wall at his left knee. It provided in-flight telephone service to the passenger cabin as well as to the cockpit with a remote handset between the pilots' seats. On the return flight from Charlotte, Martin had needed only a moment to replace the cabin's base unit with his own.

A tall man appeared from under the wing of the Cessna. It occurred to Quinn that he'd never seen Bakker in the flesh until now. Dressed in a tan leather flight jacket, white polo shirt and chinos. Gold-rimmed sunglasses. All airs and graces.

Martin sipped his coffee. He had studied the Cessna's planned flight for the day. Depart White Plains at two o'clock. A quick turnaround at Charleston, South Carolina, airborne again at 3:45 local time. Arrive in Bermuda, 1,037 miles over water, at 7:45 p.m. New York time. Leave Bermuda at 8:30 with a 700-mile flight back to White Plains, arriving around 11:30 p.m.

His arrangements with Sal had been set on the previous afternoon. If he paged him today, they were to meet as planned at Sullivan's Bar in Hell's Kitchen. No later than 8:30. Sal was to bring the Judge if he agreed to come.

Bakker had just completed his walk around as a Mercedes limousine glided onto the ramp. It stopped near the Cessna.

What the fuck is this? Quinn got an unsettling feeling.

Passengers? No, no fucking passengers!

A woman got out of the limo and walked toward Bakker, who stood at the plane. She had a small suitcase in her hand.

Quinn moved to the railing, dread welling inside him.

He watched as Penny Luscombe approached Bakker and stood for a moment at the side of the aircraft. The pair spoke together. Spoke for too long. No, goddammit! Martin quickly decided that it mustn't matter. This was on for tonight whether or not he was flying alone. Seconds passed. He saw Penny pat Bakker's hand and give him a hug. She handed the suitcase to him and, with a parting word, turned and promptly returned to the car.

"Thank you, Jesus, Joseph and Mary."

Bakker climbed aboard and pulled the air stair door slowly closed. With a whine, the Cessna's turbines began to spool up and its props began turning as the Mercedes was leaving the ramp.

The aircraft lurched forward and taxied away from its parking position. The Irishman stayed at the rail and watched as it moved to the north end of the field. Moments later, NC214T lifted from the runway, its landing gear quickly retracted and the airplane disappeared from view, climbing away to the southeast on the first leg of its journey.

He retrieved his cellular phone from his satchel and punched in the number for Luongo's pager.

Done, and done.

Chapter 36

"BRING ME A large Jameson and a Rolling Rock back, would ya, darlin'?" asked the Irishman, who was taking a booth at the back of the bar. Molly Geary smiled, she knew that tongue. The barmaid swept coal black punk-cut bangs from her eyes as she studied the stranger. Well fit, so he was. She chewed on a glistening lower lip.

"Bandit Country," she declared, setting down a paper coaster imprinted with the Smithwick's Ale label.

"D'you reckon?" replied Martin Quinn, returning her once-over survey with one of his own. He grinned. The girl was a beauty in some thoroughly unwholesome ways, with the body and brass of an exotic dancer.

"Portadown," she said. "It could be Newry, but that's Armagh I'm hearin'. Myself, I'm over from Crossmaglen."

Martin's grin quickly faded.

"Aye. Good place to be from, so it is."

She smiled a wry smile. Molly knew what he meant. Her hometown in border County Armagh had seen more than its share of horror during the Troubles, and with the worst of it said to be over, Crossmaglen remained a sectarian tinderbox. She had fled the village a year ago now for the tranquility of New York.

"And you?" she enquired, too innocently for an ex-pat who should have known better.

"Your ear's perfect," Martin said, smiling warmly again. "But it's best all you know is my preference in drink."

Molly understood but she still feigned a pout.

"The night's early, Paddy," she said as she turned toward the bar. "Night's early."

❧

TED BAKKER STARTED the engines of his Cessna Conquest on the civilian ramp at Naval Air Station Bermuda. It was a half an hour past sunset and the airfield on St. David's Island was a twinkling pattern of blue taxiway and white runway lights. It was 9:12 local time in Bermuda, past midnight Greenwich or Zulu, and 8:12 p.m. in New York. He keyed the transmit button on the controls and spoke into his headset's boom mike.

"Bermuda Ground, Cessna Conquest Two One Four Tango, ready to taxi."

"214 Tango, Ground, roger," acknowledged the American ground controller in a West Texas twang. "Your airways when ready to copy."

"Go ahead," Bakker replied, a pen poised above the clipboard strapped to his right thigh.

"ATC clears Cessna 214 Tango to the Westchester County Airport via direct the GABES intersection, direct DASER, Lima 459, your flight planned route. To maintain flight level two-two-zero. Depart runway three zero, climb runway heading to four thousand, turn right, climb on course."

Bakker read back the clearance for the final leg of his round-trip flight. His flight plan had the turboprop Conquest flying waypoints to a virtual highway in the sky that ran from the Caribbean to Bermuda to New York. At a cruise speed of 260 knots, depending on traffic and winds, he would arrive in White Plains at 11:15 p.m. local time. Just under three hours.

"214 Tango, Ground, the altimeter two-eight-niner-seven. Cleared to taxi to runway three-zero via taxiway Alpha."

The Cessna picked up speed as it crossed the ramp.

Five minutes later, Bakker held short of the mile-long runway at its easternmost end and notified the tower that he was ready to depart.

"214 Tango, Tower, cleared takeoff runway three-zero, wind calm."

The Cessna lined up at the end of the runway and Bakker shoved the thrust levers forward. The jet turbines whined as he released the brakes and the turboprop Conquest sped down the undulating runway. In ten seconds it was airborne. Bakker flipped an illuminated lever and its landing gear rose, tucking away into its wells with an audible clunk.

"Cessna 214 Tango, Bermuda Tower, contact departure on one-one-nine-decimal-one, good night."

"Fourteen Tango, thanks, switching."

Climbing out on the runway heading of 300 degrees, Bakker activated the aircraft's flight director, an autopilot coupled into its inertial navigation system. His first waypoint, an intersection named GABES, was 121 nautical miles ahead to the northwest. The Conquest veered slightly to the right, steering toward it. He reduced power from takeoff to climb and the whine of the twin Garrett jet turbines settled down to a hum. He would reach his planned altitude of 22,000 feet ten minutes after takeoff.

"Departure, Cessna 214 Tango, airborne at 0024 Zulu, with you through four thousand for flight level two-two-zero, estimating GABES at 0102."

THE BLACK CAPRICE stopped in the 600 block of 10th Avenue and nosed into a spot at the curb near the corner of West 45th Street. Jimmy Kenneally walked from a darkened doorway and got into the car.

"One-way streets in this town!" groaned Kevin Ahearn as he switched off the ignition. "Had to circle twice through four blocks. How'd you guys ever run any rolling surveillance?"

Kenneally smiled. He nodded to the vacant lot opposite the car on the west side of the street. A sign proclaimed it as the future site of another Hess filling station.

"That rubble field over there?" he said. "Summer of '86. We're all over Kenny Shannon, a Westie chieftain. Gang task force, double teaming with four rolling units. He makes a big coke deal up in the Bronx and is heading back to the Kitchen in his Lincoln limo. OCB has three cars of their own on Kevin Kelly, his partner in crime. The two Westies met here. Two o'clock in the morning."

Kenneally began to snicker. "We all came together in one giant cluster. Seven unmarked units, circling like clown cars in a Shriners drill team."

The image of that had Ahearn in stitches.

"So then what's the trick then?"

"Besides coked-up targets who don't notice? You do it like this. Two men, one car. Bigger teams always get burned."

Oh, the wisdom.

"So where's our boy, Quinn?" asked Ahearn.

"Bar on the corner," his partner replied, pointing across the intersection to a pub called Sullivan's. "He went straight in alone."

So they'd followed an Irishman to an Irish bar.

"Your message said you had a hunch. Were you planning on filling me in?"

Kenneally handed his partner the camera, a Nikon with a telephoto lens.

"Give it time. I'm still hoping I'm wrong."

Well, *that* had an ominous tone.

Ahearn muttered misgivings as he checked the focus on the entrance to Sullivan's Bar.

Minutes passed. Kenneally spotted an old Jeep Cherokee making the turn onto 10th, then signal to park halfway up the block. It was dusk, nearly dark. He strained to observe the Jeep's driver, now walking back toward the corner of West 45th. Shit. Half his hunch had been right.

"One male Caucasian approaching. Leather jacket," he said to Ahearn, who refocused the camera. Its motor drive whirred and the shutter clicked three or four times.

Then a moment of silence.

"Jesus Christ, it's Luongo!" yelped Ahearn. His target stopped at the door to the bar and lit a cigarette. He lowered the camera and glared at Kenneally.

"When were you planning on telling me this?"

"Surprise!"

"For Chrissakes, Jimmy! How long ... Who ..."

"Keep watching the door, Kev. It could get worse."

"Worse? Goddammit!" Ahearn was peering again through the Nikon's viewfinder. "C'mon, Jimmy. Spill!"

Kenneally sighed.

"Since you put me on Quinn, and thanks a fuck of a lot, by the way, I've been on his tail on and off every day. Never much to report. Then Tuesday, we cross lower Manhattan to Foley Square and he meets up with Luongo."

"Not a chance meeting, then?"

"Went straight to Sal's cart. Greeted each other like pals from the Knights of Columbus."

Kevin fumed.

"Jesus, Jimmy, you should've told me."

"Hey! We all have a lot on our plate! Anyway, I had my long-distance ears and Quinn mentioned this place. Sullivan's. Made arrangements to meet here tonight. Thought we should set up and see what plays out."

"Nothing good comes from those two together!"

"Yeah ... well, we introduced them."

They watched Luongo, nervously smoking outside the door to the bar. He checked his watch. Ahearn checked his own. It was coming up half-past eight.

"How does this get any worse? I'm afraid to ask."

Jimmy gritted his teeth.

"This afternoon, Larry from I-and-A tells me Testaverde's in town. Here to see his orthodontist."

"What? What am I, a fucking mushroom?"

"Keep your hair on! Nothing ties them together."

"What? Are you drunk? Mob family ties? The IRA? Our pensions, my ulcer ..."

"There's nothing that ties them together tonight."

"Right, but you had a hunch," said Ahearn.

"Yeah," Jimmy commiserated.

A yellow cab swung around the corner from West 45th and stopped, doubled-parked in front of Sullivan's Bar. A man exited the driver's side rear and was met by Luongo. They shook hands and spoke for a moment.

Ahearn's camera whirred and clicked.

"Who the hell's he?" he wondered aloud.

"No fucking idea."

White male, maybe sixty, open-collared checked shirt under a jacket, a worn New York Mets baseball cap. Gaunt with an angular face. Rimless eyeglasses.

"Sure as hell ain't Cousin Gino."

The pair entered the bar.

Ahearn sighed as he lowered the lens.

"No, thank Christ. Go on, you might as well get your ass in there. I'll keep an eye out for goombahs. Keep your damned pager on vibrate."

SULLIVAN'S BAR WAS typical of Manhattan watering holes, most occupying a street level space in narrow 19th century brick tenements. As such, its floor plan was a rectangular box; a bar with stools along the right-hand interior wall, a dozen tables opposite, each seating four. The rear half of the tavern had booths in an inverted L around a pool table. At the back, a narrow hall to the restrooms, the office, a store room, and a barred exit into the alley.

Typical too, Sullivan's had a wood-paneled interior that was brightened by brass fittings. It had hanging Tiffany lamps stained by decades of cigarette smoke, and walls festooned with the bric-a-brac of an Ireland few of its patrons had seen. And, of course, Irish tunes on an endless taped loop that blared as you came through the door. Lively jigs with drums, pipes and whistles, alternating with the melancholy of rebel laments. Just as Jimmy Kenneally expected.

Sullivan's was as noisy as it was busy. Friday night on the Labor Day weekend. Kenneally cast a skilled eye around the room and spotted Luongo making his way from the restroom to a booth in the far corner. He chose his spot, a standing space halfway down the crowded bar, next to the server's station. There he had a clear view of the corner booth, reflected in the mirrored wall behind the bartender.

"Kilkenny!" he said, shouting his choice to the burly young man pulling pints.

"Molly! C'mon!" the bartender hollered to the serving girl in the back. "We got thirsty people up here!"

Kenneally followed the bartender's eyes. A pretty brunette with a jagged punk hairdo was giggling as she loitered near the pool table.

The girl frowned as she made her way to her station.

"Where the fuck's Laura?" Molly sniped on arrival.

"On her smoke break out back! Wall Street at three and four is waiting for another round," pleaded the bartender, nodding toward two tables near the bar's entrance.

"Yeah? And they don't fuckin' tip!" she complained, loudly enough for the young stockbrokers to hear.

"Set me up three more Jamies, two bar Bush and a half dozen Guinness," she continued. Then she rolled her eyes, acquiescing, and headed off to the front of the bar.

"Sweet girl," said Kenneally.

"Molly?" replied the bartender, drawing the Guinness. "Bitchy, but one helluva rack. Accent that rakes in the tips. Still, find a Mick right off the boat? Like Bono there in the back corner? She goes into heat. Over here nearly a year and she'd still rather polish shillelaghs. Right? Go fuckin' figure."

Kenneally studied the back corner booth in the mirror.

Yeah. Go fucking figure.

☙

"SO YOU'RE BOTH fans of this ball team, the Mets? Do you hawk tube steaks down at the ball field as well?" asked Martin, sipping his Rolling Rock lager.

Luongo bristled. "What kinda question is that?"

The Irishman apologized quickly.

"I'm sorry, no, Salvatore, don't get me wrong! Just me wondering how such an unlikely pair got together. Back home your street vendors don't meet many judges unless they're handcuffed in the dock. Incongruous that, so it is."

Sal blushed.

"I thought you were yanking my chain."

"Curiosity, Sally, is all."

Randolph Elliott had said barely a word since he shook hands with Martin. He'd simply sat in the booth looking pained, having downed his first Jameson in one swallow. He chose to explain.

"I am a man of routine," Elliott said quietly. "For six years, I bought my lunch every Friday from Sal, at his cart, in the square outside the courthouse. He came to know me rather more than I him. After my loss, we came across each other by chance at a ballpark. That's where we connected, both as Mets fans and friends. Friends ever since. Does that clear up the issue?"

"Indeed." Martin nodded.

The Judge's eyes narrowed.

"Why exactly did you ask us here?"

Martin glanced at his watch. It was nearly five minutes to nine. He produced his cellular phone and set it on the table.

"We're here to do what we've planned."

Sal looked confused.

Martin paused as Molly returned with a fresh tray of whiskey and beer. The server was rushed off her feet.

"Ta, darlin'!" the Irishman said, smiling as he covered the round with two twenties. An eighteen dollar tip. She blew him a kiss and rushed quickly away, leaving a note on the back of a coaster: 'I get off at ten!'

"Here to do what?" Luongo persisted.

"This!" Martin replied as he picked up his cellular phone. "Our wee chore."

"Here? How?"

"Technology, mate."

Martin listened for a dial tone, punched in a series of numbers and returned the phone to his ear.

The connection was made and was ringing.

"Bakker," a male voice answered brusquely.

"Mr. Bakker, hello," Martin replied.

Sal's jaw dropped and the Judge looked alarmed.

"Pete Dye?" Martin heard.

"I'm sorry?"

"Pete Dye, the course architect. I've been expecting his call for two days. Who's this?"

Martin covered the mouthpiece with his palm.

"He thinks I'm his golf course designer!" he sniggered.

"Mr. Dye cannot come to the phone."

"Who the hell's calling?"

"I'm sorry, sir, would you hold for a message?"

Martin heard a tirade about time being wasted as he passed the phone to the Judge.

Randolph Elliott was in shock, gingerly holding the phone like he'd been handed a live hand grenade.

"Go on, now!" prodded Martin. "Talk to the man!"

The Judge pressed the phone to his ear and heard an angry voice cursing.

"Is this Ted Bakker?" he managed to ask, finally mustering courage. "Theodore Rumsfeld Bakker?"

"Yes, goddammit! Who the fuck are you? How did you get this number?"

The voice sounded distant and hollow. There was a low background droning of engines. A spark ignited inside him. His heart began to pound in his chest.

Martin was beckoning to him.

"Excuse me," he said instinctively and lowered the phone.

"Jesus!" Martin chuckled. He pointed out the pound sign on the keypad. "With him on the line, press that key twice. *That* key. Press it twice. *Go on!*"

Judge Elliott looked confused, then his eyes opened wide. He returned the phone to his ear.

"Are you there?" he asked politely.

"Yes, goddammit! Are you one of Dye's people?"

"No, Mr. Bakker," Elliott said abruptly. "But I will tell you this. I am the last voice that you'll ever hear. So long, you bastard, I'll see you in hell."

He pressed the pound sign, and again.

He listened closely, concentrating; a look of shock spread across Elliott's face. There was a loud indistinct sound and, in the same instant, what he thought was a cry or a scream. Then there was nothing at all. The line had gone dead.

Six hundred miles away, over the open Atlantic, an eight-ounce stick of C4 plastic had exploded. It blew the Cessna in half just ahead of its wings. The force of the blast caved in the cockpit bulkhead, pinning Bakker over his controls and against the instrument panel, dazed but conscious as the aircraft flew apart and tumbled in pieces toward the dark ocean. He would have still been alive, falling for nearly four miles, his mind racing, pulse pounding. Surface impact would have been instantly fatal.

Sal looked puzzled.

"What happened? What's going on?"

Martin raised his whiskey glass in a toast.

"Fire in the hole," he said, downing the drink.

"So that's it? It's done?"

"Ask our client."

The Judge had been drifting, unfocused. "Yes," he said, quickly back in the present. "I believe that it is."

Randolph Elliott felt ill. He rose from his outside seat in the booth and apologized, telling Martin he needed to leave. Sal was begging off too.

The Judge smiled weakly and shook Martin's hand.

"Thank you for this."

Sal told Martin in parting he'd call him tomorrow. After the five o'clock news.

The pair left with no further ado, making their way through the crowd, leaving the Irishman in the booth on his own. He swirled the remnants of a whiskey shot and threw it back, smiling. It's done. He'd felt that rush before, perhaps once too often. The only difference was that this time he felt … wealthy. But enough about that. He would turn his attention for the rest of the evening to a comely young lass over from Crossmaglen.

ॐ

"DIDN'T GET A whole hell of a lot," Kenneally said as he returned to the car.

It was 9:12 p.m.

"Quinn's still inside, working on getting laid. Sal and our mystery guest had two drinks with him in a booth. Polite conversation. Nothing animated. Couple of drinks, Martin makes a phone call, and Sal and the other guy leave. That's it."

"They went their separate ways," Ahearn added, chewing it over. Then he slapped his palm on the steering wheel.

"A judge!" he said, a Eureka moment.

"Number Two? He's a federal judge!"

"You sure about that?" asked Kenneally.

"I've seen his face in the papers. New York Southern District. I'm certain, just can't place the name."

"What should we make of that?"

Ahearn scratched stubble on his cheek.

"Okay, Quinn and Luongo get friendly. Could be nothing. Luongo and this Judge clearly have a connection. But the three of them together? Like you said, nothing jumps off the page. Could be it was an innocent drink. Could be they killed Jimmy Hoffa. Who the fuck knows?"

Ahearn started the car.

"So, do we report it to Coultart?" asked Kenneally.

"No! For Chrissakes, we leave it. At least for now. He's convinced that Spring Board won't get past 'Go' without Quinn. And that's straight from Paris. You'll just have to stay on him. Make sure nothing goes south."

Kenneally absently tapped his notebook as they gathered speed along 10th Avenue.

"Okay, how am I writing this up?"

Ahearn pondered the question as he turned onto West 46th. "Try something like this. 'Close surveillance on Sal Luongo with news that Testaverde's in town. We set up. He's a no-show and nothing pans out.' A short sheet report. Filed into Luongo's jacket and that's that."

Still," Kevin added with a grin, "There's the good start to a joke for you, Jimmy. A Judge, an Irishman and a Hot Dog Vendor go into a bar ..."

Chapter 37

Saturday, September 2, 1989 – 4:55 p.m. EST
21 Rye Road, Port Chester, New York

"THERE WAS NOTHING in the papers," Sal Luongo said as he paced in the Judge's study. "This morning, I bought them all. The Times, the Post, the Daily News. Not a word. I just figured there would a been something, you know?"

Randolph Elliott listened to Sal droning on as he stuffed cherry tobacco into his favorite pipe, the straight-stemmed Saddle Bulldog that Diana had given him on his 48th birthday. Or rather, the pipe that Charlotte had bought and wrapped for Diana to give to him at dinner. Diana would have been eleven. Or had she been twelve? In any case, it would have been at that age when she first had begun to ignore him. Before the first so-called trial separation. Before all the hostility. Elliott sighed remorsefully. We reap what we sow.

"Most go to press between midnight and three," he said, fanning a match and exhaling a plume of smoke. "There would've been nothing in the morning papers."

Sal shrugged and helped himself to a drink.

"You know, I never would a guessed that he'd do that thing with the phone," he said, still amazed by their bar encounter with Martin. "Or hand it to you like he did? That's gotta be a first, a friggin' do-it-yourself contract hit."

Luongo continued to pace, edgy and prattling on.

"And him? Cool as a cucumber. Fire in the hole!"

Elliott picked up the television remote.

"Sal? Have a seat, would you? Please!"

Sal apologized and turned a chair to face the television.

The screen came to life with the fast-cut montage intro to WABC-TV Eyewitness News at Five and its pounding news-teletype theme. A dolly zoom through the program's set drew in on the news anchor—chiseled jaw, blond hair perfectly coiffed—who turned to the camera on cue.

"September 2nd, 1989," he said with polished aplomb. "I'm Jonathan Price in New York, and this is Eyewitness News at Five."

Behind the anchor's left shoulder appeared still images of George Bush and Mikhail Gorbachev.

"Making headlines today, the Bush Administration announces work on a new strategic arms proposal that could pave the way for a first summit between President Bush and Soviet leader Mikhail Gorbachev later this year."

Next appeared video of a sea of protesters marching through a South African township. "Tens of thousands march in a protest in Johannesburg, this in the wake of the arrest yesterday of Anglican Archbishop Desmond Tutu, a vocal opponent of the South African regime's policy of apartheid."

The video gave way to an aviation news graphic with "*Presumed Lost?*" in bold lettering and the inset photograph of Ted Bakker.

"And locally, mystery surrounds the disappearance last night of high-flying Manhattan financier, Ted Bakker. These stories and more in three minutes on Eyewitness News at Five. Stay with us."

The program's theme returned as the screen image cut to a prime view of the news desk with its team of four, and quickly cut to commercials.

Randolph Elliott was numb.

Sal sat gaping at the television, briefly speechless.

"Holy Mother! We really did it. *You* really did it!"

Elliott had known from the moment he put down that cellular phone. Knew what he had heard, knew what he had done, and the totality of it had preyed on his mind ever since. He hadn't slept. He hadn't felt the exhilaration that he expected, and he'd had every right to. He hadn't despaired his decision, even though in his heart he imagined he would. The numbing detachment he felt had begun even then, after pressing that key, sensing death in his own private moment of absolute certainty.

Sal had continued to natter.

"Come on, Desmond friggin' Tutu?" he groused at the television. "Tell me that cross ain't solid gold Gucci. Okay! Okay, here we go! Crank that sound a bit, Randy!"

The aviation graphic returned behind Jonathan Price.

"FAA officials are investigating the disappearance of former Pan Am CEO Ted Bakker, whose plane went missing last night on a flight to New York from Bermuda," the anchorman said. "News Nine reporter Veronica Gamble is in White Plains with more."

Elliott remembered the name and instantly recognized the attractive brunette as she appeared with the airport's busy tarmac as her backdrop.

"An extensive sea and air search continues today off Bermuda for any sign of a plane flown by Ted Bakker, the Manhattan millionaire at the center of lawsuits surrounding his leadership at Pan American Airlines and its loss, last Christmas, of Flight 103 to a terrorist bomb over Lockerbie, Scotland."

Video cut to a man in his mid-forties with a military demeanor, crew cut and tanned, wearing a polo-shirt with an FAA emblem. Electronic on-screen text introduced him as Bill Kalbfleisch, FAA Spokesman, New York Region.

"Mr. Bakker is a seasoned former air force and airline pilot. He was flying his Cessna propjet alone on a personal flight which left Bermuda last night at 8:24, New York time, expecting to arrive in White Plains at 11:15 p.m. He did not. His first and only radio contact was just after take-off, indicating an estimate for his next ATC checkpoint of 9:02 p.m. If made, that report was not heard. New York Center in Islip implemented lost contact procedures at that time. At midnight the aircraft was declared overdue. And at 2:30 this morning, the extent of possible flight with its available fuel, the aircraft was declared missing. It is presumably down at sea west of Bermuda."

The FAA spokesman went on to explain that NAS Bermuda terminal radar followed his flight until 8:45, finding the aircraft on course and at its assigned altitude of 22,000 feet. It did not appear on New York Center radar as expected at 10:15. No distress call had been received, and there had been no radio hit from the Cessna's emergency locator transmitter. Investigators believe, he said, that the aircraft went down for unexplained reasons within one hundred miles of Bermuda, in the first forty-five minutes of its flight.

"The problem that we're facing now," Kalbfleisch said, "is Hurricane Gabrielle. It has grown to Category Four in the past twelve hours and is presently five hundred miles due south of Bermuda, tracking northeast. Our search area is already affected by storm force winds and high seas. I'm advised that all search activity will be suspended as of midnight tonight."

Veronica Gamble reappeared on the screen.

"Former Pan Am chief Theodore Rumsfeld Bakker, a decorated combat pilot, missing and presumed lost on a flight from Bermuda," she said, with a hint of suspicion in her sultry voice. "He was on an unscheduled flight which, sources say, had no real business purpose. There are more questions than answers tonight. And the search continues. For Eyewitness News, I'm Veronica Gamble."

Elliott melted into his chair, eyes closed for a moment. He exhaled and they opened, clear and dry—crow's feet at the corners betraying the subtlest hint of a smile.

Monday, September 11, 1989 – 11:00 a.m. GMT -1
1701 Quai d'Orsay, Paris, France

NICOLA FRY NEEDED to vomit. She could barely control the urge rising through her as she sat in the hallway outside the *grande chambre*. She wasn't alone. There was the smiling girl at the desk at the door, seated maybe twenty feet away.

"*La toilette, s'il vous plait!*" Nicola groaned.

"*En bas, vers la gauche,*" the young woman replied.

Down there, to the left.

Nikki rushed down the hall, endlessly it seemed before finding the poorly-signed women's public washroom.

She knelt at a porcelain bowl and wretched.

It had been eight hours since she had left Malta, the only passenger aboard a chartered jet. Five since landing in London. Four hours since her initial debrief at Lancaster House. Three since she and Jamie Mayhew had departed by helicopter to cross the channel. And for the past fifteen minutes she'd sat outside the doors to the grande chambre at 1701 Quai d'Orsay, Paris.

She wretched again and again. Nothing, no relief.

Nikki splashed cold water over her face and in time she returned to her seat in the hallway.

જ

"WE CANNOT HAVE unsanctioned killings," Hervé de Villiers said emphatically. "I had hoped this was clear from the start. We, the committee executive, decide who will die, not our field agents. Otherwise we have chaos."

Jamie Mayhew was exhausted. He rubbed the bridge of his nose and sighed. Around him at the conference table in the grand chamber sat De Villiers, Sir Michael, the German, Kleist, and the American, Charlie Watt. They had all been in Paris for their scheduled monthly meeting.

"Nevertheless, I support Dancer's actions," Mayhew said. "Process, not outcome, is at issue here. He was a belligerent. A conspirator in acts of mass murder. In her place, I'd have happily shot him myself."

"Might he have had further value? Perhaps lines of inquiry you hadn't considered?" asked the German.

Kleist had a point. West Germany had a keen interest in Libyan support for terrorism, with its own irons in the fire and its own unanswered questions.

"Possibly," Mayhew conceded. "But under a certain level of interrogation, one's veracity becomes doubtful. Dancer had reached that plateau with the prisoner. I agreed with her assessment at the time that to proceed any further was pointless. If not inhumane."

De Villiers nodded. The issue of sanctions would be tabled and he asked the Briton to call in his agent.

Nicola was escorted into the room, where she took a seat facing De Villiers with Mayhew at her side.

"Dancer," said the Frenchman, "please recount for us your operation."

Nikki ran her fingers through her hair and sweat sprayed in a plume.

"The Libyan, Jamil al-Salabay," she began. "We took him on Malta on Thursday, 6 September, shortly after 1700 hours, as he left his office in central Valetta. Two teams for the snatch, one German, one British. This phase went as planned and without incident. The subject was transported to our secure site, a farmhouse outside of the village of Rabat, on the west end of the island. I led the interrogation team, French, as you know, one of Algerian descent and all four fluent in Arabic. The others took up support and site security roles. I had overall charge, in contact with London throughout."

Nikki sat upright and swallowed a mouthful of water.

"The subject al-Salabay was a fit forty-two year old male, university educated, a secular Muslim, not particularly religious, and a married father of three. By profession, an administrator, employed as security chief for *al-Khutut al-Jawiyah al-Libiyah*, Libyan Arab Airlines, a position to which he was appointed in 1981 through nepotism, being married to the niece of Musa Mansour, former JSO intelligence chief."

Al-Salabay, she went on to explain, had his primary office at Tripoli airport, with a second in Malta, above the airline's travel agency storefront in downtown Valetta. He divided his time between the two locations, with a preference for Malta's more cosmopolitan atmosphere. He drank and was unabashedly self-promoting on the island's society circuit, drawing on the mystique of intelligence service.

"Was he open to alternative coercive methods?" asked the American, Watt.

"No," Nikki replied. "I determined this during our July surveillance. He had no useful sexual predilections. If anything, he presented as disinterested. He had personal wealth and no debt. He enjoyed the casino and racetracks, more for making a presence than to gamble. No pecuniary vices or leverage there. He lived well, craving status and social acceptance. Love life itself, and the prospect of untimely death is your weakness. Fear for his life was his Achilles Heel."

"How did you proceed?" asked de Villiers.

The Englishwoman recounted four days of the Libyan's interrogation, paraphrasing for the Olympiad Council her phased application of fear.

The first few hours of his captivity were spent in the farmhouse cellar in the hands of his four hooded captors. Angry English and German male voices, spouting venom as they rejoiced in their success, having seized a high-ranking Libyan terrorist. Facial and soft-tissue beatings with al-Salabay tied to a chair. Orchestrated 'discord' among his tormentors—death now, or retribution for his innocent victims with torture? Repeated execution scenarios played out to the click of a gun's empty chamber. His bickering captors kept openly drinking. Batteries and electrical leads were laid out in plain sight, along with the sharpened implements of a hide tanner or butcher. No suggestion of questioning to this point.

Next came eighteen hours of "stress positioning"—on his toes, suspended by his wrists from a hook in an overhead beam. Left in the darkened basement, alone with the significant exception of rats. No food, only brackish water to sustain him and to introduce cramps. Sleep for six hours came unfettered, naked in a dark closet the size of a wardrobe, outfitted with a bottle of water and a pail.

The first questioning session came at the end of the second day and lasted twelve hours with al-Salabay again naked and bound in the chair. It was the first time that he'd heard Nikki's voice, a woman, behind him and out of sight. In English, which he knew well enough, she instructed a series of hooded interrogators, each patiently relating her questions in Arabic. There was no threat or use of physical force. Simple questions. Details of his personal life. His role in planning airline bombings against the west. His knowledge of any involvement by Gadhafi, Musa Mansour or Malik Abu-Asara. She wanted names, dates and details around the bombing of Pan Am Flight 103.

Al-Salabay had said nothing at all. Not a word, not a whimper. He was returned to the closet to sleep for another six hours.

Prior to his second questioning session, 'discord' among his captors was reintroduced. In English, his Arabic-speaking interrogators expressed their frustration and recommended torture. Hers was the voice of moderation. With patience he might prove accommodating, she suggested, perhaps even accede to "London's plan" to turn him as an informer inside the Gadhafi regime. He might accept their inducements. Her minions scoffed. An hour passed before he was roughly dragged from the closet and returned to the chair.

The same questions were repeated as if on a taped loop. Again, Nikki had sat unseen behind him. The first French interrogator 'lost his patience' after an hour and struck him across the face. He was summarily relieved and the questioning resumed. And again, after eight hours, al-Salabay had said nothing at all.

"Did you consider water-boarding?" asked Watt.

Nikki studied the American wearily.

"Yes," she said. "It is a useful technique. But I find desert people aren't as threatened as we are by the prospect of drowning. It's foreign to their experience."

He had simply been returned to the closet again. This time, he would have heard that perhaps their 'other captive' might prove less defiant.

That hand was played over six hours that followed. The interrogation of their 'other prisoner'—played by a German team member of Libyan birth. He proved even bolder and more resistant. The violence of his 'beatings' was mortifying. He shrieked with animal sounds as the electricity was applied. In the end, their efforts proved fruitless. He refused to accept London's offer and his anguish was ended in an instant with the sound of one shot. Nikki was heard to admonish the shooter for spattering brains on her table. An hour later, Jamil al-Salabay was dragged again to the chair, now sticky with congealing blood.

"Such an excellent ruse," de Villiers said. "With it, I once had to butcher a pig. And you, Dancer?"

"A chicken," she replied. "I collected its blood in the yard." It had been on the morning of the fourth and final day. Al-Salabay was wild-eyed in the chair and he wouldn't shut up. His interrogators were removed. Nikki herself sat before him, unmasked and temperate in her demeanor. The two spoke together in English. She recorded their session on cassette tape, stopping his agitated stream of admissions and starting again from the top.

"He gave up everything," she said. "It's all in the transcripts. Names, dates, decisions, more names and more dates. We sought and received tacit verification throughout. Reliability high."

"And the salient points?" asked de Villiers.

"On or about March 20, 1987," she began, "Gadhafi ordered the JSO in a written directive to take action against American interests. In particular, a bombing campaign against U.S. aviation. A memo to that effect was followed up in a meeting between Gadhafi and Musa Mansour. Our subject had seen the memo himself."

Two weeks later, she continued, Mansour tasked his deputy, Malik Abu-Asara to put together an oversight committee which he chaired. The committee met over the course of two months, laying the groundwork for a bombing campaign. It sought technical options and decided by the fall of that year to employ a high technology solution, as had been detailed by Martin Quinn.

"In fact, his account at this point matched our Irishman's version almost word for word," Nikki said.

She said Jamil Al-Salabay had revealed that a lag on the technical side, dragging into the summer of 1988, had infuriated Gadhafi. Under pressure, Abu-Asara had set a deadline for the end of the year to bring down an American airliner. At this point he drew Al-Salabay into the planning process. A Pan Am flight out of Frankfurt at Christmas. That was the order and it had been Jamil who had put a plan together. Malta, the luggage transfer, the team make-up and planning. He gave up the names of the bombers—two of his JSO functionaries—along with the whole support infrastructure. Libya's ties to the Lockerbie bombing had been delivered, lock, stock and barrel.

De Villiers softened. "You haven't been debriefed as yet, and we appreciate that you are fatigued. Jamie says you have new information of urgent importance. Would you please proceed?"

Nikki Fry looked entirely spent.

"Two things came to light during my interrogation," she continued. "First is that Malik Abu-Asara has more than one team pursuing concurrent plans. Pan Am 103 was just one operation. Al-Salabay believed that another such bombing is set for this month. A target date this September, he thought, although he wasn't privy to useful detail."

She took a sip of water.

"Secondly, his version of events diverges from Quinn's on the matter of the Irishman's involvment. Al-Salabay said the technical delay was a result of incompetence on the part of their expert, Dr. Iqbal Aziz, who subsequently was shot. Jamie has verified this. Quinn, it seems, volunteered at this point to return to the project. And it was Quinn, in the end, who made the technology work. Well before Lockerbie."

De Villiers blanched.

"Then we've given succor to their mastermind?"

"We acted on our best information," said Mayhew. "That's the business we're in. We make hard decisions."

De Villiers frowned. "Your decision, Dancer, to execute Al-Salabay? It was completely contrary to your standing orders."

"He had exhausted his value, *Monsieur le Directeur*," Nikki coldly replied. "To me and to us. Was there an alternative? Certainly none we had planned, and it would have ultimately been down to me. I was the one looking him in the eye when I ended his life. *My* fate. *My* decision."

Chapter 38

Tuesday, September 19, 1989 – 5:20 p.m. CST
Los Cabañas Azul, Santa Marta, Colombia

IT WAS TWO hundred and fifty dollars a night, apiece, for three beachfront *cabañas* at the hotel's off-season rate. Five nights. So, that's what? Just over four thousand U.S. with taxes. Even so, it's a bargain, thought Steve Smith as he stepped from the porch of his thatched beachfront cottage into sand that warmly flowed through his toes.

He cracked a cold bottle of Costeña lager and looked out across the blue waters of Taganga Bay, a quiet cove on the northern outskirts of Santa Marta.

In Jamaica, he correctly suspected, cabins at a resort like this would cost twice as much. But this was Colombia. Santa Marta, a port city of 150,000 on the Caribbean coast had a rich history dating back to Columbus as well as picturesque natural beauty. It attracted tourism from throughout the region but not much from abroad. Jamaica had crime, but it didn't have death squads routinely culling the locals, or rebels who swooped from the hills to nab foreign contractors for ransom. Give it time, Steve concluded. Things here will settle down and this place will be crawling with fat sunburned Anglos, just like Cartagena—Colombia's jewel on the sea, one hundred miles to the south.

A hotel tab of maybe five grand? It amused him that Coultart had thought it a little excessive. Management typically sweating expenses. Spring Board was going to set New York back over $300,000 and accommodation was not going to be a significant cost.

Smith sipped his beer, his twenty-cent beer, awaiting the arrival of his single greatest expense, the third and the last of the Three Stooges—Moe. Larry and Curly were already inside, knocking back Costeñas at the rate of about two bucks an hour.

The Stooges. Spring Board would not have got to the pad, let alone prepped to launch, without the trio of former CIA contractors whom Steve had come to know as players down here. Larry Espinosa and Joao "Curly" Ribeiro were gunmen. They met as Marine Security Guards at the U.S. Embassy in Bogota. Both had returned to Colombia upon their discharge from the Corps to lucrative work in personal protection, augmented from time to time with a CIA tasking. The pair became "Stooges" the first time they partnered with Morgan MacLeish, who from childhood had answered to Moe.

It was Moe MacLeish who had become central to Steve Smith's operational plan.

The native Alabaman had been an Army pilot with four tours on Hueys in Vietnam. More than 6,000 helicopters had been lost during that conflict and a joke circulates that Warrant Officer MacLeish apologizes but he did try to save at least three. In fact, he had been shot down or brought down in combat nine times. He was awarded two Bronze Stars for Valor, a Silver Star, and the Distinguished Flying Cross for heroism as an aviator—these along with the Purple Heart for his wounds.

Still, Moe MacLeish kept returning to war. His wife back in Fort Campbell, Kentucky, left him during his first tour in 1967. Five years later, with the war grinding down, he was grounded—having coldcocked a major who commandeered his chopper from a medevac run to airlift staff officers back to Saigon. When he returned to the States, it was discreetly decided that WO1 MacLeish should simply resign.

It had been his unit Exec at Fort Campbell who had picked up a phone to a CIA buddy, and within a month, Moe MacLeish was flying an unmarked chopper out of Vientiane, Laos. Fifteen years later, with nearly twelve spent on CIA operations in Latin America, Moe had seized the opportunity to try out civilian life. He accepted a job in early 1988 as a helicopter pilot with Exxon-Mobil at its coal mining operation at Cerrejón, in northern Colombia. Moe had his own Bell 205 under contract and, from the mine site near the Venezuelan border, he routinely flew it home to an oceanfront villa near Santa Marta. It was there that Steve Smith had found him three weeks earlier. And there that a plan reuniting The Stooges had quickly begun to gel.

"Afternoon, Skipper. Admirin' my view?" came a voice up the path to the cabins.

Steve smiled. He was. Nothing warmed a Californian beach boy's heart like low rolling surf on a pristine blue bay.

"It's even better at dawn," he replied without looking away from the sea.

"It is that," agreed Moe MacLeish, stopping beside him to share his friend's moment of Zen.

"You're late," Steve said, clapping Moe on the back.

"I believe your invitation said five for five-thirty?" said the pilot. "Y'all know I don't drink, so by my watch I'm ten minutes early."

Smith slipped back into his sandals and the pair joined the others inside.

Introductions were made, first names only. Kevin, Jimmy and Martin had arrived in Bogota from New York on Friday, and had flown out to Santa Marta with Steve on Monday afternoon.

"Y'all Interpol boys like this young shavetail grunt?" Moe asked genuinely as he shook hands in turn. All replied with a nod, even Martin.

"Getting' up in the world, Stevie boy!" Moe said with a grin, popping the top on a Coke. "Always knew you'd do better than alphabet soup."

Martin drew a blank. "I'm not catching your meaning."

"CIA, DEA ... *SOL, RIP.*"

They all laughed. Even Larry and Curly, who had arrived over land from Cartagena that morning.

The team got straight down to the business at hand. Steve flipped back the first page of a newsprint tablet on an easel the hotel's banquet manager had provided. Taped to the next sheet were Xerox copies of photos he had taken at Puerto Mara. One showed the compound from the gated entrance, with the *Petroleos Vargas* warehouse to the left and the CITGO fuel cache to the right. Beneath it was a shot of the dock on the river—a blurred image, enhanced from high-speed film.

"Situation," he began, to catcalls from Larry and Curly. You can take the boy out of the army, but not the army out of the boy. "Captain" Smith was going to deliver his briefing in the standard military orders format—with the acronym SMEAC—details broken into digestible segments: Situation, Mission, Execution, Administration and logistics, Command and communications.

"Situation, *gentlemen*," he continued. "Carlos Perez-Garcia of the North Coast Cartel is a known dealer in terrorist arms. Interpol has information that a consignment of military weapons—including M-72s and Claymores—has been sold to the IRA, and will ship from this warehouse in Puerto Mara, Venezuela on the night of 21 September. Day after tomorrow."

He went on. It was expected to transport aboard a Catalina flying boat owned by a cartel pilot, a Canadian, now flying it up from Argentina. Steve had received word from Maggie and Tinker in Buenos Aires that the Canadian— Peterborough Pete—had received his Argentine export permit and flight authorization on Friday. His flight plan had been filed, VFR, mostly flying at night.

"The Catalina departed at 1430 yesterday from Buenos Aires, with its first destination, Rio de Janeiro," he said. "It leaves Rio today for Caracas, Venezuela, with a planned twelve-hour stopover on arrival. He intends to leave Caracas at 1530 hours on Thursday for a quote 'refueling stop' at the CITGO fuel dock in Puerto Mara at 1830. The flight plan has him leaving that evening on a northerly track through the Lesser Antilles."

With that information, Operation Spring Board would proceed exactly as planned.

"Mission," he said. "The team will go to Puerto Mara on 21 September and destroy the arms warehouse, along with the IRA shipment aboard the plane."

Steve flipped the tablet to the next page, displaying a map of northern Colombia and Venezuela. Highlighted was Santa Marta, the Cerrejón mine—120 miles to the east; the border with Venezuela—thirty miles further on; and Puerto Mara, another twenty-five miles past the border. Two positions were also shown on the map. The first, marked "A", was just north of the mine site. The second, point "Z" was above Puerto Mara, off Route 6, on the Venezuelan coast.

"Execution," he continued.

Phase One of Four. He along with Kevin, Jimmy and Martin will arrive at the Exxon-Mobil hangar at the Santa Marta airport at 1500 hours on Thursday. They had entered the country as geological surveyors under contract to the mine. Larry and Curly will already be there with the stores including radios, weapons and explosives.

At 1530 hours, the team will depart aboard Moe's Bell 205—in its Exxon-Mobil colors—on a one-hour flight to Point A, an abandoned airstrip thirty-eight miles to the north of Cerrejón. It was one of four fields that had been used in the early 1980s during construction of a 150-mile narrow-gauge railway connecting the mine to a deep sea coal port at Puerto Bolivar on the Colombian coast.

"Phase Two, Staging," Steve said. "At Point Alpha, Martin and Jimmy will prepare the explosives. We kit ourselves out, check the gear and our weapons. Larry is providing silenced Heckler & Koch MP5 submachine guns. Each of us has two thirty-round mags. We're not here for a gunfight. Questions to this point?"

"How much C4 will I have?" asked Martin.

"One case," Larry said. "Twenty-five pounds."

"Grand, that is. More than enough."

There would be four devices. Three set with two-hour timers for seeding the warehouse. One with a barometric trigger, set to detonate as the Catalina climbs through 9,000 feet above sea level. With the type of aircraft, the anticipated weather, and a VFR night flight, an eventual cruising altitude of between 7,000 to 11,000 feet could be expected. Detonation in these parameters would occur well offshore.

"And if he's a wave hopper?" asked Curly. Good question.

"Getting airborne will activate the mercury switch on a secondary one-hour timer," Martin answered proudly.

"Sweet."

Phase Three, Insertion.

"At 1700 hours, the team leaves Point Alpha by air. We fly due east across the border to Point Zulu, a gravel pit a mile inland from the highway. Eighteen miles north of the target. Our ETA at Zulu is 1730," Steve said, indicating the route on the map.

Point Zulu was chosen for staging as the flight route from Alpha would be over uninhabited jungle. In the region, a low-flying helicopter with oil company markings wouldn't raise an eyebrow on either side of the border. But its sound likely would on their return after dark.

"At Zulu we will be met by Maggie and Tinker. They will arrive in Maracaibo on Wednesday on a commercial flight, and will rent two passenger vans. Maggie will deliver the Strike Team to the north side of the bridge. Tinker, with the Cover Team, heads to the access road south of Puerto Mara. Teams in position by 1815."

Steve flipped the page to a map of the area around Puerto Marta, highlighting the coastal highway, the bridge crossing the Rio Limon, the island, highway access to Puerto Marta, and the positions of the warehouse, the wharf behind it and the CITGO fuel cache.

Phase Four, the Assault.

"Timing? The plan presumes that the aircraft will arrive on schedule at 1830. Fuelling and loading should take no more than an hour. Sunset is at 1827 and we will proceed ASAP after dark," Steve said.

"Rules of engagement? Weapons silenced at all times. No first shots except to defeat an immediate threat. We will assess every contact as it develops."

The Strike Team—Steve, Kevin, Jimmy and Martin—will move in two fishing canoes to the mid-river island by 1845. The aircraft should be loading at the foot of the dock.

"Larry, Curly and Tinker will set up in cover positions on the fence line to the south of the compound," he said.

Steve and Martin would then proceed ashore with Kevin and Jimmy providing cover from the island. Martin will set his four charges. The first three among the fuel barrels of the CITGO cache. Then a charge aboard the aircraft. This would be placed between the spokes of one of the Catalina's main landing gear wheels—which, with the seaplane afloat, will be in their retracted position, above the waterline on either side of the fuselage. If the dock-facing side proved unsafe, Martin would be in for a swim. On completion, they will withdraw to the island and, with Kevin and Jimmy, cross by canoe back to the north shore.

Phase Five, Departure.

"If all goes to plan? Teams return to their vehicles and make their way back to Point Zulu. Our ETA should be no later than nine o'clock. We then fly back across the border to Point Alpha and remain for the rest of the night. Maggie and Tinker return south with the vehicles to San Rafael de El Mojan, six miles from the site. Here they observe the boom and report it, flying out of Maracaibo in the morning."

The team studied the map.

"If things go for shit, we bug out to the north. Both vehicles make their way back to Zulu and we abandon them there. The latest Moe leaves is 0430. He doesn't come back. Anyone left behind? Make your way into San Raphael. Hole up there, contact New York. Anybody gets hurt? Deal with it. We stick to the bug out plan."

Administration and logistics. Their identification remains behind at Point Alpha. Nothing was to leave an American imprint. All kit would be issued by Larry. Command and communications? Steve was in charge, after him, Kevin, and then anyone else from New York. All would be equipped with Harris personal tactical radios with earpieces and spaghetti mikes. First name call signs. Plain language voice procedure.

Steve finished his beer as the others studied the pages that he was about to destroy. The soldiers in the room had liked what they heard. Good old khaki planning. This thing might even work.

ે

Tuesday, September 19, 1989 – 6:25 p.m. EST
201 Varick Street, New York, NY

"LONDON! GOOD TO see you transmitting again," said Linc Coultart, relieved. "Do we expect Paris to come back on line?"

"Yes," replied Jamie Mayhew, whose image flickered on the video screen in New York. "The techies assure me we'll all be back up in a shake."

There had been absolute panic since morning, made worse by the sudden loss of their satellite feed. Grim news had broken at 10:15 a.m., New York time—a French DC-10 jumbo jet had gone down over the Sahara desert.

Union des Transports Aériens Flight 772 had been on a flight from Brazzaville, Congo, to Paris via N'Djamena, Chad. There had been 170 souls on board, including the wife of the American ambassador to Chad, and national security hotlines around the Atlantic had been abuzz ever since.

Linc was in the command seat in the New York operations room with Ray Morgan at the controls. Beside him was Charlie Watt, solemn and silent.

So far this much was known: UTA Flight 772 had left Brazzaville that morning for Paris, landing in N'Djamena, the capital of Chad, at about 1130 GMT, 7:30 a.m. New York time.

It left N'Djamena at 1213 GMT for Paris-Charles de Gaulle, a flight of just over five hours. Its last contact had been at 1234 GMT, with ATC requesting a position report over the Sahara in thirty minutes time. The request was acknowledged and the flight leveled off at its cruising altitude of 35,000 feet, crossing into airspace over the neighboring country of Niger. Nothing had been heard from it since.

When the position report wasn't received at 1304 GMT, regional ATC made repeated calls, to no avail, and the flight had been declared missing. There was no radar coverage and little traffic over this remote stretch of the Sahara. UTA 772 had vanished and by 10:00 o'clock in Manhattan the story was already leading the news.

Video 1 in New York was the live feed from London. Jamie Mayhew sat alone, fidgeting and giving instructions to minions off screen. Video 2 continued to display nothing but bars of gray rolling static. Seconds later it cleared, showing Hervé de Villiers in Paris, with Sir Michael McPhail to his left and Jurgen Kleist to his right.

De Villiers looked more haggard than he had seemed two hours earlier. It was now after midnight in Paris.

"Hello again, gentlemen," he began, "I have Sir Michael and Jurgen with me. This continues our briefing, hopefully without further technical difficulties. As you know, the French air force had sortied a reconnaissance aircraft from its base at N'Djamena. You all heard the pilot's initial assessment, radioed at the time from the scene."

Those early details had been bleak.

The French Mirage F1-CR reconnaissance jet had launched within an hour of lost ATC contact, with an escort of Jaguar fighters. The formation had flown at supersonic speed along the prescribed route of UTA Flight 772 and tragedy had been quickly confirmed. Five hundred miles to the west, in the Tenere desert region of Niger, it came upon wreckage that was spread over an area thirty miles long by ten miles wide. The largest debris field was found concentrated near the Kanuri tribal village of Bilma and the region's only significant landmark, the low craggy face of the Kaoaur Escarpment. After completing two photo runs, the flight had returned to base low on fuel. Its unprocessed film was then expedited to Paris.

"We now have these images," de Villiers said, nodding to a technician off screen.

A streaming video sequence of air photos began to display on the Paris feed. Black and white and macabre. Low altitude images of wreckage scattered along the desert floor, here and there an identifiable shape: a wingtip, a turbofan engine, sections of seats, some clearly still occupied. The sheer scale of the crash site became the strongest impression the pictures conveyed, with mile after mile of widely-dispersed debris. The video concluded with high-altitude images revealing a sadly familiar linear pattern. These were the remains of an aircraft that had come apart seven miles in the air.

De Villiers and company returned to the screen.

For a moment no one said a word.

"I understand, Hervé, there are soldiers on scene?" asked Mayhew, who looked equally weary.

"Yes," the Frenchman replied, "for five hours now."

Within an hour of the reconnaissance flight finding the wreckage, a platoon of French paratroops was enroute from their garrison in N'Djamena aboard a Transall C-160 transport. They parachuted onto the main concentration of crash debris, twenty miles southwest of the village of Bilma. Here, the Sahara desert was truly an ocean of sand—the Erg of Bilma, as it was known—two thousand square miles of windswept featureless dunes which, from space, looked like a bronze storm-tossed sea. Following was a flight of Puma helicopters, ferrying troops who would establish a camp to support the inevitable team of investigators.

"Two hours ago, authorities here received their first briefing from the commander on the ground," De Villiers said.

"There is no chance at all of survivors. As with Lockerbie, it is a scene from hell."

"Initial indications?" asked Charlie Watt.

"A bomb," Hervé said. "The evidence is subjective, of course. Early days, but with what I have seen with my own eyes? You with yours? This is the event we'd been told to expect. I have no doubt about it."

"I agree," Watt replied.

Linc Coultart glanced curiously at his Olympiad boss. There was something here that he was missing.

"We have taken a vote here in Paris, Charlie," De Villiers said. "What say you?"

"I vote yes," the New Yorker replied.

"Then we're unanimous. Contact Boxer."

Chapter 39

Thursday, September 21, 1989 – 6:58 p.m. CST
Puerto Mara, Venezuela

MARTIN QUINN WAS panting, painfully out of breath as he paddled toward blackened timbers. He forced himself to breathe evenly through his nose, quickly feeling the effect on his heart rate, and the canoe slowly slid to a stop in the forest of pilings supporting the dock.

Steve Smith turned to him from the bow. He gestured with a hand signal, first to his eyes, then toward the activity on the barge, secured and riding low in the river at the north side of the dock. Through the pilings, about one hundred feet away, they saw the starboard side of the Catalina with its cargo hatch open. There were two men on the barge passing wooden crates to a pair inside. A fifth, out of sight overhead on the wing, was hand pumping fuel into the plane's tanks from drums on the dock. Carefree words were exchanged in Spanish, the unseen fuel man sharing his with a flat Anglo accent. That would be the Canadian pilot, he supposed.

Steve pointed to an algae-slicked wooden ladder that rose up an outer piling nearby. Martin nodded and the pair made their way silently to it and up its rungs to the top. The dock's timber surface spread at least 150 feet to its eastern extent, and was maybe a hundred in width from the rear of the warehouse to the river's edge. It was cluttered with crates and fuel drums, more tightly along the windowless wall of the warehouse. Good cover for movement and it was poorly lit, with a single lamppost on the far northeast corner. Steve signaled for Martin to follow and scrambled to the nearest crate with the Irishman close on his heels.

"All stations, Steve," whispered the leader into his spaghetti mike. "We're on the dock. Southwest corner. We have good cover to the east side of the warehouse. Give me an all clear."

Kevin Ahearn scanned the scene from the island through his night vision goggles. He and Jimmy had a clear view of the rear of the aircraft, the barge and the wharf. The men loading and fueling the Catalina were absorbed in their work and no threat. He increased magnification and could see Steve and Martin huddling behind a crate.

"It's Kevin, you're good from the river."

There was no need for light amplification at the front of the warehouse. Its doors were wide open, spilling light from inside, and the CITGO compound was lit by incandescent yard lamps. There was activity inside the warehouse. Three men in view. Two were armed guards with M-16 carbines slung over their shoulders. The other was in coveralls and a ball cap, with a crate on a hand truck dolly. Chatting and laughing. Suddenly, two more men strolled from the bowels of the warehouse to join them.

"Holy shit, Steve-o!" Tinker's voice blurted on the radio. "Carlos is here with what looks like his driver. Inside the warehouse, up front."

"You certain?" Steve's thoughts were suddenly racing.

"Yeah. Man, I could tap him right here."

"Negative!" he quickly replied. "Unless he's here for two hours, this is his lucky day. Are we good from the yard?"

"Roger," Tinker replied. "Good from the yard."

"Steve-plus-one, roger, we're moving now."

The pair scampered across the wharf from crate to crate to a collection of drums, Steve with his MP5 at the ready, and Martin clutching his waterproof satchel. They stopped just short of the northeast corner of the warehouse, tucked in behind crated glass containers marked 'Sulphuric Acid' and plastic drums of Sodium Bicarbonate. Chemicals for refining cocaine. The American smiled. The sonofabitch would be losing it all.

"Steve-plus-one in position. How now?"

"Still good from the river," replied Kevin. The loading of crates seemed to be completed and the men on the barge began to manhandle fuel drums into the plane.

"You're still good from the yard," whispered Tinker.

Steve surveyed the east side of the warehouse, facing the CITGO yard. It was a maze of fuel drums stacked on pallets as much as six high, encroaching on its neighbor with a roadway to permit access to and from the dock. Drums were piled against the east wall of the warehouse along its 200-foot length. Seeding this would be easy.

"We won't have to go far," he whispered to Martin. "Plant them quick and we're out."

"Aye," the Irishman replied, his heart pounding again. "One would be enough. You could send up this place with a cigarette."

"Steve-plus-one, preparing to move along the east wall to set charges."

"Good from the river."

"You're good from the yard."

They quickly moved forward, a third of the way down the wall before following a lead through the maze of drums to the side of the building. Steve kept watch from behind as Martin pulled a charge from his bag. Four eight-ounce sticks of C4 taped together with an electrical detonator wired to a digital timer—all wrapped in a Ziploc freezer bag. He pressed a button and a green light came on. He pressed it again and "2:00:00" appeared in LED numbers. Once more and the green light switched to flashing red and the time sequence began to count down. He placed the charge gently between the wooden slats of a pallet of gasoline drums.

They made their way back twenty paces and tucked in again to repeat the process.

"Steve, number two set, we're backtracking."

"Negative! Hold your position!" Tinker's voice crackled on the radio net. "You've got company coming, north down Park Avenue. One guy with a crate on a dolly, one armed guard beside him. No, wait one! ... Now Carlos and his wingman are tagging along. Hold in place until advised!"

Steve and Martin tucked in out of sight. Steve watched with the butt of his MP5 at his shoulder and a finger along its trigger guard. The foursome sauntered past, barely twenty feet away, with Carlos boasting in Spanish about his expansion at last into Europe. Into Britain's civil war.

Kevin Ahearn watched in pale green amplified light as the group appeared on the dock. Workers manhandled the crate to the barge as the one figure in a light business suit stopped to speak with the man who had been fuelling the plane.

"You're good from the river," he reported.

"Good to go from the yard."

"Steve-plus-one, backtracking to our final set."

They hid among fuel drums at the northeast corner of the warehouse and Martin set his third charge. He pressed its timer button, the green light came on and he set it to "01:55:00"—synchronizing the charge with the others, and pressed it again. The digital timer began to count down.

"Kevin, Steve. Are we clear to return to the ladder?"

"10-4," the cop replied. "Everyone at the plane has gone down to the barge."

In less than a minute, Steve and Martin were back in their canoe. They watched as the men on the barge concluded their business. Handshakes. The Catalina's cargo door being closed. Steve had a moment of panic, which evaporated when he heard Carlos and the pilot discuss payment. They were heading back to the warehouse. In a moment they were gone and the barge was left vacant.

"Steve-plus-one, ready to move on the plane. Confirm that we're clear?"

"Negative!" Ahearn replied. "You've got an armed guard on the dock. Right now he's at the nose of the plane, taking a piss over the side."

Damn. Steve whispered to Martin that the outside wheel would be their only option. He'd have to swim. They would glide out from the pilings, he would drop him at the end of the barge and back off down the shoreline to give him cover. Was he up to it? Martin assured him he was. He had expected this all along.

Steve maneuvered the piragua out from under the dock, briefly into the glare of the lamplight from above. He tucked in under Mangrove limbs overhanging the bank and they watched as the guard moved away down the dock. Martin slipped into the water, anxious about the caimans he had seen on the river's north shore. Steve handed him his satchel and the Irishman swam slowly away, his head above water, into shadow under the seaplane's massive tail.

"Head's up! The guard on the dock is returning your way!" warned Kevin Ahearn.

Steve back-paddled silently, moving farther away, deeper into the river bank's jungle cover.

Martin swam through the shallows, soon guiding himself with a hand along the boat-like fuselage of the Catalina. It surprised him that when he arrived at its port side wheel, he could stand with his feet on the river bottom. Its water barely reached to his chest. Now, if those fucking alligators didn't kill him, he could finish this thing. This mission, he knew, would secure him his freedom. Two undertakings. And with this one so risky? He could write his own ticket with Diver on their return to New York.

He gripped the hull of the aircraft just below its huge port side wheel, his feet unsteady in mud. He found the position he needed, peering through its mammoth spokes, past the rim and into the void behind the brakes. He steadied himself and pulled the last package from the satchel over his shoulder. Another plain plastic bag, containing four sticks of C4 with an electric detonator and two triggers—the first, barometric. He twisted a knob on the barometer's face, aligning its clock-like hands to zero-feet above sea level. He blew into its static tube to ensure it was clear. Then he pressed a button and

"9000-FT-MSL" appeared on its trigger's digital screen. He pressed it again and the screen now read "ARMED".

What a fucking adrenaline rush!

Martin hadn't felt so alive since the time he had snorkeled to Mountbatten's yacht. Wouldn't his Nicola frown? Sweet Penny Luscombe or young Molly squeal? Yeah. Wouldn't those two get off? He wiped river brine from his eyes and reached across the seaplane's bulbous tire, feeling inside, between the spokes of its massive forged wheel. Room enough for the package to fit snugly, securely for takeoff.

He stuffed the package into the void in the wheel and pressed the button again through the plastic to set the one-hour delay for the secondary trigger.

He was startled to see the green 'safe' light turn instantly red. And the timer flash "00:00:05"—*counting down.*

00:00:04

"What the hell?"

He slipped and regained his footing again.

00:00:03

"FUCK!" Martin jabbed at the button and missed.

00:00:02

"GOD DAMN YOU, YOU BASTARDS!"

00:00:01

His heart slammed against bone in his chest. And in an instant, the Catalina disappeared in a blinding flash. On the island, both Kevin and Jimmy slapped away their night vision goggles in pain.

A fireball rose into the night sky, quickly bettered by successive explosions just seconds apart. Fuel drums from the engulfed dock flew like fireworks through the air, raining down on the CITGO yard and the warehouse.

"Take 'em all down!" Tinker shouted, opening up with his MP5 on the frozen shapes silhouetted inside the warehouse.

Larry and Curly joined in a split-second later, and the figures—six men, including Carlos and the Canadian pilot—spun grotesquely as bullets struck silently home.

"Steve, South Cover Team! We're out of here!" shouted Tinker, and the trio turned and ran headlong through the bush toward the highway.

On the island, Ahearn and Kenneally anxiously scanned the river as the whole of Puerto Marta began to explode. From a distance of barely one hundred yards, it was a front row seat to epic destruction. Ahearn struggled to replace his earpiece and tapped sand from his mike.

"All teams, Kevin, bug out! Move now!"

Jimmy Kenneally scrambled up next to him and nudged his shoulder. Movement in the river! Someone was swimming toward them. Kevin reseated his night vision goggles, which whined as they recalibrated. It was Steve, struggling in the tidal current. The pair ran to their canoe and quickly shoved off, paddling toward him. In a moment they glided beside him and dragged his limp body aboard.

"Kevin, Tinker! Your status?"

"We have Steve from the river. We're making our way to the north shore."

"Roger that," Tinker replied. "We're just crossing the bridge and will rejoin Maggie in about a mile."

"You okay?"

"All good. But listen, a bunch a trolls from the bridge are bookin' it south to the scene for a look. Stay clear of the parking lot. A few are out looking for missing canoes."

"10-4," Kevin's voice crackled. "We'll make our way through the woods."

The explosions at Puerto Mara got bigger and worse once the warehouse was fully involved. The scene was volcanic. Flaming fuel barrels rained from a towering column of roiling orange and black, some even reaching the river's north shore.

Steve was dazed but unhurt. The three beached the stolen piragua and scrambled up the north bank escarpment, heading north through the jungle on an angle toward the highway. At just after eight-thirty, they emerged within fifty yards of the rest of the team.

Maggie and Tinker had their vans tucked in on a highway maintenance side road, hidden by mounds of stockpiled gravel. It was 20:44 by everyone's watch, twenty minutes from Point Zulu. Time enough for a breather.

"What the fuck happened?" asked Maggie, giving Steve a first aid once over, checking his pupils with a penlight. He sat slumped in the front seat of her van with all of the others crowded around.

"Shit happened," he said, wiping grit from the corner of his mouth. "Martin swam out to the plane. I'm maybe fifty yards back from the dock. He's wading around the tail. Standard pause of two-three and the next thing, ka-fucking-boom! I'm guessing he screwed something up."

Curly smirked. "Ya think?"

At that moment they heard, and then felt, an enormous concussive explosion. More than one mile away and trees swayed around them. That was instantly followed by an endless series of loud detonations.

"There goes the warehouse," Larry said. All agreed it was time to get moving.

"Do you think we got Carlos?" asked Steve as the group began to disperse to their rides.

Tinker smiled. "About that... Sorry, boss, made a command decision. We took all six of 'em down in the doorway."

Thirty minutes later, the team, including Maggie and Tinker, lifted off from Point Zulu, having disposed of the vans in a pond in the quarry.

"Looked to me like your Fourth of July show came early," said Moe MacLeish, as he caressed the collective and his Huey skimmed the jungle canopy.

Smith managed a weary smile in the seat beside him. "Mission accomplished. Not quite as I'd planned it."

"Was losing somebody a part of the plan?"

Steve had to think about that.

"If it was, partner, nobody told *me*."

Moe snickered.

"Fought a whole war like that, Sonny Jim. Nobody shares secrets with soldiers."

❧

OVER MANY MIMOSAS at brunch, the team stalled its goodbye to The Stooges. Steve had slipped a thick envelope to Moe MacLeish. Two hundred grand: $125,000 for him for the chopper, and his patience in putting the whole thing together; $50,000 to Larry for logistics support, he got everything back but the plastic explosives; and $25,000 to Curly Ribeiro for five days of familiar work. They had come back minus one. No sweating that, all had been there before and probably would be again. A toast to the Irishman and his bad luck, and then it was on to *cervezas* with the champagne and orange juice gone.

They had encountered no problems getting back to Santa Marta and Bogota. Maggie and Tinker had new papers on the way from New York and would fly out on Monday. Steve recovered from a mild concussion almost overnight, no more pain than he'd ever endured in the past. And Ahearn and Kenneally, being cops, were just glad that they'd never needed to fire a shot.

Brunch had left them all sentimental, half cut, and The Stooges left smiling back into their Colombian lives.

It was just after noon when Jimmy Kenneally rapped on the door to Kevin's room. He had brought up the luggage dolly that he had just used to haul gear to the lobby. A grunt from Kevin beckoned him in.

Ahearn was on the phone to his wife Valerie in New York.

"Yes, sweetheart, we're just leaving Dallas," he said, rolling his eyes. "I'll be home tonight. Yes. I know it's Siobhan's big art show in Chelsea tomorrow. No, darling, I promise. Okay. Love you, bye."

Kevin pinched the bridge of his nose.

"Got any Aspirin? Like a whole bottle?" he asked.

"None, sorry," Jimmy said. "Headache, pal? A whole bottle of scotch headache?"

Ahearn groaned.

"Naw. Got this goddamned pain in my back. Had it since we left that island. Like I'm some kinda voodoo doll, run through by a needle. I can tell you it's friggin' annoying."

They loaded Kevin's luggage on the trolley and left the room, quickly riding down to the lobby.

Kevin settled his bill at the desk as Jimmy pushed the cart out onto the street. Steve was already waiting outside with their airport taxi on order.

Kevin emerged through the revolving door looking pale. He was sweating. He stopped beside Jimmy and fumbled to light a cigarette.

"You alright?" Jimmy asked.

"This pain in my back! Going right through me like a hot friggin' poker."

"That smoke should help," Jimmy said, smiling.

Kevin stumbled and grabbed his friend's shoulder.

Kenneally struggled to keep him steady. It didn't help. Ahearn collapsed onto his back on the sidewalk and gasped like a fish out of water. Unable to catch his breath.

"Kevin! Fucksakes!" Jimmy shouted, twisting to kneel at his side. His friend sputtered and choked, rapidly turning gray. Ahearn wheezed in pain, clutching at his chest.

"Jesus, Jimmy!" Ahearn gasped, gargling his words. "I can't get ... I can't ..."

Then he wheezed loudly and fell silent, staring unfocused up at the sky. The pain on his face ebbed away as its muscles went flaccid. He wasn't breathing.

"No! You sonofabitch!" Kenneally shouted, pounding him hard on the breastbone. Ahearn turned gray-blue, pupils fixed and dilated.

Jimmy knelt beside him and felt for a carotid pulse. Nothing. He cupped the back of his neck in his hand and tilted his head, his lips closed over Kevin's slack mouth, puffing once. Then he closed his palms together and pressed on his chest, again and again. "One, one thousand, two, one thousand, three, one thousand ... Steve, get an ambulance! ... four, one thousand, five, one thousand ..."

He blew again and repeated the count.

A crowd grew around them, upset and uneasy in Spanish.

Kenneally continued to perform CPR until the ambulance arrived and the Colombian paramedics brushed him aside. To their credit, they kept at it, all the way into the back of the bus. No use, Jimmy knew, Kevin was already dead.

"Fucksakes!" he angrily shouted, kicking over their luggage with tears welling up in his eyes. And he sat on the sidewalk outside the hotel and wept.

Chapter 40

Wednesday, September 27, 1989 — 8:18 p.m. EST
Shea Stadium, Brooklyn, New York

IT WAS SETTING up to be the lackluster end to a lackluster season. Third place in the NL East, seven-and-a-half games back of the San Francisco Giants with five games left to play, the best that the Mets could do was to take second place. Even that, a diehard fan like Sal Luongo figured, would be a bit of a stretch. Final home game of the season. Last of a three-game stand against the Phillies, which so far was split. A 2-1 loss on Monday, a snore fest, and a 3-zip win on Tuesday which was pretty much done by the top of the fifth. There was no friggin' offense at all.

Tonight? The Phillies had brought their offense to Shea. Top of the first, facing Darling—bam, bam, bam. He walks Herr, the second batter, and the third man in the order, left-fielder Johnnie Kruk, nails a fastball on his first pitch, flies to the left-field corner, scoring Herr from first base. Three plays later, Phillies' right fielder, Von Hayes—a six-foot-five streak of misery from Stockton, who had been having a hell of a year—flies a homer into the center right stands with Kruk scoring from third. Three-zip, top of the first. Darling pitched like he was just up from the minors.

Phillies' starter, Kenny Howell, a right-handed kid from Alabama, goes through the Met's batting order like that. Three innings passed, no runs, no hits, no errors. The kid's a freakin' machine. Darling stays wobbly but gives nothing up.

Bottom of the fourth. Howell walks right fielder Mark Carreon, the third batter, after two easy outs. Then he faces shortstop Kevin Elster and gets a bit rattled. His fourth pitch, a slider, and *WHACK*—Elster flies over the left field wall and scores Carreon. Mets going to the top of the fifth a run down, 3-2.

"That's more friggin' like it!" shouted Sal Luongo, on his feet and cheering as Elster rounded the bases.

He turned to scan the stairs for a beer boy when he saw Randy descending the steps to his row. Sal had been sitting next to an empty seat from the start of the game. He grinned. Randy had hot dogs and beer.

The Judge excused his way precariously down the row of seats to his own, greeting his friend with a smile.

"Sorry I'm late, Salvatore," he said with a lopsided grin. "Got held up at my club."

The pair awkwardly transferred Randy's cache and took their seats as the fifth inning started.

The Judge tried to sip his beer and spilled foam down the front of his shirt. He giggled.

"Jesus, Randy," Luongo observed. "You're pissed!"

"Pretty much, my friend, pretty much. And these plastic goblets aren't really that sturdy. Ever notice they flex?"

"Been celebrating?"

"Oh yeah! That's the word, celebrating."

"Gonna tell me about it?"

"M-mm-hmm," replied the Judge with a mouthful of hotdog. "How we doing, by the way?" he eventually asked.

"Down 3-2. They gotta pull Darling, he sucks."

"M-mm-hmm."

Darling again faces Herr and this time strikes him out, swinging hard on a 3-and-2 fastball.

"Yeah!" Sal shouted, jumping to his feet with the majority around him. Maybe they were wrong about Darling tonight.

Judge Elliott finished his hot dog, wiped crumbs from his lips and drank a mouthful of beer.

"I'm selling my place in Port Chester," he said, to a cheer as Johnny Kruk grounded out to first base.

"What?" Sal asked, surprised. "That beautiful house?"

"Bought a brownstone on East 57th," Randy said. "Has views of the park."

"Moving into the city."

"Yeah. You know? I'd rather have tossed it all and moved down to Port Lucie? But she wants me to stay in Manhattan. To stay on the bench. You can't argue with single-minded women. Know what I mean?"

Ricky Jordan, the Phillies' first baseman, singles to center field on the second pitch, a sloppy inside curve.

"Makes sense, you return to the bench," Sal replied. "It's what you do. You're too young to retire."

Elliott took another mouthful of beer.

"Maybe, but you know what?" he said, beaming. "I'm fucking rich! Not as if I have to work. And I've decided I love Liv Geller. There! I said it. Does that make me a bastard? I mean, Charlotte's been gone for nine months and I'm in the sack with my boss. But the thing is, I do love her, Sal."

On a 2-1 pitch, Darling delivers a peach to Von Hayes and he too singles out to center field, moving Jordan to second. Groans ripple through the stands.

"Think it'll work?" asked Luongo, sincerely.

Randy Elliott nodded. Hell yes, he thought it would work. Liv Geller had become that important. It shocked him to realize it, but that's where it was, where things stood. No reflection on him. Nor on the love that he did have for Charlotte. That part of him simply was gone, in the past, and he had to move on. He could accept it now, having moved past his grief. It could work. It will.

A big hitter, Phillies' catcher Dutch Daulton goes to the plate and stares down two fastball strikes. Darling gets a fastball signal from Mackey Sasser, but he thinks better of it and throws a tight inside curve. Daulton line drives into right field and Jordan scores from third. A wild throw from Carreon misses HoJo at third.

"Oh, you freakin' apes!" screams Luongo, spilling his beer as Hayes scores on the error.

Steve Jeltz, the Phillies' shortstop, grounds out on a 2-1 pitch to leave the Mets down 5-2 at the top of the fifth.

"What about you, Sal?" asked Randy, draining the last of his first cup of beer. "Settled on any plans?"

"Well, your check cleared," Luongo said with a grin. "I had a few bucks saved, and now I'm what you might call officially wealthy. I'm gonna retire. The first of October, I'm selling my cart to my sister's boy, Tony. And get this! For a buck! Gonna give him a leg up in life. The kid deserves it."

"You're a good man, Salvatore," Randy said, and he meant it. "You deserve to retire."

"Fuckin' eh! Gonna settle down in Florida. Get in all those spring training games. Maybe if I get bored, I'll get into the dog and bun rackets down there in Port Lucie. You gonna come south this winter, Judge?"

"With bells on, Sal," he replied. "Great big goddamn bells."

Mets manager Davey Johnson finally yanks Darling from the mound after the fifth inning, replacing the big right-hander with the leftie reliever, Jeff Musselman. He carried the day through the top of the eighth inning, giving up nothing. The rest of the game was strategic, three relievers thrown in to knock off Phillies' hitters. It worked. But why bother? The season was over. The game ended as it had been decided at the top of the fifth inning, 5-2, Phillies over the Mets.

There were four more games in the regular season and the Mets went on to clobber the Pittsburgh Pirates four straight.

They ended up two games back of the Giants—who would lose 4-zip to the Oakland A's in what would be called the "Earthquake Series"—with the Loma Prieta Earthquake devastating San Francisco during Game 3—October 17, 1989, televised to the world as the quake rattled Candlestick Park.

Still, for two Mets fans at least, the year would be ending infinitely better than it began.

Chapter 41

Monday, March 12, 1990 – 10:40 a.m. EST
26 Federal Plaza, 23rd Floor; New York, NY

SPECIAL AGENT WINTERS left Jimmy Kenneally with Fat Boy and the Tall One and disappeared from the room. Kenneally stared out the window and began to wonder just who exactly the other two were. Fat Boy? Pasty and balding, perhaps forty and at least eighty pounds overweight. An ill-fitting suit. A gold badge that Kenneally didn't recognize hung in its leather wallet from the man's left breast pocket and, like the Tall One, he was wearing a visitor pass. Now, the Tall One was harder to read. A bean pole, a bit younger, a bit better dressed. Buddy Holly glasses. No visible shield. Nope, for all his experience and intuition, Jimmy had no bloody clue who the Tall One might be, or why he was here. He could ask. Naw, fuck it, Kenneally decided. At this point in time, he didn't much care.

Winters returned with a another FBI file in his hand.

"Detective Kenneally," he began as he sat and placed it on the table. "I'm curious ..."

Jimmy raised his catcher's mitt of a hand.

"I'm gonna stop you right there," he said. "First of all, it's no longer Detective, it's Mister. I know that you know I've retired from the force."

Winters smiled thinly.

"Yes, that's right, but you're still on the payroll at One Police Plaza. Until, when? End of June?"

Kenneally fumed. "Accumulated annual leave. I turned in my shield and my gun in November," he said.

"Still one of New York's finest. Technically."

"And that matters?"

"It might. But if you're more comfortable with it, Mr. Kenneally, I'll drop the reference to rank."

Winters shifted in his chair, changing gears.

"As I said, I'm curious ..."

Again, Kenneally raised his hand to protest.

"Second of all, why the fuck am I here?"

The Tall One whispered again to Fat Boy.

"And thirdly," Kenneally said, this time his voice and his ire slightly raised, "if you don't introduce these assholes, I'm leaving. Are we communicating, Davis?"

Winters actually blushed. What a sap.

"I'm sorry," he replied, possibly genuinely.

He pointed to Fat Boy, who had clearly been rattled by the exchange. The man straightened in his chair, anticipating his introduction.

"This is Agent Walter Kuchapsky of the Immigration and Naturalization Service," he said.

Fat Boy offered his hand and Kenneally shook it.

The Tall One leapt up of his own volition and extended a palm across the table.

"I'm sorry, Mr. Kenneally. I'm Dick Benedict, IRS."

Jimmy shook his hand too. At least this one didn't have a grip like a maiden aunt.

"Nice to meet you, Dick!"

Greetings dispensed with, Kenneally returned to staring down Winters.

"Now, answer my second question and I might stay."

It looked almost as if Winters was growing a backbone. Hard to tell with that beady-eyed squint.

"Answer one for me first," Winters said flatly.

"Fine. Tit for tat."

Winters opened his FBI file and studied the top document for a moment—an old interview dodge, reasserting his primacy. It could have been a Chinese takeout menu for all Kenneally knew.

Davis re-engaged his eye contact.

"Your surveillance that evening. You were on secondment to an ... Interpol task force. What can you tell us about that?"

"Tell you?" Jimmy replied without skipping a beat. "Probably next to nothing. As for Dick and Walt, here? Probably even less. What would you like to know?"

"You know. The W-Five ... And spare me the national security crap. This investigation has clearance."

Amateur. Kenneally saw the look in his eyes. Had to get defensive, had to brag. These weren't simply enquiries. He'd tipped his hand and Winters knew it the moment he did.

"Well," Jimmy said, "The who? Interpol. A collective of international police agencies, headquartered in Lyon, France. No police powers really, a support organization, facilitating investigations across international borders. Yeah, facilitators. That's the latest buzz word."

Winters darkened.

"What did you do during your Interpol secondment?"

"I *facilitated*," Jimmy replied.

"You're damned close to obstruction, Kenneally! Give me a straight answer, or ..."

"Or what? Get to the goddamned point!"

Winters just sat there and fumed. And then he composed himself and perused another document in his file. "Have you heard of Theodore Rumsfeld Bakker?" he asked flatly.

Kenneally thought about whether he had. He hadn't.

"No. Why?"

"A millionaire businessman, hated by many. On September 1st last year, he goes missing on a flight to New York from Bermuda. Vanished," said Winters, snapping his fingers, "just like that."

Kenneally brightened.

"Is that what this is? Look, if you're investigating the Bermuda Triangle, I'm afraid I'm a non-believer."

Winters groaned. "Yeah, that's funny. Same night Bakker goes missing, you were surveilling a known IRA bomber at a bar in Hell's Kitchen."

Kenneally's boyish grin subsided.

"Don't get the connection. I told you we never ID'd him."

"Right, right. You were on Ahearn's low-level mafia snitch. Nice piece of detecting."

"Fuck you."

Winters pulled a couple of photographs from the file and handed the first to Kenneally. The photo was from a Customs port-of-entry surveillance camera at Newark airport and was time-stamped: 10:34:05 EST 05/13/1989. It showed Quinn casually standing at Customs, next in line with a confident smile on his face.

"Same guy as your Irishman in Sullivan's bar," Winters continued. "Am I right?"

"Could be," Kenneally replied, turning to Fat Boy. "Looks like one got through your net, Walter. *Tsk.*"

Kuchapsky blushed but stayed silent.

Winters continued.

"He entered the country from Rome on May 13th last year, using a British passport in the name of Martin Robert Catesby. INS shows he was admitted on a six-month tourist visa, with an initial Manhattan hotel address. No reason, of course, for him to report his movements after that."

He produced another photograph, nearly identical and time-stamped just moments later. It showed a striking blonde following Quinn to the same Customs agent. The contractions wracking Jimmy's gut didn't show on his face.

"Nicola Jeannine Fry. Seems to have arrived with your man. Same hotel destination. You know her, Kenneally?"

"Wouldn't I like to!" was his non-reply, tossing the photo back onto the table.

"You wouldn't tell me if you did, would you?"

Kenneally shook his head slowly, feigning dismay.

"Entered the country on a British diplomatic passport, according to INS records. Stays a couple of days and flies back to London. Turns out she's MI5 and on a secondment to Interpol. Now there's a coincidence, eh?"

"Yeah. Spooky."

Fat Boy and the Tall One looked like they were going to explode. Kuchapsky was actually chewing his fingers.

"So Bakker goes missing. An FAA investigation turns up nothing. His plane likely crashed. But the thing is, Hurricane Gabrielle comes along and the ocean's swept clean for a thousand miles. Never turned up so much as a sliver. The guy's left everything behind. All his riches intact, well, at least those that he hasn't hidden off shore. And here's where Dick and the IRS boys come in," droned Winters.

The Tall One stiffened proudly and straightened his tie.

"A month ago, IRS agents are going through Bakker's business affairs, and one of his pilots mentions a contract that had come up last August. Just before Bakker disappears. An Irishman, he said. Charming guy. Sought to contract both of Bakker's aircraft for some upcoming business charters. A man named Martin Quigley. Turns out his Irish company never existed. INS has no record of a Martin Quigley from Dublin having entered the country. So Dick, here, calls me."

Kenneally nodded approvingly at Dick Benedict.

Winters continued.

"We discover this Quigley had chartered the same plane that went missing three times in the two weeks before it vanished. Including a flight to Charlotte the day before Bakker supposedly crashed. The pilots who flew Quigley, half the gals at Bakker's Manhattan office, including his personal assistant, all identify Martin Quinn from the photos."

Fuck. He was crossing the line.

"So that's pretty much it, I suppose," Winters said smugly. "September 1st? Your surveillance at Sullivan's Bar. Interpol secondments. Special guest spooks escorting IRA bombers into the country? Bakker. Quinn renting the missing man's plane? And you ask why you're here?"

Jimmy Kenneally was stone-faced.

"We tracked a mafia contact to a Hell's Kitchen bar," he said, repeating himself. "He met with some federal judge and they drink with an Irish stranger who might have been Quinn. If Kevin Ahearn was still alive, he'd tell you the same story. We got nothing. You've got nothing."

Winters sneered.

"Really? Ahearn, I nearly forgot. Tell me, Kenneally, where exactly where you when your partner dropped dead?"

A younger Jimmy Kenneally would have punched the sonofabitch right there. He was much more reserved now that he was retired.

"Davis? You want to be careful with what you say next."

Winters wasn't that smart. He was too fucking keen.

"Bogota, Colombia? A bit far afield for a couple of washed-up facilitators from Midtown, don't you think?"

To this day, Jimmy Kenneally has a recurring dream where he propels the toothless Davis Winters through that twenty-third story window, with Fat Boy and the Tall One guessing they're next. It's a good dream, as dreams go.

"Those two, out! And get your supervisory agent, now!" Jimmy said, unsmiling but not at all flustered. He had to repeat himself only once.

Fat Boy and the Tall One loitered in the hallway, visible through the glazed office walls, and Winters returned promptly with the SSA, having had to pull Bill Findlater from a meeting. The SSA wasn't happy.

"This had better be good," Findlater said, craggy cheeks and the tip of a twice-broken nose turning red.

Kenneally told Winters to pick up the phone and ask his switchboard operator for a line to the White House, its general number would do. Winters blanched and Findlater's owlish eyebrows arched with surprise.

"You're connected?" asked Kenneally. "Good. Now tell the gal you'd like extension 6929. Good job! Now give the phone to your boss."

Findlater took the receiver. He nodded, acknowledging a voice on the line.

"Bill Findlater, Supervising Special Agent, FBI Region New York. Yes, thank you, I am. How do you do, sir? Pleased to ... Yes, just one moment," he said, agitated.

The FBI veteran lowered the receiver and covered the mouthpiece with his palm. His eyes bored blazing holes into Winters' thick skull.

"Name?" Findlater hissed.

"Davis Winters."

"Not you, asshole! Him!"

Jimmy chuckled. "Tell him Jimmy Kenneally. New York."

Findlater flushed red and returned the phone to his ear.

"Kenneally, sir," he continued, listening for a moment and his florid complexion quickly draining through normal to pale. "Thunderbolt? Yes sir, I understand. I will need a confirmation message. Thank you. I'll see to it. Bill Findlater. My pleasure."

It was clear at this point that the line disconnected. Findlater replaced the receiver and sighed.

"That was Dr. James Brace, the Deputy National Security Advisor. A personal friend of the President, and of yours, apparently, Mr. Kenneally."

"No sir, we've never met. I did work for him though. Suppose we all do, in a way," Kenneally replied.

"True, that's true. Winters? My office. Bring all of your files in this case."

"But sir, we ..."

Findlater glared and Winters evaporated.

Kenneally rose and extended his hand to the man who might have been his double.

"Tough row to hoe," he said with a smile.

"Yeah," Findlater agreed. "We do what we can, don't we? I heard that you worked with Kevin Ahearn in this. Partnered up for a while?"

"I did. And we were."

"Lucky man. You've got my respect, brother. Sad day when I heard that he died. You were with him?"

Kenneally nodded. "First time I lost a partner. Makes you rethink your future."

"Yes, indeed. It does that," said Findlater. "Did you know? He would've just found out that his kid, Patrick, graduated from Quantico at the top of his class. Posted with the Bureau out to Los Angeles, so I've heard."

"He never told me."

"Well, Kenneally, I'm glad to have met you," Findlater said as they walked from the room.

"Listen, this would be a real favor," he said, "but if you happen to see his wife Val in your travels? Tell her Bill and Millie Findlater say hi."

Epilog

Wednesday, May 9, 1990 – 1:25 p.m. GMT +1
O'Shea's Hotel, Lower Bridge Street, Dublin, Ireland

THE SNUG AT O'Shea's Merchant Hotel, in the city center of Dublin on the River Liffey, did much to suggest it had been serving drink since its first had been poured in 1793. And for Jimmy Kenneally, the pub had the feel of Sullivan's Bar in Hell's Kitchen, New York, except here it was real. He had returned for the first time to his native land—well, close enough, to the Irish Republic—late the previous day.

He had selected the modest hotel from a brochure at the airport upon his arrival. No advance booking. A taxi had taken him to it and, to his luck—this being the height of the American visiting season—one of its twenty-five rooms had been available for the entire week he was planning to stay. He had settled right in, finding his way to its quiet pub within minutes of stowing his bags in his room. In the pub he had stayed through a rollicking evening until, as he could barely recall, the barman called for last orders at midnight. And this morning, he awoke in his bed fully clothed.

Five days in Dublin was all that he planned. Get a feel for the capital first, then it would be off on a train ride to Cork and a bus to Fennell's Bay—a seaside village on the western approaches to Cork Harbour. It was there that a realtor in Manhattan had found him a cottage on a half-acre of land with "sea glimpses". The details and photographs that had been provided by an estate agent in Cork had all but sealed the deal. This was where he would retire. His for one hundred thousand U.S., all in, subject to his inspection on site.

Retirement to Ireland.

His sister Sinead had thought he was crazy. Still, what was he leaving behind? Sad memories for the most part. Two brothers he hadn't been very close to or seen all that often for years. They had their own lives. And a sister, his reminder that pity's a virtue and sadness a sin. Three thousand miles would be barely enough of a distance between them.

Fennell's Bay, Ireland. It had a ring to it that sounded like home. In a week he would know if it really rang clear.

"So it's hair of the dog, Mister Jimmy Kenneally?" asked the serving girl who arrived at his table.

Jimmy looked up red-eyed at the young woman he vaguely remembered from the previous night. Annette? Annabelle. He remembered he'd charmed her. He had charmed everyone within earshot, buying copious rounds of whiskey and beer for pub patrons around him—mainly students from Trinity College, he recalled. Young and vibrant and thirsty. Good company for someone who's come home.

"Yes darling," he said bashfully, "and I'll apologize now for forgetting your name."

"Niamh!" she said, pronouncing it 'Neev'. "I was so sure you'd remember! A large Paddy neat?"

"Niamh, yes!" he replied cheerily. "And no, not a whiskey. Could you bring me a pint of light lager with some tomato juice on the side."

The girl wrinkled her nose as she marched away. "Ah, you American Irish! Amateurs when it comes to the drink."

The pub was nearly empty. Early afternoon sunlight streamed through its windows, reflecting on cocktail glasses that hung above the bar. Delicate floating dust hung suspended in its golden rays. Pop music played softly from the pub's sound system, in contrast to a night that had been too loud, too lively.

"Boxer?" asked a feminine voice approaching behind him.

Jimmy looked up to find Nicola Fry at his table. He was startled to see her.

"May I sit?" she asked.

"Yes, of course!" he replied, rising gentlemanly.

She did, just as Niamh arrived with his beer and tomato, and she sent her after a glass of white wine.

"Sorry to surprise you," Nicola said.

Kenneally was struck dumb for a moment. As much by this ghost of his immediate past—he was no longer Boxer—as he was by the beauty of Nicola Fry. She was no longer starkly platinum blonde, having returned to her more natural color.

"How did you find me here?" he sputtered.

"You're not in hiding."

True enough.

"Should I be?"

Nicola smiled politely. "No, not at all. I'll get straight to the point. Paris wants you to reconsider your retirement."

Jimmy sighed. "Oh, I don't think so! For f ... *pity's* sake, it's barely begun, and if you knew ... well, it was no small decision to leave New York and my whole life behind."

The server returned with the wine and a withering look.

Nicola smiled.

"There's something I've wanted to ask you since we first met in New York. Mr. Happy? A personal question," she said, and took a sip of Chablis.

"Go ahead," Kenneally replied.

"Did you know that Martin and I had been lovers?"

Jimmy felt instantly apprehensive. It wasn't her tone, but the question itself.

"We'd been briefed. Those of us who needed to know."

She sighed.

"You've lost people you loved? Or had become close to?"

"I have," Jimmy said. "We all do."

"Dead by your own deeds. Your own hand?"

She looked away wistfully.

He studied the woman's face, forlorn, wracked with sadness. What the hell was she after?

Jimmy knew she had been MI5 and hardcore; knew what he'd seen and he'd sensed when he met them together. He had been briefed on their background, on Rome the first time when she'd turned him, and again when she'd drawn him back in. He learned all about Malta after the fact. He had to come clean.

"It was me," Jimmy fumed in a whisper. "I was the one who killed Martin, rigged a timer to blow prematurely. Is that what you wanted to hear?"

"I knew that, Boxer," she sighed. "I knew before you did. Killing Martin had been my presumptive duty the moment we met. Before we became lovers. And when I brought him to New York, I was relieved to be passing it on. If it's any consolation, it was my hand in the end as much as it might've been yours."

"Really?" Jimmy said, broken hearted. "You know, the bitch of it is that I liked him. I grew to respect him, in our perverse way. It was a sanction that Paris had ordered. An instruction to no one but me, the only one on our team who had become his friend. The sonofabitch trusted me. Which made it simple, not easy."

Nicola's focus returned. She looked at Jimmy clear-eyed.

She took a mouthful of wine and savored it for a second.

"I do understand, I just thought you should know."

Jimmy was thankful for that.

Nicola's eyes brightened. She reached into her purse and retrieved an envelope. "Our last order of business," she said, passing it to Kenneally.

"Fresh orders?" he asked, looking the envelope over. It was thin, of plain business stock with no markings at all.

She shrugged.

He opened it with growing curiosity.

It contained a cashier's check, drawn on the *Banque de France*, in his name, with an imprint: 3,000,000 Francs.

"What the hell's this?" he asked, with fingers beginning to tremble.

"A cheque for three million Francs."

"I can see that, what's it for?"

Nicola smiled.

"After the bombing of Flight 772," she said, "France secretly authorized a reward of three million francs for the capture or 'judicial disposition' of Martin Quinn. Station Paris convinced the French government that his disposition had been satisfied, based on your report of his death. The reward, as a result, was summarily issued to you. It cannot be returned or reversed, apparently. Legal issues. And now, as you have retired, Paris wants you to have it. Officially."

Jimmy studied the check warily, rubbing it between his fingers, holding it up to the light.

"Are you worried that it's blood money?"

Slowly Kenneally managed a smile.

"It wouldn't matter to me if it was," he replied. "Three million francs. What is that in ..."

Nicola smiled wryly.

"Real money? Three hundred grand, pounds sterling," she said. "More than a half-million in American dollars, I'm told."

"And it's mine?"

"Yours absolutely."

"An inducement for me to return to the game?"

Nicola signaled to the girl with her empty glass.

"None implied or intended," she said. "Those were exactly the words out of Paris."

"Really," Jimmy Kenneally said as the server returned.

"Niamh, dear, I think I'll be having that large Paddy now."

The End

Made in the USA
Charleston, SC
23 November 2013